Gold for Prince Charlie

In 1745 the Highlanders limped away from the bitter field of Culloden. Soon the Duke of Cumberland was offering a huge sum for the capture of Prince Charles, dead or alive. Duncan MacGregor, great-nephew of Rob Roy, volunteered to join the small band of men escorting the Prince to safety.

Just one day after the Prince's escape, a large amount of French gold was landed at the very spot from which he had sailed. Thus it was that Duncan became involved in a desperate attempt to save Prince Charlie's gold, helped by beautiful, headstrong Caroline Cameron.

Gold for Prince Charlie

Nigel Tranter

CORONET BOOKS
Hodder and Stoughton

CHAPTER 1

'BLOW, damn you – blow!' Glengyle cried. 'If you call your-selves pipers, pipe now, by God! And no dirge, no lament! Give us . . . give us *The Gregorach's Challenge!* Aye – give us the *Challenge.* As you've never blown it before. Yonder's the Prince. Let him hear that MacGregor is with him yet. That all is not lost. Blow, in the name of God!'

Even Gregor Black Knee MacGregor's great voice was hoarse and uneven with much shouting and much emotion. Red Knee indeed would have been an apter description of him this day, for the famous black mole on his left knee was completely hidden under the dried and caked blood which coated the entire leg below a bayonet thrust in the thigh, that had also torn a ragged rent in his kilt. Limping, he gestured forward, with the stained broadsword that he had not yet thought to sheath, towards a cot-house beside a group of wind-blown stunted trees across the high moor, where a scattering of horses and men were grouped.

At Glengyle's broad back, his son spoke thickly. 'They cannot do it. They're done. Done, I say – finished! It is more than flesh and blood . . . '

'As Royal's my Race – they can! And shall!' The big man turned round fiercely – though he did not leave hold of the semi-conscious figure that slumped only approximately upright on the plodding garron at his side – turned, he to whom fierce-ness of manner had never come naturally despite his style and reputation. 'Lord – must I play them my own self? 'Fore God – have we come to that!'

It would be an exaggeration to say that this aroused a smile, a single smile, in all that weary, tattered and blood-stained company; but sunken heads were raised momentarily, dulled and hollowed eyes gleamed here and there. And from some-where in the stumbling trudging throng, the first uncouth wails and groans of filling bagpipes sounded. One man handed over to another the arm of a comrade whom he had been supporting, and reached across to a baggage pony for his pipes.

7

Another, who had been staggering along with difficulty on legs lacerated by grape-shot, had himself hoisted on to the broad back of a second garron, already overburdened with two wounded men, and perched ludicrously thereon sought air to fill his instrument. Slowly, unsteadily, amidst outlandish discords and howls, the three pipers strove to respond to the summons of their colonel and chieftain.

Only three sets of pipes, it seemed, had survived the holocaust – or only three pipers.

Gradually the painful caterwauling evened and steadied and merged into something recognisable, though still quite fantastic in the circumstances, into the savagely martial strains of a ranting march, a proud, swaggering, damn-your-eyes flourish that was not so much defiant as purely, scornfully triumphant. Louder and stronger the music swelled as the instrumentalists forgot their pain and hunger and wretchedness in their playing, and all along the shambling ranks teeth gritted, drooping shoulders squared, strides lengthened, and defeated, shocked and betrayed men became fighters again, the warriors that their name and fame demanded.

Up at the front of the straggling column, the young captain immediately behind Glengyle – who was in fact his youngest son Duncan MacGregor, sometimes called Duncan Beg or Little Duncan because he lacked fully three inches of his father's six feet four – Duncan MacGregor was behaving strangely. Stripping off the red-and-green plaid which he had worn folded about his torso and one shoulder, he began to turn around in little circles even as he walked. Men near him looked at him askance, as though the sights that they had so lately left behind had turned his head – as well they might. Then it was seen that he was in fact unwinding something from his body – the colourful silken tree-and-sword banner of Clan Gregor, soiled and rent, which had been wrapped shaftless around his person. He drew his claymore, and thrusting the bloody point through and through like a skewer beside the torn socket for the shaft, he raised sword and standard arm's length above his head.

A ragged snarling sound, part growl, part cheer, issued from hoarse dry throats behind him.

And so, pipes playing and banner flying, after a fashion, the remnant of Glengyle's Regiment of the army of King James the Eighth and Third, marched, not off the field of Culloden – for they were already a couple of miles from that shameful blood-soaked place – but across Drummossie Moor to where rumour said that the Prince had halted.

Duncan MacGregor kept his arm held high, although presently it demanded his other hand to support it thus.

The thin rain, now and then laced with sleet, blew chill in their faces off the grey shrouded hills.

Despite the wet, the party for whom they headed were congregated outside the lonely cot-house, not within it, under the doubtful shelter of the dark dripping Scots pines. All there were far past noticing the effects of rain or cold, that late afternoon of the 16th of April, 1746. In twos and threes and little groups they stood or sat or lay about, in various attitudes of exhaustion, anger or despair. Yet however preoccupied they were, each and all, in their own distresses, it was very noticeable how frequently all eyes turned in the direction of one man who sat alone, a little way apart, on a fallen tree-trunk. Head in his hands, he crouched, a picture of utter despondency.

Apparently it took the sound of the pipes some time to penetrate to this man's inner consciousness, deep sunk as he was in grief and dejection. When at last, affected more perhaps by the cries of his companions than by the message of the music, he looked up, it was to reveal a handsome sensitive face, too young, at twenty-four, to be so drawn with hurt and care, large eyes ringed with fatigue, high forehead bruised from a fall and streaked with dirt below natural fair hair sadly in need of powder and curling-tongs.

Heavily those tired, rather prominent brown eyes stared, and lightened a little at what they saw – though only a little. Charles Edward Stuart rose to his feet, however, a graceful well-made figure of a man, with a strange distinction of bearing by no means always to be observed in royalty, tall, slender, bare-headed, dressed in long tartan jacket and tight riding-trews, with a buff waistcoat, and no single indication of his rank and position. Shaking his head, he awaited the Gregorach.

By the time that the clansmen came level, two or three others had joined the Prince – O'Sullivan, the Adjutant-General and Quartermaster; old Sir Thomas Sheridan, Charles's second-cousin and former tutor; and Lord Elcho, commander of cavalry. When Gregor of Glengyle held up his

9

hand to halt his followers and still the pipes, it was indeed O'Sullivan who spoke, frowning, before his Prince.

'Very stirring, i' faith, Glengyle – very dramatic!' he said, in his curious Frenchified Irish, into the hush. 'But have you no thought for His Highness's safety? Do you want to bring Cumberland himself and all his baying pack down upon this wretched spot, with your brayings and squealings? It has been sore enough, by the Blessed Virgin, to bring him so far, undiscovered, without your shouting aloud . . . !'

'My God, sir – is that the way of it now!' Gregor Black Knee burst out, hotly. 'Is our Prince sunk so sudden from Captain-General of his army to a skulking fugitive who hides from his own fighting men . . . ?'

'Gentlemen! Gentlemen!' Charles Edward intervened. 'What talk is this? Be silent, both! Colonel O'Sullivan – you forget yourself, I think.' His attractively musical voice, with its foreign intonation, was unusually strained, with an edge to it. 'I still command here, God pity me!' Then quickly he relented, he whom many blamed for being ever too ready to trust and overlook and forgive. He touched his friend's arm lightly. 'Though well I know, John, that it is but anxiety for my safety that moves you.' Turning back to the huge Mac-Gregor, he mustered a smile – and he had a particularly sweet and disarming smile, however wan and brief it was today.

'Glengyle – I rejoice to see you,' he said. 'If joy is a word that I may ever use again, *mon Dieu!* Your coming thus lifts my heart . . . a little. I had feared that you, too, were, were . . .'

'We are fewer than we were, Highness – but still at your service,' Glengyle told him, simply.

'Aye, *mes braves* – I should have known that if any could cut their way out of that sorry ruin it would be my gallant MacGregors . . .'

'Provided always that they left in good time, of course!' a voice murmured from behind the Prince, where Hay of Restalrig, the Military Secretary, had come up.

There was a choking indrawing of breath from every Mac-Gregor near enough to hear. Hands dropped to broadsword hilts, involuntary paces were stepped forward. There was little love lost between the Highland and the Lowland components of that army – or indeed between many of the units of either persuasion themselves – witnessed to by the sourly laughing

10

voice that spoke as Captain Alexander MacLeod, aide-de-camp, came strolling over even as Charles Edward raised a hand to still them all.

'You have your clans mixed, I think, Colonel Hay! It was the MacDonalds´who were, h'm, over dainty on this occasion!'

'Aye – they would not fight! They would not charge, damn them! Because they had not the right of the line, by all the saints!' That was O'Sullivan again. 'And who denied them it? The Lord George. The Lord George again! For his accursed Athollmen ...'

'Sawny! John! Peace – I command you!' the Prince cried, and now his voice was vibrant with emotion. The fine eyes flashed, the glazed weariness momentarily gone. 'This is insufferable! Enough of it! Has there not been hurt enough, sorrow enough, for one day ... ?'

'Aye, sir – and treachery enough, too! The Lord George knew well that the MacDonalds would not fight, denied the right of the line. I heard Keppoch tell him so, with my own ears. Yet he took it for himself ...'

'Christ God!' Glengyle roared, that quiet giant who could out-shout them all on occasion. 'Who talks of Clan Donald not fighting, Storekeeper? If they were slow to charge, they were slower still to leave the field! They did not leave the field, I say. They have not left it yet, whatever. Because they are dead, all dead. They died where they stood, I tell you, around Keppoch and Lochgarry and the others, because they would not run Keppoch is dead ...'

'Keppoch!' the Prince cried. 'Keppoch, my good friend ... !'

'Aye. And most of his own and Clanranald's and Glengarry's officers with him. Those that did not die then are being butchered now, my God! Cumberland's Hessians are butchering the wounded and the prisoners, like dumb animals. Now, at this moment, they are dying like slaughtered cattle.' Glengyle's voice broke. 'I ... I have never seen the like, nor heard it.'

'Yes. Yes we ... we heard of it.' Charles nodded, biting his lip. 'It is monstrous, beyond all belief. *Ma foi*, they are barbarians, brute beasts! But, you – you escaped?'

'By holding together, just. By holding close, we fought our way out. Some of us.' Gregor Black Knee glanced back at his ragged battle-worn veterans. There were perhaps one hundred and twenty men there, mainly MacGregors, many of them Rob Roy's former freebooters, but with forty or so of the hundred Perthshire Stewarts who had been attached to the regiment. Few there were wholly unscathed. 'These, out. of four hundred! We Gregorach have been cutting our way out of ill places from our mothers' knees. But not as today. Never the like of that!'

'No. No – it is a cataclysm, a disaster! And Locheil? My good brave Locheil? Do not tell me that he has fallen, *mon Dieu*? And the Duke? My lord of Perth? You were brigaded with him, in the centre, were you not? What of the Duke?'

'I think that he escaped, sir. I saw his brother, the Lord John, leading him off the field. They tell me that Locheil fell, both ankles shot with grape. But his Camerons carried him off in time. They were on the right. I did not see . . . '

Captain Duncan MacGregor touched his father's arm, and gestured behind him, wordlessly. Glengyle nodded.

'But, sir – my men are in no state to be standing by, while we talk here. You can see their need. I ask Your Highness's permission that they may stand down. Rest for a little . . . '

'*Certainement*, Colonel. Forgive me . . . '

Both Elcho and O'Sullivan spoke at once. Elcho, son to the Earl of Wemyss, prevailed.

'Your Royal Highness – this is folly!' he exclaimed. 'All these men will but bring down Cumberland upon us. Your immediate safety is all-important, now, if the Cause is to be saved. That is why we brought you here. Already there were over-many of us. My pickets tell me that dragoons are scouring all around for you. Videttes are all over the moor, searching. Already they may have spied us. These MacGregors will bring them down on us like a swarm of locusts! You must order them to leave us, Highness. At once.'

'God in Heaven – is that what you think of the Gregorach, now!' Glengyle cried. 'Is his Highness safer in the midst of a hundred MacGregors, every one of whom would die for him? Or amongst a wheen Sassunach secretaries and storekeepers!' And his hand swept in scornful gesture over the dozen or so of the Prince's company.

'Gentlemen – I pray you! A truce to this talk . . . '

'His lordship is right, Highness,' O'Sullivan insisted. 'In this matter, at least. The fewer men about your person now,

12

the better. What could a hundred of infantry, MacGregors or other, do against a regiment of dragoons? Yourself it is that Cumberland wants – the rest he can hunt down at his leisure. Send them away, sir.'

'Very well, gentlemen. Glengyle – you will take your gallant regiment yonder. Behind these trees there is a hollow where a stream runs. Take your men there, Colonel. Rest them in that hollow. They will be out of sight. Then yourself come back here. For a council.'

'But, sir – here is no time nor place for a council!' Elcho protested. 'You should be gone. Ere this. As far from this fatal place as is possible. Southwards into Badenoch. To join up with Cluny. To Ruthven . . . '

'My lord – your advice will be welcome. At the council. Others give me contrary advice. We must decide what is best. What is wisest. What is possible, *mon Dieu!*' Charles drew a hand over his bruised brow. 'Glengyle – you have your orders.'

'Yes, sir.' The MacGregor hesitated for a moment. 'Highness – might I ask? For my men. Your Quartermaster – has he any food? Any provisions? Anything . . . ?'

'Alas, Glengyle . . . '

'I have nothing, sir. Nothing nearer than Inverness,' O'Sullivan said.

Gregor Black Knee inclined his head. The entire Jacobite army had had one biscuit apiece for sustenance that whole grim day. And not much more the day before – with an all-night march of abortive folly in between. 'Your servant, sir,' he said. 'I shall be back.' And raising his voice. 'Pipes! *Dia* – let us have the pipes!'

' 'Fore God – not again!' Lord Elcho burst out. 'Not again, Glengyle! No more of that damnable noise . . . !'

The rest of his protest was lost in the clansmen's growling wrath and contempt, and in the bubbling ululation of the bagpipes.

In a fold of the high moor, eight hundred feet above the sea, where a burn ran down towards the River Nairn, Glengyle left his men to bathe their wounds and fill their empty bellies with water if with nothing else, and limped back towards the cot-house, taking his son with him. Four miles away to the north, down at sea-level, the towers of Inverness Castle could

13

just be distinguished through the grey curtains of the rain squalls. Beyond, although the massive outline of Ben Wyvis itself could not be seen, the stark white streaks of snow in the mountain's corries stood out strangely.

Under the dripping trees the MacGregors passed Charles Edward's personal bodyguard, dismounted and waiting, sixteen troopers of FitzJames's Horse. Their French officer eyed the two bare-kneed Highlanders with unconcealed scorn, and offered no greeting.

Back at the Prince's party, they found the council already in progress, after a fashion. Another couple of officers had arrived – Major Maxwell of Kirkconnell, of Elcho's Horse, and the Master of Lovat. Tempers were brittle, and words were high.

Young Lovat was speaking, son of the wily Fraser chief. ' . . . nor do I trust Cluny. He has held off all day. He is but six miles off, with five hundred Macphersons. He might have tipped the scales had he thought fit to join us. It would be folly for Your Highness to turn south into his country.'

'How do you know that Cluny is but six miles off?' Lord Elcho demanded. 'The Lord George Murray left him yesterday at Ruthven, fifty miles away . . . '

'This is Fraser country, my lord. I learn quickly all that passes in it.'

'Then perhaps, Master of Lovat, you could tell us where the rest of the great Clan Fraser is hiding? Only two hundred men were here to face Cumberland . . . !'

'Damnation, sir! Do you jest – or must I teach you that in Fraser country no man speaks so to . . . ?'

'My lords! Gentlemen!' the Prince intervened wearily. 'May I remind you that this is a council-of-war – not a tavern brawl? Here is Glengyle. And Captain Duncan. Sit in, Colonel. You are wounded, I see. Your leg . . . ?'

'A scratch, Highness – no more. A bayonet prick.'

'You were at close quarters, then?'

'Oh, aye – we were close enough. Too close for Barrel's fusiliers, I warrant you! But yourself, sir? Your head? Your brow?'

'Nothing, *mon ami.* A bump, a bruise. My horse was shot under me – that is all. No more honourable scar! *Alors* – we have but now heard more of the battle, from the Master of

14

Lovat here, and Major Maxwell. And ill tidings they bring! The Mackintoshes are cut to ribbons. The Chisholms died where they stood, like the MacDonalds. Dillon's Regiment is no more. The Drummond Horse were decimated by cannon-fire and grape, and my Lord Strathallan is dead. As is Mercer of Aldie. My Lords Kilmarnock and Balmerino are prisoners. All gone. My brave army is no more. There is nothing left – nothing!'

The MacGregor shook his head, fair still, the golden hair only faded a little by silver-grey. 'It is bad, sir – bad. But there is much left, see you. A battle lost, it is – not a campaign. Och, sir, the half of your army were not here, at all. No more than four or five thousand men faced Cumberland this day, and him with twice that number.'

'And there we have it!' Hay of Restalrig interjected. 'Your Royal Highness had twelve thousand at Perth. Many more than that at Edinburgh. Where are the rest?'

'Aye, sir – there's the rub,' O'Sullivan nodded. 'Sure, more than a battle is lost.'

'I fear that you are right, John.'

'But much may yet be saved, Your Highness,' Elcho insisted. 'Go south to Ruthven. That is where Lord George and his Athollmen are making for. And the remnant of Drummond's Horse. With the Duke. Both your Lieutenants-General. It is Cluny's country . . . '

'And claim you that as recommendation!' Young Lovat cried. 'The Lord George Murray and Cluny! My beloved brother-in-law. Better put your life in the hands of honest men . . . '

'Like my Lord of Lovat?' Elcho gave back.

The Prince had to beat on the tree-trunk with his sword-hilt to quell the uproar.

'I will have none of my good friends and faithful officers mis-called!' he exclaimed. 'We have had that, a-plenty! I seek true and wise counsel, not raillery and malice.'

'There is but the one true and wise counsel for Your Highness in this pass,' O'Sullivan declared earnestly. 'Go back to France, sir. King Louis has promised men and arms and money. If we had waited, and brought them with us at the first, this whole endeavour would have turned out differently, I swear. Go back to France and raise them now. Then return with them. Next year, mayhap. There is the only wise and practical course, sir.'

'And what of the men who have come out for your Cause, sir?' Glengyle demanded. 'If you sail away and leave them, for France? What is to become of *them*?'

'They will disperse to their homes. Such as have not already done so!' Hay said. 'I agree with the Adjutant-General. The only sound course is to return to France . . . '

'Sound for whom?' the MacGregor cried. 'My God – think you that there is any safety in their homes for the thousands you leave behind? Think you the Government will forgive and forget?'

'And King Louis has been promising men and money for years, Your Royal Highness,' Maxwell of Kirkconnell pointed out. 'You still have an army, if you will but collect it, re-assemble it. Scattered wide it may be, now. But it can come together again. Go to Ruthven in Badenoch. Assemble there.'

'Or in Lochaber. In Cameron's country. Better there, in the West. It is more remote. Bid the clans assemble there,' Young Lovat proposed.

'Safely away from *your* doorstep . . . ?' MacLeod the aide suggested softly.

'Damn you, sir . . . !'

'There should have been a rendezvous appointed,' Elcho interrupted, looking accusingly from the Prince to O'Sullivan. Of them all, Elcho had ever been most critical of Charles's leadership and his Irish friends. 'That was elementary. Had there been such, we should not be in this pickle, at least. But since neither Captain-General nor Adjutant-General ordered a rendezvous in case of defeat, surely it behoves us that we all seek to join the two Lieutenants-General. Lord George has left word that he is making for Ruthven, with the Duke of Perth. To Ruthven, therefore, all should go. And swiftly, before Cumberland thinks to close the passes of Moy and The Slochd.'

'I agree,' Glengyle said, although he frowned. 'That is what an army should do. Not that I wouldn't sooner see your Highness making for the north-west, for Kintail and Torridon and Gairloch – the wild MacKenzie country where the Redcoats could never come at you. The Earl of Cromartie is north of Inverness, with eight hundred Mackenzies, watching Sutherland. MacDonnell of Barrisdale likewise. I left them there

16

but two days ago. I say, go south now to Ruthven, and join Lord George and the others. Then head you north through the mountains, by the Corryarrack Pass, Fort Augustus, Glen Moriston and over to Kintail, with your men. I will guide you by high ways where no dragoons nor fusiliers may follow. Bring in Cromartie and the others to join you there – and you have an army again. The summer is coming . . . '

'Och, heed them not, me boy,' old Sir Thomas Sheridan, at the Prince's back, said in his thin reedy Irish voice. 'Ye will not turn the clock back, thus. The die is cast. 'Tis France for ye now, lad. The only thing, at all, at all. 'Tis but foolishness to be knocking your dear head against the wall . . . '

'God in Heaven – the *Tutor*-General now!' Elcho snorted.

A new uproar sank and dwindled at the hollow beat of horse's hooves on the heather. A single rider came pounding across the moor from the north-east, from the direction of the battlefield, on a shaggy and sweat-lathered Highland garron. A tall lean handsome figure this, dressed in MacGregor tartans and a major's insignia.

'James Mor!' Glengyle exclaimed. 'So we have not lost him yet!' Gregor Black Knee muttered something else below his breath, and he and his son exchanged glances.

'I sent him back to endeavour to reach Locheil,' the Prince said. 'To bring him here, if he might. Alas, it appears . . . otherwise.'

The newcomer flung himself dramatically off his foundered pony, and came swaggering up to the waiting group. Everything that man did was done with a swagger – whether it was leading a charge, seducing a woman, cutting a throat, or merely undermining confidence in lesser men than himself. His bonnet, with its single eagle's feather, now swept low in an exaggerated yet somehow fleering obeisance to the Prince.

'I thank God for your safe return, Major MacGregor,' Charles said – who, unlike some others, esteemed him highly. 'But . . . you are alone, I see!'

'And, on my soul, devilish lucky to be that itself, Highness!' the horseman replied, grinning. 'But, then – the devil aye looks after his own, does he not? Eh, Gregor?' And he glanced side-long at his cousin. 'You preserved your soul also, I see. And even dear Duncan Beg here, likewise!'

'And Locheil?' the Prince asked urgently. 'We have just

17

heard, from Glengyle, that he is said to be wounded. But in the hands of his own people . . . '

'That is more or less the way of it, yes,' the new MacGregor agreed, elaborately stifling a yawn. 'Locheil sends suitable greetings, Highness, and suggests that he will see you another day!'

'Another day? You mean . . . ?'

'I mean, sir, that Locheil is off home to Achnacarry on Loch Arkaig-side as fast as some hundreds of running Cameron heels can carry him. And the Camerons were ever good at running!'

'James Mor will have his little jest, sir,' Gregor of Glengyle interpreted quietly. 'If Cameron of Locheil is shot in both ankles with grape, then he is in no state to be sending greetings, nor yet ordering his clansfolk. And Achnacarry is the best place for him, whatever – and the faster there, the better. Ewan Cameron is as true and sure a man as your Highness commands.'

'Yes, indeed, Glengyle. I know it well . . . '

The two MacGregors looked at each other. They were full cousins, although James Mor was considerably the younger – only a little older, indeed, than Gregor's son, the Captain Duncan. He was a dark, sardonically good-looking man, hawk-faced with just a wicked wisp of moustache and beard, almost as tall as Gregor although less broadly built. He was a son of the famous Rob Roy, now dead some eleven years, but a very different man from his father. Nominally second-in-command of Glengyle's Regiment, which he had led with great gallantry and no less than five wounds at Prestonpans, he had latterly spent most of his time in the Prince's personal entourage as a sort of extra aide-de-camp and courier. His cousin made no complaint at this development – nor his second-cousin either.

'Do not tell me that your own self and Duncan are the sole survivors of our graceless band, Gregor?' James Mor asked.

'There are some six score behind the trees younder. We cut our way out. You were . . . otherwise engaged, I take it, James?'

'Exactly.'

'Have you heard aught of Glencarnock? How his regiment fared?'

There were two MacGregor regiments in the Prince's army, for the clan was split. A part of it recognised Balhaldy as chief of the name of MacGregor, long with King James in France, and of these Glengyle was the foremost chieftain; the other part claimed the leadership for Murray MacGregor of Glencarnock, and he had brought his own following to the Jacobite array. It had been brigaded with the Mackintoshes in the centre of the first line.

'They fared but ill, I fear,' James Mor said. 'Unlike the MacDonalds, the Mackintoshes charged too soon. And Glencarnock with them. Ah, well – they paid the price of impetuosity! Glencarnock ever lacked judgement, did he not? Though they say that he is a prisoner, himself . . .'

'Your Highness – may the MacGregors be permitted to discuss their private affairs on some other occasion!' Lord Elcho interrupted. 'At the moment we have more urgent matters to decide. We have lingered here too long already. At any moment the dragoons may be upon us. A decision must be reached, sir.'

'Yes, yes, my lord.' Charles pressed hand to head again. 'Jamie – did you see aught of skirmishers? Videttes? Are Cumberland's dragoons indeed anywhere near?'

'I dodged three or four parties, yes, on my way back,' the Major said. 'I came by Aultlugie and Daviot Castle. A picket was at the castle – I saw their red coats. And I saw a troop cutting down stragglers along the Nairn's banks below. Another troop were shooting what looked like Menzies men – bright red tartans, at any rate – that they had cornered just over yonder ridge . . .'

'Lord – so close!' the Master of Lovat exclaimed. 'Then it is time that we were gone, by the Rood! Sir, to horse, I say!'

'Indeed yes, Your Highness.'

' 'Tis folly to remain here longer.'

'Very well, gentlemen.' The Prince rose to his feet. 'So be it. If the dragoons are already along the Nairn at Daviot, then the route to Ruthven and Badenoch, by Moy and The Slochd, is already closed. To go northwards again, the way we came, to Inverness, would be foolishness. It is what Cumberland will expect, where he will look for me. He will make for Inverness, certainement. We part here, therefore, gentlemen – to my sorrow. I go south by west, up Strathnairn, as the Master of Lovat advises, for Fort Augustus, the Cameron country and the sea. Whence I came. God pity me!'

'And at Ruthven . . . ?' Elcho demanded. 'The Lord George and the Duke? Cluny Macpherson and the rest? What of them?'

'You will convey to them my love and devotion and grateful thanks, my lord. And my last orders – that they disperse forthwith to their homes.'

'Then . . . Lord God above! All is over! Done with! The Cause is lost – and Scotland with it!'

'I am sorry, my lord – desolate. But . . . I have no choice.'

'You have choice enough, sir – but you choose ill!'

'Enough, sir! You forget yourself. My father's cause will be saved now in France, not here. Not here.'

'Thank God that your Highness has listened to reason!' O'Sullivan cried. 'To wise and proper counsels.'

'A hundred MacGregors, yonder, would not call them that!' Gregor Black Knee said heavily.

'I grieve that you think not, Glengyle. But I must do what I believe is best,' Charles Edward told him. 'For yourself, you also will do what you deem best. For you and for your regiment. It is now every man for himself, I fear.'

'I have no doubts, sir, as to what is best for me and mine. We march north to Inverness, picking up such other stragglers as will march with proper men. Food there is there, and food my men must have. Inverness is still your town, with a garrison and provisions. Cumberland will not take it tonight, with his own wounds to lick! Then we march ever north, into the Mackenzie country of Cromartie and Seaforth. None shall take us, there. Nor take *you*, if you will but come with us . . . ?'

'No, my friend – that is not how it must be. For me. For yourselves, God be with you. We shall maintain contact, for so long as I am in Scotland – for, who knows, I may need your gallant Gregorach yet. No doubt Major Jamie will be with me, to serve as courier between us, if need be . . . '

'Alas, Highness, I think not!' James Mor intervened lightly, smiling yet. 'As you yourself so aptly put it, now it is every man for himself. Myself, I confess that I'd sooner trust my skin to one hundred MacGregor broadswords, in Cumberland's Scotland, than to, h'm, your royally select band! I pray to be excused the honour!'

The Prince looked at him steadily for a moment, brown eyes into black. 'I see,' he said.

Quietly Duncan MacGregor spoke into the brief silence. 'I will come with you, sir. To serve as link,' he said.

His father opened lips to speak, and then closed them again. 'Valiant cousin!' James Mor murmured.

'Very well, Captain,' Charles said. 'That is all then, gentlemen, I think. This is ... farewell. God's blessing on you all ... and the undying gratitude of your Prince. And of your King. I ... I ... ' His voice broke, as he held out his hand to Glengyle.

That man stooped low, to kiss it. Others formed up to do likewise – but not all. Elcho bowed stiffly, from a little way off.

Charles Edward Stuart turned quickly away, and went striding through the trees, towards the troopers of FitzJames's Horse, Young Lovat, Sheridan, O'Sullivan, Hay and Captain O'Neil following. Also, at a decent distance, Ned Burke the Prince's valet.

Duncan MacGregor looked at his father, and clasped his hand silently. Then he glanced at James Mor. 'I will take your garron,' he said. That was all.

Vaulting lightly on to its lather-flecked broad back, he rode after the Prince.

CHAPTER 2

DUNCAN MACGREGOR had to drive the stocky short-legged Highland pony hard indeed even to keep in sight of the Prince's fast-riding company, mounted as they were on tall and comparatively fresh horses. Heading almost due south, they skirted a number of small lochans and peat-pools amongst the heather, making for the long southwards slope towards the River Nairn. They thundered past many fleeing Highlanders, singly and in pairs and small parties, not a few of them carrying or supporting wounded comrades, but stopped for none of them. Duncan noted one party of horsemen on the skyline to the east, but whether they were dragoons or some of their own leaderless cavalry he could not tell, with a storm of sleet lowering its grey curtain between them. The troopers of FitzJames's Horse formed a tight cordon about Charles and his group, and drove their mounts unmercifully.

They reached the river in the vicinity of Faillie and galloped along past the ford of the same name, the water running high and yellow with the rains. The floor of the strath, on both sides of the river, was dotted with hurrying fugitives from the battle, of various clans. Of a company of Frasers, in better order than most, his own people who, like himself had arrived too late to take any notable part in the fighting. Young Lovat demanded in the Gaelic whether any of Cumberland's dragoons had been seen thus far up-river – to be told that a troop of light cavalry in blue tunics, Brunswicker hussars by the description, were indeed in front on this side of the Nairn, ignoring the fleeing infantrymen and apparently making each laird's house in the strath their target. Duncan came up on his pony while this information was being translated, and saw the effect of it upon Charles and his companions. It was decided to turn back a little way, and to cross the ford.

By the time that they had splashed across the river, making a difficult task of it in the flood-water in which they could not see the bottom, the Prince had come to the conclusion that he would be safer without his bodyguard, the sixteen troopers being liable only to draw attention to his little party, whilst being insufficient to protect them against any formation of the enemy that they might be expected to encounter. They were instructed to take themselves off, therefore, to head straight into the trackless mountains of the Monadh Liath south by east, to make their way as best they could to Ruthven. Duncan MacGregor at least was sorry for them; mainly Spaniards and Frenchmen, he believed that their chances of reaching Ruthven, fifty terrible miles away, were slender indeed – even if they never saw a Redcoat.

The Master of Lovat now led the Prince's party of eight. They went more discreetly, no longer in headlong gallop, by little-used tracks and by-ways. The main route up Strath Nairn followed the other bank of the river, and this side was more broken, wooded, and with less of habitation – more apt for fugitives altogether, although innumerable burns coming in off the mountains had to be crossed, often in deep and precipitous ravines and with never a bridge to any of them.

Some five miles up the strath they came to the house of

Mackintosh of Tordarroch. The laird himself had last been seen, wounded but still swording, on Culloden Moor. His house, however, provided his Prince with no sustenance that night, for it stood dark and shuttered, with every appearance of having been but recently and hastily abandoned. Whether indeed anyone lurked within, they could not tell; none answered their banging at the locked and barred doors, at any rate, and all cattle, horses and even poultry were gone from the out-buildings.

It was dark, and raining steadily, before their guide brought them to the next hoped-for sanctuary, some eight miles further – the House of Aberarder. They were in Lovat's own clan territory here, but although the Master had sought Aberarder's aid only the day before in enlisting a second battalion for the Fraser Regiment, tonight his house was as black and deserted as that of Tordarroch. Clearly word of the defeat had preceded them, with the uncanny swiftness by which news can travel in the seemingly empty Highlands – with this result. The implications, the acceptance that all was lost and only savage reprisals could now be expected, did nothing to cheer hungry, weary and disheartened travellers.

'By the Cross of Christ – they have not waited long before scuttling into their hills!' O'Sullivan exclaimed, disgustedly.

'Would you – with German Cumberland charged to teach Scotland a lesson?' Sawny MacLeod demanded.

When, at Farraline, another Fraser house a few miles further, and over the watershed into Stratherrick, they discovered the same state of affairs, Young Lovat, crestfallen and angry, came to a decision. They would make for Gortlech House, across at the other side of Loch Farraline, even although it would involve a long and arduous circuit of the loch. They would find that house open and occupied, at any rate – for no less a person than the great MacShimi, his father the Lord Lovat himself, was presently lodging there. That he had not proposed to conduct his Prince to Gortlech and his father – who held a Jacobite lieutenant-general's commission from King James – before this, might have appeared a little strange in the circumstances; but perhaps the Master had his own reasons, and moreover knew the great MacShimi better than most.

Heavily, wordlessly now, the tired and dispirited party splashed and floundered and stumbled its way around the flooded boggy shores of Loch Farraline, the horses now as weary as their riders. Indeed, in the pass, Duncan MacGregor's sturdy garron made the best showing, making up in stamina for what it lacked in pace and style, sure-footed and with an apparent ability to see in the dark. Until near the house itself, on rising ground to the west of the loch, Duncan led the way in fact.

The Master had been right. Lights shone in friendly fashion from the windows of Gortlech House. Nevertheless, the little company's welcome was less than reassuring, warm as it might be. When still approaching uphill through dripping birch trees and shadowy junipers, the horsemen were suddenly and without warning surrounded by a horde of Gaelic-shouting fighting-men who seemed to rise out of the very ground at their horses' hooves, swords and dirks in their hands. They had old Sheridan, O'Sullivan and Ned Burke dragged off their mounts and naked steel at their throats before the Master of Lovat could make his identity recognised. The Prince and O'Neil were hurriedly drawing their own swords and at the same time seeking to control their rearing steeds, when MacLeod and Duncan Mac-Gregor managed to convey to them that these were only MacShimi's guards and loyal Frasers all.

In an atmosphere compounded of relief, resentment and lingering suspicion, all came to Gortlech House.

Fraser of Gortlech himself appeared to be a man torn by conflicting emotions. When the quality of his guests was made known to him, he most evidently did not know whether to express first his sense of honour, his commiserations or his own agitation and alarm. That he also had heard the news of Culloden was apparent — and the fact that he had had a son in the battle, of whose fate the Master could tell him nothing, did not help to soothe him. He and his lady, in fact mislead by a garbled report of the supposed success of the Jacobite army's abortive night venture against Cumberland's birthday celebrations at Nairn, had that day been preparing a great feast to celebrate the Prince's anticipated victory, and his old chief's imminent translation to his coveted dukedom. Now, in incoherent gabbling perturbation, he led Charles and his followers upstairs to the principal room of the house.

There was nothing of incoherence or apparent perturbation about the man who sat at ease, decanter in hand, alone at the head of a long and groaning table therein. Coming in out of the wet and windy night, after that prolonged and perilous flight from horror and disaster, the quiet comfort, plenty and air of assured and established well-being in the lamp-lit and richly provisioned apartment, was sufficiently striking to bring up the dishevelled and travel-stained newcomers with an almost physical start.

As indeed did the appearance of the room's sole occupant. Simon Fraser made an extraordinary figure. Squat and heavy and immensely broad, almost toad-like, he sprawled there, gross, repulsively ugly in form and feature, yet of an undeniable and strange distinction. Sagging-bodied, blotchy of face, physically corrupt, but shrewd-eyed, glittering-eyed indeed, his thick gouty legs stuck out before him like great logs, he was slovenly clad in a mixture of Highland and Lowland dress, the tartans so stained as to be unrecognisable, the disordered lace at throat and wrists torn and discoloured, wig askew, small-clothes undone. An old man, nearing his eightieth year in fact, he sat there dissipated, potent, ageless.

'MacShimi,' his son announced, from the Prince's shoulder. 'His Royal Highness the Prince of Wales, Duke of Rothesay, and Chevalier de Saint George.'

Lovat stared, silent for a moment or two, and then made a mere gesture at rising to his feet – an action of which he was obviously incapable without assistance. 'My esteemed and beloved sir, my precious Prince and true paladin,' he said. 'Scotland's fair hope and future King – behold your most humble, loving and devoted servant!' That was enunciated in courtly French, in a voice singularly and unexpectedly musical, clear and youthful-sounding. 'I rejoice that these old eyes should be thus blest. Your Royal Highness – will you come close that these poor lips may kiss your hand?'

Charles Edward, distrait and weary as he might be, was not a man who could fail to respond to such a greeting. Lack-lustre eyes lighting warmly, he strode forward beside the table to its head, hand outstretched, smiling. 'My lord,' he exclaimed, 'I rejoice that we meet at last! I have heard much of you . . . '

'And not all of it to my credit, I swear, lad!' the old man took him up swiftly, kissing the royal fingers. 'Wae's me, there's a-many who would see me low that they might ride higher – many who would make bad blood between MacShimi and your gracious father, to their own advantage.' He continued to hold and plant kisses on the Prince's hand, in embarrassing and almost maudlin fashion – but his shrewd little eyes darted and probed.

'My father, like myself, is assured of your faithful love and devotion, my lord,' Charles declared. 'I would only that I came to assert it on a happier occasion.'

'Aye – so does MacShimi, lad! So does MacShimi! An ill night, this, for true men, by all accounts.' Lovat cast a quick glance at his son. 'There will be a price to pay for the day's work, I warrant. That some of us will pay dearer than others! Who have less to lose! Were you in it, at all, Sim? Were you in it? I'm thinking likely you would not have been in time to be actually drawing a sword, at all?' There was little doubt as to the answer that he hoped for, in that.

'All was lost by the time that I came up,' the Master told him. 'As you know, I had been raising a second battalion. I was only in time to strike a blow or two. And help cover His Highness's retiral . . . '

'Fool!' his father spat out unexpectedly, almost viciously. 'What good in that? To draw sword when a fight is lost is the work of a half-wit! Naught is achieved, save to bring down punishment upon the innocent and the helpless!' He gestured, and most clearly included his own gross helplessness in the sweep of his hand. 'There is a time to strike – and a time to withhold, 'fore God!'

'Your lordship knows well, sure, the difficulty of nicely judging such time,' O'Sullivan mentioned tartly, from down the table – in scarcely veiled allusion to Lovat's own long-delayed and indeed only recent public commitment to the present Jacobite venture.

The great head jerked round with almost reptilian speed. 'To whom have I the honour to listen, Your Highness?' he snapped.

'To Colonel O'Sullivan, my Adjutant-General and Quarter-master,' the Prince informed. And quickly. 'Here also is Sir Thomas Sheridan, Colonel Hay, Military Secretary, Captains O'Neil and MacLeod, aides, and . . . '

'Aye, aye – to be sure. Wórthy warriors all, I'll be bound! Welcome to MacShimi's poor table, gentlemen. It was prepared to signal your victory – not your defeat! But draw in, draw in – we must e'en do as we're done by. Your Highness – a glass. Fill up. We shall drink a toast to better days . . . '

'My lord,' Colonel Hay said stiffly. 'The Prince – all of us – have not eaten more than a biscuit all day. Nor much more yesterday, indeed. This food . . . ' He waved at the laden table, all but licking his lips. 'I . . . we . . . '

'Why – set to then, gentlemen. God save us – set to! Victory or defeat – and I'm waiting to hear why it was the latter, mind – victory or defeat, the belly must be served. Highness – sit you here, by me. Gortlech, man – fetch more meats, cates, provision. And the claret's low. Though poor MacShimi may die for it, none shall say that his Prince came to his table and was not filled, sought shelter and was turned away!'

'It is only a bite and a sup that we seek, my lord,' Charles told him. 'We must be far from here before the night is out, I assure you. I must reach the sea, the Western Sea, as soon as may be, to my sorrow.'

'Say ye so?' Lord Lovat considered the younger man thoughtfully.

The others, without ceremony or delay, fell upon the spread food.

The pangs of his hunger appeased for the moment, Duncan MacGregor sat back in the lowest place at that table, and eyed his host and provider with but little of the gratitude that would have been seemly. He did not trust the noble mountain of flesh one inch further than his broadsword tip would reach – being a MacGregor and of an uncomplicated mind. The man had changed sides so often, was so well known to have sold the Stuart cause time and again, that this guest at least wondered indeed how the Prince could have anything to do with him. Presumably it was because he was still one of the greatest chiefs in the Highlands, and could raise a thousand Fraser swords. Could – but would he? Ever? He was clever, too – too clever by half; but had he ever turned either his talents or his power to any purpose other than his own private satisfaction or advancement? The Gregorach would have known how to deal with MacShimi.

But Charles Edward, as ever, was apparently prepared to believe the best of him. As he ate and drank he answered Lovat's probing questions about the battle unreservedly, accepted his belching strictures and improved strategy patiently, and only gently corrected the Fraser when his outspoken denunciation of practically all others exceeded the allowable. Duncan marvelled

27

at his forbearance – and would not believe it weakness.

Suddenly Lovat changed his tune. 'And what's this about making for the sea, young man?' he demanded. 'The sea will be winning you no battles. What is your meaning?'

'My meaning, sir, is to return to France. French ships were to keep patrol along that seaboard, where I landed those months ago. To seek to prevail upon King Louis to honour his pledge and send us the men and arms and money which he promised. That, as I see it, is the most effective way in which I may serve my father, and you all, in this pass. I cannot . . . '

'France, eh?' the old chief interrupted. 'You are for France again? On which knave's advice would you be fleeing away to France, man? Will you leave your loyal and faithful Highlands, because of one reverse?'

The Prince frowned. 'You call this day's disaster but a reverse, my lord . . . ?'

'A ruffle, sir – a ruffle, no more. There are as many bold lads in the heather within fifty miles of this house as Cumberland can count in all Scotland!'

'But no guns for them, no ammunition, no provisions, no money. And but few trained officers,' Charles shook his fair head, heavily. 'I have discovered, my friend, that more than bold lads are needful to win a throne, and to defeat trained and disciplined soldiers . . . '

'They did it at Prestonpans and Clifton, did they not? Even at Falkirk . . . '

'At Preston they were fresh, light-hearted, full of confidence, of hope. We all were full of hope. Today, it is . . . otherwise. We have retreated six hundred miles, from Derby, six hundred long miles. Have you ever been in a very long retreat, my lord? I think not.' Even Charles could sound bitter, on a rare occasion. 'We have been losing men, whole companies, by desertion, through offence, through petty squabbling, for months. *Ma foi* – today's ruffle, as you name it, was the end, the culmination, of many reverses, not the first.' The Prince's voice wavered, and his head sank forward almost to his arms upon the table.

Lovat's urgent glance considered him, and all of the other heavy-eyed, weary and dishevelled men around his table, probing, calculating – and Duncan MacGregor, of them all, watched him. Then the old man's great swollen hand clapped down on the younger's shoulder.

28

'Och, och, lad – you are tired, that is all,' he cried. 'Here is no way for Scotland's future King to talk! Damnation – your great ancestor talked not so, sir! King Robert Bruce, who lost eleven battles yet won Scotland by the twelfth! Take heart, man!'

Charles slowly raised his head. 'You think . . . you believe . . . that I can yet rally the cause? At this late hour?' he faltered. 'That there is still support for me in Scotland, to win the day? *You* think that?'

'By the Mass, I do! Would MacShimi, with his own head and fortune and a province to lose, be sitting here persuading you to it, otherwise. Hech, hech, sir – what do you take me for?'

That question more than one man was asking himself, at Gortlech's table, Duncan MacGregor not the least searchingly. He who would die for his Prince, doubted strongly whether the Lord Lovat would do so. Why then was he counselling resistance? Duncan himself, like his father, was for the continuance of the fight, at all costs, and should have welcomed this powerful ally. But why did MacShimi so urge, when clearly the fight would be long and arduous, and success far from assured? He, who knew only too well the difficulties, the weaknesses of the clan system, the fatal jealousies of the chiefs, the unending intrigues – he, indeed, who had instigated so many of the intrigues himself? Lovat had delayed to the very last moment, before reluctantly joining the Prince – and even so, maintaining a loophole of escape by pretending to the Government that it was really his headstrong son's doing against an old man's wishes. Why should he now talk as thought victory could be just behind the next hill?

Charles himself, it seemed, however forgiving, was not wholly blind to this curious contradiction. 'And yet you, my lord, not so long ago, were naming me . . . what was it? A mad and unaccountable gentleman, I think. Yes, such a one, for coming to Scotland at all, without a French army, urging me to return thither, and assuring that all that you could offer me, in these circumstances, were your prayers! Here is a notable change, to be sure?'

For a moment Lovat's extraordinary face was wiped clear of all expression. Then he smiled, almost reproachfully. 'Your Highness will be recognising that circumstances can alter prospects, whatever! You have proved, bonny sir, that you can win battles as you can men's hearts. That the Highlands will rise for you – even if the Lowlands and the Englishry will not. That MacShimi was mistaken yon time. Sink me, lad – now that Cumberland is at our very doors, will not the Highlands rise the more readily? If ten thousand rose to march with you away to yonder London, how many more will rise to defend their own glens, their own rooftrees?'

'I would that I could believe you, my lord . . .'

Duncan thought that he saw it now. The phrase of Lovat's – now that Cumberland is at our very doors! Was that the key to it all? Nearer to Clan Fraser's doors than any other. That could be the reason for MacShimi's fervour. He would have the Rising prolonged, the clans reassembled, the battle renewed – to save his own territory from being over-run, his own rooftrees spared. That made sense out of MacShimi. It was entirely in character for the man to seek to sacrifice a host in his own protection.

Perhaps even MacGregor was not wholly unbiased in this conclusion – and something of Prince Charles's problem in holding together a clan army exemplified.

It was noticeable that the Master of Lovat uttered no words in his puissant father's presence.

'His lordship's faith is touching, sir – but, I fear, too late!' O'Sullivan put in, out of a full mouth. 'A thousand Frasers yesterday – and all might have been otherwise!'

'The Irish, I have ever observed, are an unhappy race,' Lovat mentioned conversationally. 'As over-ready with their tongues as they are backward in judgement. And manners, forby . . .'

'Sir!' O'Sullivan's chair scraped back over the floor abruptly. 'I will take such words from no man, by God! Not even you . . .'

'At MacShimi's table, eating MacShimi's victuals, you have scant choice, man! Sit you down and fill your belly, Quartermaster. Belike you'll travel far and fare worse!'

'Your Royal Highness, I protest!' That was Captain O'Neil rising in support of his fellow-countryman.

'Gentlemen, gentlemen!' Almost automatically, and so very wearily, the Prince called his followers to order – as he had been doing for nine months. 'We are beholden to Lord Lovat, and our need is great. His lordship did but jest, I am sure. We have no time to waste on such foolishness. We must be gone forthwith. We cannot linger here.'

Lovat turned back to the speaker swiftly. 'Where?' he demanded. 'Where go you now?'

'Where, but through Locheil's and Glengarry's country, to the sea?'

'Not waiting for the clans to assemble again?'

Charles shrugged his shoulders, helplessly, hopelessly.

'See you,' the old man pressed. 'Send you out orders, from here. Now. My gillies will carry them. Through our own country. Into Lochaber and Locheil and Ardgour. Into Glengarry and Glenmoriston. Into Badenoch and Atholl. To rally to Your Highness. Not here – not just here, mind. This is not a convenient place, at all. At Fort Augustus, maybe. Aye, at Fort Augustus – that would be best ... '

'I have not the time, my lord. I must be well beyond Fort Augustus by daylight. You do not understand – Cumberland's dragoons are at our heels. They are scouring the country. *Mon Dieu* – some of his light cavalry was actually ahead of us, coming up Strath Nairn!'

'*Dia* – you say that? They were that far?'

'They were. I cannot wait for the clans to reassemble. Long ere they could do so, I would be in Cumberland's bloody hands.'

Lovat's thick fingers beat a tattoo on the table. 'What of Cluny? My good-son. Cluny and his Macphersons cannot be that far away ... ?'

'No doubt they are now hurrying back into their own mountain fastnesses in Badenoch. They may have joined with the Lord George and the Duke, making for Ruthven.'

There was a sombre pause. Into it, since no one else saw fit to speak, greatly daring, Duncan MacGregor raised his voice.

'Your Highness,' he said. 'MacShimi. There is a middle course. Whereby much may be saved, much gained – and Your Highness's person preserved from capture. Your army, your officers, scattered as they may be, will be looking for orders from their Captain-General – nothing is surer. Send them orders, from here, sir, as MacShimi says, by his gillies. To assemble in two days, three days. Somewhere that is suitable and safe. In the Cameron country – Loch Arkaig. The dragoons will not dare to penetrate yonder for some time, where they could be trapped like rats. And for immediately, tonight, tomorrow – have MacShimi's runners go out to his own people. And to others near at hand, Glengarry's people, Grants of Glenmoriston, and to the Keppoch country. Ordering them to meet with you at Fort Augustus. At dawn, if you wish it. The hour is barely nine. By dawn, in eight hours, many could reach Fort Augustus.' Duncan looked directly at Lovat. 'I have no doubt that the great MacShimi alone could have five hundred Frasers there by then! With these, your Highness could then retire westwards meantime, safe into the Cameron country. Then join the main assembly at Loch Arkaig or elsewhere, later.'

Lovat glowered at the MacGregor heavily. 'Here's a young cockerel crows loud and clear!' he growled. 'Out of a Gregorach roost, by the colours of him! Cattle-thieves, of course, are aye apt for night work and dodging in the heather!'

Duncan's knuckles gleamed white as he clenched his fists on the arms of his chair. But he held his tongue.

'And yet, my lord, Captain MacGregor – who is son to Glengyle – speaks good sense, does he not?' the Prince observed. 'And largely in accord with your own suggestions, it seems?'

The old man pulled at his fleshy chin. Although superficially Duncan's proposals might seem but an extension of Lovat's own, in fact they were quite otherwise. Quite clearly the course that the younger man envisaged would drain Fraser manpower away from Fraser territory, committing Lovat to a major role in any resurrection of the campaign, and at the same time leaving his own lands largely unprotected. It did not demand any great percipience to recognise that this was a very different matter from having the Jacobite army reassembling at Fort Augustus, less than twenty miles away on the verge of Fraser country, where it would serve to keep Cumberland's marauding cavalry at a distance. Minds round that table, of course, were sluggish and fogged with fatigue.

'Ah. H'mmm.' Their host cast darting glances round them all. 'I will do what I can. What I can. Och, yes – MacShimi will do what may be done, whatever. But . . . what sense is there in getting swallowed up away yonder in Locheil's country? Barren empty mountains, just . . . '

'But secure, my lord – secure. Hemmed in and guarded by the same barren mountains. The enemy may only approach yonder by one route, which is easily guarded.'

'Aye. But once in there, the clans themselves will be trapped.

Better assemble in some more central place, Highness. Where all may readily come together. Fort Augustus, I swear, would be the best . . . '

'For Augustus will be warming with Redcoats by noontide tomorrow, sir. No – if assembly there shall be, it had better be in the west. Loch Arkaig is as good as any.' Charles Edward stood up – and perforce all others, save only Lovat himself, must do likewise. 'Let that be the way of it, gentlemen. Though God knows if aught will come of it!'

'How shall all these be fed? In these so notoriously barren mountains, sir?' O'Sullivan demanded.

'They must just fend for themselves. As ourselves must do . . . '

'Let the orders command those coming from their own homes, at least – the Frasers and others – each to bring a pouch of oatmeal enough for a week, sir,' Duncan advised, quickly.

'Orders . . . !' The Prince ran a hand through his hair. '*Ma foi* – never did I feel less like writing orders. Sawny MacLeod – write to Cluny. And to Lord George. To meet at Loch Arkaig in three days. I shall sign it. You yourself will carry the message. See as many chiefs and commanders as you may. You understand?'

'Yes, sir. And what of those to the north? Beyond Inverness? Glengyle's and Barrisdale's Regiments? My Lord Cromartie's force . . . ?'

'I shall go for them,' Duncan said.

'No,' the Prince decided. 'There is no time for them to come. Inverness and all around it will be in Cumberland's hands by morning, by now it may be. To reach these others, and bring them all the way south and west to Loch Arkaig, round through the Mackenzie country, would take many days. Let them remain north of Inverness meantime, as a threat to Cumberland's rear. Sawny – write your orders, and I shall sign them. My lord – you need no written orders from me to your people? To have them at Fort Augustus by the dawn? In eight hours. You will send them your own instructions?'

Lovat toyed with his wine-glass. 'No doubt you are right, Highness,' he said at length. 'Aye – MacShimi will send his own instructions.'

'Very well. Then, as quickly as we may, gentlemen, let us be

33

on our way. With our grateful thanks to my Lord Lovat. And to the Master.'

The old man cackled a laugh.

CHAPTER 3

THE little group of men huddled together behind the broken ramparts of the fort, to gain such shelter as they might from the thin driving rain. None had spoken for the best part of an hour, other than to mutter a curse or two. In the grey light of early morning the scene was as desolate as were their spirits. The shattered walls of Fort Augustus, named after Cumberland himself and strengthened and enlarged by General Wade only six years before, had been stormed and demolished by the Frasers only a month ago – the sign and symbol of Lovat's belated public adherence to the Jacobite cause. Today, however, they spoke nothing of victory, or triumph; only of dripping ruin and owl-haunted desolation. The surrounding hillsides were blotted out under low mists and rain. Some of the men had dozed, as they crouched there, at the first, all but stupefied by lack of sleep; but the chill had soon awakened them again to their miseries.

It was only a small company that waited there. Captain MacLeod had departed southwards, with a Fraser gillie as guide, making for Ruthven by Glen Tarff and the Corryarrack Pass – no easy journey in such conditions. The Master of Lovat had remained behind at Gortlech with his father, meantime. Only the Prince, Hay of Restalrig, and three Irishmen and Ned Burke the servant, apart from Duncan MacGregor, kept their trying vigil by the ruined fort.

That it was a vigil as fruitless as it was trying, had become ever more evident as the comfortless minutes had lengthened into hours. No one had been found there when the royal party had arrived, at around three in the morning; no single man had approached the rendezvous since. The seven fugitive were quite alone in the grey cold world of the mountains.

The Prince had been fretting almost from the start, his reluctant agreement to an attempt to resume the campaign fading like snow in summer. Nor did the three Irishmen, Charles's closest intimates, seek to maintain his resolve – nor yet Colonel Hay, whose views were quite otherwise. Only the young Mac-Gregor sought to counter the tide of reaction and pessimism, and that with the inevitable lack of authority of a very junior regimental officer – although he was in fact a couple of years older than the Prince himself. Even Duncan fell silent as time wore on.

At last Charles would stand it no longer. '*Dieu de Dieu* – this is intolerable!' he cried. 'What profit is there in further waiting? Are we lepers, to lurk and skulk here, shunned of all? None come. None rally to us – not one man! So much for Lovat's bold clansmen! A thousand Frasers within a few miles of me, and not one will rally to my banner! Not one to draw sword for his King!'

'Belike scarce one knows that you are here, sir,' O'Sullivan said. 'My Lord Lovat may have changed his mind, I think! Not for the first time!'

'The old fox has sent out no orders, at all, I swear!' Hay asserted. 'He has held his hand, curse him! I never trusted the man. Though it was but a crazy project from the first . . . '

'Even in his disappointment and despondency, Charles would not hear so ill of the Fraser chief. 'No, no, my friends – Lovat would not act so ill,' he declared. 'He is a strange man – but one of my father's oldest friends and supporters. It will be his people. They will have perhaps fled into the hills. Left their homes. For fear of the dragoons. That will be it. His messengers will still be seeking them . . . '

For once, Duncan MacGregor tended to be in agreement with O'Sullivan and Hay – although he did not say so. 'No doubt Your Highness is right,' he acceded. 'And eight hours is but a short time, at dead of night, to arm and leave all and come here . . . '

'But we dare not wait longer here, Charles.' Old Sir Thomas Sheridan had roused himself and risen, still bent and aching, from the fallen masonry on which he had been sitting. 'You have delayed overlong already,' he said, his teeth chattering. 'Danger there is, all around us, here. The main road, it is, between Inverness and Fort William. Cumberland is bound to effect a junction with his garrison at Fort William, forthwith. Sure, it is madness, lad, to linger here.'

'That is true, sir. Your Highness's safety demands that we go from here. At once . . .'

'Yes, John. Yes. We shall go. Forthwith. To Glengarry's house. It is not any great distance, I believe. Our beasts can do it – and so can we. How far, Duncan my friend?'

'Eight or nine miles, perhaps. No more.'

'Better that we do not halt there, sir – that we go on westwards,' O'Sullivan objected. 'We should still be on this same road from Inverness, at Invergarry. Better to go on through the Cameron country, to the sea. I' faith, the sooner we reach the sea . . .'

'No, John. I told Lovat that I would move on to Glengarry's house from this rendezvous. His people may reach us there.'

'And others, likewise, Christ God!'

'I think not. Not so soon. It lies more secure than this, if I mind aright? How think you, Duncan?'

'I do not think that dragoons will reach Invergarry today, sir. Nor attack the castle if they do. It is in a strong position. And since Your Highness said that you would go there . . .'

'Very well. So be it. Gentlemen – to Invergarry. And, pray God, a bed!'

The rain had stopped and the sun had risen above the mountain ramparts to the east before the fugitives reached the long narrow sheet of Loch Oich, further down the endless gut of the Great Glen. It transformed all the upheaved world of the high places into a wonderland of colour and dazzlement, of light and shade, of the deep sepia of old heather streaked with the emerald of moss and bog and the crimson of raw red earth, of the bottle green of the old Scots pines and the tender verdance of the budding silver birches, the blue of the loch and the white mist-wraiths rising out of the high corries, water glistening and gleaming everywhere and the heady sweet scent of the bog-myrtle ascending like incense to the praise of the new day.

All this brilliance but little lifted the spirits of the travellers, however – more especially when, midway down the west shore, on a jutting green peninsula where the turbulent River Garry joined its peat-brown waters to the loch, they saw the tall reddish-grey walls of Invergarry Castle rising forbiddingly before them, and not a plume of smoke from a chimney, not a flicker of movement from window or doorway, nor any sign of life about the place. In silence they rode up to the obviously empty, barred and deserted stronghold of the Glengarry chief.

It was a doubly bitter moment for Charles Edward Stuart. Here, within these walls only eight months before, he had been welcomed and feted by young Aeneas MacDonnell – who now lay buried at Falkirk. His father, John, twelfth of Glengarry, was a less successful fence-sitter than Lovat, and, unknown to his would-be guests, was even now lodged securely in Edinburgh Castle. His elder son Alastair, Young Glengarry, was still an officer in the French service. But Aeneas, nineteen years old, had brought out six hundred of the clan for the Cause. Here, last August, the Clanranald MacDonalds and the Appin Stewarts had also joined the Prince's standard, amidst high hopes. And now – this.

Sleep they must have, however. Unable to gain entry to the securely locked and barricaded castle, they hid the horses in a deserted stable and bedded down near-by in a loft and sweet-scented bog-hay. Duncan MacGregor volunteered to keep the first hour's watch.

For most of that day they lay at Invergarry. They were neither disturbed nor reinforced. No dragoons came near; no armed parties of clansmen came to join them, Frasers, Mac-Donnells or other; no living soul indeed approached that green peninsula in the blue loch. In the afternoon, Duncan, waking refreshed and hungry, searched the place for possible food – and found nothing. He did, however, notice salmon-nets permanently staked out in the loch across the mouth of the in-coming Garry. Taking a chance, he threw aside the clothes which had not been off his back in ten days and nights, and plunged into the water, gasping at its chill but glad of its cleanly purging. He was fortunate enough to find two salmon caught in the stake-nets, and brought them back to the shore in triumph. Although neither were monsters, they were quite substantial fish. Ned Burke cooked them on a modest fire of twigs and driftwood, roasted on spits. None complained that they were charred on the outside and under-cooked within. They were all the hospitality that Invergarry offered the Prince that day.

There was no argument, this time, as to moving on. That they could not stay here was self-evident. With the sun low over the massed abruptly rising hills to the west, a start was made. They turned south again, down the lochside, heading for Loch Lochy, the next sheet of water, where they could turn away westwards out of this Great Glen which cut Scotland in half, off through the narrow defile of the Dark Mile, into the Cameron country. They planned to ride all night again, towards the Hebridean Sea.

They had gone no more than a mile or so down the shore of the loch when they were abruptly brought to a halt. From the high rocky bank on their right fully a dozen armed men leapt down on to the drove-road at their sides, broadswords and dirks in hand. Ahead, a group of men appeared, kilted and plaided, barring the way.

'Stand, you!' a voice commanded fiercely, in the Gaelic. 'And never a hand on your weapons at all, if you value your lives!'

Twisting round in their saddles, the horsemen perceived three more Highlanders standing where they had just ridden, cocked pistols in hand.

Duncan MacGregor, unlike O'Neil, did not waste time in seeking to draw his sword. In the same motion that he whipped the plaid from around his shoulders, he flung himself bodily off his short-legged garron and on top of the nearest attacker. Two pistol shots cracked out as he plunged down. One ball tore a hole in the flapping corner of the plaid.

The folds of loose tartan cloth enveloped the unfortunate ambusher below, engulfing himself and his upraised broadsword even before Duncan's body knocked him flat on the ground. The MacGregor fell with him, inevitably, and the two men immediately became a struggling, rolling entity of flailing limbs and heaving tartan – into which none of the others might plunge steel for fear of striking the wrong man.

Captain O'Neil was indiscreet enough to unsheath his sword. One of the pistols had been aimed at him. The shot went low, scored a glancing wound along his horse's croup and went on just to sear the skin of O'Neil's thigh. With a whinny of pain the beast reared, throwing its rider sideways out of the saddle, and cannoning heavily into the Prince's mount. Charles, tugging at his own sword, was all but unseated, and found the retaining of his balance as much as he could do before half a dozen fierce hands grasped him and pulled him down to the road.

O'Sullivan, who had been shouting to the Prince to spur and

bolt forward, to ride down the men in front, at sight of his master's downfall, cursed, folded his arms, and so sat. Hay and old Sheridan prudently did nothing.

On the ground near-by the struggling pile had become larger, for Duncan, perceiving a pair of dancing feet near his head and assuming that they represented menace to himself, had thrust out an arm to encircle their owner's ankles, and brought down a second attacker with a crash upon himself – thereby unfortunately partly winding himself.

The MacGregor's object in all this, of drawing the onslaught of as many as possible of their aggressors upon himself, in order to allow the Prince to effect an escape, although it did not gain its ultimate aim, certainly attracted attention. When, in fact, no other fighting was going on, fully half the score or so of assailants were able to concentrate on him. That his somewhat ridiculous situation ended with a crack on the head from a pistol-butt wielded by the leader of the company, rather than many dirks being thrust into his body, was significant for more than Duncan Beg. (However it struck the others, its significance eluded the MacGregor just then.) His twisting thrashing body suddenly went limp, and his consciousness slipped away into welcome darkness.

Turning to the rest of the Prince's party, the spokesman of the enemy considered them all briefly and barked some orders in Gaelic, which evidently had to do with the holding and quietening down of the alarmed horses. Then, in English, he spoke – and it was noticeable that it was to O'Sullivan that he addressed himself.

'You are my prisoners, gentlemen,' he said, and it was apparent that the language did not come easily to him. He was a small wiry man, with a pronounced limp, dressed in a mixture of tartans, keen-eyed, swift of movement, with something of the aspect of a lame terrier dog. 'If you will not be foolish at all, no hurt will be coming to you. Come down from your horses, if you please.'

Those still mounted did as they were ordered.

'Are you Campbells, from Loudon's Regiment at Fort William?' O'Sullivan found his voice to demand.

The small man did not answer. He issued more swift orders to his followers, who proceeded to relieve the prisoners of their

39

weapons and hemmed them in in a tight group. Others picked up the unconscious MacGregor, and threw him unceremoniously, like a sack, across the back of the most convenient horse, which was his own short-legged garron. Some took the other horses in charge, but none mounted. The leader put two fingers to his mouth and blew two ear-piercing whistles. In a few moments two men came running to them from around the twists of the drove-road, one from up-loch and one from down. Obviously they had been pickets set to watch the road for possible interruption. When these had joined them, without any further delay or discussion the small man led the entire company off the road, directly up the rocky bank at the west side and into the birches and alders of the steep wooded hillside above. The Prince and his companions had to use their hands, and sometimes even their knees, to aid them up the abruptly-rising and broken slippery slope, and the led cavalry horses made but a poor task of the ascent unlike the sure-footed pony that carried Duncan MacGregor.

No delay of man nor beast was permitted.

It was quite high above the road in the valley floor before they were granted a respite, very near the tree-line indeed, and the prisoners were panting heavily, Sir Thomas Sheridan especially being in much distress. There was a fairly well-defined track up here, running parallel with the road below but quite hidden from it. Along this, northwards again, the company turned. It was only on protests from the Prince and O'Sullivan that their principal captor agreed to a brief halt.

'Where are you taking us?' Charles Edward asked, of the leader, breathlessly. 'Why are you forcing us to climb this hill? Can you not see that it is too much for this gentleman? He is no longer young . . . '

The Prince was interrupted by Duncan MacGregor, coming to himself draped over the garron's back, and being violently sick. Charles promptly transferred his attention to him, aiding him down off the pony and supporting him as he staggered dizzily.

'My poor Duncan,' he said. '*Mon brave, mon ami* – you will feel very ill. See – take this. It will help.' And he drew a slim silver flask out of the capacious pocket of his long-skirted jacket of Stewart tartan, unscrewed the cap, and set it to the other's lips. 'Drink!'

Duncan sipped the fiery whisky gratefully. There was not a lot left in the flask. As, choking a little, he was handing it back to its owner, the small limping man stepped forward and snatched it from them. Briefly admiring the handsome craftsmanship and the Prince of Wales's feathers engraved thereon, he thrust it inside the folds of his own plaid, and turned away, pointing forward peremptorily.

'You are welcome, of course, friend,' Charles commented, shrugging, with a half-smile. 'So long as you will spare us the contents. Sir Thomas Sheridan, here, could well do with a mouthful, I swear.'

O'Sullivan who, like the other prisoners, had taken the opportunity to sit down amongst the young sprouting bracken, spoke up. 'That is no way to behave towards His Royal Highness, fellow!' he protested.

'Royal Highness . . . ?' the other repeated, looking from the speaker to Charles, and back. 'Are you not then the . . . the *Prionnsa*?'

The man looked along at the tall but slight and graceful figure supporting the unsteady MacGregor. It was perhaps not altogether strange that he had made his mistake. O'Sullivan was considerably older than the Prince, with a haughty and authoritative manner. The way that he had sat his horse, arms folded, after the attack, had been dignified, whatever else it was. Charles had lost his bonnet on Culloden Moor, and wore no distinguishing marks of his rank; and he was the one who appeared to be concerned for the welfare of the rest, rather than the master of them all. Their captor stared at him thoughtfully – and then turning about abruptly, gestured for the march to be resumed, and went striding ahead at a great pace.

Willy-nilly the prisoners followed, the Prince still assisting Duncan – that is until the leader, glancing back, noted it and sent a gillie to take the MacGregor's arm instead. When Charles called out that Sheridan would delay them less if he was mounted on the garron, since they seemed to be in an unconscionable hurry, the small man nodded shortly. Sir Thomas was allowed to ride thereafter.

Thus, with the gloaming all about them, they travelled northwards, dipping down presently through thicker woodland, to cross the rushing Garry by a dangerous-seeming ford perhaps a mile above the loch, the gillies plunging in up to their waists without the least hesitation, although the saddle-horses required a deal of coaxing, with the Prince's party mounted again for the moment. Beyond, they entered the cover of the woods once more.

It was dark by the time that they crossed to the other side of the Great Glen, avoiding the Bridge of Oich and fording that river considerably further up, an unpleasant proceeding in the gloom. Then, despite protests from the tired and stumbling captives, they turned due eastwards up the long slow slope that lifted eventually, beyond the tree-level, to a bare shoulder of heather hill. All made it unmistakably clear that they were in no condition for hill climbing – not that they seemed to make any impression on their captor, who appeared to be tireless despite his limp. He pressed on down into the deeper shadows of a lesser glen beyond.

'This must be Glen Tarff,' Duncan told them. 'General Wade's new road runs up it, on the way to the Corryarrack.'

'What do we here, then?' the Prince demanded. 'Where are we being taken?'

Nobody answered him that.

Sure enough, presently they came down to the long pale scar of the military road, which after reconnaissance by their guards, they crossed and without delay plunged into a country of more woodland, scattered lochans and innumerable hummocks beyond. They had to stumble and flounder through almost a couple of miles of this before the small man acceded to the pleas of his prisoners and made a camp for the night.

They were back into the Fraser country again.

Round a fire of resinous and aromatic pine branches they sat thereafter, fed after a fashion by their escort on tough dried venison and *dramach*, or oatmeal and cold water mixed in an unappetising paste. Some of the gillies were posted as sentries, but most just cast themselves down amongst the blaeberries and slept without ceremony, but close to their captives. These continued to sit around the fire, and discussed their plight, at first in lowered tones. Only a few yards away the small limping man sat and watched them, alert, silent. More than once the Prince sought to question him, to engage him in the conversation, to find out where he was taking them – but without avail. He had a great gift for silence, that man.

'Clearly we are not being taken to Fort William,' Charles

declared, outspoken now. 'Nor yet, it seems, to Inverness. We have been avoiding all roads where we might meet with Cumberland's troops. Or our own. *Ma foi* – it is a mystery, is it not?'

'Perhaps Lord Loudon has moved on up Laggan-side? For Badenoch and Ruthven,' Hay suggested. 'To attack Cluny and any of our people who may have gathered there. It may be that we follow him. By the Corryarrack.'

'Would you not believe that they would lodge us more secure at Fort William, than following a fighting force half across Scotland?'

'Perhaps it is intended that we strike south, beyond the Pass, for Breadalbane. That is Campbell country. These may think that Your Highness would be more secure there. While there are still pockets of our people in Lochaber and Badenoch. It would be a likely course for Campbells to take.'

Duncan spoke. His head was splitting, seeming to open and shut to a curious steady rhythm of its own. 'These are no Campbells, I think. They wear half the tartans of the west – but I have seen none of Campbell amongst them.'

'Then who ... ?'

'My friend,' the Prince called out, to their watchful warden – though almost certainly he had heard every word that they spoke. 'Tell us – are you of the Clan Campbell? Like my Lord Loudon, Inverawe, and so many others in the Government service?'

The man, although he would answer none of the others, did not wholly ignore the Prince when he spoke to him. 'My name is my own, sir,' he said, tight-voiced.

'Undoubtedly, sir. But, as a gentleman, you will agree that it would be fair that we should know into whose hands we have fallen. As prisoners of war, I presume?'

Beyond the fire the other inclined his head at that, but made no comment.

'You will get nothing out of these barbarians, Highness,' O'Neil declared sourly. His wound, though only superficial, was very painful, and bound up only very roughly. 'They are no doubt some independent brigands, who will sell us to Cumberland for what we may fetch! Savages would be more to my taste ... '

'You will be well acquaint with savages and barbarians, Captain – in your Irish bogs?' Duncan asked.

'Curse you, MacGregor . . . !'

'Felix, *mon cher*,' the Prince said. 'Your leg – does it pain you? You should seek to sleep. Like Sir Thomas. Lie down here . . .'

'I thank Your Highness – I do very well as I am.'

'*Eh bien* – as you will.' Charles Edward reached into a pocket for his snuff-box. Before taking any himself, he offered it to O'Neil and then passed it round the company. Only O'Sullivan and Hay partook. The Prince was about to take a pinch with his own fingers when, recollecting, he rose to his feet and went round the fire to offer the open box to the man who sat alone there. 'Pray, sir – join with me, if you use snuff,' he invited courteously.

The Highlander sat motionless for a moment, before getting up suddenly, without a word, and stalking a little way off, his limp pronounced, there to stand with his back to them. The Prince, sighing, returned to his seat beside the others. Their captor turned to watch them, just outside the circle of the firelight.

For the best part of an hour they sat there, weary dispirited men, hunched around the fire, coughing now and again with its acrid smoke, staring into the flames and seeing therein all the ruin of their hopes, their careers, the possible ending of their lives indeed. All save Charles Stuart, who chose to talk rather than merely to stare. He chatted easily, genially, but at length, recalling other camp-fires that he had sat beside, in this present campaign, at the Siege of Gaeta and in the Italian wars, re-counting anecdotes of his father's impoverished Court at Rome, and of the serio-comic straits to which the royal exiles' household were constantly put to preserve even an illusion of dignity. Frequently he laughed softly. Clearly his theme and object, however lightly implied and hinted at, was the necessity for a philosophic attitude towards human fortunes and misfortunes, and the temporary nature of both trumpets and reverses. Per-haps he was talking as much to himself as to his companions – none of whom joined in on the royal reminiscences. Indeed, it would have been hard to say who were actually listening and who were either deep in their own thoughts or three-parts asleep.

Indeed, the main effect of the Prince's monologue appeared to be upon their dark kidnapper. Coming back to the fire with an armful more fuel, he sat down again, clearly listening intently. In the flickering firelight his black eager eyes seemed to be concentrating on the royal lips. Perhaps it was necessary for him to attend thus if he was going to understand fully the foreign accent of a tongue with which he was not greatly familiar anyway. More than once Charles, smiling slightly, quite evidently addressed his remarks to him.

At last the speaker fell silent. O'Neill, at his side, was lying muttering in his uneasy sleep. The faithful Ned Burke was snoring heavily. Of the others, only Duncan MacGregor looked up, raising an aching head from between his hands.

It was then that their captor rose to his feet, in his abrupt jerky way, and began to limp back and forth at the other side of the fire. He might have been chilled or stiff from long sitting, or merely keeping himself awake — save for some tension, some urgency, in his uneven pacing. For a time he strode thus. Then halting for a moment, he swung round and came over to the Prince, his features working strangely.

'Highness,' he said, 'I cannot do it. No. It is not possible. *Och, ochan! Mise'n diugh.* You understand? *Tha mi'g iarraidh maitheanais.* I ask your pardon.'

Charles looked up, perplexed. 'What is this, friend? What ails you?'

'*Cha'n fhiuling mi sin.* It is not to be borne.' The other struck a clenched fist against his kilted thigh. 'You are free, Highness.'

'*Dieu de Dieu!*' The Prince got to his feet. 'Are you ... are you crazed, man?'

'No. No. It is the truth. *Tha mi cur romham. 'Sann orm tha naire. No dean tair orm.* You will go. *Na h'uile le gu math duit.*'

'*Ma foi* – what is all this? Duncan – what does he say? What is the man at? Has he taken leave of his wits?'

The MacGregor had risen now. 'It is most strange, sir – extraordinary! He is telling us to go. That he is sorry for what he has done. He says that we are free to go.'

'But ... this is incredible! What is the meaning of it? Tell him ... tell him, Duncan, to speak slowly. To speak plain. Slowly, man. You understand?'

Duncan spoke in Gaelic to their agitated captor, who presently nodded, seeming to take a grip upon himself.

'Highness,' he said, almost bringing out each word separately. 'A great wrong I have done to you. My heart is sore. I did not know you. Did not understand. What I had to do, I cannot do, at all. You shall not suffer by my hand. Go you. Where you will.'

The Prince stared, from the man to MacGregor. 'You mean . . . you mean that you are changing sides? Now? At this late hour? When so much is lost?'

'I have no side. But. . . . I cannot sell my Prince,' the other said simply.

'Sell . . . ? Then O'Neil was right? You intended to sell us? To the Government?'

The man inclined his head, unspeaking.

For a moment or two Charles Edward was silent, also. 'I do not know what has changed you, my friend,' he said at length. 'But I thank God for it.'

'You, it is. *You* have changed me, Highness.'

'I? How can that be?'

'I was not knowing Your Highness. When I came to do this thing. Now I see you. Now I know you. I know you as my Prince. Och, I cannot do it, at all. It is not possible. The money – it would be choking my throat.'

'I rejoice to hear it, *mon ami*. But . . . this money that you speak of? You must have been very sure of money, to do all that you have done . . . ?'

'The man Cumberland, Highness – he will give a great lot of money for you. For your body. *Dia* – much gold. Thirty thousands of pounds, no less. Be Your Highness dead or living.'

'*Mortdieu!* Money? For my person? Dead or alive? *Ciel* – this is beyond all belief!'

'Thirty thousand pounds!' Duncan MacGregor exclaimed. 'Lord preserve us – to seek to buy Your Highness like, like a stirk at a mart! To buy a Prince . . . !'

'At least, it is a princely sum, Captain!' Charles observed grimly.

'It is monstrous! The work of a huckstering German pedler! Does he think that, in Scotland, in the Highlands, your Highness can be, can be . . . ?' MacGregor looking at their captor, faltered and was silent.

'*Exactement*, Duncan!' the Prince murmured. To the small man he said, 'Your masters, sir? When you return to them, without me – how will you do then?'

46

I do not serve any master, Highness. I am a Highland gentleman.'

'Ah, yes. Of course! Forgive me.'

'Go you now, sir, if you would be safe out of this country by daylight. You should not be slow, be lingering.'

'No. That is true.'

'A gillie you shall have. To guide you to the Cameron country.'

'Ah – so you know that is where we go, do you?'

'Yes. And, Highness – do not go to Arkaig by Lochy and the *Mile Dorcha*, the Dark Mile. As you were going, I think. There are Redcoats. The Campbell, Loudon, has there a troop. Go you by Garry.'

'I see. You are very good, sir – very kind. If I might have your name? To thank you.'

'My name, Highness, matters nothing. *Tha mi duilich.* Only that the wrong is . . . only that I make right the wrong that I have done to you.'

'Fear not for that. It would seem that I am *your* debtor. My thanks, friend – your Prince's grateful thanks.'

'You will go, now?'

'But yes. At once. Duncan – rouse the sleepers . . .'

As the somewhat bemused and astonished party was at length marshalled and about to move off into the night, their late captor, whose only wish now appeared to be quickly quit of them, came limping over to the Prince's horse.

'Highness,' he said, eyes lowered, head down – and held out the silver pocket flask.

'Why, sir,' Charles exclaimed. 'On my soul, I had forgotten it, quite. Keep it, friend, I pray you – as a momento of this occasion.'

The other shook his dark head wordlessly, and thrust the thing at the Prince's hand.

'No. I swear, I will not take it. Keep it, sir. I'faith, that is a royal command, do you hear? A souvenir. Instead of thirty thousand pounds, *mon Dieu!*'

The Highlander bent and kissed the outstretched fingers.

CHAPTER 4

BACK through the night they went, across Tarff and Oich and lesser streams, mounted again, with O'Neil riding pillion to O'Sullivan – who, as befitted the Quartermaster-General, had the best horse in the army. Ahead, apparently tireless, trotted the running gillie who was to guide them beyond the Garry.

Picking their way in the dark precluded talk, but did not prevent even sleep-clouded minds from turning over curious circumstances and possibilities.

When the party was safely back across the ford of the Garry, with the wilder roadless country ahead, the Prince called a halt. 'It is time to consider our future progress, gentlemen, I think,' he announced, dismounting. 'It would be wise to weigh well the lessons of this adventure.'

By the splashing headlong river they gathered round.

'We must change our mode of travel, my friends,' Charles went on. 'If I am considered so valuable to the Government that they will spend thirty thousand pounds on my poor person, then most clearly I must deny them the satisfaction of laying hands on me. Equally certain, however, is the fact that with such splendid fortune available for so slight a labour, many will be seeking swift enrichment. Is it not so?'

'Every accursed soldier in Cumberland's army, to be sure, will already be accounting himself rich as Croesus,' O'Sullivan agreed. 'And worse, every peasant and cottager of this benighted land, likewise – and that's the devil of it!'

'I think not,' Duncan said shortly.

'They are not all going to change their minds at the last moment, MacGregor!'

'Nine out of ten would not be needing to, Colonel.'

'Either way,' Charles intervened, 'it behoves us to take precautions the more stringent. My father's cause demands it. We may not proceed as now – we are too apparent, too noticeable. We must separate, gentlemen. We must go more discreetly. We must seek other clothing. And for myself, I go afoot from now on. Horses are a luxury I cannot afford, unfortunately.'

'You would skulk, Charles – like any common fugitive?' Sheridan protested, shocked.

'I would indeed, Cousin. The commoner the skulker, the more likely he is to reach France alive.'

'I cannot go trudging the heather, Highness,' O'Neil declared. 'My leg . . . '

'Do I not know it, my good Felix. For you rest is necessary. And also a horse. You will return to Invergarry Castle, to wait there for a day. To direct any of our people who may come to the meeting at Loch Arkaig that they avoid this Dark Mile, where Loudon's troop waits. Thereafter you must find your own way to Arkaig.'

O'Neil did not look as though he relished these orders.

'Thomas, you require to ride. Skulking in the heather is not for you. Nor for Colonel Hay, I think.' Something, possibly the curious demonstration of his own influence back there in Glen Tarff, had revived Charles Stuart, given him back his powers of leadership which weariness and dejection had sapped. 'You will go together, mounted, to Arkaig. There to supervise the meeting. Duncan – you best know the country. How shall they ride, to avoid this Dark Mile? There must be a way?'

'There is, yes. Six or seven miles further south, three miles beyond the foot of Loch Lochy, there is another way through. By Glen Loy. Ride to the head of that, and over the little pass into Glen Mallie. That will bring you down to Arkaig beyond Locheil's house of Achnacarry.'

'Good. That is your road then, gentlemen. You hear?'

'Sir,' Duncan interposed. 'Most of those who will answer your message to come to Arkaig will be coming from Ruthven and Badenoch. Down Loch Lagganside and Glen Spean. They will know nothing of this danger at the Dark Mile. If Sir Thomas and Colonel Hay are to be riding in that direction anyway, would they not wait awhile within the mouth of Glen Spean, to warn at least the first comers . . . ?'

'Well thought of, Captain. You understand, Colonel? At the mouth of Glen Spean.'

'But, Highness,' Hay objected. 'It is no more than ten miles yonder, I vow, from Fort William itself! On the very road to the fort. To linger there would be as good as to surrender ourselves. By daylight, every trooper of Loudon's garrison will be scouring the country for this money on your head. It may be that they are doing so now. To say nothing of Cumberland's dragoons following us down.'

'Not so, I think,' Duncan asserted. 'How shall they know that His Highness is in this part of the country, at all? Or even, as yet, of the damnable reward?'

'Eh? This fellow we have just left knew it, did he not? Knew of our route exactly, enough to ambush us yonder . . . '

'Aye – and there's the whole point,' the MacGregor said grimly. 'How did he know so well, so exactly? And so soon?'

'Damme – how can we tell that? But knew he did. And if he knew, others knew. Why not the whole garrison?'

'It depends, does it not, who gave him his information, Colonel?'

'Why – who but General Lord Loudon? Or one of his staff.'

Duncan shook his head again. 'How could he? We rode fast from Culloden. No courier of Cumberland's could have so greatly outdistanced us as to reach Fort William last night. To have received the news of Cumberland's victory, to have discovered that His Highness was in this district, to have planned and despatched that expedition against us, and for it to come north to here – that would all have taken a deal more time than Lord Loudon has yet had.'

'He is right,' the Prince said. 'It could not have been Loudon's doing.'

'Whose, then?'

'Some independent group of clansmen. Campbells probably. They had stumbled on the information . . . '

'Those were no Campbells, Colonel,' Duncan assured. 'Nor was the information such that they could stumble upon. They knew that the Prince was making for Loch Arkaig and the sea. Where would they have learned that?'

'Christ God!' O'Sullivan burst out. 'Lovat! The double-dyed traitor! The old dastard!'

'No! *Mon Dieu* – no!' Charles cried. 'I will not believe that. Lovat would never do that. It is not to be considered.'

'Thirty thousand pounds is a lot of money, Highness. Even to Lord Lovat!'

'It need not have been Lovat himself,' Duncan agreed soberly. 'But only at Gortlech House was it known that Your Highness was in this district, that the decision to make for Arkaig and the sea was made. And at Gortlech House, I mind a small limping man calling off those guards who attacked us when we arrived!'

50

'Mother o' God!'

'They were Frasers, then . . . ?'

'I do not know that they were. But it seems likely . . . '

'The guide,' O'Sullivan exclaimed. 'Put it to the guide, MacGregor. We shall get it out of him, 'fore God!'

But their silent shadowy guide, when they looked round for him, had gone.

'Frasers were coming back from the battle, to the Gortlech district,' Hay pointed out. 'Some could have arrived, bringing the word of Cumberland's reward. If he had announced it at once. Almost on the field . . . '

'Frasers, or not,' the Prince said strongly, 'they did not betray me. Tempted they may have been, and sorely – but, my friends, in the end they did not betray me, for the gold.'

'That is what I say, Highness,' Duncan declared. 'They did not – whoever sent them. Nor will most in the Highlands, of whatever clan, I think.'

'Of whatever clan! There you have it!' O'Neil put in bitterly. 'Faith, it could have been the Clan MacLeod as easily as the Frasers! Captain Sawny MacLeod also knew all this, did he not? He departed over the Corryarrack, for Ruthven. He could have been captured . . . and talked!'

'Save us all . . . !'

'Damn you, O'Neil . . . !'

'I never trusted the man. He was altogether too smiling. And his chief, the Laird of MacLeod, is a perjured turncoat, as we all know. Like so many another. Trust none of them, I say. As we should not have trusted the MacDonalds, back at Culloden Moor. Traitors all . . . '

'*Diabhol!* I will not hear such talk from any man!' the MacGregor cried. 'If you were not wounded, O'Neil, you should pay for those words in blood! Highness, I . . . '

'Be silent, MacGregor! And you, Felix – for shame! Were you not injured and, as I believe, scarce in your right mind, I could not forgive your folly. The clans have spilled untold blood for my father's cause and for me – the MacDonalds in especial. Sawny MacLeod is my friend. You shall apologise to Captain MacGregor.'

'I desire no apologies from such as O'Neil . . . !'

'Be quiet, sir! *Mortdieu* – here were we, but two short days ago a band of brothers, comrades in arms, who had fought the

51

length of Scotland and half of England together. And now — this! Only suspicion, treachery, the black shadow of treachery over us! If this is the first fruits of defeat, *Nom de Nom* . . . ! But, enough. This talk profits us nothing. Better that we should be on our ways. You have your orders, gentlemen. O'Neil, here, to Invergarry. Sir Thomas and Colonel Hay to Glen Spean, and thence by Glen Loy and this other glen, to Arkaig, to await the Lord George, the Duke, and the others. And later bring their word to me.'

'And yourself, sir?' Hay wondered.

'With John here, I shall make for the sea forthwith. For Arisaig, where I landed. One of Sir Anthony Walsh's French privateers was to be ever patrolling there, to slip in to land at Loch nan Uamh each second night or so. Such was the arrangement.'

'Then you do not come yourself, to the meeting at Arkaig, sir?'

'No. Better that I should not be there, I think. Better for all. Safer for all, also. But I shall not be far off. Arisaig is in Clanranald's country, but I shall also be near Locheil and yet suitably far from Fort William — at least for the time being. You will send and let me know how matters stand, and whether my friends can undertake to continue the struggle. And, meanwhile, at the least guard some corner of the country to serve as a base. If they believe that they can do this, then it is best, I think, that I go myself to France. At once, or as soon as may be. We have no money, nor arms. Without these it is impossible to keep together or to subsist. No — I will go myself. I will then bring succour of money and men. I believe that my presence will do more to move His Majesty of France than anybody that I may send.'

A silence fell upon them all, as what this implied sank in.

'I shall take Captain MacGregor with me, meantime, since we cannot speak the Erse. And Ned Burke, of course. MacGregor tells me that there is a track, half-way up Loch Garry, that leads over the hills to Arkaig. It is no road for horses. That way we shall go. Is all understood, my friends?'

Hay still wondered. 'If Your Highness is to be at Loch Arkaig, somewhere. If you are to be there anyway, would it not be best that you should attend this meeting in person? It will be expected, sir. And you might sway many.'

The Prince shook his fair head sadly. 'Yesterday I would have agreed with you, Colonel. But not now. Not tonight. Now, there is thirty thousand pounds upon my head. A fortune. It behoves me to put temptation in the way of as few as possible. To my sorrow, the fewer who see my face hereafter, the better. Accursed be the mind that conceived this foul thing, and the hurt and dark suspicions that it must breed. How malevolently understanding that mind was, *mon Dieu!* But the deed is done. Even amongst ourselves here the poison has begun its work of base mistrust. You have seen. I shall not add to the trials of my good friends by imposing this new burden of temptation on them and theirs. You understand, gentlemen?'

Wordless now, men eyed the ground. There was nothing to be said, to that.

'So it is *adieu*, my friends. Here we part – let us pray to meet again in happier case. Till then, may a kinder Heaven guide the steps of each of you. Go with God.'

Charles held out his hand to Sheridan, Hay and O'Neil. Sheridan sought to say something, but his tremulous old voice choked on his emotion. The other two kissed the outstretched hand in silence.

Abruptly the Prince turned away, and went to his horse, to remove the tiny bundle of his effects from its saddle. Then, without a backward glance, he set off on foot up the wooded side of the rushing Garry. O'Sullivan and Duncan MacGregor were behind him. Ned Burke, a faithful shadow, brought up the rear.

CHAPTER 5

WITH the early morning sun flooding golden glory at their backs, and setting ablaze all the head of long Loch Arkaig, the four men trudged wearily up the gentle grassy slope towards the pleasant white house that sat so snugly in the mouth of the narrow glen ahead, backed by its ancient trees. That house seemed to have beckoned them for the last hour, as they rounded the marshy meadows at the head of the interminable loch.

When, still a mile away, they had perceived the blue column of peat smoke rising from its chimney, against the dark brown of the heather hill behind, it had been the first lift to their hearts for hours. Someone there was stirring, and the smoored and banked overnight fire had been replenished for the new day. Involuntarily they had lengthened their limping, lagging strides.

For three out of the four were indeed limping. They had covered nearly twenty long and gruelling miles from the Garry in eight hours of benighted walking, the last ten of them along the northern shore of the loch – and only the MacGregor's feet were proof against such treatment. O'Sullivan was in particularly poor way. Time and again his companions had urged the Prince to halt and rest, to seek shelter and food at one or other of the many little townships of scattered cot-houses which they had so cautiously skirted and avoided in the darkness. But always Charles had insisted on pressing on. They would put Loch Arkaig behind them, he declared, with its populous northern braes, before they sought rest. On occasion he could be extraordinarily obstinate.

Now, that resolution had faded somewhat. The long trough of Arkaig between its massed mountains, forked into two narrow side glens at its head, with the great thrusting prow of Monadh Gorm between – Glen Dessary and Glen Pean. It was into the latter that they headed, facing south-westwards towards Morar and the sea. Within the jaws of it, this goodly house was as a magnet to their dragging feet. So normal-seeming, so secure, speaking to them of friendly settled living, of ease – even of a cooked breakfast. Charles had declared that they must avoid all substantial houses, all townships and clachans, lest their passage should be traced, lest the dread contagion of reward-seeking should be spread; they must call only at isolated humble huts and remote sheilings. Yet here they were, passing by the scattering of cabins and blackhouses of this Glen Pean, and making directly for the long low two-storeyed whitewashed house of what must be a laird of some substance.

None had actually voiced the decision that they might halt at it, admittedly.

It was a pair of great grey wolf-hounds that came loping down towards them from the house, baying the heavens, that settled the matter. To turn away now would brand them as furtive fugitives, inevitably. Without debate they pressed on, even though the dogs looked less than welcoming.

Then, above the deep baying another sound reached them – the clear high belling of a woman's voice upraised. At its insistence the hounds fell silent, and halted.

A young woman had appeared at the porch of the house, watching from under a hand that shaded her eyes against the glare of the early level sunlight pouring in from the east behind the newcomers. Under her scrutiny the four travellers approached, unconsciously squaring their sagging shoulders.

'You speak with her, Duncan,' the Prince directed. 'In her own tongue. We are travellers who have lost our way – innocent travellers. Seeking refreshment. For which we will pay . . . '

'You are in Cameron country, sir. None here will think ill of us for being what their own chief, Locheil, is – part of Your Highness's army.'

'Nevertheless, you will do as I say. What the good people do not know, they cannot bear witness to. And, *mon Dieu* – no more of this Highnessing and Sirring! Or we are lost.'

The tall hounds stalking stiff and suspicious behind them, to Ned Burke's distinct alarm, they approached the house. The woman proved to be little more than a girl, and a bonny one – a warm-eyed, well-built creature with a mass of auburn hair which the streaming yellow light turned into a gleaming halo, dressed neatly but serviceably in a gown of bottle-green handspun stuff, shorter skirted than was the southern mode, worn over a white linen bodice, brief sleeved and generously open at the neck, the white spotless enough to emphasise the honey-brown of arms and face and neck, to where it faded into white between her breasts. Her dress was caught round the slender waist with a broad scarlet girdle, and with it she wore a white apron. This also was notably clean, like the bodice – as indeed was everything about her, even to her bare feet. Her glowing cheeks and general air of new-washed freshness, in fact, were almost an offence in the lack-lustre eyes of the jaded, grimy and travel-stained men, unshaven and dishevelled, so early in the morning.

'Good morning,' she called out, in English, before Duncan could address her in the Gaelic. 'You come early to Glen Pean, gentlemen. But you are welcome, if you come in honesty –

even though you are not those for whom I looked.'

Charles Edward, clad now in Ned Burke's plain grey coat, gave her a courtly bow but left Duncan to do the talking.

'We are travellers making for Arisaig and the islands, lady,' he said. 'We fear that we have gone much astray from our road. We have had certain misfortunes, owing to the unsettled state of the country. We seek, of your kindness, only refreshment and direction. You need not be afraid of us, I promise you . . .'

'I am not afraid of you, sir! But one word from me, and my hounds would have their teeth in your throats, faster than you could draw that pistol that I see hiding in your Gregorach plaid!' Those warm eyes could flash as fiery as her hair. Young and fair she might be, but it was apparent that she considered that she was well able to look after herself.

'I beg your pardon,' Duncan said, hurriedly. 'I had forgot, ma'am – "Sons of the hounds, come and eat flesh!"'

She laughed at that, pleasantly, the Clan Cameron's age-old slogan. 'You are not wholly without knowledge of the country you are in, sir, lost or not!' she said. 'But your Lowland friends must not think that we feed our dogs on strangers, as of habit!' Looking at the others, and particularly Charles Stuart, the girl's wide-open hazel-green eyes changed expression – a thing that they could do, apparently, with as great clarity as speed. 'You are tired, gentlemen – weary. You have travelled far and fast, I think?'

'Far, yes,' Duncan admitted cautiously.

'And fast. Those who fall into bogs, as you have done, do so by night. And those who travel by night in this country do so for good reason. Is it not so?'

'Mistress – how we travel, and where, surely is our own concern,' O'Sullivan said tautly. 'If you prefer not to offer us the refreshment we require, then faith we must press on . . .'

'I said before, sir, that you were welcome to Glen Pean – if you came in honesty. I think if you were truly honest with me, you would tell me that you had come hot-foot, and from somewhere nigh to Inverness! And that white cockades were probably in your pockets!'

None of the four answered a word to that.

'I am right, then. Or I hope so – for I am a Cameron, and would not like to think that you were of the other persuasion!'

'You are indeed right, Mademoiselle,' Charles said then,

with his engaging smile. 'We should have declared it at the outset. We are of King James's army, and hasten to Arisaig where we have business . . . ah, on his account.'

'Where two French ships have been sighted, off and on, this past week and more, I am told!' the young woman added, significantly.

'You say so? Is it a fact?' The Prince looked at once disconcerted and enheartened. 'It is known that they are there, Mademoiselle?'

'Why yes, sir. Also that three Government warships keep chasing them around the islands and the lochs in a cat-and-mouse game.' She shook her head. 'But, come inside, gentlemen. My father would not have any of the Prince's army kept standing on his doorstep. He . . . he is not here to welcome you in person, I fear, for he is himself with the Prince.'

'Oh!' Charles said. 'I . . . ah . . . am distressed to hear it.'

Quickly she looked at him. 'Distressed? Then . . . then it is true? That there has been a great battle, and that our cause is sore stricken? Only last night we had grave tidings. We heard that Locheil, our chief, was sore wounded. That the Prince's army had been defeated, near Inverness.' Her words tumbled out now in a rush. 'I feared, when I saw you coming. It was my father whom I was looking to see. And my brother. My father is Donald Cameron of Glen Pean, a captain in Locheil's Regiment. And my brother Colin is an ensign. You would not know . . . ? You will not have heard . . . ?'

In silence the men before her shook their heads, or looked down at the grass.

'We did not know whether or no to believe the word of it,' she went on. 'Ill news travels fast, they say. It was but a few words that reached us here. But now, you . . . you make it true by your presence, do you not? That you should have come so fast, so far. And in such state -- you who are clearly officers. Was it -- was it so great a defeat? A disaster?' That was almost a whisper.

Charles swallowed. 'It was an undoubted set-back,' he admitted.

'The Prince's cause will recover from it, never fear, ma'am,' Duncan assured stoutly.

'Yes. Oh, yes. Pray God it be so. If Locheil was sore wounded, then his regiment must have been . . . have been . . . ?'

'They were hard engaged, yes,' Duncan told her, as gently as he knew how. 'But many escaped. They carried Locheil off the field – both ankles shot. Your father and brother may well have been with them. It is likely . . .'

She bit her red lip, nodding her head a number of times, jerkily, determinedly. 'Yes. Yes indeed. No doubt you are right, sir. But – come inside. I have kept you standing here too long as it is. You will be hungry, and very tired. Only my two young sisters are at home. Lazy they are – not yet out of their beds . . . !'

In the pleasant and comfortable old house, unpretentious but commodious, the newcomers were offered unstinted hospitality by their young hostess. Breakfast had indeed been a-cooking, and more oatmeal was added to the porridge-pot and more eggs and smoked salmon to the frying-pan, which, with milk laced with whisky, bannocks and heather-honey, would keep them in being, as the girl declared, until she could cook them a regular meal. In the interim, they should wash and tidy themselves somewhat, and she would make up beds for them while they did so.

Charles, heavy-eyed as he was, demurred. Her kindness made them eternally her debtors – but they would not sleep under her roof. It must have seemed a curious scruple to Caroline Cameron, as the young woman named herself, that although her visitors would partake heartily of her provender and the other facilities of her house, they insisted on sleeping outside, in any shed or outhouse, apparently solely on account of possible repercussions by the authorities on people who sheltered rebels – a narrow distinction, perhaps, in the house of a militant rebel, to his own daughter. It was the Prince himself who insisted on this – or Monsieur Dumont, a French officer, as Duncan introduced him, along with Mr. Butler from Ireland, a commissary, Ned Burke and himself retaining their own identities. Caroline Cameron eyed them all a little thoughtfully thereafter.

It was after they had fed and washed, their entire bearing and appearance quite transformed and spruced up thereby, that the keen-eyed young woman, whilst Charles and O'Sullivan were inspecting a hay-barn in which it was proposed to bed down, drew Duncan aside.

'Mr. MacGregor – or Captain, should I say? I have no reason to doubt your word, or that *you* are what you say – an officer in Glengyle's Regiment. Or that Mr. Butler is not an Irishman, and may well be a commissary, for all I know of such. But your Monsieur Dumont is a different matter, I swear. He has an extraordinary manner. For a mere French officer, you treat him with notable deference. When he speaks, no other speaks. He must sit first at table – and when he half-rose to collect his eggs from me, tired as you are you were all on your feet in a moment. Is it not so?'

Duncan coughed. 'He is a, h'm, an important French officer,' he said.

'So I must believe! Even so, I would not have thought that a Highland officer, *any* Highland officer, would have been so respectful towards any mere French mercenary! Or has the Prince's army French generals now?'

The MacGregor was silent. His mind was much too heavy with fatigue for this sort of thing.

'Moreover, I would not have you think that I am part-blind, Captain. Do I seem it? When you emerged from washing yourselves, your Monsieur Dumont was a different man! And a *young* man. So young to be so important. Not much older than myself, I vow. Younger than your sober self, I think? And that fair hair, that noble brow, that commanding countenance? Captain MacGregor – if I have the honour to have His Royal Highness in person under the roof of Glenpean House, pray tell me so!'

Duncan all but choked. 'Ma'am ... Miss Cameron ... you go too fast. Altogether too fast. You must not be carried away by, by such imaginings. Monsieur Dumont is ... '

'Is *not* the Prince?' she put to him squarely.

He bit his lip. 'Ma'am, surely it is no part of our travellers' duty to provide you with papers of identity to support our statements ... !'

'Hoity-toity!' Caroline Cameron said. 'But you do not deny it, I see! Here he is. Now we shall see!'

Charles and O'Sullivan came out of the barn. Without a moment's hesitation, the girl ran forward and took his hand.

'Is it permitted that I kiss your fingers, sir?' she asked.

The Prince, startled, stared at her, and then swiftly turned on Duncan. 'Captain MacGregor!' he exclaimed. 'What is the meaning of this? Your instructions were sufficiently clear, I thought...?'

'It is no fault of the Captain's, Your Royal Highness,' Miss Cameron intervened sweetly. 'He is painfully concerned that I should believe you to be some junior French mercenary officer. His fault is that he does not credit me with eyes in my head or any modicum of wit. He would have me believe that a prince, Scotland's own Prince, is a prince only in name! That by giving him the name of Dumont he transforms him into merely some ordinary Frenchman. Surely you, Highness, know better than that? Think you that the Highlands would be willing to die for any such changeling?'

Charles shook his head helplessly, wordlessly. Then with a Gallic shrug of the shoulders, he smiled at her ruefully but engagingly. 'I capitulate, Mademoiselle. And apologise. I am Charles Stuart, yes – and yours to command.'

Caroline Cameron dropped in a swift but deep and graceful curtsy, and pressed her lips to those outstretched fingers. When she rose, she looked at none of them. She turned away quickly – but not before Duncan MacGregor at least had seen that her hazel-green eyes were swimming with tears.

She hurried back to the house, and, somewhat sheepishly, the men followed her.

Now that she knew that it was the Prince whom she was entertaining, their young hostess would not hear of him sleeping in any hay-barn. On the other hand, Charles was adamant about not sleeping in the house – explaining the significance of the £30,000 reward and the hue-and-cry which would inevitably take place, and what might be expected in reprisals from a commander-in-chief who could conceive such a thing, and slaughter the defeated wounded and prisoners on a field of battle. Moreover, there was the little township of cabins and cot-houses near by; their dwelling here in the house could not be hid from the clansfolk there, and however loyal and true they might be, their presence represented exactly the situation that the fugitives had made up their minds to avoid. The girl's indignant protests that these were the very families from which her father had taken a score of men to fight for the Prince, could not alter his stubborn although courteously expressed decision.

A compromise was reached – since Charles recognised that not only must they have a period of rest and refreshment forthwith, but that somewhere in this vicinity it was necessary for him to wait awhile for news of what transpired amongst the other leaders of his cause. There was a more secure place, a lonely shieling or summer lodging for the upland pastures, another four or five miles up the glen, near the head of the pass over into Morar. Unoccupied at present, here the travellers could lie up safely – yet near enough to be supplied daily with food from the house. Although O'Sullivan for one groaned aloud at the thought of those additional four or five miles, all agreed that this appeared to be the best solution.

Miss Cameron insisted on escorting them in person to this refuge. Moreover, she provided sturdy garrons for the journey, so that at least they did not have to walk. Declaring that the cottagers below would merely assume that she was hospitably setting the travellers on their way over the long steep pass, she led the way, skirts hitched high on shapely legs straddling the broad-backed pony, the two wolf-hounds bounding joyfully ahead.

O'Sullivan fell asleep twice on his mount's back on that ride up the lovely quickly climbing glen of the River Pean, the second time actually tumbling off into the old bracken, fortunately without hurting himself although a heavily built man of middle age. Even Duncan had much ado to keep his eyes open, Charles, however, riding ahead with the girl, seemed to be able to exchange chatter with her readily enough, to his companions' wonder.

The shieling proved to be admirably suited for their purposes. It was a stone-and-turf cabin of but the one simple room, with a thatch of heather, hump-backed and so much part of all its surroundings as wholly to fade into the hillside, a few hundred yards above the track and a small blue lochan. Behind it rose the two enormous three-thousand-foot peaks of Sgor Thuilm and Sgor nan Coreachan, and, across the glen, the long long ridge that ended in Monadh Gorm, the Blue Mount, above Gleanpean House. From its door indeed they could see all around, both far and near, a whole world of the high places – and notably in both directions from which danger might come, east down to Loch Arkaig and west towards Morar and the sea. The interior, although windowless and dirt-floored, strewn with heather, was clean, there was a central fireplace with a hole in the turf roof above for the smoke to escape, and there were built-up shelves or benches, with deerskins stuffed with heather-tops as mattresses. A sparkling burn splashed past down to the lochan, and there was bog-pine outcropping from all the hill-side around about for fuel.

The visitors scarcely appreciated the full excellence of this sanctuary at first sight, however. Somewhat owlishly they stood, swaying slightly, whilst Caroline Cameron demonstrated its advantages. Once inside, nothing would bring them out into the sunlight again, those built-up mattress benches seeming to have a hypnotic effect upon them all. When at length the young woman turned away back downhill with her horses and hounds, promising to come back again in the evening, her charges collapsed on the bunks like men felled. All except Ned Burke, that is, who knelt first to ease off his royal master's boots. Before he had so much as undone the second spatter-dash, Charles had dropped solidly sideways, asleep.

He was barely the first, at that.

Eight hours later, Duncan MacGregor was swimming in the lochan below the shieling, swimming vigorously for the peat-stained amber water was icy cold, fed from the snows not yet melted high on Sgor Thuilm above. Surface-diving, blowing water like a grampus, turning on his back and kicking up water-spouts with his feet, he was alone, with his companions still asleep in the cabin – or thought that he was. About to clamber out on to a thrusting rock, preparatory to a deep dive, he suddenly was aware of the sound of clapping hands and the tinkle of laughter. And seeing who sat the pony up there, between the two panting hounds, he slid down into the brown water again, hastily.

'Bravo, Captain MacGregor!' she called. 'You swim mightily. Like the monster, the water-horse! Are you trying to catch the trouts – or to frighten them out of the water?'

'I am trying not to freeze to death!' he answered her, pant-ingly. 'If you can do better, come you and join me! Warmer with the two of us!'

'I do very well watching you,' she assured. 'I prefer to do my swimming some months hence, when the water is warm. I shall wait here and guard your clothes for you, sir!'

'No, no. Go away. I want to come out.'

'But I have brought you whisky. And new-baked cakes. Would you not be wise to have one now, Captain? To stop you shivering.'

'No.'

'Or do you not shiver? The Gregorach – perhaps they are too hot-blooded to shiver?'

'Go away.'

'You are most discourteous, sir. When I hold you all in the hollow of my hand!'

'Go and tell that to the Prince. Woman, I warn you – whether you go or stay, I am not remaining in this water another moment!'

Laughing, she turned and rode up the hillside.

Wrapped only in kilt and plaid, he came up with her as she waited outside the cabin.

'They are all still asleep,' she told him. 'You, it seems are the only lively one.'

'They are *Sassunach* – Lowlanders,' he pointed out, explaining all. 'This country is hard on them. And there has been little enough sleep for any of the army these last six days. Let them sleep.'

'Very well. But I brought you news, see you. Good news. At least, for me and mine. For the Camerons. Locheil is back at Achnacarry, and my father with him. But not my brother. He is wounded, poor Colin. But left secure in the house of some Macpherson in Badenoch. He will be safe. It is not good news? I am so very happy. See – have a cake. Take a drink of this. You *are* shivering, I vow.'

'I thought that you sounded in good spirts, Miss Cameron! I am happy about your father . . .'

'Yes. It is wonderful. I have been very anxious. Now I could dance! And sing!' She trilled a laugh, gay, infectious, her eyes flashing and sparkling with joyous relief. When this young woman was happy, it appeared, she was very happy. Indeed, whatever she did she seemed to do with all her heart.

'Have you seen your father? Did you tell him about . . . us?'

'No. He is still with Locheil. Only a gillie brought us the news. He came for clothes and gear and money. This afternoon.'

'And did you hear have any others reached your country?

From Badenoch? From Ruthven? The Lord George Murray? the Duke of Perth . . . ?'

'The gillie did not say so. He was concerned only with Locheil and my father.'

'If Locheil, crippled, could be brought thus fast, others surely could have come also. It is important that the Prince should know . . . '

'What is so important to me, my friends? Miss Cameron – you catch us at a distinct disadvantage, of which I am grievously aware. My humblest apologies.' Charles Edward, crumpled, tousle-headed and flushed with sleep, stooped in the low doorway, smothering a yawn.

Caroline Cameron curtsied. 'Your Highness – I am sorry if I disturbed you. I but brought up some more provisions. I should have been quieter. I brought some Cameron plaids to wrap around you all. And a kilt of my brother's. Which may enable you to attract less notice in this country . . . '

'You are kind. Thoughtful. But, *mon Dieu* – in this matter of attracting notice, will you not pay heed to your own self, Mademoiselle? For you, like my friends here, these salutations and talk of Highness must cease. My name is Charles. And if Dumont displeases you, then I give you leave to choose me another.'

'But . . . but, sir . . . !'

'No "sirs" either. Not said that way, at any rate.'

Duncan intervened. 'Miss Cameron has brought news. Locheil is back, and Glenpean with him. At Achnacarry. Others no doubt. But the messenger did not say.'

'Ah – say you so? My brave, good Locheil! Praise God for that. He will give me good honest advice. Always he has done so . . . '

'What better advice can Locheil give you, if he be honest, than to reach the Court of France with all possible speed?' O'Sullivan's voice came thickly from behind. 'Locheil, nor any other, can alter the fact that we have lost this throw. Lost totally. And without money and arms, we cannot make another throw – not another that has any hope of success.'

'These French ships in the offing, John, may be bearing arms and men.'

'May be – or may not. That remains to be seen. Even so, the

64

sooner you are aboard one of them, the better for King James's cause, sir.'

'You . . . are not *leaving* us?' the young woman burst out, staring. 'You are not going away again, sir? To France?'

Charles frowned a little, and plucked his unshaven chin. 'I must do what is best for all. Or for most. Take the longer view. Think you I would not rather stay, *ma foi*? Here, with my brave and loyal Highlanders. But . . .'

'Wait a while, at the least, sir,' Duncan urged. 'Until you know the true position clearly. Until . . .'

'Until Cumberland's dragoons, or his filthy money, catch him, you mean, MacGregor? If Locheil can reach Arkaig from Culloden so fast, wounded as he is, how far behind ride Cumberland's cavalry thirsting for a fortune? If the Prince is taken, all is lost — once and for all. No waiting, I say. Let us press on to the sea at Arisaig, and seek these ships with all speed. If they are being harried by Government frigates, they may not tarry much longer. Faith, it may be too late, even now. They may have been caught. Or sailed back to France. I say move on tonight. Now.'

The Prince paced a turn or two outside the cabin, running a hand through his fair curls.

Caroline Cameron looked from one to the other, unhappily now. 'At least eat, gentlemen,' she said. 'While you decide what is best. I have brought your supper . . .'

Over an adequate meal, spread before the shieling in the vivid sunset light that streamed through the pass to them in gold and crimson glory from the Western Sea, they came at length to a compromise. Duncan MacGregor should hurry down Arkaigside through the night, to Achnacarry, to find out what he could of the true position, and consult Locheil in the Prince's name. Charles and O'Sullivan would wait here at the shieling until dawn — for the route over the pass was very rough, and inadvisable in the dark anyway — and then proceed down to the lower ground of Morar, and on as best they could to the sea at Loch nan Uamh, near Arisaig. Here it was that they had landed all those eventful months before. It was Clanranald's country, and Young Clanranald himself might well have reached home, by then, if he had escaped from Culloden. Anyway, MacDonald of Borrodale would shelter them, as he had done when they had arrived. He would know about the French ships, if anybody did. Duncan should rejoin them, as quickly as he might, between here and Borrodale, with his tidings.

None were satisfied with this arrangement. O'Sullivan's age, experience and authority undoubtedly had a greater weight with Charles than could have the representations of the young Mac-Gregor or this mere girl.

And so, in the lovely quiet half-light of the north, aftermath to the blaze of the sunset, Duncan strode down the glen at the side of the young woman's pony, very conscious of her presence above him, of the distracting nearness of a long shapely leg which she made ineffective attempts to cover with a skirt stretched tight by the garron's broad back, of her mood of thoughtful quiet that had succeeded the happy gaiety of her coming – yet himself preoccupied with oppressive thoughts of the sorrowful fruits of failure, the suspicion of motives, and ashamedly, of just the first faintest stirrings of the canker of doubt as to the moral strength and fibre of the so gallant, admirable and gracious prince whom he had so nearly worshipped.

The bitter fruits of failure, indeed.

CHAPTER 6

DUNCAN neither rode nor walked down the rough dozen miles of Loch Arkaig, that night – he rowed. It was Caroline's suggestion that he take one of the Glen Pean boats, and so spare his limbs. She offered the aid of one of her gillies as boatman, to spare his arms also, but this he refused. It was a long long row admittedly, but the simple square sail hoisted, and the prevailing breeze which blew unfailingly down the lengthy funnel of the valley from the south-west, should be a help. For coming back, she advised a garron borrowed from Locheil.

For a MacGregor, used to boat-work amongst the strong currents, great depths and unpredictable winds of Loch Lomond, Arkaig was comparatively uncomplicated. He indeed enjoyed the soothing slap-slap and creak of his progress down the loch, and the feel of oars in his hands again – even although a prolonged neglect of such useful implements, for sword and pistol, produced blisters in due course. It was a fine star-lit night, and the great silent hills crouching black against the deep blue of the sky spoke their age-old peaceable message to him, as did the whispers of the many waterfalls cascading down to the shore on the steep south side, the sigh of wind over endless leagues of heather, and the lowing of cattle from the water-meadows of the northern shores. The loch was nowhere more than a mile wide, and frequently only half that, and no problems of navigation obtruded.

He reached the foot of Arkaig before midnight, in just under three hours – which was a deal less, he reckoned, than he would have taken with a garron over that broken stream-furrowed terrain. Hiding the boat in a clump of water-side alders, he made his way along the river-bank to Achnacarry Castle.

Duncan did not gain Locheil's house without being challenged, but he managed to convince the Cameron guards of his status as a bearer of important tidings for their chief. House servitors declared that Himself and the gentlemen were not yet retired for the night, and the newcomer was led upstairs to the first floor hall of the castle, a modest place enough by southern standards but palatial compared with the Prince's sanctuary, and ushered into the great smoke-filled chamber.

Quite a gathering sat around the long table or about the flaring fire of pine logs. Donald Cameron, nineteenth of Locheil, a fine-looking leonine man of middle years, with the calm reflective eyes of a scholar rather than a warrior, sat on a settle near the fire, his bound-up legs outstretched before him. Although Duncan had seen him often, as a regimental officer he had never had occasion to speak with so great a dignitary; but Locheil welcomed him courteously, even warmly, apologising for being unable to rise to his feet to welcome an honoured guest and a son of Glengyle to his house. He was hospitably offering food and drink, and enquiring after his visitor's journey and comfort, when interrupted by many of those around him, demanding to know the state of Prince Charles, his whereabouts, intentions and plans.

True to traditional Highland civilities, the young man ignored them all until he had assured his host of his well-being, of the honour he felt at coming under so notable a roof, and asked politely for the chief's wounded legs, the safety of his sons, and the general welfare of his people.

Many of the company chafed observably but ineffectually at

this display of Gaelic manners. Donald Cameron might be known as the Gentle Locheil, but he was not a man with whom any would trifle, especially in present circumstances or in the heart of the Cameron country. Despite his preoccupation with his host, Duncan's keen eyes had not failed to note amongst the other guests Sir Thomas Sheridan, Colonel Hay and Captain O'Neil, as well as the impetuous cavalryman Lord Elcho and his friend Major Maxwell of Kirkconnel.

At last, due courtesies over, the MacGregor informed the company of the Prince's situation and proposed programme. His Highness sought Locheil's advice in this pass – but no doubt MacDonuill Duibh would give him that later, and privately, to transmit to the Prince?

This assumption by no means precluded a large part of the assembly giving their own advice vigorously there and then. The sum of it all seemed to be fairly evenly divided, the fighting men, plus Elcho and Maxwell, considering that Charles must stay in the Highlands to rally his scattered forces, and the staff officers counselling an immediate return to France to replenish the sinews of war. It was evident that these two courses had already been the subject of hot debate.

Waiting patiently for the clamour to subside somewhat, Locheil at length intervened. 'I am privileged that His Highness should seek such poor advice as I may be able to offer him, Captain MacGregor,' he said. 'But I could have wished – we all could have wished, I am sure – that he could have come here, under my roof, honoured my house, to receive it. Since he is here in my country.'

Duncan nodded. 'I said the same to His Highness. But he is determined that he will endanger no man's roof by sleeping under it, MacDonuill Duibh. He believes the Government will wreak unmerciful vengeance on any who are thought to have sheltered him. He will not further imperil any, he says.'

'The Government will seek to do so, no doubt – although they do not need the Prince's presence for excuse, 'fore God! They burn and slay and harry already, indiscriminately, without distinction. Young and old, women and children. Even the houses of those who have ignored the Prince's cause are not safe, we hear. Cumberland and his jackals are behaving like madmen.' Locheil paused. 'But surely, if the Prince will but draw his strength to him again, make a stand with such as he can assemble still, he will *save* the houses of his friends, not destroy them?'

Duncan was in no position to controvert that, since it was his own strongly held opinion. 'How many men can I tell His Highness can be assembled to make such a stand, MacDonuill Duibh? At once, I mean?' he asked.

Locheil looked away, across the room at the tight group of his own Cameron lairds who sat around the foot of the long table – not a few of them still bandaged from the battle. The Mac-Gregor noted and recognised amongst them Locheil's sons John and Charles, Major Cameron of Erracht, second in command of the regiment, Cameron of Glenevis, of Torcastle, and others. No doubt Caroline Cameron's father was there too. The chief sighed.

'We have suffered sorely. I have sacrificed so many of my people. God forgive me. Hundreds. Yet . . . ' A low rumbling growl from the foot of the table seemed to hearten him, for he raised his head perceptibly. ' . . . yet we still can fight. I think . . . yes, I think I can promise two hundred men by this time tomorrow.'

'Three hundred, Donald,' Erracht said.

'More, by God!' Torcastle amended.

'That is worth the hearing!' Lord Elcho cried. 'That is how King James will gain his own again – not by talk of defeat and pleas to the King of France.'

'How will three hundred men serve against Cumberland's thousands?' Colonel Hay demanded.

'We have heard the like before,' O'Neil observed. 'My lord of Lovat made some such pronouncement, I recollect! But not one man arrived at the assembly.'

'Sir – have you the effrontery to doubt a Cameron's word!' Erracht cried, half-rising from his chair – and others with him.

'I but speak from recent experience,' the aide said. 'Lovat urged His Highness to fight on. But I do not see a Fraser here! Any more than at Fort Augustus.'

'To what other chiefs can the Prince look for men, in this pass?' old Sir Thomas Sheridan intervened hurriedly, probably seeking to pour oil on troubled waters. 'The MacDonalds? Clanranald and Glengarry and Keppoch?'

There was a moment's pause. Tempers were still somewhat sore over the Clan Donald's role at Culloden; Locheil's Regiment, like others, undoubtedly had lost heavily on account of the MacDonalds' offended failure to charge. Moreover, both Clanranald and Glengarry were rather too close neighbours of the Camerons to be the best of friends.

'How many of the MacDonalds escaped?' Duncan asked. 'They were dying fast, it seemed, as we retired.'

'Many of their officers, of all three regiments, are dead, undoubtedly,' Locheil nodded. 'But some survived. Young Clanranald himself passed here this very afternoon on his way home to Moidart.'

'Young Clanranald? He escaped, then?' the MacGregor exclaimed. 'That is good news. I had feared otherwise. So had the Prince.'

'He could raise another two hundred, at least,' Erracht declared.

'His cousin Kinlochmoidart's company will still be intact,' Locheil pointed out. 'They have been keeping Loudon and his Campbells pinned down at Fort William. There should be a hundred-and-fifty men with Kinlochmoidart, never at Culloden.'

'And would you trust MacDonalds again? After Culloden?' O'Neil demanded. 'And now that treachery is to be rewarded by £30,000!'

There was a sudden and complete silence in that room, so that only the hiss and spurt of the burning logs sounded. Then Erracht's chair toppled backwards with a crash as he leapt to his feet. 'God in Heaven – this is too much!' he cried. 'I am no MacDonald – but my wife was a daughter of Keppoch. Does this . . . this parlour-soldier judge Highland gentlemen by his own Irishry? Does he believe that any would sell the Prince for dirty money . . . ?'

'If they will do it for pride and vanity . . . !'

'Silence, fellow – or a Cameron will teach you manners . . . !'

The sharp crack of his chief's hand smacking down on the settle halted the speaker in mid-phrase. 'Cousin – Captain O'Neil is my guest, I'd remind you,' Locheil said evenly. 'Also he is a wounded man.'

'Then let him not presume upon your hospitality! Or on his scratched leg, by the Powers!'

'My *guest*, I said, Donald! And as such, secure at my table.'

'Then I will no longer sit at your table with such a guest, sir. Goodnight to you, MacDonuill Duibh!' Erracht clapped on his bonnet and stormed out of the hall.

'Goodnight to you, Eoghain 'ic Eoghain,' Locheil returned, but sadly.

Most of the other Camerons rose, saluted their chief, and stamped out after Erracht.

'My apologies, gentlemen,' their host said to his remaining guests, quietly. 'Such displays do credit to none of us.' His level glance rested directly on O'Neil. 'The Prince needs our united strength – not foolish strife and suspicion. But we are all tired, my friends – over-taxed. And the hour is late. I advise that we take to our beds. Who knows whether we may be so fortunate as to have the opportunity again! My gillies tell me that the troop stopping the entrance of this valley, at the Dark Mile, was reinforced at dusk by a full squadron of dragoons under no less a scoundrel than Major Lockhart. Tomorrow, it seems, we probably shall be in the heather!'

'Dare they attack you here, sir?' Duncan wondered.

'I think they may. They know that we are without ammunition – that we have only swords and dirks against their guns. I shall not attempt to defend this house. My grandfather built it for prospects of peace, when our old stronghold was cast down. It is not sited for war. We shall do better in the heather when it comes to fighting.' He gestured towards his bandaged legs. 'Even a cripple!'

'I shall not avail myself of your bed, Locheil,' Lord Elcho announced. 'I have travelled through these last two nights, and shall travel through this. I go on to Kinloch Moidart, where at least I can join a body of armed men – a disciplined unit, Mac-Donalds though they be. I shall endeavour to bring them here to Arkaig, to join you.'

'As you will, my lord . . .'

One by one the others bade their host goodnight, until only Duncan was left. The older man eyed him closely.

'You are not one of the Prince's regular aides, Captain MacGregor,' he said. 'Have you replaced your cousin, James Mor?'

'After a fashion, I have, sir. He has, h'm, rejoined the regiment.'

'I see.' The other sighed. 'So His Highness seeks my advice? Do you believe that he will heed it – with Colonel O'Sullivan at his other ear?'

71

'I do not know, MacDonuill Duibh.'

'Nor do I! O'Sullivan's advice is unlikely to be mine.' Locheil shook his greying head. 'The Prince's Irish friends, Captain, are loyal. They love His Highness. But they do not love Scotland. And, God save us – they are but doubtful strategists!'

'I know it, sir . . . '

'Aye. What to tell the Prince, then? Tell him that I believe that he can have five hundred fighting men in a week. Two thousand in a month. But, until ammunition comes from France, they can only serve as a threat to Cumberland and a bodyguard to himself. Tell him that, somehow, although we have not a penny-piece left in our sporrans, we will manage to hold the men together until the promised aid arrives. But not if the Prince leaves Scotland. His presence is essential. We shall never hold them, otherwise. Tell him that my country of Arkaig and Locheil will support and hide him meantime, with Clanranald's Moidart and Glengarry's Knoydart – but that he and his gathering forces should move north and still north. Into the Mackenzie country of Ross and Kintail and Torridon. It is remote, easily defended and untouched by war. The Mackenzies of Cromartie and Seaforth can there bring him another thousand men, at least. That is my advice.'

'And what of Lord George Murray? The Duke of Perth? Cluny Macpherson? We had hoped that they would be here by now, from Ruthven. The Prince sent Sawny MacLeod to bid them come here.'

'No doubt they will come.'

'But if you could get here, wounded, by now . . . ?'

Locheil shrugged. 'They hold it against His Highness that he did not appoint a rendezvous in case we lost the battle. That not having done so, he did not come to Ruthven where his two Lieutenants-General went. Give them time, lad . . . '

'Time, sir! Time is what we have not got! If one thing is certain, it is that the Prince will not wait for long. That I prophesy.'

'A week. Ask him for but a week, MacGregor. Aye – and tell him to send O'Sullivan and O'Neil and the rest of them to France, to talk with King Louis! As his ambassadors. Not to go himself. Give that as my advice also, man!'

'As you say, sir . . . '

When Duncan MacGregor left the house to collect the

72

garron which Locheil was going to lend him for his return journey, he found a man waiting for him at the door. He proved to be Glenpean, a broad stocky man of similar age to Locheil, who had walked out of the hall above with the others, behind Erracht. He spoke to the MacGregor, there in the dark.

'My friend,' he said. 'I believe that you are to be happier than I in that you will be passing my home within a few hours? That you have seen my daughters? Indeed, that the Prince is even now in my shieling of Allt Ruadh? You are carrying a message to His Highness from Locheil – will you carry one to my girls from their father?'

'Assuredly, sir,' Duncan declared. 'I saw your daughter Caroline this very evening. She lent me the boat by which I came here. And the other two I saw early in the morning. All were well and in good spirits. And . . . and very bonny.'

'Aye, bonny. I had hoped to see them – but every Cameron sword is like to be needed here in the morning. A company of foot, we have just heard, is making a night march up Lochyside. From Fort William. With Lockhart's squadron at the Dark Mile, it can only mean an attack on Arkaig.'

'You think that they know of the Prince's presence here?'

'It is possible. But not necessarily. Enough that they should know that Locheil is home. Loudon has sworn to have Locheil's head.'

The younger man bit his lip. 'I should be staying here with you,' he said. 'One extra sword. It is a bad business when a MacGregor turns his back on a fight . . .'

'Your duty is to the Prince, not to Locheil,' Glenpean said. Duncan could sense the smile that he could not actually see. 'And even a Gregorach sword might not wholly turn the scales! *Dia* – if only we were not devoid of powder and shot, Camerons would be *rejoicing* that the Redcoats should pay a visit to Arkaig-side!' He sighed. 'But, enough of this. Here is my message. It is to Caroline, for the others are too young to understand fully. Tell her that if she hears that the Redcoats are nearer than half-way up the loch, she is not to wait. You understand? Not to wait an hour longer. She is to take to the heather with her sisters. Deep into the hills. The deeper the better. To leave all. And to send all our people away also. She is not to let the soldiers come nearer Glen Pean than half-way. On no account. She is to be ready to leave . . .'

'Young girls, sir?' Taking to the hills? In April . . . '

'Yes, by God! There are scores this night, hundreds, who will be wishing that they had done just that, in Badenoch and Strathnairn and Lochaber. Those who are still alive! I have seen . . . Lord forgive these eyes for what they have seen! I was behind Locheil's main body on my journey here, you understand, with just two gillies. We had been settling my wounded son in a safe place – I pray Heaven that it *is* safe – high in the Badenoch hills. So that Cumberland's savages had got before us down Spey. We saw . . . ' The other swallowed audibly. ' . . . we saw bonny young women's bodies lying in the heather, naked as the day they were born, with bayonets between their thighs! We saw women who had been burned alive in their houses. We saw children with their brains dashed against rocks . . . '

'Good Christ!'

'Aye – well may you say it! We saw a minister of the gospel crucified against his own church-door. And everywhere, the dead, the wounded and the survivors, stripped naked of every stitch. Women raped and mutilated, even those big with child. Men shot dead while at work in their fields. And, see you – these were, in the main, Strathspey Grants, who had never come out for the Prince, people of the Laird of Grant who supports the Government, a curse on him!'

'But this is unbelievable! In a Christian country . . . '

'Christian! MacGregor, Cumberland is said to have given orders, not only that there was to be no quarter on the battle-field but that the Highlands are to be made into a desert. He says that the only way to ensure that the country will not rise against the Hanoverian again is that there should be no one left to rise! So . . . so, you will carry my message carefully, will you, Captain? And see that my daughter understands. In case it should so be that I cannot myself come to them in time . . . ' Glenpean's voice quivered, and he gripped the younger man's arm tightly.

Duncan wrung the other's hand wordlessly, and turned away.

'And . . . if you would convey a father's affection, my friend . . . ?'

The young man rode up the dark lochside thereafter, and knew none of the night's peace that had encompassed him on

74

the way down. For too long, it appeared, he had been looking at war like a part-blind man, first from the viewpoint of a fighting soldier and these last days from that of the generals and leaders; now he was seeing it for the first time as the people, his own Highland people, were being brought to see it. And the sight affronted him, sickened him. That men could so act . . . !

The picture of such as Caroline Cameron and her sisters, lying before the smoking ruins of Glenpean House, projected itself unbidden time and again upon the shocked retina of his mind's eye – and he bore the leaden nausea of it in his belly all the way up Arkaig.

Duncan came in person to Glenpean House again in the grey hour before sunrise – and had his weary approach trumpeted by the baying of the hounds. Before he could dismount, the door was opened and the young woman stood waiting for him, rosy with sleep, her hair a tumbled glory, but fully dressed and with a plaid around her shoulders. Obviously she had not undressed all night; by her swift appearance at the door she had probably been sleeping in a chair downstairs.

'You are back. And . . . and alone?' she welcomed him.

'I am sorry,' he said. 'I would have brought your father back with me if I might. But Locheil – he needs all his support . . . '

'I know, I know. It was not to be thought of. But come away in. You will be tired. It is a long weary ride back. I have food for you, ready.'

'Always you are for feeding us, woman!' he smiled. 'I think that the Camerons must be a hungry clan – those hounds ever eating flesh! But I will not come in, no – lest I fall asleep at your kind table. I must get to the Prince. He was going to start for Morar this morning.'

'But that is so foolish,' Caroline exclaimed. 'Where could he be safer than at the Allt Ruadh shieling? Have you not brought word that will keep him? From Locheil?'

'That remains to be seen. I do not know. I hope so, but . . . ' He shrugged. 'Anyway, I must press on.' Duncan hesitated, 'But, before I go, I promised your father that I would deliver you a message, *mo caraidh.* Indeed more than a message – a command. A father's command.'

She laughed at him. 'La, sir – how solemn-sober! That, Captain, for your solemnity!' And she snapped her fingers. 'As for my good father's commands! I was twenty-one nearly a year past – probably he has forgotten! He needs reminding, does he not, that I am not one of his poor gillies?'

The man pulled at his lower lip. 'This is no jest, Miss Cameron,' he assured. 'You will please pay heed to it. The Redcoats – Cumberland's dragoons – are massing at the Dark Mile. Your Camerons, like the rest of us, have nothing but swords and dirks to fight them with. Most had neither powder nor shot even at Culloden Moor. So that there is no certainty that the soldiers will not reach here, even – to Glen Pean.'

She nodded, silent now.

'Your father's commands, in that case, are certain. And very emphatic. You are to take to the hills, with your sisters, before ever they come near. Before they get more than half-way up the loch. You are to wait for nothing. You must arrange for signals to be sent to you from down the loch. You are not to let them nearer than that, before you go. And see that the rest of your folk go likewise. Deep into the hills. Be ready. You understand?'

She searched his tired face in the grey half-light, all the laughter drained from her eyes. 'You mean . . . ?'

'I mean that we are dealing with brute-beasts, not men! No – that is unfair to the beasts, whatever! Even a cat with a mouse, even the ravens with a deer-calf, would not do what Cumberland's pitiless dragoons are doing. By order. In the name of King George! If God Himself can forgive them, I . . . !'

'Hush!' the girl protested. 'Surely, surely you make too much of it! You have been listening to tales. Such rumours grow . . . '

'It is what your father has seen with his own eyes. Do not ask me to tell you of it, girl. I would not have you even begin to imagine it. Just believe that it is so. And promise me that you will do what your father says.'

'Yes,' she whispered. 'Yes. If it is . . . if it is so, of course I promise.'

Almost fiercely the MacGregor glared at her. 'I should not be leaving you. If it was not for the Prince, I . . . I . . . could at least keep watch for you. Provide one sword to guard you. Aid you, if it comes to the heather. But . . . '

'How foolish! Of course your duty is with the Prince. Foolish to fear for me also – for us. I am very well able to take care of

76

myself, on the hill. We have been going to the shielings, at the high pastures, all our lives: In summer time. If . . . if we have to go, it will be just a month or two early, that is all. And up there, we do not need wild MacGregors, with swords, to protect us from the deer and the eagles!' She mustered a smile again. 'But – thank you, Gregorach, nevertheless.'

He shook his head, wordless.

Caroline turned away. 'See you – if you will not come inside for a bite, at least you shall take as much of it with you as you can. There is cold meat and bannocks . . . '

So, provisioned again, but strangely leaden-hearted, Duncan rode away once more from that hospitable house under Monadh Gorm. He had meant to leave the garron there, but the young woman said to keep it for the extra miles up the glen, and if the Prince should insist on going on over the pass to the sea, to leave the beast tethered at the shieling. She would ride up in the evening, as before, and could bring it back.

He turned and waved, once, some little way from the house, and thereafter did not look round again.

Five miles further, he came to the shieling above the dark lochan by the tumbling Allt Ruadh, just as the lemon-yellow sun was piercing the slate-blue cloud-banks low behind him on the jagged horizon of the Lochaber mountains. No drift of blue smoke yet lifted from the hole in the turf roof. A tired man's momentary resentment at the prolonged sleeping of others changed abruptly as he dismounted and stooped in at the dark doorway.

The cabin was empty. The ashes of the central fire were almost cold. No other trace of his companions remained. They had not waited for sunrise, or even dawn; they had been gone for hours.

Perhaps it was his weariness, but to Duncan MacGregor there seemed to be an ominous significance about that precipitate departure which struck him like a blow.

For a while he stood heavily outside the hut, staring westwards, biting his lip. Then, tethering the garron to a bog-pine root, he removed the folded handkerchief that Caroline Cameron had insisted on him using to cover the sticky patch amongst his hair that a pistol-butt had broken, under his bonnet. Over at the uncaring chuckling burn he washed it clean; he would have liked to have kept it, with its C.C.

initials stitched in one corner. Taking off the signet-ring with the MacGregor crest of a crowned lion, indicative of their royal descent from Kenneth MacAlpine – a thing that his father had given him on his reaching man's estate – he threaded the wet linen through this, and placed it inside the leather satchel that had contained his breakfast. He hung this from the cabin doorpost. She would understand.

He turned to look eastwards, down towards Arkaig, sketched a salute with his hand, and then set off heavy-footed in the opposite direction up the stony pass that crossed the watershed between this country and the sea.

CHAPTER 7

It was almost exactly eight days before Duncan came back to the head of Glen Pean, although just a little later in the morning. Eight days of fretting inaction, frustration, alarms and disappointment. Eight days whilst the balance tipped and swung and wavered, finally to come down to sound the knell of Jacobite hopes for many a long day to come. Prince Charles Edward had given Locheil the week that he pleaded for – and one day more. Now, alone and disillusioned, Duncan Mac-Gregor came trudging eastwards over the high stony pass again, and headed down by the side of the bounding stripling Pean. No sun shone this morning up the long deep trough of Arkaig.

He was skirting the lochan in the floor of the glen, where he had swum nine evenings before, and in two minds whether to press on the five more miles to Glenpean House or to climb up to the shieling above and rest there, even on an empty stomach – for he had once again walked all night – when a faint sound on the still morning air caught his attention. He heard it only for a moment, so brief was it – but he was fairly sure that it had been the high baying of a hound, muffled and somehow swiftly cut off.

That halted him. Stare as he would he could see nothing to account for it amongst the heather and bracken around him. The shieling up there was not in sight from the track or the lochan – one of the distinct advantages of its position. He started to climb the hill.

He reached the cabin, and paused a little way off. Its doorway stood dark, empty. No sign of life showed there, no sound emerged. He noted that the leather satchel was gone from the doorpost. Then, on a sudden impression, the man knelt down – in order the cause the roofline to be outlined against the brown heather rather than the leaden sky. Sure enough, there was just the faintest eddy of bluish smoke lifting above the chimney-hole. His hand on his sword-hilt, Duncan stepped forward softly.

A cry from the heather stopped him. 'Duncan! Captain Duncan! Captain MacGregor!' Out of a fold in the hillside fifty of sixty yards above, Caroline Cameron came running, skirts kilted high, holding the wolf-hound back with one hand and dangling a pistol in the other. Behind her, after a moment or two, appeared her two younger sisters, Anne and Belle.

He started towards the young woman, long-strided – and stopped short. She, who ran as though to hurl herself headlong upon him, stopped short also. So they stood, only a couple of yards apart, the girl's breathing unsteady, her breasts heaving, her eyes filmed – and the hound reached out between them to bridge the gap.

Duncan looked from Caroline to the pistol in her hand, over her shoulder to her sisters, and back to the cabin with its telltale wisp of smoke.

'What does this mean?' he asked, throatily. 'What do you here, all of you?'

'We have been here three days,' she said, panting a little. 'We came . . . because it was as – as you said.'

'You mean . . . ?'

She nodded. 'They came. The soldiers.'

A sort of groan escaped him. 'You were in time?'

'We were in time. We did not wait.'

'Thank God! And your home? Glenpean House?'

She bit her lip, blinking hard, and then shook her head, wordless.

'My dear,' he said. 'I am sorry. More sorry than I can say, whatever. I did not know. I thought that . . . all was well. I saw your father but two days ago, at Borrodale. He said that the Redcoats had not come as far as the head of Arkaig, that they

79

had burned Achnacarry and Muick and Achnasaul – but that he had been home and seen you, and that Glenpean was untouched...'

'They came the next day. After he had gone. They were making for Doctor Archie's house in Glen Dessary. They burned it, too. And all the cot-houses – his and ours.'

'I see. And your people? You got them away in time also?'

'Yes. Father had warned them all the day before. They are scattered about the hills, now. There is one family up behind us here, in a sort of cave on Sgor Thuilm. All are safe. Save... save old Seana.' The young woman's voice faltered. 'She went back. For something that she had left behind. She ... she was not very right in the head, you see. And old. They caught her. And they ... old as she was, they ... ' Caroline shook her auburn head, glancing back at her sisters, and left the rest unsaid.

But the girls had heard. Belle, the youngest, a plump and vivacious nine-year-old, spoke up in shocked excitement.

'We found her. Old Seana. The next day, when we crept down for some things. When the soldiers were gone. She was bent right over her table. Out on the grass. She was tied that way. With ropes.' The child giggled unevenly. 'And she had no clothes on! Not even a plaid!'

'She was dead,' Anne, the elder by three years, declared reprovingly. 'You should not laugh, Belle.'

'Hush, dear God – both of you!' Caroline said. 'Come you and pay your respects to Captain MacGregor, properly. Aren't you glad to see him? Belle, pull your skirt down. We ran from the cabin in a great rush,' she explained to Duncan. 'Luath must have scented you, and began to bay. I had to quieten him at once – he would have given our presence away. But at least he warned us of someone approaching...'

'Cuilean is dead,' the factual Belle informed. 'The soldiers shot him too.'

'We found his body. At the door of the house,' Caroline explained jerkily. 'They had been away somewhere – the two hounds. When the soldiers were signalled. We could not wait for them. Luath came up here to us, later. Alone. Following our scent. But not Cuilean. Poor Cuilean, he was ever the headstrong one...'

'Cuilean was brave,' Anne said. 'He could run down any deer. I loved Cuilean very much.'

Duncan stooped to take the pistol from Caroline's fingers, as a diversion. 'And this?' he asked, glancing at it and shaking his head. 'Unloaded? Unprimed?'

'We have no powder and shot either. But it might have kept a soldier away. For a little. So that we could run.'

'We could run faster than any Sassunach soldier in a red coat, I swear!' Anne asserted stoutly.

'And Caroline has a *sgian dubh*, too – a little dirk,' Belle informed, confidentially. 'She keeps it in her . . . '

'Belle! For Heaven's sake!' her elder sister cried. 'Off with you! Into the cabin, and get the fire going again. Quickly, now. The Captain will be wanting his breakfast.' Flushed a little, she turned to Duncan. 'We had just new-made the fire for breakfast. When Luath barked, I covered it over, to hide the smoke, as best I could . . . '

'It was the smoke that warned me that you – or someone other – were here, nevertheless,' he told her. 'It could be a danger. There is a trick that we have in the Gregorach that I will show you.' Deliberately he smacked his lips at them all. 'But I am hungry as any horse. Always I come to you for food. Let us get that porridge boiling.'

It was time that the subject was changed.

The interior of the cabin was transformed from the some-what stark appearance it had worn when the man had last seen it. The girls had managed to bring up many items salvaged from the wreckage of their home to give the place a domestic and lived-in air, with the indefinable touch of feminine occupancy about it – however dark and constricted it must remain. Plaids hung against the bare stone walls, deer-skins, most of them burnt and charred in places, strewed the earthen floor and that was also now coated with rushes from the lochan. There were wicker baskets of clothes, which presumably had been ready packed for their flight. Even a mirror, broken admittedly, was set to gain the best light opposite the doorway, and a jug of yellow cowslips from the crannies of the hillside lit up a dark corner.

The man was moved. Here was quiet courage, a clear deter-mination not to dwell on sorrows and discomforts. He did not voice his recognition thereof, however.

Bustle and assist as he would at the remaking of the fire and the preparation of breakfast, the inevitable question was not long in coming.

'The Prince?' Caroline asked. 'How is he faring? Where is he now? And how comes it that you are back here alone? Are you carrying messages again?'

'After a fashion, I am,' Duncan admitted heavily. 'The Prince has left me a mission to perform for him. For he no longer needs me . . . where he has gone.'

'Gone? He has gone?'

'Aye. Last evening, with the sunset, he set sail in an eight-oared boat from Loch nan Uamh. For the Outer Isles. For Loch Boisdale. I watched him go.'

'But . . . but this is folly, is it not? Duncan – here is madness, surely? How will he serve his cause yonder? It is here that he is needed, the leader, where his men are to gather. He will gather no army on Lewis.'

'He is not going to gather an army. He has gone seeking the French ships. Word came that they were hiding from the English frigates in Loch Boisdale. Lewis is but the first stage on his journey to France.'

'So-o-o! It is done, then? He has left Scotland.' The young woman gave a long quivering sigh. 'After all. All! So all is over – save paying the price!'

'He will be back.' Strongly, loyally, Duncan declared it, to himself as much as to his hearers. 'He goes only to win the aid that we need. From King Louis. Money to pay his regiments, to buy provisioning. Guns. Ammunition. Powder and shot . . . for such as this pistol.'

'Could someone else not have done that? His own father, even? King James? Is he not the one to have gone to the King of France? The Prince's place is here, with those who have fought for him . . . would fight again . . .'

'Think you that we did not tell him so? Young Clanranald told him, pleaded with him. Locheil sent him that advice, by myself. Elcho arrived two days ago, with Kinlochmoidart, and said the same – although he said it differently, wrongly unforgivably; for he is a passionate, impatient man and he has ever criticised the Prince. He said . . . what he should not have said.' Duncan ran a hand through his hair. 'But others spoke more suitably, reasoned with him. Your Doctor Archie Cameron of

Glendessary – who cannot have known that his house was burned. You father was with him. And others. It was of no use. The Prince – he has a stubbornness, and obstinacy, at times, that there is no moving. And the Irishmen were ever at his private ear.'

'Are they false, then, think you?'

'No, never that. But they see it all differently. It is all just politics to them, a sort of game that they play for high stakes. But it does not mean to them men's lives and homes, the fate of Scotland. Adventurers they are, without a country – more French than Irish, indeed . . .'

'They are with him still? Have gone with him?'

'Yes. O'Neil joined us again at Borrodale. That is where the Prince has been waiting these last days, in a shieling near MacDonald of Borrodale's house. Waiting for these ships, waiting for word that the clans were gathering, waiting for Lord George and those who went to Ruthven. Doctor Archie and your father brought O'Neil and Sheridan from Achnacarry. But Sheridan did not sail with them. He was ill again. He is too old for this kind of life. Locheil sent them because he is now taken to the heather himself . . .'

'Yes. Achnacarry Castle is no more. There has been fighting. But Locheil seeks not to come to blows until he has been able to gather the clan again, and equip his men in some fashion, my father told me. He has abandoned all the strath of Arkaig to the dragoons, but they dare not follow into the hills themselves.'

'Where is Locheil hiding, then? I have to find him.'

'Father said just above his own house of Achnacarry. Up the hill, in a cabin like this. He cannot travel easily, injured as he is. But his men are not there. Most of them are in the high valleys between here and Loch Eil itself. A party passed here yesterday, from the north, to join them. Forty men from Glen Kingie. Old men and boys. We were frightened until we knew that they were our own people.' She stirred the phuttering porridge. 'Your mission, then, is to Locheil? Not back to your own MacGregors?'

'It is not to Locheil himself, no. It is a curious matter. While we were waiting in Glen Borrodale, one of Glengarry's people brought the Prince word that a courier, Young Scotus – he will be MacDonnell of Scotus itself now, for his uncle, cousin to Glengarry, fell at Culloden and he is heir – Young Scotus is bringing money to the Prince from his brother the Duke of York. How much money is not known for sure. He came in a small vessel from France, meaning to put in at his own Glengarry country at Loch Nevis. But Government ships chased them and they had to flee far to the north, landing in the end up in the Mackenzie country. This Scotus was making for Inverness, to the Prince, when he learned of the battle. Not knowing then where to find His Highness or to take his money, he made for his own country. Lochgarry, colonel of Glengarry's Regiment, heard of him on his return home from Culloden – I had been told that Lochgarry was dead, but it seems that he was only wounded. He sent one messenger after Scotus, to bring him to the Prince, and the other to tell His Highness himself.' Bitterly Duncan shrugged. 'I do believe that it was the waiting for his money that kept Charles at Borrodale biding as long as he did!'

'But it did not come, the money?'

'No. At length he would wait no longer. That is the mission that the Prince has put upon *me* – to find this Scotus, and get the gold. To keep it safely for him, until he sends me instructions.' The man grimaced. 'It is not an employment that I esteem!'

'It shows that His Highness trusts you. Trusts you more than this MacDonnell of Scotus, it seems. Or many another.'

'That may be. But I am a soldier, not a banker! I would rather that he had chosen someone else. Or left the gold with Scotus – who after all must have been sufficiently trusted by the Duke of York, and has brought it all this way.'

'What do you now, then?'

'First I must see Locheil. Scotus may have come to him, at Achnacarry. He is now the recognised leader of the cause, the most respected man left, whom all trust. Round him all circulate. If he knows nothing of MacDonnell, then I suppose that I must go to Scotus itself, seeking him. It is on the Knoydart coast, opposite to Skye.' Duncan sighed. 'Chasing gold pieces!'

Caroline laughed – the first laugh of the morning. 'Some do nothing else all their lives!' she pointed out. 'But before you do that, or anything else, my good banker, you will eat your breakfast. And then you will sleep. If you have come from Borrodale, then you have covered a score of the roughest miles in all Scotland, and by night. You look as though you have, too. You are

not the man you were, even when first I saw you. Rest you need
– and this is as good a place for it as any. We shall keep watch
for you . . .'

'You are kind,' he said.

Duncan found it a pleasant interlude indeed, up there in the lap
of the mountains, and a most welcome change from the atmosphere of manoeuvre, perplexity, anxiety and mistrust in which
he had been living these past days and nights. A joy also to
relax in easy idleness after all his hurried and furtive travelling
– however soon it was to resume.

Not that the girls lived a life of inactivity up at the Allt Ruadh
shieling. When the man awoke, in the early afternoon, it was to
find Anne Cameron rooting about in the heather near by for
bog-pine roots, relics of the noble forests which had once clothed
all the Highlands, even up to these altitudes far above the present tree-level. These, when dried in the sun, made excellent
fuel, being impregnated with resin, burning with a hot flame and
a minimum of smoke. Caroline and Belle apparently had gone
for the milk. This involved climbing up the broken hillside
above into one of the high hanging corries of the mountain in
which some of the Glen Pean cattle had been temporarily pen-
ned, well out of the way of marauding Redcoats – with whom it
was a major point of policy to round up and drive off all stock,
to whomsoever it belonged, as a means of starving the country-
side, and at the same time feeding and enriching themselves. It
seemed that the Cameron cattle were in fact scattered all over
these lofty and inaccessible pastures, in little groups, and the
people likewise. It was as well that this enforced dispersal had
not been imposed upon them in the autumn or winter, when,
apart from the cold and the snows for the refugees, there would
have been no herbage for the animals; now, the new growth was
already burgeoning, and would provide excellent feeding until
September. That indeed was the object of the shieling system –
the annual migration of the young people, with the flocks and
herds, to make use of the brief rich summer growth of the high
places, and thus preserve all that could be grown in the little
fields of the lower glens for essential fodder during the long
winter months.

Duncan went down to the lochan in the pass to wash and
refresh himself with a swim, and then set out over the heather,

85

on Anne's directions, for the corrie about a thousand feet above. Here, in a great cauldron scooped out of the summit massif of Sgor nan Coireachan, ringed with frowning cliffs but floored in bright green grasses and wildflowers, he found not only about forty cattle, cows and calves, but almost a dozen people, living in improvised caves amongst the great rock-falls that choked the mouth of the place – including amongst them a wounded survivor of Culloden.

Caroline, chiding him for not having slept longer while he had opportunity, made him known to her people – who seemed on the whole surprisingly cheerful considering the circumstances and the burnt-out state of their homes down in the glen. Then, shouldering the leathern bottles of milk, and a shoulder of venison from a young stag which one of the men had managed to trap in a pit, they headed downhill again, Belle and Luath the hound running before.

On the way down, the young woman took him to another hidden hollow in the long hillside, not a corrie this time but rather a widening of a deep ravine scoured by a tumbling torrent, where another little party was ensconced. Instead of cattle these had a herd of goats and three or four garrons. It was one of the ponies that Caroline wanted, for Duncan's nocturnal visit to Locheil. That man was relieved to know that the three girls were not quite so isolated and alone as they had seemed.

Later, as Duncan's suggestion that some fish might provide a welcome change to the necessarily somewhat restricted diet that oatmeal, milk, dried beef, fresh venison and honey produced, they all trooped down to the River Plean. Throwing off all but his kilt, the man stepped into the rushing peat-brown waters, encouraged vociferously from the bank, and sought to balance precariously on the slippery river-bed pebbles. In his boyhood he had been an acknowledged expert in the gentle arts of tickling, gudding, or otherwise extracting trout from their element without the aid of lines and hooks. Now, feeling cautiously around boulders with both hands, crouching under the overhang of the banks, testing the eddies, concentrating all his senses in his finger-tips with head on one side as though he listened, eyes half-shut, mouth half-open, he proceeded to demonstrate that he had not entirely lost his cunning – whilst pointing out to his admiring gallery that these Cameron trouties were wee, terrible wee, compared with the giants of his own native Glen Gyle far to the south.

It was not long before he had first Belle and then Anne in the water beside him, modesty cast on the winds, and producing much squealing and splatter if not actual fish – and challenging, daring their elder sister to do better. She came in, too, after a suitable display of reluctance, and with stern warnings to Duncan MacGregor to keep his roving eyes steadily upstream and not down in her direction, under direst penalties – a precaution which she quite omitted to see stringently maintained in the subsequent excitement and thrill of the hunt, even to the extent of summoning the man urgently to her side on one occasion to assist in cornering a monster which, unfortunately, escaped through a certain preoccupation on Duncan's part. All this with her skirts tied approximately round her middle.

Altogether a stirring and enjoyable afternoon, far removed from thoughts of war, suspicion and treachery – and productive of more than brown trout.

It was with much disinclination, then, as the sun sank behind the high pass to the west, that Duncan gave ear to the call of duty, in opposition to the siren-songs of his eloquent hosts and tempters – the two younger of whom punctuated his pleas for delay with giggled wonderings as to the propriety of a man sleeping overnight in the one room with themselves, but deciding magnanimously that, since one room was all that the cabin contained, it was that or poor Captain MacGregor catching his death in the dewy heather outside, to the general hurt of the Stuart cause. Duncan declared that it was clearly high time that Donald Cameron of Glenpean was home to keep his daughters in order – but asserted that he must go, nevertheless.

Caroline, leaving Luath with her sisters, accompanied him down the glen; she wanted to see if her cat, which had been missing since the day the soldiers came, had returned to the vicinity of the house. So they rode down through the gloaming on garrons, now side by side, now one behind the other.

Although they started out smiling and at ease, a silence and a sombreness descended upon them as they neared the foot of the glen and the long trough of Arkaig. The realities of their situations came flooding back upon them both.

Even so, the sight of Glenspean House came as a shock to Duncan MacGregor. He had accepted that it had been burned, devastated, but the sudden recognition that those black-stained, roofless, gaping walls, surrounded by heaped rubble and charred timbers, were all that remained of the fair white house with its garden and trim farmery, brought a lump to his throat and a swift blinding fury to his heart. For a few moments he did not trust himself to speak, nor even to look at his companion.

Caroline Cameron did not speak either.

They scanned the area before them carefully, beyond the house and the scattered ruins of the crofts, to all the open ground about the head of the pewter loch and the wide mouth of Glen Dessary opposite, before emerging from the last trees of their own glen. No sign of life showed therein.

Duncan was still racking his brains for something to say to her, anything, that would not sound either hopelessly shallow or quite unsuitable, as they rode up to the broken premises themselves, still yielding up the evil smell of fire, when the girl herself found words.

'I do not see Min. Mineag, the cat. Do you?' she asked, in a flat factual voice. 'Small. Black-and-white.'

'No. No, I do not.'

'I suppose, if she is here, she will be . . . inside.' Caroline dismounted, and moved towards the gaping doorway, stiffly, unsteadily.

The man came after her.

At the threshold she paused, staring straight ahead of her. For moments she stood so, her back to him, rigid, still. Then, after one or two false starts, she got out a husky uneven call. 'Min! Minnie! Mineag – come, puss . . . ' Her voice broke.

Duncan's hand reached out to take her forearm and grip it.

Twisting round abruptly she buried her auburn head against his chest, and her body shook to great sobs against his own.

Holding her tightly there in the doorway, the man stroked the down-bent head, wordless yet. He saw them both standing in this same doorway last time he had been here, refusing to come inside, saying that it was his duty to hurry on after his Prince. He saw Charles himself standing here, declaring that they must not sleep in this house lest harm come to it and its occupants. And he did not know how hardly he gripped the young woman as he thought of it – so that she stirred and looked up at him, blinking away her tears.

He was not looking down at her – for something else had

caught his blackly frowning glance. He gazed over her head, northwards, towards the mouth of Glen Dessary, out from the dark gut of which a group of mounted figures had just appeared, shadowy in the dusk.

'Men!' he jerked. 'Horsemen. Coming out of the glen.'

She turned, to stare. 'I . . . I cannot see.' She wiped her swimming eyes with the back of her hand.

'There are four or five, I think. It is difficult to tell in this half-light.'

'Are they Redcoats? Dragoons?'

'I think not. I think that I would see scarlet. But all Cumberland's cavalry do not wear red coats.'

'We must not be caught here, Duncan.'

'No. But they may well be going down the north shore of Arkaig. If so they will not come near here. It is the best road, after all. They probably have not seen us, amongst all these broken walls. But if we ride off now, they are bound to see us.'

'What is best, then?'

'Inside. Quickly. The garrons too. They will not see us then. Even if they come this way they will not likely trouble to look inside this burned house. They will have seen many such . . . '

So into the shell of Caroline's home they moved, pulling the reluctant ponies in after them, to stumble over the charred fallen rafters and pathetic rubble within, into a corner that had once been part of the kitchen. There, amongst the debris, they waited, the garrons restless, the girl holding herself tightly under control.

An empty window space allowed them to peer out, northwards. Soon they perceived that the newcomers had not in fact turned eastwards down the north shore of Arkaig, but were coming across the marshy flats at the head of the loch, towards them.

'Surely, if they were Government soldiers, they would have gone by the north shore,' the girl said tensely. 'Where the road runs. It may be that they are our own people?'

'May be. But I think that the man who rides in front is dressed like an English officer, nevertheless.' Duncan was straining his eyes in the gathering gloom. 'Yes, I am sure of it. There are three mounted gillies and two pack-ponies. But the leader is a Southron.'

The horsemen were perhaps a quarter of a mile away. They rode ploddingly as though after a long journey. Soon it was perfectly clear that the foremost was dressed in military clothing with gold facings and a cocked hat. His three followers wore dark tartans and seemed to be armed to the teeth. Equally clear was the fact that not only were they coming in this general direction but that they were actually heading for Glenpean House.

'We . . . we would have been better to have bolted,' the girl faltered. 'While we had opportunity. Better still, perhaps . . . ?'

The man shook his head. 'Their horses are better than ours – long-legged beasts, not garrons. They could ride us down easily. Save on very rough ground.' He looked around him, in that desolate shadowy place, urgently. 'See, Caroline,' he said. 'We cannot get the garrons out of here now, unseen – too late. But *we* can get out. Through those windows at the back. Facing the loch. Once they are a little nearer, so that they cannot see the back part of this house, we will climb out. Then, keeping the bulk of it between us and them, we will hurry down to those alders and bushes by the loch-shore. In the dusk we should get away without being seen. Into the trees and then round to the mouth of your glen again.'

'Yes. Yes. They will find the garrons, but . . . '

'Come, then.'

They scrambled over the debris to a shattered window of the rear wall. Assuring himself that they would be hidden from the approaching riders, Duncan helped his companion to climb through, and then followed her. They crouched down behind the walling, hands blackened with soot. The angle of the building to the nearest cover of bushes was such that they could not risk a dash into the open until the horsemen were very near the front of the house. It was unfortunate, for it meant that if they were spotted they would be the more easily captured.

Fretting, they waited there. By peeping through their window, in alignment with another at the front, they could see some of the space before the house. And here in a few moments, they saw the newcomers pull up and dismount, and gaze towards the burned-out buildings. The leader was a handsome young officer clad in what had been a very fine and elegant uniform, now somewhat travel-worn, the long-skirted coat deep-blue with white-and-gold facings. His supporters might have belonged to any dark-tartaned clan. As the fugitives watched, the officer pointed to the house doorway, and came towards it, followed by two of his men. The other stayed with the horses.

Duncan came to a swift decision. Somehow, he had to aid the girl's escape. 'Quick! Off with you now,' he commanded. 'Run. To those bushes. No — alone. Go, now. I will join you later.' And as she began to question his purpose in a whisper, 'Quickly, *mo caraidh*— or it will be too late.'

Obediently Caroline rose, and bent almost double, an ill posture for any well-made woman, ran for the nearest alders, perhaps a hundred yards away.

Duncan did not wait to watch her progress. Crouching still, he edged to the gable-end nearest to the horses. Peering round, he saw the three men staring in at the door of the house. The garrons inside were restless and uneasy at the smell of fire, and even Duncan could hear them. The fourth man, over at the horses, was watching his companions.

As the group at the door stepped in over the threshold, Duncan darted forward and half-right. The barn, in which the Prince had once thought to sleep, was there. He was behind it, unseen, in a dozen strides. He now had cover. Rounding the corner of the wrecked barn and the byre beyond it, he was behind the cluster of horses. Moreover, the beasts were between him and their guardian.

The man did not hesitate for even a moment. Drawing his dirk, he raced forward lightly.

The stirring of the six horses covered any sound of his approach. He was amongst them in only two or three seconds. Edging between the beasts, he worked his way into position directly behind the unsuspecting guard — who stood holding the reins of the four riding horses in his hand.

Even as something of an outcry from within the roofless walls of the house seemed to indicate that Caroline's flight had been perceived, Duncan leapt. One arm encircled the gillie's neck from the back, and the other hand crashed down the hilt of the dirk on precisely the right spot of the unfortunate man's head, bonnet or none. With an incipient cry that choked off into a long shuddering sigh, the fellow went limp in his assailant's arms, still clutching the reins. For any MacGregor weaned on Rob Roy's tactics, it was child's-play.

Letting his stunned victim fall, Duncan vaulted up on to the back of the nearest horse. Kicking out with his brogans and waving his arms, he sought to stampede the other beasts away from the scene. He was successful with the more highly strung saddle horses – but the stolid garrons stayed where they were. He had no time to waste on them. Digging his heels into his new mount's flanks, he dragged its head round and sent it plunging after its fellows.

Cries arose behind him, tenor notably changed from a moment or two before. It was not these, however, that made the man look back. It was the hollow pounding of hooves immediately at his back.

The two pack-ponies were hurtling along at his very heels, their short legs going furiously, the basket-panniers which were slung on either side of them joucing about crazily. This phenomenal display of fire and energy was explained by the two leading-ropes which stretched forward from the beasts and tied somewhere to the saddle of his own horse. He had selected the wrong steed, apparently.

Duncan could not see, at the moment, just where the ropes were hitched; possibly to the buckles of the stirrup-leathers under the flaps of the saddle. Nor could he spare time to stop, investigate, and unhitch them. He must just put up with the garrons meantime.

This resolution was reinforced a moment or two later by the sharp crack of powder and shot. That would be only a cavalry pistol, he imagined, and no great threat at this range; but when, thereafter, a vicious whistle to his left and a louder report came practically simultaneously, the man crouched low in the saddle and pricked at the horse's rump with the tip of his dirk. That was a musket – a different matter altogether.

Only one more shot came after him, however, and not very close. Presumably the marksmen were not very swift at reloading. Better that they should be shooting after him than at Caroline, at any rate. And so long as they were shooting, they were not catching their errant horses for pursuit.

Presently Duncan decided that he was out of musket-shot. Glancing over his shoulder, he perceived three men running hither and thither, not far from the house, undoubtedly seeking to corner their mounts. Since the beasts could not be seriously upset, that would not take very long.

Pulling his borrowed horse's head round, he headed his trio for the mouth of Glen Pean, going as hard as the garrons' drag on his mount would allow.

It was Duncan's intention to go far enough up the glen to be well out of sight, and then to climb up the hillside to the south, to circle round and back, higher up, to try to pick up Caroline. She would have seen what he was doing, and presumably would be looking out for him.

It was just after he had turned off from the narrow floor of the glen, that it happened. The steep braeside meant that the panniers on the two garrons were unbalanced and askew – and no doubt they were already strained and displaced by the rough treatment they had received on that headlong career. At any rate, as one of the ponies stumbled on a loose stone and saved itself from falling only by a mighty scrabbing, the fastenings of its left pannier snapped with a jerk, and the basket fell to the heather.

The impact burst the wickerwork lid open, and out spewed two or three bags. They all looked identical, not very large, made of some sort of cloth, probably linen. One of them, rolling and bounding downhill, struck a corner of rock, and split open. Out therefrom spilled a stream of coins – that even in the fading light gleamed golden.

Duncan pulled up, staring. Many gold pieces were rolling down.

There is something about gold, about money, that few can resist. The sight of it, in large quantities, will even seem sometimes to alter a man's whole character. If it did not do that to Duncan MacGregor, at least it had him down off the horse and grasping for the errant coins in the instant. He picked up two, three. All were of a sort – *louis-d'or*.

'Lord!' he gasped. 'French! French gold *louis*!'

He hurried to the broken pannier. It was almost full of the little linen bags. He weighed two of them in his hand. They were very heavy, and the coins within chinked metallically. He looked into the other pannier, still attached to the garron. It contained only clothing and personal gear. So did both those on the second pony – the effects of an elegant man who liked his comforts even when travelling. A folded paper lay amongst them. It was written in French script.

Duncan turned back, thoughtfully, to gather up the spilled gold. One pannied filled with coin – reason enough for it to be the one that broke loose, heavy as it was and therefore lacking balance. French gold! Could it be, then, that he had made a mistake? A grave mistake?

He stared away down the glen.

Even as he looked, a mounted figure came into sight round a bend down there, riding hard. The pale breeches at least stood out in the gloom.

'So be it,' Duncan said.

CHAPTER 8

It was less than pleasant just to stand there waiting for the irate rider – but Duncan obscurely felt that he owed it to him, somehow. He had moved down to the track in the floor of the glen once more, with the three animals, and now stood in front of them, arms folded on his chest to proclaim, if possible, his present inoffensiveness. He had taken the precaution of pinning his white cockade, distinguishing emblem of the Jacobites, prominently on his bonnet. He hoped powerfully that the approaching man, even in the dying light, would notice all this and not merely pistol him out of hand.

The officer slowed down from his furious gallop as he approached. Undoubtedly it must have seemed a strange development, and probably he feared a trap or an ambush. One of his kilted supporters, mounted again, had now appeared far in the rear.

Duncan raised his hand and waved it.

About one hundred yards away, the horseman pulled up, and drew his pistol, obviously nonplussed.

Duncan raised his voice as well as hand. 'Sir,' he shouted, 'my apologies to you if you are King James's man. If not – shoot and be damned to you!' He was ready, at the first raising of that pistol, to dodge behind the nearest garron.

The other did not answer. He sat there uncertainly, on restless mount, as well he might.

Duncan tried again. 'Are you French? *Fraşçais, Monsieur?*'

'I am not,' came back shortly. 'And who the devil are you, to ask?' That certainly did not sound like a French voice. Nor yet, indeed, despite the language, an English one.

'I am an officer of Prince Charles Edward's army. Sir . . .

could it be . . . is it possible that you are Young Scotus? Mac-
Donnell, younger of Scotus?'

'Aye. I thought that was it, by God!' The question seemed
to further infuriate the newcomer. 'Another rogue in need of
shooting, curse me!'

Duncan hesitated. 'But you *are* Scotus?' he insisted.

'What if I am, damn you! Does that make *you* any less of a
thieving robber?'

'I think so, yes,' Duncan cleared his throat. It was tiresome,
this long-range shouting, and the mounted gillie was coming up
fast. 'My name is MacGregor. Captain MacGregor . . .'

'Well I believe it! Always the MacGregors were thieves and
caterans!'

'Also an extra aide to His Royal Highness. Charged to find
Captain MacDonnell of Scotus.'

'What . . . ?'

'It is the truth, sir.'

'You have an uncommon strange way of carrying out your
charge, then!'

'It was a mistake, Captain. I apologise. I took you for an
English officer. Your clothes. None of His Highness's officers
dress so . . .'

'I am an officer of the Irelanda Regiment of His Catholic
Majesty of Spain.'

'No doubt. But you looked devilish like one of Cumberland's!'

The other turned to glance behind him, saw that his hench-
man was in close support and evidently decided that he could
risk coming near. He moved forward, pistol notably at the
ready.

Duncan stood still, arms folded again.

The gillie came thundering up just as his master reached the
MacGregor, very fierce with musket in right hand and drawn
broadsword in left. Duncan could see now that the fellow was
wearing the dark Glengarry MacDonnell tartan. No doubt he
thought that his superior had been successful in cornering the
miscreant.

With one looking down at him on either side, neither kindly,
Duncan smiled. 'Your money is all safe, Captain,' he said. 'It
was the gold that opened my eyes. A pannier fell off, and one of
the bags burst open. Only one man is like to be travelling the

Highlands today with all that French gold – MacDonnell of Scotus, the man His Highness set me to find. So it is well met, sir.'

Scotus rubbed a pointed chin with the back of the hand that held the cocked pistol. 'I suppose that I must believe you,' he said.

'Indeed you must! I have a paper signed by the Prince . . .'

'His Highness – is he near, then? Near here? I have had conflicting word – that he is with Locheil in Arkaig and again with Borrodale in Arisaig . . .'

'Unhappily he is neither. By now he should be at Loch Boisdale in South Uist. He sailed for the Outer Isles twenty-four hours ago.'

'Good Lord – what does he do there?'

'He seeks ship to take him back to France.'

'But . . . Saints of Mercy! To France? The Prince? How will that serve him? I have just come from France. His place is here. What a plague means this?'

'Well may you ask. Many sought to dissuade him, I assure you.' Duncan sighed. 'But it is a long story, and better places for telling it than this. Moreover, I have a friend that we must find. I was not alone in yonder burned house of Glenpean's. His daughter was there also – Miss Caroline Cameron. Her home it was. We were looking for something there, when we saw you coming. Taking you for one of Cumberland's officers, we hid – for I have no powder or ball for my pistol. I sought to draw you off – and succeeded. Now we must find her.'

'*Dia* – Glenpean's daughter! And his house destroyed. I knew nothing of it. Who did this thing? Why? I intended to pass the night there. Doctor Archibald Cameron's house of Glendessary is also burned. What is the meaning of it, sir?'

'The meaning is that there is much in this sad realm of Scotland today that you will require to learn, Captain. Much of it that stains the very name of common humanity. But that can wait. Here is your second gillie. I hope that I did not damage your third too sorely? Let us be off down the glen, to find him. And Miss Cameron too. When your man has put his pannier to rights . . .'

They found Caroline readily enough, by means of Duncan hallooing and shouting her name every couple of hundred yards or so down near the mouth of the glen. At his fourth or fifth cry they heard her answering call, and she rose up out of the hillside heather some way above them, eyeing them doubtfully. At Duncan's beckoning and reassuring wave she came down to them.

Whatever doubts MacDonnell himself might have about the MacGregor, he appeared to have none at all regarding the young woman. He was off his horse in a trice, bowing low and kissing her hand, and apologising profusely for having inadvertently frightened her. Flushed, breathless and distinctly dishevelled as she was, he most evidently approved of her – for which Duncan should not have blamed him. He was a very personable, gallant and good-looking young man indeed, though his Frenchified manners Duncan felt to be excessive.

Caroline did not appear to share his insular bias, however, and after only a brief period of introduction and explanation, was quickly on easy terms with him, laughing and bright-eyed. Duncan was vaguely resentful, and felt that it was all slightly unsuitable.

Scotus and his gillies were hospitably invited to the shieling up at Allt Ruadh – an offer accepted with alacrity, and seemingly taken as a personal compliment by the former. There was now no need for Duncan to go seeking Locheil, so, after returning to Glenpean House to pick up the third gillie – now fairly well recovered but eyeing his former assailant without love or understanding – and the two garrons, they all made their way up the dark glen once more.

Luath bayed her warning to the mountains long before the party reached the shieling, and, true to their instructions, Anne and Belle were nowhere to be seen when the newcomers arrived at the cabin. Caroline's call brought them swiftly out of the heather, however, small dark shadows wrapped in plaids, and the nound with them. Astonishingly soon their excited laughter resounded on the night, the fire was blown up and revived, and food produced. The Cameron daughters, it was apparent, seldom actually dwelt on the more sombre aspects of life.

Scotus was a success from the beginning, treating the girls like three princesses – with one of whom at least he might almost have been contemplating seduction.

With the gillies bedded down outside in their plaids, the talk went on in the cabin, by the flickering light of the bog-pine fire, well into the night. Suggestions that the youngsters should go to sleep were treated with the contempt that they deserved, and Scotus's assertion that no beauty sleep was required in this company received with acclaim. Duncan MacGregor became a very secondary figure on the shadowy scene, and John Mac-Donnell took the stage as to the manner born, ably supported by Caroline.

The newcomer's account of himself was as enthralling as it was well and dramatically told. Without his actually saying so, it was clear that he was cast in a pleasingly heroic mould, suitable to his appearance, and if King James's cause had had more like him for support, matters would have been in a very different state by this time. It seemed that he had been expressly recommended to Henry Duke of York, Charles Edward's brother, by Marshal Saxe himself, and had been seconded for this very important mission by the Spanish king. Prince Henry had collected, with great effort, no less than two thousand *louis d'or*, to assist his brother's campaign, and Scotus selected as the trusted courier . . .

'Two thousand!' Duncan interrupted, a little sourly. 'Two thousand is a vast deal of money, and could have made a great difference to the Prince's army – had it arrived in time. But, Captain – there is not two thousand gold pieces in those bags in your pannier, I swear!'

'There is not, no – because they have been stolen, sir!' the other returned warmly. 'Stolen by our own rascally knavish people. By MacKenzies, of my Lord Cromartie's force. Fight as I would to save them.'

'Stolen . . . ?'

'Aye, by God! My ship, a small French barque, had the devil's own luck, buffeted by gales and harried by the English men-o'-war that blockade this coast. We were weeks at sea. It was intended that I should be landed at my own house of Scotus on the north shore of Loch Nevis, but we could not come near it, and the only place where we might eventually put in was far north at Loch Broom in the MacKenzie country of Dundonnell in Ross. A curse on them! At first they received me fairly enough – but when they found that I was carrying this money to the Prince, damn them if they did not attack me violently, while at table, truss me like a fowl, and steal it all! In the house of Laggie, where I landed. On Loch Broom.

And Colin Dearg MacKenzie, who was host to me, leading the assault! Every gold piece – of their own Prince's money! It is scarce to be believed . . . !'

'It is, indeed!' Duncan observed grimly, above Caroline's incredulous cries. 'But you still have a few left, friend – a pannierful. Have you forgotten them?'

'I got those back. After much trouble I recovered five hundred *louis*. With the aid of my cousin, Coll MacDonnell of Barrisdale, I . . . '

'*Dia* – that . . . that . . . !' The MacGregor controlled himself. 'Are you cousin to Barrisdale?'

'Our fathers were both brothers to Glengarry,' the other informed haughtily. 'The Prince had attached Barrisdale to Cromartie's force, in some capacity. He came to Loch Broom when he heard of my landing. With his help, as I say, I recovered around five hundred *louis*. That was all. Of the rest – *pouf!* Nothing! All gone into black MacKenzie sporrans. Lost without trace.'

'But this is monstrous!' Caroline exclaimed. 'What sort of scoundrels, dastards, could do such a thing?'

'MacKenzies could, and did! Devil-damned rogues! Officers of Cromartie's, as I said. The whole clan of them as thieves, ruffians, like . . . like . . . ' He glanced sidelong at the MacGregor.

The man smiled thinly. 'The MacDonnells have never loved the MacKenzies,' he murmured obliquely. Lochbroom and Lochalsh and Dundonnell in Wester Ross had once been Mac-Donnell country, before the MacKenzies took it from them. The very name Dundonnell told its own story.

'It is beyond all understanding,' the young woman said. 'The money that the Prince needed so desperately! His army unpaid and starving. A gold *louis* is as much as a guinea, is it not? Two thousand guineas . . . ! What might it not have done?'

'Even yet, it might have worked wonders. Served to hold the clans together,' Duncan said, frowning. 'Properly used, two thousand guineas at this juncture might keep much of the Prince's army in being until it can be equipped again and . . . '

'Might or might not,' Scotus doubted. 'It was never expected to hold together a defeated army. But whether it would or no is of no matter now, since most of it is gone. Five hundred certainly will not . . . '

'Gone? You have not said goodbye to it so soon, so entirely, surely? Fifteen hundred *louis* will not disappear into the ground like a burn in summer! Gold pieces will not be so thick amongst the MacKenzies that such a flood of them will not leave any trace. It should be possible to recover much of the money, I would say.'

'How could that be done, man? Who will take it from them now, in their own country? Think you that I did not try . . . ?'

'My father will be with Cromartie's force by now. Glengyle's Regiment – what is left of it – is up there. He could find most of that gold, I swear.'

'Good God – MacGregors, now!' the other exclaimed. 'You propose that a regiment of MacGregors should go looking for gold pieces amongst the MacKenzies! And expect that any should come out of it, for the Prince? Save us, man – you cannot be serious . . . !'

'Sir!' Rising from a deerskin rug on the floor to one's full height in a single outraged movement is no mean feat, but Duncan achieved it like a spring uncoiling. 'Damn you, Mac-Donnell – watch your words!' he cried, hand on dirk. 'As Royal's my race, I'll listen to that from no man – much less a Frenchified dandy who is cousin to that time-server Coll of Barrisdale . . . !'

'Duncan!' Caroline pleaded. 'Gentlemen! Please – do not speak so. Peace, I pray you . . . !' She started up in turn, and came round the fire to clasp Duncan's arm. 'Here is no way to behave. You are my guests – both of you.'

Wide-eyed, the two younger girls stared from one man to the other.

Duncan swallowed, his glance flickering round them all. 'I . . . I am sorry,' he got out. 'But I will not hear the MacGregor name insulted. By . . . by . . . '

Scotus had risen now, also, without haste and gracefully. He bowed to Caroline, and then to her sisters, smiling. 'My profound apologies, ladies. I am desolated that you should have been alarmed. I was but so taken aback at the notion of MacGregors handing over gold pieces to anyone, that . . . '

'*Dia* – it is a notion that you will have to get used to sir!' Duncan broke in. 'For it is your own position, entirely. You are

100

to hand over the moneys that you have brought, to me. That is why I was seeking you. On His Highness's instructions.'

'To you? Never!' Scotus declared. 'Great God above – do you think that I have brought it all the way from France to hand it over to the first MacGregor I meet?'

'It is the Prince's command,' Duncan said gratingly. 'I have the paper here, signed with his own hand. Read it.'

'No! I tell you, no! I care not what paper you have. I will not do it. His Highness of York gave the gold to me with *his* own hands. I'll not deliver it to any save the Prince of Wales himself.'

'But he has sailed for the Isles, man. On his way to France. I told you. You cannot follow him there, with it.'

'Then I shall keep it until he comes back.'

'That was His Highness's command to me – to hold the moneys safe for him, until he sent me instructions.'

'And think you that you can do that any better than I can, sir?'

'Perhaps – since you already have lost most of it! But that is not the point. It is the Prince's orders. Written here . . . '

'Your orders, perhaps – but not mine. I am an officer of the King of Spain, in the Duke of York's service.'

'But . . . you cannot just carry all that gold around the country with you!'

'And what would *you* do with it?'

'I would hide it somewhere. Safe. Send a courier after the Prince. And await his instructions.'

'I propose to do likewise, sir.'

The two men glared at each other, the tall dark MacGregor and the slender fair MacDonnell.

Caroline stepped between them, biting her red lips. 'See you – this is folly. And worse,' she asserted. 'How shall King James's cause be served thus? The money was sent to aid that cause, was it not? And the cause needs aid, desperately. Even five hundred guineas might do much.'

'I do not dispute it, Miss Caroline,' Scotus acceded. 'But if the Prince is not here to receive it . . . '

'Then give it to someone else to use, in the Prince's interests. Give it to Locheil. All know him to be trustworthy – a good man. The best of the Prince's leaders, it is said. You were going to see Locheil, Duncan. Go, and Captain MacDonnell with you. Together. Give him the gold. He will know best what should be done with it. Surely it is not for either of *you* to decide . . . ?'

'The Prince's orders . . .,' the MacGregor began.

'My mission is to the Prince himself,' the MacDonnell declared.

'Oh, do not be so stupid!' the girl burst out. She took hold of Duncan's arm and shook it exasperatedly – though she did not do the same for Scotus. 'What stiff and stubborn infants men can be! Anne and Belle, here, could show more sense, I do declare! I will not listen to more of this. I am going to bed. You will kindly go outside, both of you, while I do so. Do not come in again until I call. And when you do, there is to be no more of this talk. Of any talk! You may bed down over there, at that side. Beside Luath. You understand? Not another word out of either of you. Or I will set Luath on you – and she can be a devil! Out with you, now. Anne! Belle! Into your bed. Quickly. Don't sit there gaping . . . '

In that tone of voice Caroline Cameron was not to be argued with. The youngsters scuttled for their bunk, and while their sister smoored and banked up the fire again, with slow-smouldering peats, for the morning, the two men hurried outside into the night. There they paced up and down, wordless, in opposite directions and at different sides of the cabin.

When at length a call from within allowed them to return, they went in discreetly, almost on tiptoe, jostling each other in the dark now that the firelight was quenched, stumbling over impedimenta and even the hound – all with muttered apologies. At one major collapse, which was Scotus falling over the legs of his companion – who, being much less elaborately clad was the quicker outstretched on the deerskins – something that might have been a sniff or even a snigger sounded from the other side of the benighted hut, but was swiftly repressed.

When silence and stillness was at length achieved, after a little a quiet 'Goodnight' came from across the floor. Duncan's brief, and MacDonnell's more comprehensive reply, brought forth no further remark.

Late as it was, Duncan lay long thinking. Perhaps he had got out of the way of night-time sleep, these last weeks. Not so Scotus, evidently, who soon was breathing deeply with the regular rhythm of a seemingly untroubled mind – even though, by earlier sounds, he had taken the precaution of tying the pannier containing the gold in some way to his person.

It was neither the gold nor yet its guardian that preoccupied the other man's wakeful mind, nevertheless. When he listened intently, very intently, he believed that he could distinguish Caroline's soft breathing. He was fairly sure that she lay nearer to the door than her sisters. The latter fell asleep as rapidly as did Scotus, he thought – but not so Caroline.

He listened, and thought and considered – and sought not to sleep, indeed. He was well content just to do that.

It was long after he was assured she slept that he allowed his own eyes to droop.

CHAPTER 9

IN a morning of bright sun, shouting larks, and the first cuckoos calling hauntingly from the trees deeper in the glen, the girls were up and about long before the men stirred. Although rumpled and unshaven and feeling by no means at their best, it became – or was made – promptly and abundantly clear to the latter that this was no morning for a resumption of the previous night's disagreements, and tacitly both recognised the desirability of a truce meantime. It was a prickly, brittle armistice, but it served to keep the peace. The understanding was that both men should indeed make their way down Arkaig the next night to see Locheil – although no assurances were exchanged as to final decisions.

Meantime, willy-nilly, they were caught up in the carefree, timeless and idyllic life of the shielings. Always, to the Highlanders, the shielings spoke of an annual release, the end of the harshnesses and confinements of winter, the long halcyon days and short northern nights amongst the high pastures, alpine, arcadian, untrammelled by so much of the restrictions, conventions and routines of ordinary settled life, a young people's elysium. As a brief release from the shadows of defeat, savagery, treachery and suspicion which haunted them, and in the company of such as the Cameron sisters, young men would have been churls indeed had they not responded.

The trouble was, to Duncan's mind, that Scotus seemed to respond too whole-heartedly altogether. Very quickly he was taking the lead in everything, all gaiety and gallantry, as free and easy with the girls as though he had known them all his life, taking liberties with Caroline which Duncan would never have dared – and being put in his place therefor with only mild and token rebukes. His effect on the MacGregor was to make him more than ordinarily abrupt, tongue-tied and reserved – which was not how he wanted it to be, at all.

They all went up to the high corrie for milk and meat, and helped to round up some of the straying cattle, Scotus in his elegant Spanish uniform looking particularly incongruous at the task. They visited two or three other encampments of Camerons, from Glen Pean, Glen Dessary and Glen Camgarry. They joined in an energetic and not very effective attempt to corner deer, by seeking to drive them into one of the many corries that scored the stern flanks of Sgor nan Coireachan, the Peak of Corries – but succeeded only in forcing one young beast over a little cliff, where its broken leg changed the girls' laughter to tears of reproach in truly contrary feminine fashion at the despatch of the poor brute. There was a proposal to go fishing again, down in the River Pean, later in the afternoon – although on this occasion, however much he had relished the business last time, Duncan was strongly against the idea, suggesting on impulse that it might be foolhardy, asking for trouble.

Nobody took this seriously, of course. Indeed, it was difficult up here to feel that anything that went on down in that other world of the valleys and lochsides and plains had any relevance, held any immediate threat.

Nevertheless, back at the cabin by the Allt Ruadh, they found a messenger awaiting them, sent by Locheil to warn his clanspeople that Lord Loudon was going to establish a line of posts based on the head of Arkaig and reaching north-west through Glen Dessary right to salt water at Loch Nevis. A barracks to act as headquarters for this force was to be erected out of the ruins of Doctor Archie Cameron's house of Glendessary. This was to seek to subdue the high Cameron hinterland, and to prevent access to the sea and possible French aid. Probably part of the intention, the messenger said, was to bar the route of the Prince's escape – which would not yet be known by the military. And it seemed likely that having decided to take these steps, the Government would not be long in setting up a similar line through Glen Pean to the sea at Loch nan Uamh.

This news was like a douche of cold water on the party. It brought the Redcoats very near indeed. It meant that Scotus, had he been but one day later, would have been trapped. It darkened the future, here at Allt Ruadh.

Scotus declared that this cabin was no longer sufficiently remote to be secure. The Cameron girls must move up to the high corrie. Caroline demurred. From here, if they were approached, they had all the wide laps of the hills to escape into; up there, there was only the other corries and the narrowing summit. Safer here. Duncan agreed. Above, they could only flee in one direction; down here many ways were open to them. Nevertheless, he did not like the notion of them being left alone. The girls might have to consider moving still deeper into the empty hills to the south . . .

Scotus found in this new situation an excellent excuse for not proceeding that night down Arkaig-side to Locheil's hiding place. Their hostesses' protection had the first priority, he asserted. Duncan found himself obliged to counter this, however reluctantly, and much as he would have preferred to stay where he was. As serving officers their first duty was to the cause; moreover, the girls were in no immediate danger. That gold could not be allowed to remain undelivered. And the sooner that something was done about that stolen by the Mackenzies, the better. It is probable that the MacGregor did not even admit to himself that he had no intention of allowing MacDonnell to stay any longer at the shieling. He insisted – and when Caroline saw that he was determined, and prepared to have another scene about it, she added her support and urged Scotus to go. Though clearly ready and anxious to do battle with Duncan, the other conceded that the young woman's slightest wish was his command, and gracefully yielded.

It was decided not to wait until dark – nor to go down Arkaig-side at all. The safety of the gold was vital, and a much less dangerous though more difficult route to the Achnacarry area could be found through the wild hills to the south, taking longer, but where they need look for no Redcoats. This was Caroline's suggestion – indeed she offered to act as guide to set them on at least the start of their journey. Duncan would not hear of this, of course, declaring that a MacGregor could find his way anywhere in the mountains.

With farewells that were as stilted and cramped on Duncan's part as they were elaborate and eloquent on his companion's, with many instructions to the girls as to what to do in various cases of emergency, the pair, with the three gillies and the two extra pannier-ponies, set out.

Their route lay slantwise, uphill not down, with the sunset at their backs, over the long flanks of Sgor Thuilm, across a thrusting shoulder and so down into a quiet valley beyond, filling with the lilac shadows of the night. This was the first of many such that they crossed, for they were going against the grain of the land. It was slow and tiring travelling for man and beast, for, most of the way, the only tracks that they might follow were deer-paths. But Duncan pressed on determinedly, anxious to get the first and most punishing third of their journey over before the short half-darkness of the May night made the going even more difficult. When they would reach the long trough of thickly wooded Glen Mallie, which ran roughly parallel with Arkaig and eventually joined it, it would be easier.

Their arrival, eventually, in upper Glen Mallie, after negotiating eight grim miles and two high passes, was noteworthy for more than mere easement of travel. They had barely entered the scattered Scots pines, black in the gathering gloom, when a baying of hounds from no great distance ahead brought them up sharp. Duncan, dismounting and listening with ear to the ground, could clearly hear the drumming of hooves, many hooves going fast. Scotus, drawing his pistol, was for hurrying back uphill whence they had come – since hiding amongst the trees would be of no avail against hounds' noses – but Duncan argued that it was almost inconceivable that anyone but Camerons would be riding up Glen Mallie at such an hour; no enemy force would dare risk night travel in such wild and ambush-favourable clan territory.

They sat their mounts, therefore, like graven statues amongst the dark pines, waiting, weapons ready. Duncan tossed the MacDonnell his own plaid to cover up the eye-catching Spanish uniform – which, though it might serve to gain for its wearer correct prisoner-of-war treatment from Government troops, was more likely to draw swift ball or steel from Jacobites mistaking its significance.

Soon three bounding slavering deerhounds were barking around them, and it was not long before horsemen were there too – Highlanders obviously, mounted on shaggy garrons similar to their own, and with broadswords drawn. With nothing to lose now, Duncan hailed them, shouting out the Cameron slogan about hounds eating flesh.

This was answered promptly – and by, of all men, the girls' father, Donald Cameron of Glenpean.

Warmly they greeted each other. Scotus was introduced. Nothing was said of the gold, meantime.

Glenpean and his men, it seemed, were acting as advance-guard for a large party of Camerons coming this way, escorting no less a personage than Locheil himself, borne on a pony-litter.

At Duncan's wondering demands as to the whys and wherefores, he gained the surprising information that the two French warships which had been for so long playing hide-and-seek with the English men-o'-war had at last managed to slip unobserved into Loch nan Uamh, and were waiting there now, loaded with guns and ammunition for the Jacobites.

Duncan groaned aloud. 'Lord – at last! And too late!' he exclaimed. 'Mercy on us – two days! Two days only, and they would have been in time! *Dia* – this is the Devil's own doing!'

'Well may you say it,' Glenpean agreed. 'Two whole shiploads of what we have been gasping for, praying for. And the Prince gone!'

'With what you have brought, this could have saved the day!' Duncan said, to Scotus.

'The Prince can be brought back, can he not?'

'I do not know. Who can tell where he may be?'

'Locheil has sent a courier after him. Hoping to find boat to take him to the Outer Isles. But . . . ' The older man shrugged eloquently.

'At least the arms will encourage the clans. Hold the army together until the Prince's return,' Duncan said.

'Even that I would not swear to,' Glenpean asserted heavily. 'Locheil is not alone, behind us. And not a few of those who ride with him are giving thanks that those ships will carry them safe back to France rather than for the arms that they bring.'

'To France? You mean that they are going? Giving up? The Irish, you mean? Old Sheridan? O'Hara?'

'Not only these, lad. Many of the Sassunach. Even some of our own people who ought to know better. There is a great cry that all is lost. Captain MacLeod, the Prince's aide, has come back from Ruthven, bringing the Duke of Perth, the Lord Tullibardine and others with him, and saying that the Lord George there, in the Prince's name, ordered all assembled at Ruthven to disperse to their homes. To make what terms they could with the Government – God pity them and Cromartie's force was surprised in Sutherland. Cromartie himself is taken.'

'Sink me – I seem to have come home to a sorry crew!' Scotus cried.

'You have come, Captain, to a broken army at the end of six hundred miles of retreat and defeat,' Glenpean informed levelly. 'But there are true men left yet, never fear.'

'I rejoice to hear it, sir!'

'Unfortunately Murray of Broughton, his Highness's Secretary, has arrived. He was ill at Inverness, but has contrived to escape Cumberland's net, and reached Locheil yesterday. In the absence of the Prince and the Lord George, he conceives himself to be the first authority. But the man is a clerk and no soldier, and I fear that his influence will not be for maintaining the fight.' The Cameron sighed. 'Ah, well – I have work to do. It will not do if Locheil in his litter catches up with his vanguard! If you wait here, you will surely meet him. I will leave a man with you.'

Duncan moistened his lips. 'Glenpean,' he said. 'Your house. Your home ... ?'

'I know it all, lad,' the other told him. 'It is hard – but not so hard as for many another. Clunes' wife and daughter were caught and ravished. He found them wandering naked, his wife completely demented. Achnasaul's lady was more fortunate – with a pistol ball through her head. Myself, I know that my girls escaped, and are safe up in the shielings ... '

'We have only just left them, sir – at the Allt Ruadh. They are well, and happy enough. Remarkably so. But this new line of posts that Loudon is to set up in Glen Dessary will make them less secure.'

'Aye. But, God willing, when we have these new guns, when we have ammunition, we may be able to do something about

108

that. Now – I am off. I will see you at Borrodale, at Loch nan Uamh ... '

With one of Glenpean's gillies, the two younger men settled down to wait for Locheil, while the advance-party trotted off westwards into the gloom.

The importance of this new development, of the arrival of the two French ships, was amply demonstrated by the fact that not only the wounded Locheil, but practically all the prominent Jacobites who had gravitated to his territories in this present crisis, were travelling that night from their hiding-places around the burnt-out Achnacarry Castle to Loch nan Uamh. The ailing Duke of Perth, formerly one of the two lieutenants-general until he had disagreed with the Lord George Murray, was there; also his brother the Lord John Drummond, colonel of Drummond's Horse. Lord Nairn was there, and Lord Elcho with his friend Maxwell of Kirkconnell, the MacKinnon of MacKinnon, Stewart of Ardshiel, Lockhart of Carnwath and Sir Stewart Thriepland. Also Hay of Restalrig, Sir Thomas Sheridan, Colonel Dillon and others of the Irish faction. It was a strange company to find trotting through wild and night-bound Glen Mallie amongst an escort of fully a hundred Camerons.

When Duncan and Scotus were brought before Locheil, it was to find the chief not really in a litter but sitting in a sort of chair slung between two garrons, a mode of transport that at best could only have been grievously uncomfortable. He greeted the two young men courteously, and on Duncan's claim that they had important information for him, invited them to ride alongside his own two beasts meantime. Unfortunately many of the other leaders were there already, or close at hand, and neither of the newcomers had any intention of broadcasting the news of the gold to all and sundry at this stage. They managed to convey this reluctance to Locheil, who however was too much of a gentleman to offend his illustrious companions by asking them to fall back out of earshot. In consequence the disclosure was postponed, and the rival guardians of the treasure found themselves consigned to a more lowly place down the column, their basket of gold with them, and riding westwards again the opposite direction to their former travelling. Something of mutual frustration perhaps brought the pair of them rather closer to each other as a result.

Distressing to an injured man as this jolting journey over rough country must have been, Locheil did not spare himself or his companions. From Achnacarry to Borrodale's house near the head of the sea loch of nan Uamh, the Loch of the Caves, was well over thirty exacting miles, with a pass between the head of Glen Mallie and that of Glen Finlay to surmount, not very high but grievously boggy and wet. It was down near the foot of the latter glen before a halt was called, at approximately half-roads, where Glenpean had surveyed a camping-place in a wood and had fires burning and hot porridge cooking for all. An hour's break was announced, to rest the garrons rather than their riders.

More than half of this period was gone before, watching their chance, the two young captains approached Locheil where he sat by a fire, for the moment alone. Barely had they begun to speak to him, however, when another man came up, a man not old but of a fleshy paunchy build with, nevertheless, a fine-drawn almost ascetic face, sallow complexioned. He was soberly dressed in Lowland clothes, but wore an air of considerable authority. When Duncan paused in his preliminary remarks, Locheil waved his hand towards this gentleman.

'Captain MacGregor – proceed. If, as I take it, your information concerns His Highness's affairs, then there is no one more fitted to hear it than Mr. Secretary Murray of Broughton. All the Prince's business, other than actual military commands, are in his hands. Speak on.'

They bowed, somewhat stiffly, to the newcomer, who for his part ignored them completely and sat down beside the chief.

Doubtfully Duncan looked at his companion, and then shrugged. 'Captain MacDonnell, younger of Scotus, here, has brought five hundred gold *louis* from the Duke of York, for His Highness,' he said baldly.

'That is so,' the other agreed easily. 'To be delivered to His Highness in person, gentlemen.'

Both older men sat up abruptly, as though electrified.

'*Louis*? From France? Gold . . . ?'

'Five hundred . . . ?'

'Five hundred, yes.'

'But . . . brought, you say? You have it here?' That was Murray. 'In gold? With you?'

'I have indeed.'

'But this is extraordinary! Magnificent!' Locheil exclaimed. 'Five hundred *louis d'or* is a fortune. It will solve many problems...'

'It is a goodly sum, at any rate,' Murray said, more cautiously. 'It will be very useful, undoubtedly.' He paused. 'I would wish to hear details as to how came this notable good fortune, sir?'[1]

His hearers listened to John MacDonnell's account of his stewardship, and the theft at Loch Broom, with varying emotions and sundry interruptions. But at the end of it all, Murray of Broughton was quite decisive and certain – and more authoritative than ever.

'I shall take charge of this money, from now on,' he announced briefly. 'And you, gentlemen, will take the necessary steps to recover such sums as have been, h'm, mislaid, *en route!*'

'No!' Scotus objected vehemently. 'The Duke expressly told me to give it only into the Prince of Wales's own hands...'

'Mine are the Prince's hands, Captain, in this pass.'

'And *I* have the Prince's own orders to take the money and hold it secure until his further instructions,' Duncan declared. 'He knew of this gold. He charged me, before he sailed...'

Murray spoke through him. 'You have heard my instructions, gentlemen.' There was some slight emphasis on the *my*. 'In the Prince's absence, I, as his Secretary, give the orders. I will provide you with a receipt for the money you have brought, Captain MacDonnell. And thereafter, that sum ...' He paused significantly. '*That* sum, whatever may be decided about the remainder, is no further responsibility of yours.'

'And if I refuse, sir?' Scotus asked, quietly now.

'Then you will be arrested forthwith, Captain. And, no doubt, in due course tried by court-martial for having mislaid

---

[1] *The equivalent of 500 golden guineas in 1746 today would be twenty times as much and more. Gold pieces, actual specie, had always been rare in Scotland, especially in the Highlands. At this time One Pound Scots equalled only 1s. 8d. sterling, a chicken might cost 6d. and a cow 10s.*

three-quarters of the total sum entrusted to your charge! Take your choice.'

'Damnation – this is too much!' That was Duncan Mac-Gregor, hotly. 'Locheil – he cannot do this . . . !'

'Locheil, as a senior officer, will you kindly inform these individuals as to their duty?' the Secretary said smoothly, rising to his feet. 'Or must I request the Duke of Perth, as former general, to take the necessary steps militarily?'

The Cameron chief shook his grizzled head unhappily. 'You have the rights of it, no doubt, Mr. Secretary,' he said heavily. 'But you are over-hard on these young men, I think. They deserve a kinder reception than this.'

'They have their duties, sir, as I have mine. Let them abide by theirs, and they need fear no unkindness from me.' Murray bowed stiffly, and was moving off when he half-turned. 'Locheil – perhaps you will instruct some of your Camerons to bring me this money forthwith? Lest there be any further . . . mischance!'

Locheil sighed. 'Very well,' he said.

When the march was resumed a little later, the two junior officers rode very far back down the column indeed, side by side but with little to say to each other or anyone.

CHAPTER 10

THE sun was well up before the weary company arrived at the mouth of Glen Borrodale and gazed out over the blue waters of Loch nan Uamh and all the sparkling vista of the isle-strewn Sea of the Hebrides. Islands, skerries, reefs and rocks, from the mighty jagged mountains of Rhum smoking with captive mists, to the tiniest weed-hung islet ablaze with sea-pinks and girt with golden tangle – all was colour and light and loveliness. Few eyes, however, if any amongst that strung out cavalcade, saw any beauty consciously that morning. All attention was concentrated on the two tall ships that lay directly below them, anchored as close to the rocky shore as they dared, hidden from seawards behind a thrusting headland of the lochside.

Young Clanranald welcomed his guests pleasantly enough to his temporary headquarters at Borrodale House amongst the slanting oakwoods – though clearly he was hardly prepared for so many of them. His father, an elderly man and 16th chief of one of the main branches of the great Clan Donald, preferred in troubled times to live out on his territories in the Outer Isles, so that in effect the son, Ranald, was captain of the clan. Grave and quiet of manner, he was one of the Prince's earliest and most loyal supporters, and his regiment had been, until Culloden, one of the largest and most gallant of all the Jacobite army. So far, the Government troops had not penetrated into this mountain-girt and secluded Clanranald land of Arisaig, Morar and Moidart that thrust like an array of spearheads into the western sea.

A clan chief's house had always to be ready for vast hospitality at shortest notice, and Clanranald did not fail to produce adequate food and drink for the invasion, even though already his resources had been tapped in providing for the ships' companies after long weeks at sea. One of the ships' masters, Captain Lemaire of the *Bellona*, was with him now. He seemed to be an anxious, not to say impatient man. He was not long in getting into earnest, excited but apparently highly secret converse with Murray, Locheil and the Duke of Perth.

Glenpean was able to give Duncan and Scotus a certain amount of information. It seemed that there were at least three English ships in this area of the Inner Hebrides, and the French captains were not at all certain that their presence in Loch nan Uamh was not suspected. Earlier that same morning a small naval sloop had loitered about at the mouth of the loch for almost an hour, before suddenly departing northwards in a hurry. Telescopes on board might possibly have picked out the Frenchmen's tall topmasts rising behind the trees of the sheltering headland. The captains therefore were anxious to be off at the earliest possible moment.

Proof of this disquiet was forthcoming in a practical fashion only a few minutes later. An order from Secretary Murray was circulated that all fit and able-bodied men, irrespective of rank or age, were to repair at once to the loch-shore, there to assist in the unloading of the two vessels. Clanranald was assembling every small boat in the vicinity to assist in the operation.

When the newcomers arrived down at the beach, it was to find a large accumulation of gear – small cannon, muskets innumerable, bayonets, swords, ball and shot, kegs of powder, blankets, clothing, saddlery, barrels of brandy and wine, and so on – already stacked on the narrow apron of shingle. The shore, however beautiful, was a wickedly rocky and broken one, and only the one little strand offered a landing-place for the small boats. The big ships themselves could not approach nearer than three hundred yards off shore. Most of this cargo had been landed the day before by the ships' own boats; now, with the arrival of more local small craft and a sizeable labour force, the work went apace. There seemed to be a vast deal of shouting wherever the French sailormen were involved.

When Young Clanranald himself, with the MacKinnon chief, threw off plaid and doublet to assist in the actual manhandling of boats and gear, Highland pride and the reluctance of most of the officers to soil hands with any sort of manual labour evaporated, and the work went with a will. Glenpean's own group of Camerons were engaged in transporting the landed cargo, on their garrons, up to well-hidden storage in a couple of the large caves in the hillside, for which the area was famous, perhaps a quarter of a mile inland. To this party Duncan and Scotus and the three MacDonnell gillies attached themselves, glad enough of the work to do, tired though they were.

It was heavy and awkward toil, and the terrain over which the ponies had to be coaxed, steep, slippery, rock-strewn and heavily wooded. Stacks of arms and provisions piled higher and higher on the scrap of beach, having to be moved back as the rising tide threatened to engulf part of the precious freight.

In the midst of all this activity, in mid-forenoon a sudden hullabaloo arose out at the ships. Swiftly the word was shouted back, via the busy ferry-boats, to the shore. Three vessels had appeared in the mouth of the loch, heading in – two sloops and a somewhat larger corvette; naval ships, and as obviously English.

Something near to panic developed amongst the voluble Frenchmen and some of the Jacobites. The shouting and excitement rose to a crescendo. Captain Lemaire, superintending the unloading ashore, went hurrying back to *Bellona*, and behind him, in a few moments, a boatload of Jacobite notables hastily put out. Others stood in apparently violent altercation, and still others ran inland in the direction of Borrodale House.

'There go those ambitious of a passage to France!' Glenpean

observed to Duncan, pausing in his task of tying a couple of powder-kegs on either side of a garron.. 'Dia – it looks as though some are in a pretty predicament. They have had enough of fighting – so to France they would go. But it seems that these French ships are going to have some fighting of their own! A sorry problem for peaceable warriors!' The Cameron sounded unusually bitter.

'What will they do?' Duncan asked. 'The French ships? Cut and run for it? Fight their way out?'

'They must,' Scotus declared. 'They have no choice.'

'If the English are only small craft – like the sloop this morning,' Glenpean said, 'our French frigates may out-gun them. But still much cargo is to be unloaded. They say not much more than half is ashore . . . '

For a little while there was chaos in the sheltered inlet, with the Frenchmen leaving everything to hurry back to their ships, Jacobite leaders demanding boat-room to get out also – although some seemed to be rowing back again. Many of the working parties ashore were tending to abandon their tasks and hurry to high ground to see what was going on. Then stern orders came from Locheil that the work was to go on with redoubled vigour. The precious cargo must be cleared and secured.

'Thank God for one man with a soldier's head!' Glenpean cried. 'Donald never loses it.' He pointed 'Though there is another who, I swear, does not lose his head either! But uses it to a different tune, I think!'

In a small boat being rowed out to the ships was the dark and sober figure of John Murray of Broughton.

'Is he going? The Secretary? To France?' Duncan demanded.

'I heard that was his intention, yes. Small loss, perhaps.'

'But . . . the gold!' Scotus interrupted. 'What of the gold? If he goes. He said nothing of this last night. God – if he takes it with him . . . !'

'He would never do that.'

Glenpean stared from one to the other. 'Gold?' he repeated. 'What gold, man?'

As the pony-party toiled up the hill towards the caves, the two younger men told the Cameron something of the business, briefly, breathlessly. But their minds were not really on what they were saying, preoccupied with the situation down at the ships and with Murray's probable intentions.

From higher ground, where they could see over the intervening headland, they eagerly turned to stare seawards. It took them a little while, against the dazzle off the water and amongst the great multitude of the skerries and islets, to pick out the English vessels – for they were unthinkingly looking for tall men-o'-war and near at hand. In fact the craft were neither large nor very near – fully two miles away, probably, and beating up and down amongst the islets, as indeed they must in a north-easterly breeze and amidst the intricate shoals and channels of the loch.

'They are not much more than half the size of the Frenchmen,'. Glenpean said. 'Their guns will be much less powerful. They will not dare to come too close.'

'Perhaps they will only block the mouth of the loch? Bottle the French,' Scotus suggested. 'Until bigger English ships can come up . . . '

'How can they inform other English ships?' Duncan wondered. 'Unless there are some near at hand. The French are not trapped yet.'

'Trapped or no, they do not intend to stay hidden behind that cape,' Glenpean observed. 'Look there . . . '

The feverish activity round the two frigates was developing now to some purpose. Anchors were up, and the small boats of each ship, with cables attached to the parent craft, were beginning to row outwards, seawards. Obviously the big ships were to be towed into more open water. One or two small topsails were being unfurled to catch the breeze and provide steerageway.

'Damn them – they're going!' Duncan cried. 'Bolting. They're off!'

'Have they got the gold aboard – that's what I want to know?' Scotus demanded. 'I' faith, if that blackguard Murray sails off with it . . . !'

'More important than your gold – those ships are still half-full of guns and ammunition,' Glenpean reminded. 'Enough to equip whole regiments. We need every scrap of it. Curse their shrinking French hides . . . !'

They were unfair to the Frenchmen, all of them. The *Bellona* and *Mars* were slowly towed out only a short distance beyond the tip of the headland, where they had an uninterrupted view, and there they hove-to, held in position by boats at bows and sterns. The double-banked gun-ports at their tall sides were opened up, and the fierce snouts of ranked cannon appeared menacingly therein. The lilies of France broke at their mast-heads and fluttered proudly in the forenoon sunlight.

'Ha – we spoke too soon, I think . . . ,' Glenpean began. 'They are preparing to fight – that is clear. But they do not look as though they intend to make a dash for it, to shoot their way out. They are furling those sails again.'

'The short boats are going alongside once more,' Duncan reported. 'It looks – *Dia*, it looks as though they are starting to unload again! Yes – see, there are barrels being lowered once more.'

'Bravo! *Vive la France!*' Scotus acclaimed. 'They have given themselves room to manoeuvre, and to sight their guns. We owe *messieurs* an apology.'

That appeared to be the situation. The unloading proceeded apace, with the two frigates held approximately stationary.

The three smaller vessels continued to beat their way up the loch, tacking one way and another, deliberately or otherwise using the scattered skerries and rocks as a screen.

The pony party had not paused in their own task of coaxing the long string of laden garrons uphill, heartened as they were by what they saw. They were unburdening their beasts in a cave entrance when a single loud cannon shot boomed out, seeming to shake the rock around them and echoing amongst all the enclosing hillsides. At the ominous sound, every man paused.

'That is one of ours. A Frenchman. Too loud, too near at hand for the English,' Scotus announced. 'Sounded like a culverin. A twenty-pounder. Just a warning shot, for the others to keep their distance.' He sounded very knowledgeable – but then he always sounded that.

On their way down to the shore again they saw that the English ships had drawn much closer; were in fact less than a mile away, and keeping as close to the north shore as they dared. Indeed they seemed to be intending to use the other side of the same headland behind which the French had hidden formerly, to protect themselves.

'What range have their guns . . . ?' Duncan was asking when

117

the shattering crash of a broadside drowned his words. The *Bellona* seemed to leap on the calm face of the loch, one side of her vomiting fire and smoke. A barrier of water-spouts rose in front of the English vessels – but a notable distance in front. That had been a gesture only; clearly the range was still too great.

No reply came from the smaller ships – save to edge still closer in towards the land and to gain the fullest shelter of the headland.

'What next?' Duncan wondered. 'What can the English do? They are held, surely.'

'They could put a landing-party ashore,' Glenpean suggested. 'To attack us from the rear. Halt the unloading, at least.'

Locheil had thought of that. He detached a party of Camerons from the unloading, under Torcastle, and sent them to man the summit of the headland ridge, where they could command the approaches from the west. He also sent word to Captain Lemaire urging him to put ashore two or three of his heavy cannon which, sited on the same ridge, could make the English ships keep their distance.

Glenpean's people worked on, and though the two young officers would have preferred more military employment they were offered none. They were setting off with another pony-train when suddenly Duncan pointed back towards a boat that was being rowed out to the French ships.

'See yonder!' he cried. 'I would know those two a mile off. There is only one man in all the army with so long a back as that. And only one who cocks an eagle's feather that long in his bonnet! Two beauties, I swear! Your cousin and mine, Scotus – God forgive us! Where have they come from? What ill wind brings them here? Those two together . . . ? I do not like it – I do not.'

'Coll!' the MacDonnell exclaimed. 'Coll of Barrisdale.'

'Aye – and James Mor MacGregor. A pair indeed!'

'Both gentlemen with gallant records, lad,' Glenpean put in, mildly reproachful.

'Oh, aye – they are bold enough, I grant you. Both of them. Nobody doubts their courage. But I trust neither. And mislike the more to see them together.'

'Perhaps they are for France? Like Murray and the rest.'

'I could hope so . . .'

'Never. Not Coll. What ails you at Coll? Scotus demanded. 'He is as brave a soldier and seasoned a campaigner as any in the army.'

'I do not deny it. Winning, I might trust him – but losing, no!'

'Stuff, man! Coll is a fighter. And a MacDonnell, whatever! He aided me at Loch Broom, there – amongst the ruffianly MacKenzies. He helped me to recover that five hundred . . .'

'You are sure that none of it stuck to his own fingers? That he did not know more than he admitted?'

'Sir! Watch your words, will you! You will not speak so of any MacDonnell. Of your own James Mor, it may well be true. You know your own clan, presumably! But not . . .'

'Gentlemen!' Glenpean intervened. 'Let it be – och, let it be! What does this serve? All know Barrisdale. And we have work to do . . .'

Colonel Coll MacDonnell, younger of Barrisdale, was indeed known to all. The tallest man in the Prince's army, and one of the most handsome, he had first commanded Glengarry's Regiment for his uncle, and later formed another MacDonnell regiment of his own. Daring, brilliant at guerilla warfare, he had actually been knighted, in King James's name, by Charles Edward, who esteemed him highly. But then, the Prince had also esteemed highly his aide-de-camp Major James Mor Mac-Gregor, whom Duncan for one did not. Indeed the two were much alike in many ways, of a sort that the Highlands have always brought forth in numbers, dare-devil swashbuckling blades, attractive, high-spirited, but perhaps a little mercurial – and only mildly troubled by conscience. Barrisdale and his regiment had not been present at Culloden, having been sent north earlier to reinforce Lord Cromartie's force holding Ross and Sutherland.

Duncan's alarm at seeing him here, without his regiment, and in the company of his own cousin James Mor – who also should have been with Glengyle's Regiment in the north – was instinctive.

A party of Camerons were manhandling two massive eighteen-pounder guns from *Bellona* up to the summit ridge of the headland, as Glenpean's pony-train came down once more from the caves, superintended by three French gunners. Glenevis, their leader, called out.

'Donald – have you heard? Of the gold? On yonder ship. A fortune, just! Gold enough to sink her . . . !'

Glenpean glanced at his companions. 'Och, well,' he answered. 'Not just that, man. Not all that much.'

'It is true, I tell you. All the gold in the world! Casks and barrels of it. In the ship.'

'Here's foolish talk, Glenevis! There is no more than five hundred gold pieces altogether. A deal of money, yes – but . . . '

'Murray *has* taken it out to the ship, then?' Scotus charged.

'Eh . . . ? Murray? No, no. How could he do that? The gold is on the ship, I am telling you. It has come from France. In barrels . . . ' Glenevis and his men were pressing on, laboriously dragging and pushing the heavy cannon up the steep hill and the difficult ground.

'Nonsense, man!' Scotus shouted after them. 'You have it all agley. *I* brought the money from France. But not in that ship. Murray has it. Five hundred *louis d'ors* . . . '

But down at the beach, the same story, or versions thereof, was on everyone's lips. Unlimited gold had arrived from France, and they were all rich beyond the dreams of avarice. The excitement seemed to quiver in the very air. The threat of the English warships so near at hand, even the importance of all the accession of arms and ammunition in the circumstances, seemed to have faded into insignificance. The thought of gold filled man's minds, gold in quantities unheard of, undreamed of, hitherto.

Much perplexed and incensed, the two younger men, with Glenpean, left their ponies and went to speak to Locheil, to get to the bottom of the matter.

'The truth it is,' the chief told them, on the grassy bank amongst the sea-pinks, where he had sat all morning supervising the landward handling of the precious cargo. He sighed. 'I suppose that I should be rejoicing, for the money is needed, without a doubt. But . . . ' He shrugged plaided shoulders. 'It will bring its own problems, I warrant. If it had only come two days ago, two short days, when the Prince was here. I could almost wish . . . ' He left the rest unsaid.

'There is much of it, then?' Scotus asked, almost aggrievedly. 'More than I brought?'

'Much, yes. More than I could have believed. Money that, two months ago, even one month, could have changed all the course of the war. What made King Louis send so much – and delay so long in sending – I do not know. But I am told that there are eight great barrels of *louis d'ors* aboard the *Bellona*. And in each, five thousand gold pieces!'

'God in Heaven!'

'Lord save us all!'

'You say . . . five *thousand*?'

'In each? Of eight? That is . . . that is forty thousand *louis-d'ors*!'

'That is so, yes, my friends.'

Stricken to silence, they looked at one another, scarcely able to comprehend the full meaning of what they heard. Forty thousand gold pieces was indeed almost beyond comprehension in the Scotland of 1746.[1]

Into their stupefaction Locheil went on heavily. 'What it could have done, all this, is almost beyond imagining. The army has not been paid for months. Payment could have held it together. We could have bought the guns that we needed – the powder and shot. Aye, and the food! Hungry men do not fight their best. Even men we could have bought – those Lowland lairds whose souls are in their pockets. And the frightened English Jacobites who turned their well-clad backs on our ragged Highland rabble! Consider proud Edinburgh, and what money could have done for us there. God – when I think of the Prince, selling even his very rings and drinking cups . . . !'

'Aye,' Glenpean nodded. 'It is hard, hard. So much, too late by so little! And yet – better now than never, Donald, is it not?'

'You think so?'

'It could be changing much, even yet.'

'Aye – nothing truer. But change it how? To what end? With the Prince gone?' Locheil grimaced slightly. 'It has changed us our Murray, already – the good Secretary! He has decided not to go to France, after all. He is for taking charge of this great wealth and remaining with it! Others may well think similarly.'

'That I can well believe!' Scotus nodded grimly.

[1] *In present-day figures, 40,000 guineas would add up to almost half a million pounds Scots; but in actual gold coin it represented considerably greater value than that. Almost certainly it was the largest single consignment of money ever to enter the Highlands. A million modern banknotes would be less resounding.*

'What is to be done with it all?' Duncan asked.

'Lord knows. Many will be asking that, I think – and offering suggestions!'

'The Prince will have to be informed. Somehow. A courier must be got to him – before he can sail for France. This could yet change all – if the Prince came back.'

'That is, I think, my own view,' Locheil agreed slowly. 'The money must be held intact, for another attempt to bring King James's cause to triumph. For that it was sent. It must be held for the support of armed action against the Elector of Hanover – either this one resumed, or another Rising later. It must not be dispersed, frittered away. It was sent for Prince Charles so to use; it must await his return – or, at least, his directions – surely.'

'Are others saying differently, then?'

'They are indeed. Already. Some are talking about arrears of pay. Of compensation. And subsidies. Inducements. Suchlike phrases – fine words that mean just money. Gold in fists and pouches and sporrans . . . '

The crash of cannon-fire halted Locheil. Up on the ridge above the inlet wisps of smoke rose above the trees. The guns dragged up there had found targets to shoot at, apparently.

Young Clanranald came hurrying up. If the firing meant that a force from the English ships had landed, then a company must be sent to deal with them. He could collect forty or fifty of his own men quickly; could he have Glenpean's score or so to add to them? If it was only at the ships themselves that they had opened up, of course, it would not be necessary . . .

The lesser booming of more distant gunfire punctuated his words. The English were firing back – individual shooting, not broadsides. It might be covering fire for a landing-party or it might not. But it gave added urgency to Clanranald's suggestion.

Locheil agreed. Glenpean hurried back to his men, Duncan and Scotus with him, none of them averse to a little more soldierly activity than pack-horse transport.

Up on the ridge, well supplied now with muskets and powder and ball for their pistols, they were able to see the English ships in a bay of the loch something less than a mile to westwards – though still out of range. Glenevis told them that they had seen small boats heading for the shore, and the French gunners had fired a few shots, not at the vessels themselves but into the intervening woodlands along the shore, to discourage any landing-parties from making their way along. The English guns had retaliated in similar fashion, firing at random into the loch-side woods at extreme range. Both sides were well aware of the danger represented by these tree-covered approaches. There the matter stood – but the boats had not put back to the English parent ships.

Having thus briefly sketched in the situation, Glenevis was clearly more interested in discussing the gold than the enemy's possible tactics.

Clanranald decided that they should wait where they were meantime. Knowing every inch of the terrain, he declared that no enemy could approach their present position from the west-wards without crossing a certain bare area of ground where a landslide of the steep thrusting hillside had scored a wide open wedge of red earth and rock, sweeping away trees and under-growth almost down to the water's edge. This, approximately half-way between the two inlets, was in full view from the ridge. Time enough to move down to the attack when they observed the sailors crossing there.

So they waited. No sailors appeared. The subject of the gold absorbed them all.

Duncan fretted, lying there in the sun, idle. Little as he enjoyed the heavy and undignified labour of transport, this pro-longed inaction seemed as unsuitable as it was wasteful of man-power. Almost a hundred men lay about the crest of that ridge doing nothing, while the precious freight continued to pile up on the shore behind – and men's thoughts dwelt almost wholly, crazily, on glittering yellow *louis d'ors*, innumerable, uncount-able. Clanranald pointed out that their presence here was not in fact wasted; since they could see the English ships plainly enough, it was certain that the officers thereon could equally well see themselves through their telescopes, a large armed body waiting and ready – which was no doubt why the shore party had so far not moved forward.

After almost an hour there was a notable diversion. Without warning, what sounded like a full broadside of French cannon crashed out, shaking the very ground beneath the recumbent warriors, and setting the gulls a-scream amongst all the boom-ing echoes. The fall of shot showed in a great line of spouting water much nearer to the English ships than heretofore.

Soon it was clear that *Mars* had left the bay, and was now in full sail out in the loch, where she was in a position to bear down directly on the enemy. Presumably she had completed her unloading and was now either going to make a dash for it alone or was deliberately challenging the English to a fight. Or perhaps trailing her coat, seeking to decoy the opposition away from their landward shelter.

Whatever *Mars*' purpose, the English lost no time in responding – as indeed they must or be trapped in their inlet. Two ships hoisted sail and put out into wider waters forthwith. The third, a sloop, was left, almost certainly to collect the shore party – and even with the breeze contrary the watchers could plainly hear the bugles aboard urgently blaring their message, presumably of hasty recall.

The situation developed rapidly, rather like moves in a game of chess, the two English ships seeking to divide and confuse the Frenchman's attention, while trying to keep out of his range. *Mars* tacked about in open water. Loch nan Uamh was almost two miles in width and roughly twice that length. She did not seem concerned with immediate escape.

Small boats began to straggle out from the shore to the remaining sloop.

The English corvette, the larger craft, was now firing tentative shots from well across the loch. Two could play the decoy-duck, patently.

Mars was forced to swing round. The English ships were lighter and faster; moreover they could risk shallower water. They would be almost impossible to bring to bay.

It was now practical stalemate. Nevertheless *Mars* was creating a diversion – which was obviously her intention, posing a threat rather than pressing an attack, giving time for her sistership to finish unloading and sail out.

Perceiving this, Clanranald decided that the main body of his men should return forthwith to transport duty, but that a small scouting party should proceed cautiously along the coast to find out whether or no any English sailors remained on shore. Duncan offered to lead this, with a local guide – and was surprised when Scotus volunteered to accompany them.

It was almost a couple of hours before this group got back, so thorough was their search. They had found no men – only six empty boats riding at anchor well out amongst the islets of the inlet. This discovery had kept them searching and quartering the woodlands, until satisfied that the boats had only been left thus because one sloop could not take them all aboard.

Although Duncan and Scotus had recognised, from a heavy outbreak of gunfire, that *Bellona* had almost certainly joined her consort, and both French ships were now probably gone for good, taking much of the Jacobite leadership with them back to France, they were quite unprepared for the situation they returned to at the beach below Borrodale House. Agitation prevailed. Not at the loss of leaders – but at the loss of gold. And not, it seemed, just at a gold piece or two a-missing. A vast amount was gone – five thousand *louis d'ors*, no less.

Almost incredible as this information sounded, it appeared to be fact. The gold had been packed in linen bags in eight great barrels – and one of the barrels was gone. Or, rather, the barrels were all ashore, but one of them was filled with stones and shingle.

Suspicion, accusation, resentment quivered in the very air.

'Who brought the money ashore?' Duncan asked the obvious question of Glenpean.

'A number of people did that. There lies the difficulty,' the older man told him. 'The barrels of gold were too heavy to put into small boats as they were. They had to be opened up, and the bags lowered into boats one by one. Then the empty barrels. Senior officers rowed back and forth with each boat – Secretary Murray himself, a Major Kennedy who came with the ship, MacDonald of Borrodale Clanranald's kinsman, Sir Stewart Thriepland, Ardshiel. Others too . . . including your friends Barrisdale and James Mor MacGregor!'

'Ah!'

'The missing money perhaps never left the ship?' Scotus put in.

'That has been suggested. But all saw the barrels opened on board and the bags lowered into the boats. All the barrels and all the bags.'

'How, then . . . ?'

'There was much confusion on shore. Guns were firing, men coming and going. Less care, it seems, was taken when unloading the gold from the boats. Some came in at different points in this bay, where there are few landing places. Other boats were

125

landing the ordinary cargo. Our people, with Clanranald's, were all up yonder on the ridge . . . '

'But, man – five thousand gold pieces cannot just be spirited away!' Duncan cried. 'Think of the weight of them! Even the five hundred that we brought in that pannier was a vast weight. Ten times that . . . !'

'Aye. Clearly a number of men were in league. One boatload, whatever.'

'The carrying of it away would be simple enough,' Scotus pointed out. 'The pack-ponies going up from the beach into the woods with the other gear, all the time. Nothing would be easier than just to join in with the rest.'

'Why are Barrisdale and James Mor here at all?' Duncan demanded of Cameron.

'They came with news of Cromartie's capture. Seeking instructions from the Prince.'

'I see. And no doubt they did not travel alone? They would have some of their gillies with them? Enough for . . . '

'I'll thank you not to couple my cousin's name with yours, MacGregor – as though they were equal rogues!' Scotus said, as in duty bound – but with rather less conviction than heretofore.

'Tut, gentlemen!' Glenpean's head-shaking protest was as automatic, conventional and weary. 'But . . . it is a bad business. A bad, bad business. Och, ashamed it makes a man. Ashamed of his own kind. *Dia* – if only the Prince had been here . . . '

'I think it as well that he is not!' Duncan MacGregor asserted grimly. 'There would seem to be too many men here in love with the chink of gold! You will recollect that Cumberland has put a price of thirty thousand pounds on his person, dead or alive! I think it is as well that His Highness got away when he did. Even though it is unlikely that Cumberland would pay his blood-money in gold!'

'Och, hush you, lad – that is a wicked thing to say!'

'My own remark entirely, but a few days back,' the younger man agreed levelly.

CHAPTER 11

'GENTLEMEN, I vow for the life of me that I cannot see the need for all this damned wearisome discussion. Since His Highness has seen fit to leave us, and even now may be on his way to France – like so many of our friends who have felt similarly impelled today – since that is the position, surely it behoves those of us who remain to deal with this money to the best advantage of King James's cause? The Prince's army – or shall we say, King James's army, since His Royal Highness has found it expedient to leave? – the army must be kept together as far as may be. For the next attempt against the devil-damned Elector. It should not be allowed to disperse, to fritter away – whatever the Lord George may say, God forgive him! To that end the money should be applied. The men must be paid, provisioned, re-armed. Only so can the regiments be held together for another campaign. I speak from experience, my friends. My own regiment is still intact – or as much so as battles have left it. It will not remain so much longer, I can assure you, unless I receive money. Few of us in the Highlands are rich men – not in money, at any rate. Myself, I have spent all my scant fortune. Give the money – or most of it – to the colonels, to keep the army in being, I say.'

The speaker was as manly and soldierly as his words – Colonel Coll MacDonnell, younger of Barrisdale, nephew of old Glengarry. An immense figure of a man, fully six feet eight inches in height and broad in proportion, he was handsome in a dark and smiling sardonic fashion, all vigorously masculine, the Highland gentleman *par excellence*, dressed in fullest gallant style to match. More than a murmur of agreement greeted his soldierly demand.

'Certain regiments and units are already dispersed and broken up,' Colonel Stewart of Ardshiel objected. 'Some, less fortunate than Barrisdale's, did not survive Culloden Moor! Others have been sent to their homes already, by the Duke of Perth and Lord George. Are these, who bore the fiercest burden of the battle, to receive nothing?'

'What of those whose houses have been burned, their glens harried, their women ravished? Are they to be forgotten?'

127

Cameron of Dungallon demanded. His own unhappy case, that was. '*Dia* – there must be compensation!'

'Aye, compensation! Some of us have lost all . . .'

'Peace, gentlemen, I pray you,' Murray of Broughton interjected, in his smooth voice. 'All such will be duly considered, I promise you. I shall make it my business to see that this money is properly used, fairly distributed . . .'

'*Your* business, sir! But is it your business, Mr. Secretary?' That was Barrisdale, smiling still, and genial, but contemptuous too. 'Is not this a military matter? The money was sent, with the arms and the ammunition, for the army. Not for, h'm, secretarial administration!'

A shout of approval rocked that crowded room. Barrisdale had the great majority of the company with him, most clearly.

There might have been more against him the previous night. Most of those like Murray, the Lowlanders, the courtiers, the political theorists, the Jacobite adventurers, had gone. Although the great apartment of Borrodale House was indeed crowded still, that evening there were notable gaps. The Duke of Perth was gone, and his brother the Lord James; Lord Elcho, and his friend Maxwell; Sir Thomas Sheridan, Hay of Restalrig, Colonel Dillon; Lord Nairn and Lockhart of Carnwath and others. The ships had carried them away – and as far as could be ascertained, safely; provided no larger English men-o'-war arrived on the scene, they should all make sunny France in a few days. Everyone in the room knew that Secretary Murray would also have been aboard, but for the gold. In the main, it was only the fighting men, Highlanders almost to a man, who remained.

'I know my duty, sir – and will perform it, with or without your advice!' Murray snapped. 'As His Highness's secretary and immediate representative, the responsibility for distributing this money is wholly mine.'

'No!'

'That's a matter of opinion, sir.'

'Let Locheil distribute the gold.'

'Aye – Locheil knows our Highland position. Better than any Lowland lawyer!'

'I want no hand in it,' Locheil said shortly, from his seat by the fire.

Into the clamour in the great room, Duncan MacGregor raised his voice, greatly daring amongst all his seniors. 'I say that it is not for any to distribute, be he secretary or colonel or other!' he cried. 'The gold was sent to the Prince. He only may say what is to be done with it.'

'What puppy barks there?' Barrisdale enquired.

'Glengyle's son,' Duncan jerked back. 'And a different man from Glengyle's cousin there!'

'Indubitably – thank God!' James Mor MacGregor agreed, smiling.

There was a general laugh at the younger man's expense. Stubbornly he went on, however.

'His Highness ordered me straightly, before he sailed, to take possession of the money that was coming from the Duke of York, and to hold it safe for him until he should come for it or direct me otherwise. That money Mr. Secretary Murray now has taken. The Prince said nothing of giving it to him, or any other. I cannot believe . . . '

'Must we look to you, young man, to interpret the Prince's policies and best interests?' Murray interrupted haughtily. 'When your sage counsel is required, no doubt it will be asked for.'

'I hold a paper bearing His Highness's signature, authorising the Duke's money to be delivered to me. The Prince did not know of this other money, but . . . '

'And I hold King James's commission as Secretary-General to the Prince of Wales!' the other returned sharply. 'Until his Majesty revokes it, I act in his name. Let none presume otherwise. The gold will be properly and fairly distributed . . . '

'But, dear God – it should not be distributed, at all!' Duncan exclaimed. 'That is not what it was sent for. To be handed out to all and sundry. It was sent to fight the Elector of Hanover. It must be kept for that. Forty thousand gold pieces could make the difference between success and failure in a new rising . . . '

'Duncan, *a graidh* – is not that what we say?' James Mor put in. 'Give the money to the colonels, to keep the army together, to keep their regiments in being. Use it, do not bury it, or hoard it up.' He could be persuasive when he liked. 'Only by holding the army together can the Elector be fought and beaten. For that we must use the money.'

'Aye – he is right.'

'That is the truth.'

129

'We did not ask for money from the Prince when we drew the sword! We fought the Elector at Prestonpans and Carlisle and Clifton and Falkirk, without payment. What has come over us now, that all must have gold? Arrears of pay, compensations, reliefs – all that will melt away this money like snow in the sun ...'

'Nonsense, boy! There is plenty for all.'

'To be sure there is.'

'I agree with Captain MacGregor,' Scotus spoke up. 'I did not bring that money from France to pay compensations and satisfactions!'

'And got rid of most of it on the way!' James Mor mentioned.

'Damn you, sir! That from you! Yourself, you were not so far away when those scoundrelly MacKenzies stole it!'

'You impudent Frenchified jackanapes! Are you suggesting ...?'

'Gentlemen! In this house you will kindly remember your manners,' Clanranald intervened sternly. 'I will have no incivilities round this table.'

'You are right,' Locheil commended. 'Let us have no unseemly bickering, my friends. We may all hold our own points of view in honesty and sincerity. For myself, I think that I agree with these young men. The money will be needed for the next campaign, and should not be frittered away. Nevertheless, there is point in what Barrisdale says – and Ardshiel and Dungallon too. If some small proportion of the gold is given to the colonels, to keep their regiments assembled, the great part of it can be held intact for another rising when the Prince returns. There need be no clash.'

'Exactly,' Murray concurred suavely. 'My own view entirely. It is in such fashion that I propose to administer these moneys. None need fear otherwise. And now, gentlemen, if you will give me your attention ...'

The door opened to admit Glenpean, who was captaining the guard.

'Doctor Archie,' he announced. 'New come from Atholl and the Lord George.'

Archibald Cameron of Glendessary, M.D., youngest brother of Locheil, and known all over the Highlands as Doctor Archie, was a fine looking man of early middle years, prematurely grey and stooping a little, but with a humorous twinkle in his eye.

Dressed now in Lowland clothes, less conspicuous for the enemy-held territory he had just traversed, he looked tired and travel-worn. He greeted the company cheerfully, however, and went over to embrace his brother warmly.

Throughout the room frowns faded and tension relaxed, for the Doctor was one of the most popular and respected figures in the entire army, a soldier as well as a medico, and lieutenant-colonel to Locheil. Where Archie Cameron was present, laughter rather than frowning was the rule. Even the burning of his home had not wholly quenched his spirits.

Nevertheless, his tidings now were not calculated to cheer the assembled officers. The news that he brought from Atholl and the south was that everywhere the rising was considered to be over and defeated, that all the Lowland levies were dispersing to their homes, and their leaders fleeing overseas wherever possible. The Lord George advised the Highlanders to do like-wise, to make whatever terms they might with the Government, and to do nothing to provoke further reprisals. As far as the Lowlands were concerned, all was lost. The Doctor's own arguments and pleas had fallen on deaf ears.

Into the gloom, ire and recriminations engendered by this announcement, the Secretary, who, with Sir Stewart Thriepland, was the only Lowlander present, judiciously informed the newcomer of the heartening arrival of the arms and money from France. The mood of the company lightened at once, so potent was the thought of almost limitless gold. Most of those present forthwith conducted and accompanied the Doctor outside to show him the treasure, if not the guns, stowed temporarily in the forecourt. Duncan, Scotus and one or two Cameron lairds were left with Locheil.

'I do not trust Murray,' Duncan declared to the chief, as soon as they were alone. 'Any more than I trust Barrisdale or my cousin James Mor. It is my belief that they will do anything to get that money into their own hands. How much will Barris-dale's Regiment see of it, I wonder? The gold has gone to their heads . . .'

'And to yours, my boy, I think,' the older man said mildly. 'To all our heads, one way or another. Here we have been arguing and squabbling over it like hounds over a carcase — while we should have been deciding on more urgent matters. Those English ships know that we are here, now. Know that much heavy cargo has been landed to us here. They will be back, bringing others with them. When they cannot catch the Frenchmen, they will come back for us. Nothing surer. We must prepare to move from here – and move the arms and ammunition also. The gold, and what to do with it, can wait.'

Duncan bit his lip, rebuked. 'That is true,' he admitted. 'You are right, sir, of course.'

The gold, however, was not to be so easily dismissed. A mounting noise and clamour outside rose to a crescendo as the door burst open and men surged into the room shouting the news. More of the money was gone. Another barrel was empty. Five thousand more gold pieces had been stolen.

Complete chaos and uproar reigned. Sane and reasonable men were smitten with a sort of madness. The precious hoard that had suddenly become all-important, a recoupment and recompense for all the loss and failure and defeat, they saw evaporating under their very noses. Ten thousand guineas gone in the first few hours! Appalled, crazed, they scoured the neighbourhood in the creeping dusk, all but pulling Borrodale House apart, searching again and again possible hiding-places, accusing each other, coming to blows, every man's hand against his fellow, suspicion rampant, indiscriminate.

It was Duncan MacGregor who discovered the powder. Searching in one of Clanranald's cow-byres, already examined by others, he noticed on the cobbled flooring a thin and intermittent trail of black powder. A mere rub between finger and thumb assured him that it was gunpowder. The rail led him to a great pile of last season's bog-hay in a corner. He himself had thrust a hay-fork into this earlier, as no doubt had others, without jarring the prongs on hidden gold pieces. Now, pulling armfuls of the hay aside, he uncovered heaps of loose gunpowder deep beneath it.

No great discernment was required to realise that the missing gold was now in the kegs from which this powder had been emptied. A feverish opening, and spilling, of powder-kegs followed, but no trace of the missing *louis d'ors* was found. Presumably they had been transported away on garrons, amongst the other stores – this work of clearing away the cargo to hiding-places having gone on continuously, even while the officers were at their evening meal in the house. The business would have been simplicity itself, for a small group of men working with the others; finding the hidden gold, however, would be very much otherwise in a densely wooded steep hillside terrain consisting very largely of great fallen rocks, with bracken-filled hollows everywhere and caves innumerable. Any thorough and intensified search would have to await the morning light.

Glenpean and his Camerons, having been on guard-duty, were the prime targets for accusation. Either they had failed in their vigilance – or they had taken the money themselves. In vain did Glenpean protest that their task had been to guard the approaches to Borrodale House from assault from without, not to watch for perfidy within, and point out that all evening working-parties had been moving to and fro with pony-trains. These assertions did little to clear the Camerons, but they did serve to spread suspicions over Clanranald's own MacDonalds who had necessarily largely manned the working-parties. Talk of the MacDonalds' failure to charge at Culloden rose again on the myrtle-scented evening air, dirks were drawn, and even some blood spilled in a minor way.

Throughout Locheil was pleading for priorities, for a council-of-war to decide matters other than financial. At length, by the device of having Clanranald bring all the six remaining barrelfuls of gold into the great room of the house itself, where it would be safely under the eyes of all, he managed to re-assemble the officers within. Though a man gentle by nature and the reverse of self-assertive, he took forceful lead now, even speaking sharply to Murray of Broughton.

How much attention was concentrated on strategy and matters military, and how much remained preoccupied with *louis d'ors*, was doubtful; but it was decided that Locheil, despite his disability, should be accepted as military commander for the time being, with Clanranald as deputy – these being the two colonels with most men presently at their command – and that a move should be made away from this now dangerous area at first light next morning. A small but trustworthy party could be left to search for the lost gold. Doctor Archie, who had travelled westwards by Loch Eil and Glenfinnan, reported enemy units as near as the latter pass; it was therefore agreed to move north into the empty country around the head of Loch

Morar, and to take as much of the arms and stores with them as was possible. And, of course, the gold . . .

Later, in the soft darkness of the May night, the two young men sat in a black pool of shadow under trees that crowned a knoll near Borrodale House. It was a carefully chosen stance. From it not only could all the sleeping house be surveyed but, owing to the configuration of the ground, anyone leaving the house area, save to the eastwards, must pass round the base of the knoll. Duncan proposed to keep watch here all night – and Scotus had somewhat doubtfully agreed to share his vigil.

Encouraged by his finding of the jettisoned gunpowder and his deductions therefrom, Duncan reasoned thus; if all were going to move away in the early morning, it was almost certain that whoever had taken that second barrelful of gold would want to have another look at its hiding-place before they left the district. It would probably have been hidden only very roughly, hurriedly, owing to the need for haste and secrecy. A more thorough hiding and covering-up would likely be called for. Moreover, did not gold always draw its hoarders like a magnet, traditionally? He believed that the thieves would visit their booty sometime that night therefore, while more honest men slept.

When Scotus objected that the guard would spot any such movement, Duncan pointed out that the guard was made up of oddments, Glenpean's group having been relieved, and they would not be apt to know who was who amongst the officers, or just what were their duties. Moreover, all would be very tired, having been hard at work all day after travelling through the previous night. Again, who was to say that the guilty men had not got themselves put on guard duty?

So they waited, keeping their own eyes open only with difficulty – for all that applied to the guard applied equally to themselves. Presently indeed Scotus dropped off, and though he made two heroic attempts to rouse himself, thereafter slept soundly, however uncomfortable his posture, a borrowed plaid around his shoulders. To prevent himself from doing likewise, Duncan rose to his feet, to move like some uneasy shade from tree-trunk to tree-trunk, in geometrical order, rhythmic, deliberate.

For how long the MacGregor kept up this grievous patrol he

did not know; it seemed to pass beyond mere time into eternity He imagined frequently that he saw figures moving in the shadows below; he imagined that he heard noises foreign to the night; he imagined that the darkness was decreasing and that therefore the dawn was near and his vigil in vain. Indeed, in time his imaginings grew so constant and graphic, and his judgement so befogged, in the agonising effort to remain approximately awake, that he was no longer in a state to decide what was real and what false. Some men can make their own hells.

Duncan was in fact fully asleep, leaning against a pine-trunk, when he suddenly jerked upright, thereby scratching his face on a projecting twig. Staring about him hurriedly, dazedly, he managed to focus unsteady eyes on two dark shapes moving below him. This time there was no imagining, he would swear. One figure was taller than the other, but it was the smaller that led the way with a gap between them.

Hastily he shook Scotus, and had the wit to put a hand over the other's mouth to prevent him from exclaiming. Urgently he pointed downwards.

Scotus came awake more completely and swiftly than his companion.

The two young men slipped down the side of their knoll. Their quarry was already out of sight in the gloom, but they had obviously been taking the path that ran up into the woodland behind the house. Along this the pursuers hurried, though cautiously.

They presently heard muffled voices of the men in front, without seeing them; here the darkness was intensified by the thickness of the trees. There was nothing about the voices to recognise, no knowing what was being said – but the murmur acted as a guide.

For some distance they followed the track, broad and churned up by the hooves of garrons. This was the main route from house to the area of the caves. Up over the first ridge they climbed, and down into a little valley beyond. They lost the guiding voices here, drowned in the splash and clamour of a swift-running burn threading the wooded valley-floor. Fording this, they pressed on up the much longer slope beyond, with the track rising towards the broken sandstone escarpment wherein opened the largest of the caves. Frequently they paused briefly, to listen.

'They seem to have stopped talking,' Duncan commented, at length. 'I have heard nothing since we crossed the burn.'

'Needing their breath for climbing this damned hill,' Scotus suggested. He sounded similarly affected, himself.

Duncan, leading, increased his pace nevertheless.

At the crest of another and smaller intermediate ridge he halted, all ears – and cursing the thudding of his own heart. No single sound, other than the faint whisper of the night breeze in the trees, disturbed the sleeping hills. Frowning, he whipped off the plaid belted crosswise over one shoulder and handed it to his companion.

'Hold it, so that it will hide a light,' he directed, panting a little. 'We have climbed fast – faster than these others were moving before. We should have come close. We should be able to hear them, at least . . . '

Drawing flint and steel, he struck sparks and blew some tinder into a flame beneath the cover of the plaid. He had chosen a wet patch of the track, of which there were no lack. No recent footprints showed thereon amongst the many broad marks of ponies' hooves.

'I feared as much,' Duncan said, quenching the flame. 'They have turned aside. We have missed them. Damnation!'

They turned back, only too well aware that their quarry could have left the track almost anywhere along nearly a mile of its course. Where their feet slipped on another muddy patch, about half-way down the slope again, they made another inspection by hidden light. Two sets of recent footprints showed here – but they identified them as their own. The men they sought had not come even so far.

'A pest! They could turn off anywhere,' Scotus complained. 'We shall never find them now, man . . . '

'They could, yes,' Duncan agreed. 'But ̇. . . I have been thinking. If they are following the route that garrons took – garrons carrying the stolen gold? The garrons could not turn off anywhere – not without leaving clear traces behind. Except in one place, that is.'

'Eh . . . ? I do not take you.'

'The burn. In the burn itself. Garrons could be led down the bed of the stream, and leave no tracks.'

'*Dia*! That is true, yes.'

136

'It may not be the burn, of course. But it is worth the trying . . . '

They hastened straight down to the stream now. A light, struck by the little ford, told them what they wanted to know. At the sandy edge new-made footprints turned off the track, down-stream, on the north bank, one set of heeled boots and the other of less clear-cut rawhide brogans.

They would have liked to hurry now, for the others had gained a substantial lead – but they dared not. They had no means of knowing how far along this burn their quarry might have gone. It was notably dark down here, in the gut of the little valley, with the trees growing thickly enough to form what was almost a tunnel. Haste was out of the question.

'This burn will be the one that comes out on to the beach – the one we all drank from today,' Duncan said. They were whispering now. 'It cannot be more than half a mile to the shore. Somewhere between here and there . . . '

'We shall get no warning in this darkness,' Scotus pointed out. He drew his pistol, and began to busy himself with the priming. 'We may find ourselves unpopular, I fear.'

The other shook his dark head. 'We do not want that. Fighting,' he declared. 'We want to win the money back. That comes first. Best that whoever stole it should still believe it undiscovered. To challenge them here will serve nothing. They, or others, will only change the hiding-place. We must see without being seen . . . '

'How in the name of mercy shall we do that, in this darkness?'

It was the same darkness, for all that, which solved their problem for them in the end – and as they were despairing of finding what they sought, fearing that the others must have turned off somewhere out of the burn's channel. They were almost down at the outfall to the beach itself when suddenly they saw a tiny light flare in the gloom ahead, quite close apparently. The air here was filled with the sound of falling water, backed by the deeper and more distant boom of the surf.

'Someone else needs to see what he is doing!' Duncan commented. 'Who would have looked for them right down near the beach? There is a waterfall here . . . '

The light disappeared as he spoke. But it came on again in a

137

few moments, seemingly in the same place. Again it died away and came on, appearing to be very low down, near the bed of the burn – lower than they would have anticipated. It must be below the fall, they decided.

They moved on, climbing some way up the bank in order to get a better prospect, drawing as near as they dared. The light came on and off intermittently – no lamp, but bunches of tinder burning out, undoubtedly. The stream evidently dropped here in a sizeable fall, just before it emerged out into the open sand and shingle of the shore, trees still bordering it closely. They could distinguish nothing of who struck the light, but got the impression of much movement about it.

They waited.

Their patience was not unduly taxed. Fairly soon the light striking came to a stop. The watchers from up on the bank could not see any figures below them, what with the gloom and the intervening foliage – and the noise of the fall drowned lesser sounds. But they both gained a distinct sense of movement away from the pool below the fall, movement which continued back upstream, whence they had come. No single glimpse did they catch of those responsible.

After a brief interval the two young men moved quietly down to the waterside, below the fall. There were only shallows here.

'*Diabhol!* They have it in the water, for a wager! The gold!' Duncan declared. 'In the pool itself. Under the fall. It will take no harm in the water – the gold. It must be that. In the pool.'

'That is it, for sure. Clever they are. Under the fall, where the foam and white water will hide it. Where better?'

'What were they doing, then? Just now? That they needed a light?'

They quickly had an answer. Grasping an alder sapling to pull himself up to the frothing pool, Duncan staggered and all but fell back as the entire young tree came away in his hand, rootless. A second grab had the same result, and ended with the MacGregor knee-deep in the water. Investigation proved that the natural screen of bushes and trees around the pool had been reinforced and thickened by a cunning insertion of boughs and fronds and leafage, some planted in pockets of soil, some just entwined amongst growth already there. The result was a sufficient density of verdure to hide the pool from all but the most determined searchers.

'They are thorough,' Scotus said. 'Who is behind this, think you?'

'My cousin, and yours, are both tall men!' Duncan answered cryptically.

'As are many others. Your own self, for that matter! And those two were with us in the house all evening.'

'Barrisdale's men were not.'

'Nor were my own!'

Within the barrier of foliage, they peered down at the foaming swirling pool. The white froth and scum eddying on the surface they could see, but all else was black as pitch. The pool was large for the size of burn – fully ten feet across, and no doubt deep, scoured by the plunging waters of the fall.

Duncan began to throw off his clothes. 'There is but one way to make sure,' he said.

Gleaming palely in the gloom he lowered himself into the chill water.

His shoulders were just going under when his feet touched the stones and gravel of the bottom. He swam two or three strokes towards the splatter and spray of the fall itself before lowering his feet again. At once his toes came in contact with something other than stone – ridged wood, rounded.

'They are here,' he gasped out. 'I feel one of the kegs. No doubt of it.'

Taking a deep breath he surface-dived and breasted his way downwards. Black as it was, his hands quickly found the kegs. They lay anyhow on the bottom, some of them under the fall itself. It was difficult to count them, difficult to stay down for any time. The pounding, rushing waters of the fall seemed to punch all the breath out of his lungs.

Soon Scotus was in the pool beside him. He was a better swimmer than was the MacGregor, diving like a seal. Between them they found nine kegs, by feel. They may have missed one or two, but not many. They could barely move them. Ropes would be required to hoist them out.

Back on the bank, drying themselves with their plaids, and shivering a little, they agreed that this probably represented only one barrelful of the stolen treasure. The powder-kegs would each hold no more, certainly, than had the pannier containing the five hundred gold pieces that Scotus had brought. Nine or ten of them, therefore, could be expected to account for approximately five thousand *louis d'ors* – but assuredly not ten thousand. This most probably would be the second lot filched, not the first.

'They are clever, whoever they may be,' Scotus said. 'To hide all this so near the beach. None would look for it so close at hand. And to use a waterfall, that must always cover its pool with foam and spume, as hiding-place. And to cover their garrons' tracks by using the burn-channel. These are no fools.'

'A pity that they do not apply their wits to better ends! It will be our task to outwit them.'

'Aye. That is easily said. But how? What do we do now?'

'I do not know, at all. Not yet. We must think of something. Something that will not only get this money away from here, but keep it safely for the Prince, too. I do not trust Murray. Where the gold is concerned, by heavens I do not trust many of them!'

'I am with you there,' the other agreed. 'Locheil, I would trust with it. And his brother, the Doctor. And Glenpean. But who else, I would not be too sure.'

They walked back to Borrodale House the simpler, more direct way, by the beach. Half-way there, Duncan paused.

'We must not tell anyone of this, Scotus,' he said. 'That we have found this gold. If we tell any, even Locheil, all will soon know. These others will be warned. We leave in the early morning for Loch Morar. The men who stole the money will seek to come back for it, later. We must come first. We must make some excuse to leave the rest – before these others do. We must come here again, get the gold up, and take it away. To somewhere where it will be safe. Until the Prince returns.'

'You mean – not give it back to Murray and the rest? Keep it ourselves?'

'Yes. The Prince is going to see but little of that forty thousand *louis*. You heard them all. It will all go, one way or another. By the time that all are satisfied there will be nothing left. I wish that it had never been sent. It will do more harm to our cause, I do believe, than did Culloden! Culloden was defeat, yes – but this gold means demoralisation, unmanning us, turning every man's hand against his fellow's.'

'Ours, also?'

'Perhaps. But at least we can save this five thousand for its true purpose. For Prince Charles. And we both have a responsi-

140

bility in the matter of gold, of money, do we not?'

'That is true. As an officer seconded to the King of France, who sent the money, I may have more responsibility than any. I owe no obedience to any here. Aye – I am with you in this, MacGregor. We shall do as you say. And *I* need ask no man's permission, need make no excuses, to leave them at Morar.'

'That may be so. But we shall have to be careful, see you – or we shall merely bring suspicion upon ourselves as being the thieves. There is a risk in all this, mind you – a big risk. If we were caught with the money, later – this five thousand – few would believe that we had not stolen it for our own purposes. We must go warily . . . '

They were in no two minds about that. Wariness hereafter would have to be their watchword. For a start, wariness about re-entering the purlieus of Borrodale House. To be challenged by the guard would involve explanations as to what they had been doing, and almost inevitable suspicions. Better to wait out here until morning, when in the bustle and preparations for departure it would be an easy matter to mix in again with the others.

The two men sought a dry bed of pine-needles beneath a tall Scots pine, and wrapping themselves in their plaids, slept at last.

CHAPTER 12

THE morning was productive of surprises. Not only Duncan and Scotus, and the men they followed, had been active that night, it seemed. Mr. Secretary Murray came out with a most extraordinary story that had the effect of considerably delaying the company's departure for Loch Morar. It seemed that he had been approached, during the night, by one Harrison, a priest, and chaplain to Dillon's Regiment, who had elected not to sail for France. This priest had informed him that a certain Irishman of the same regiment had admitted to him, in the Confessional, that he and another had stolen the gold. This appeared to be the first theft. They had been working on one of the pony-trains, and had taken the bags of money from one

141

of the barrels and mixed them with bags of musket-balls very similarly packed, and so carried them away with the rest. The gold was still stowed away, it seemed, in one of the caves, amongst the ammunition. Which cave was unspecified. The Irishman, whom the priest refused to name because of the sanctity of the Confessional, had suffered a change of heart apparently occasioned by the subsequent attitude of his companion in sin, a junior officer, ensign of the same unit. He suspected that this officer intended to make away with all the loot. It might seem an inadequate reason for Confession to a priest – but such was Murray's story. They should be able to test the validity of it, at any rate, by searching amongst the caves for the missing money-bags.

In the excitement and indignation, the demand for an immediate court-martial and enquiry was put forward. This sort of thing must be nipped in the bud. Barrisdale was particularly urgent on this score, particularly indignant. Despite Locheil's assertion that their survival, in the face of the possible return of the English warships, was more important than this missing money, immediate steps were taken to find the culprits, while a large party of officers hurried up to the caves to ransack the stored ammunition.

There had been a number of Irishmen left behind – it had been only senior officers who had been able to obtain passage in the French ships. It was fairly quickly ascertained that one of them was missing – a corporal by the name of O'Rourke. Search produced no trace of him. His accomplice, however, was more easily found. The priest had revealed that this man was an Englishman, a Lancashire adherent; and the only English ensign who had been working with the ponies was a man named Daniel.

Ensign Daniel was arrested forthwith.

Barrisdale had his way, and a court-martial cum court-of-enquiry was instituted here and then. Messages from the caves area indicated that no money had yet come to light. Daniel, a hulking man of apparently scant intelligence, declared vehemently that it had all been O'Rourke's idea, and that he himself had thought it best to seem to go along with him, and thus be in a position to know where the stolen gold was hidden so that he could dutifully reveal this to his superiors – a thing which he had been about to do as soon as he had had his

142

breakfast. It was in a separate small and inconspicuous cave a little way apart from the others. He was prepared to show the court just where if they would deal kindly with him in consequence.

Being in something of a hurry, the court ingloriously agreed.

Daniel duly conducted them to a well-camouflaged and isolated small cave, and there, sure enough, amongst the bags of musket-balls were other bags of gold pieces. There were only nine of them, however – although Daniel insisted that there should be ten. And one of them was not much more than half full. It seemed that the missing O'Rourke had not departed entirely empty-handed. The full bags were found to contain approximately five hundred *louis d'ors* each, the part-filled one only three hundred. Presumably seven hundred were missing.

In the circumstances, and largely at Doctor Archie's urging, it was decided to waste no more time in any search for this moiety; what was to be done with Daniel could be decided later. There was no sign of the English ships, but they might appear at any time. Orders were belatedly given to pack up and the garrons were loaded, every beast that Clanranald could produce being pressed into service.

It was then came the morning's second surprise – for Duncan and Scotus, at least. It was decided that *they* should stay behind, with the three MacDonnell gillies, to look for the five thousand gold pieces still missing. They had anticipated that there would be some competition for this duty. There was none. No doubt any volunteering for the task would be looked upon with grave suspicion. It was Locheil who declared that the two young men were the obvious choice, with no other duties to perform. Indubitably it was a sign that the chief trusted them – however much askance they were looked at by many others. There were murmurings and objections – but then, there would have been these for whoever was left behind for the search.

Scotus was elated, seeing this as solving their problem about getting away from the others later and coming back for the sunken money. Now they would have a free hand to get it up and away. Duncan was less pleased, however. This was, in the long run, going to add to their difficulties. It would single them out. When the culprits who had sunk the treasure in the burn came back and found it gone, they would have a very shrewd idea as to who had taken it. They themselves would have to deny, to Locheil and the others, having found it -- which was bad. Duncan went to Locheil and asked that they might be relieved of the duty.

The chief would not hear of it. They owed it to the Prince, did they not? Who more fitting than themselves? It was an order. They must search the entire area. The gold could not be very far away. They should look out for garrons' tracks in unexpected places, since it was certain that such an amount could only have been carried away on horseback. And might fortune smile on them.

Feeling guilty as sin itself, Duncan acquiesced.

They watched the entire company move off, about two hundred strong, with its long strings of laden pack-horses – watched with mixed feelings. Borrodale House and its vicinity was left to the care of some old servitors, and themselves. If some of the others would have changed places with them, without a doubt the majority preferred to keep company with the certain thirty-four thousand three hundred guineas rather than go searching for the doubtful five thousand.

A discreet distance behind the main company, Duncan Mac-Gregor climbed alone up Glen Borrodale to a point sufficiently high to be able to watch the long train of men and horses heading away northwards across the tumbled watershed of barren rocky hills. He had to be sure that none, on any pretext, turned back. Satisfied, at length, he returned to the low ground. Three sails, he noted, were showing faintly on the far horizon, near the low Isle of Muck.

Scotus had managed to obtain ropes from a fisherman's cottage. With his three gillies and the seven garrons, they set off into the woodlands, taking the same secret route to the hiding-place as had the original conspirators. Their recovery operation was to be as secret as was the depositing.

At the waterfall they carefully dismantled some of the artificial screen of foliage, for replacement later. Then the two young men threw off their clothing and jumped into the swirling peat-stained water, to commence the quite difficult and exhausting task of diving with ropes down to the floor of the pool, against all the pressures caused by the weight of falling water, looping slip-knot nooses round the kegs, and having them hauled up by the gillies. It made a lengthy proceeding – although in daylight it was possible vaguely to see the kegs under water when close to them. There proved to be ten, after all, representing the entire missing barrelful. They had one keg opened, for a check, and found a sealed bag of five hundred pieces intact therein.

It took them more than an hour to recover the lot. Carefully re-erecting the leafy barrier of boughs and saplings, and loading the kegs on to the garrons, hidden under sacks, plaids and the like, they led the beasts back upstream, splashing along the bed of the burn, they hoped and believed unobserved.

Although Duncan and Scotus found much material for argument and discussion in most things that they did together, in the matter of where they should go now, with their precious freight, there was no question, nor even talk. The shieling of the Allt Ruadh up above the high pass between Arkaig and Morar beckoned them both like a magnet.

Their route was east with a little north to it, keeping to the thickest woodland until they were well away from Borrodale, and avoiding the direct road to Loch Morar at all costs.

'If we *should* meet anyone – any of Locheil's people, for instance – what do we say?' Scotus wondered.

'Nothing,' his companion declared. 'We admit nothing, give no account of what we do.'

'That is not so easy, as I found to my cost. Any man can see that we are laden with more than any personal baggage. If they ask . . . ?'

'Then such ill manners must be discouraged, whatever! Better that we see to it that we meet no one, I agree. We must go by round-about and difficult ways. If one always rides well in front, to scout and give warning . . . '

Thus they did travel all that day, by lonely hill tracks and remote valleys, by Glen Beasdale and little Loch na Creige Dubh, by desolate Loch Beoraid and the narrow gut of Glen Caeol. Here they really started to climb in earnest, and as a windy sunset stained all the westermost faces of the hills, they mounted and mounted to the lofty knife-edge ridge between the giants Sgor nan Coireachan and Sgor Thuilm, and looked down into the fair sanctuary of Glen Pean, now filling with the violet shadows of night. Apart from the peat-smoke of a cot-house or two seen at a distance and avoided, the only signs of life that they had encountered throughout were the deer and the grouse, the ptarmigans and the blue hares, with the circling specks that were a pair of eagles following their slow earth-bound progress on tireless wings for many leagues.

Once beyond the ultimate skyline no travellers could remain unobserved, and it was not long before sundry Camerons had spotted and stalked and recognised them. The fact that they had only that morning left Locheil, Doctor Archie and Glenpean assured them of a welcome, and they gathered quite an escort as they proceeded downhill. Duncan's tentative suggestion that Scotus and his gillies might suitably prefer to remain with the larger group of refugees in the high corrie, on account of the limited accommodation at the Allt Ruadh cabin below, was not even granted the favour of an acknowledgement.

The girls spied their approach from afar and came running – Caroline by no means the hindmost until, almost up with them, she recollected her dignity and smoothing down her skirts sought to look ladylike. Her sisters suffered from no such inhibitions, and hurled themselves bodily upon the newcomers, who had hastily dismounted. Somewhat embarrassed, Duncan gave ground a little before the onslaught. Not so his companion; Scotus swept up Anne in one arm and Belle in the other, returned their kisses with interest, and then advanced upon their sister. Undoubtedly his stature grew in the presence of the other sex proportionately as Duncan's diminished.

Caroline did not seem to object to the MacDonnell's embrace – even if she only offered a firm but rather shy handclasp to the MacGregor.

Flattering as was this welcome, after a mere forty-eight hours absence, just a little of the cream was skimmed off it by Caroline's first words – or at least the first she was permitted to enunciate properly.

'Oh, I am glad that you are safe,' she panted. 'So glad. I . . . we were so worried. And Father? Is he safe too?'

'Of course he is, my dear,' Scotus told her genially. 'Why not?'

'The battle,' she said. 'We heard about the battle. Yesterday. We were so anxious. Almost I decided to try to come myself. To find out . . .'

146

'Battle?' Duncan repeated. 'What battle? You mean the ships? The gunfire . . . ?'

'We heard it. In the distance. Boom, boom, boom!' Belle cried.

'Just the echoes of it . . . '

'Did you win?' Anne demanded. 'You beat them, didn't you? Did you kill lots of Englishmen?'

'Anne! Hush! Think shame!'

'Was it exciting, Duncan?'

'But . . . there was no battle. No fighting. Only a few cannon shots exchanged.'

'Oh, but the man told us there was. A great battle. He had just come from it. With French ships and English ships. And many soldiers.'

'Yes, but it came to nothing.'

'What man was this?'

'A soldier who came through the pass. Earlier today. Going east. He said French ships came into a loch at Clanranald's house – Borrodale on Loch nan Uamh, that would be. And the English ships came in after them. There was much fighting, he said. And we heard the echoes of it, even all this way off.'

'Much gunfire, yes. But most of it out of range. The English ships were smaller than the French. They dared not come too close. No blood was shed. Not on our side, at any rate.'

'None?' Anne demanded. 'All those booms and no one hit, at all?'

'I fear not, my trout!' Scotus laughed. 'All noise and bluster. Are you much disappointed?'

'She is a foolish child. Thank God that it is all right – that you are all safe. You saw Father . . . ?'

'Yes indeed. We worked together all yesterday. Like slaves, like very bondsmen. My back is sore, yet.'

'He is well,' Duncan told her. 'Locheil keeps him busy. He asked us many things about you. About you all.'

'Did you give Locheil the gold?' Anne demanded. 'What did he say? Was he pleased? All that money . . . !'

'H'mmm.' Duncan glanced from the questioner to Scotus and Caroline. 'That is rather a long story, I fear.'

'Tell us,' Belle supported her sister imperiously.

'Well . . . another time, perhaps.'

'You shall hear all our adventures in due course,' Scotus

assured. 'Give us but a little time.'

'I do not believe that you gave him the gold, at all!' Anne accused. 'I believe that you just kept it!' She pointed dramatically at the string of ponies behind them. 'What is all that you have got? You have as much tied to those garrons as you took away! More! I believe that you have kept the money! You weren't even at the battle!'

'I think so too,' Belle agreed.

'Anne! Belle! This is insufferable!' their elder sister exclaimed. 'Go back to the cabin, if that is the sort of manners you are going to display.' She turned. 'Forgive them. They are running wild, and it is difficult. But we will all go back. You must be tired. If you have come all the way from Borrodale . . . ?' There was just a hint of a question in that last, nevertheless.

To produce a diversion quickly Duncan changed the subject. 'This man you spoke of – the soldier who told you that there had been a battle? Who was he? How did he come to be here? Was he one of your own people? A Cameron returning home?'

'No, no. He was a stranger. A rough kind of a man. Irish, I would think, by his voice . . . '

'Ha! Irish. And alone? His name would be O'Rourke, for a wager?'

'I do not know. He did not tell it.'

'Had he a garron with him? Was he carrying anything? Anything heavy?' Scotus asked.

'He had two, yes. One laden, very much like your own. The other he rode.'

The two men exchanged glances.

'How long since he left? And which way did he go?' Duncan demanded.

'He was here in the afternoon. We gave him food. I said that he should stay and rest. for he seemed very weary. But he would not wait. He said that he had a very important message to deliver – about this battle. To whom, he did not say. He must press on, he said. He went on down the glen, towards Arkaig. I warned him that the Redcoats were apt to be met along the north side of the loch, where the road is. Some were in Glen Dessary yesterday.'

'Afternoon, you say? Late or early?'

Surprised, the girl looked at Duncan. 'Is it important? It was fairly late, I think.'

'How many hours ago? Three? Four?'

'About that, yes. What is it, Duncan?'

'Just that we must catch that man. He has seven hundred gold pieces with him. Stolen. The Prince's money.'

'Seven hundred! All your gold, and more? Oh, the scoundrel, the blackguard! You are sure? And to think that we gave him food and drink! Helped him on his way! All your precious gold gone . . .'

Duncan cleared his throat. 'Have you fresh garrons for us? These are tired.'

'You mean – to follow this man? Yourselves? Now?'

'Yes. If he has four hours' start, there is no time to be wasted.'

'But . . . surely it can wait awhile? You are tired yourselves – you both look weary. Given rest, you will travel the faster. And the man will have halted for the night by now, will he not?'

'All the more reason to be after him at once. Before the Redcoats get their hands on him – and on the gold.'

Scotus opened his mouth to speak, but closed it again.

'You think that is likely, Duncan?' the girl asked.

'Of course I do. The way that you say he is going, the fool is riding straight into trouble. He is not a Highlandman – he cannot know the country. He will take the south shore of the loch, no doubt, you having warned him. But at the end of it, he will be in territory where Loudon's forces are thickest. He must be stopped before he gets that far.'

She shook her head. 'I have only the one garron, just now. The others are away with a deer-hunting party.'

'One will be enough,' Duncan returned briefly. 'A Mac-Gregor does not require help to deal with one Irish corporal!'

Scotus laughed. 'You are welcome to the task, friend. Myself, I feel that you are perhaps over-zealous in this!'

'I have my reasons,' the other answered. 'If we can lay hands on that seven hundred *louis d'ors*, it could ease our situation greatly . . . in other ways. We could return it to Locheil!'

'Eh? Locheil? Ah . . . mmmm.'

'At least you must eat, Duncan, before you set off,' Caroline insisted.

'Always you are thinking of our bellies, woman!' he declared, but not unkindly.

With the two younger girls sent to catch and bring in the fresh garron, and Caroline bustling about the cabin at the preparation of a hurried meal, out of a muttered consultation with Duncan, Scotus spoke up.

'Caroline, my heart,' he said. 'We have something to tell you. Something for your ear alone. We could not speak of it in front of the young ones. But they were right, after a fashion. We have, not five hundred gold *louis* tied to our beasts out there – but five thousand!'

'You have *what*? Mercy to goodness – what are you saying?'

'Plain facts, my dear. We lost our five hundred. To the Secretary Murray. But we have brought back ten times as much!'

She turned from him to stare at Duncan, unbelieving.

'It is the truth, *a graidh*,' that man assured. 'The money – more French gold – is out there. Tied to the garrons in ten gunpowder kegs. Five thousand *louis*.'

'But ... but ... !'

They told her the story, as briefly as might be, and their reasons for their actions. Appalled, the young woman listened to the tale of greed and folly and treachery.

'It is ... it is beyond all belief!' she declared, at length. 'That men who have given their all for their Prince, risked their lives, shed their blood – that such should act so!' She shook her head, helplessly. 'But why – why have you brought it here? It is evil, that gold – evil! Why bring it here?'

'Because you we *can* trust,' Scotus told her. 'Here we can hide it, but keep an eye on it. Where none will look for it.'

'There is nothing evil about the gold itself,' Duncan asserted. 'Only its effect on men. Some men.' He smiled. 'We do not believe that it will have this effect on you, Caroline! If we can keep it safe for the Prince, it will yet do much for His Highness's cause. It is our duty, whatever.'

Doubtfully she looked at them both, her lovely eyes troubled.

'Tonight,' Duncan went on, 'When Anne and Belle are asleep, you two, with the gillies, must hide the gold. As well to learn from those others, and hide it in water. Less difficult and noticeable, it is, than digging holes. Down at the lochan there, would do. There are overhanging trees at one corner – under them and their roots might serve.' He paused. The thought of Scotus and Caroline together on such a secret employment in the dark, gave him no pleasure. But he shrugged away the mind-picture this conjured up. 'The gold will take no harm in the water. So long as it may be recovered again without over-much difficulty.'

'And you . . . ?' the girl asked. 'With all this money saved? And all that the others have? Must you go hot-foot after this seven hundred?'

'I must indeed. Seven hundred guineas is still a lot of money. But, more important – if I can get it, then we can take it to Locheil. The seven hundred. Somehow we must give an account of ourselves to him. If we take him this, then we shall have justified ourselves in some measure. In accounting for it, we may be spared accounting for the five thousand, mean-time . . . '

She stared, as though seeing the man with new eyes.

'Man – you are a true MacGregor, after all!' Scotus declared, slapping his thigh. 'I would never have thought of that.'

'I am not proud of the notion,' the other said shortly.

It was Caroline's turn to change the subject. 'Here is cold venison. And oatcakes and honey. And whisky. I think that I hear the girls coming . . . '

CHAPTER 13

THE man rode alone down the shadowy glen, in no contented frame of mind. How much he would have preferred to remain at the shieling he dared not admit even to himself. He found himself to be almost hating Scotus, dwelling upon his in-sufferable good looks, his deplorable charm and smug superior-ity, his dandified Continental manners. Was he not positively betraying Caroline Cameron by leaving her to the mercies of such a one? Why could Scotus not have volunteered for this task? Why had it got to be himself . . . ?

Duncan MacGregor was dog-tired.

At the foot of the glen he made no move to :wing out to-wards the wide levels at the head of the loch, northwards, in the direction of the dimly seen jagged remains of Glenpean House. The Irishman was almost certain to have followed the roadless south shore of Arkaig. The loch now gloomed slate-grey and uninviting before him. Mallard beat up from the shallows at its head on whistling pinions. Due eastwards, along the waterside, Duncan headed his mount, trotting wherever the terrain allowed.

He was in little doubt as to the line on which to look for his quarry. Though there was no road on this side, there were paths, deer and cattle tracks winding hither and thither amongst the rock-strewn and broken wooded hillsides. No man in his sane senses, no stranger to the area in especial, would follow any other save that which, intermittent and sketchy as it frequently was, yet clung fairly faithfully to the loch-shore itself. Along this Duncan pressed, watchful. Here and there, in muddy stretches around the innumerable burns that poured down to the loch, he could distinguish, even in the gloom, the hoofmarks of two garrons, recently made.

He calculated that O'Rourke would not be so vary far ahead, now, in spite of his long start. His beasts were bound to be worn out, especially that carrying the gold. With the fellow no hillman, he himself must be nearing the end of his tether. The wonder was, indeed, that he had got so far. He must have been travelling solidly for almost twenty-four hours, over terrible country. Duncan was prepared to come on him, bedded down in the old bracken, round any bend of the loch-shore. His pistol was primed and ready in his hand, and his broadsword loosened in its scabbard.

Despite all this readiness, the MacGregor was quite unprepared for the fashion of the encounter when it did take place. He was nearly half-way down that interminable loch when, following the narrow path through a very dark stretch beneath trees, his hitherto stolid garron suddenly whinnied in fright, and without other warning reared up on its hind legs, throwing its rider backwards to the ground, before bolting sideways off the path and uphill through the dark pines, as though the Devil himself was at its heels.

Much shaken, and with a jarred shoulder and hip, Duncan staggered to his feet, cursing. He had dropped his pistol. Tugging out his sword, he crouched on guard, peering around him. Warily he backed to a nearby tree-trunk, for possible support and cover.

152

Nothing moved around him, no sound reached him other than the tinkle of burns, the night breeze in the trees and the lap-lap of wavelets on the loch-shore.

He waited. The other man could move first. He guaranteed that he would hear him the moment that he did so. He was a fool not to have clung to his pistol.

After a while, with the hush continuing, Duncan stooped very slowly, picked up a fallen piece of wood at his feet, and tossed it into the dark of a juniper bush some distance back along the track, where it made a distinct stir.

No reaction being provoked by this, presently he edged forward again to the path. He wanted that pistol. Ready to flatten himself on the ground at the least hint of movement, he scanned the area where he had been thrown.

He saw the body, lying, booted feet to the path, only a darker shade, more substantial, amongst the shadows in the young brackens.

He stared, and his sword-tip sank. It was no Highlander who lay there – and the ragged uniform and broken boots would not belong to any soldier of the Government. Undoubtedly it was the man he sought, the Irishman. And by his every aspect, dead.

Only a moment or two's closer inspection was required to confirm this. O'Rourke, even in the half-light, was not a pretty sight. One half of his face was quite shot away, indeed. But two other bullet wounds showed, one in the back and one just above the left knee, blackening the clothing with blood. No weapons remained about the body, or lay near.

Straightening up, Duncan looked about him thoughtfully. No sign of any garrons. He walked slowly further along the path to where he could hear the nearest burn chuckling its way down to the loch. Where the path crossed this there were tracks in plenty. It did not require any great perception to recognise that these were mainly of shod and narrow hooves, not the broad almost circular unshod marks of Highland garrons.

Duncan did not even have to make a conscious reconstruction of what had taken place, it was all so obvious. O'Rourke had been ambushed, or perhaps had merely blundered wearily into a patrol of the Elector's cavalry. Unhorsed, probably by the shot in the knee, he had sought to bolt one foot into the thickets. He had been shot in the back as he ran. Then, later, he had been shot in the face at closest range by a pistol, no doubt as he lay on the ground, and to save the trouble of caring for a wounded prisoner. His weapons had been taken, but his tattered clothing was not worth removing. Both his garrons, with their burdens, were gone.

With the example of his own beast's abrupt bolting before him, it could not be taken as certain that the Redcoats had the Irishman's garrons, and therefore the gold; but it seemed highly probable.

Duncan went back, and dragged the body the few yards down to the shore, where he heaped loose stones on top of it, in lieu of a dug grave. He repeated the Lord's Prayer over the sad pile. It was the best that he could do. O'Rourke had paid heavily for his cupidity, despite the tentative Confession half-way.

The MacGregor found his pistol, but was less successful in recovering his pony. Although he searched the seamed and wooded hillside for some considerable time, he discovered no trace of the brute; frightened by the smell of blood, it might have run for miles.

Duncan had climbed quite high, to get above the tree level and so to somewhat wider prospects, before he recognised the hopelessness of it all, and turned back. It was then, as he began to head downhill again, that he noticed the red gleam of light, far below him along the loch-shore. A mere pin-point, it was fully a couple of miles off, he reckoned, well to the east of where O'Rourke had met his end. This would be his killers, for sure – bivouacked for the night, with a camp-fire to cheer them. Only Government troops, secure in their domination of a cowed country, would light open fires in such a situation.

Purpose about him again, Duncan MacGregor changed his direction half-right, eastwards, and went downhill long-strided, his weariness forgotten.

That fire must have sunk down considerably from its first viewing by Duncan, for it was no more than a glowing red heap of embers when cautiously, stealthily, the man crept closer and closer to it. The soldiers slept, then, no doubt. But equally without doubt there would be a sentry.

The encampment was in a little open bay of greensward and

shingle where one of the myriad burns entered the loch. Apart, some distance from the glowing embers, a group of horses stood out, a dark mass in which numbers could not be distinguished – though Duncan believed that there could not be very many. Various black shadows on the ground would be recumbent dragoons. For the moment, at that distance of fully a hundred yards, he could perceive no sentries, no movement.

As he began to work carefully round for a better and closer inspection, a chop-chopping noise to the right, inland, turned his head. A crack of splintering wood followed, confirming Duncan's impression that the first sound had been made by an axe. As far as he could see, the noise disturbed none around the fire.

Then came the sound of something being dragged – the chopped wood. Duncan waited. Presently a dark figure materialised out of the shadows of the surrounding trees to the right, pulling behind him what presumably was a bough. One man only.

Over to the fire this individual drew his wood. There followed the sound of more chopping and the snapping of twigs. Then suddenly the scene was illuminated, as the fire blazed up. The stoker had tossed on to the smouldering ashes what must be the top of a dead pine-branch; only large quantities of resinous needles, dead and dry, could have produced that abrupt flare-up.

All was, for the moment, comparatively clear. There was much vivid red about the scene, the red of the busy soldier's coat, red covering the outstretched sleepers. No other men appeared to be on guard; this was the only sentry, intent on improving a fire that he had allowed to sink. Possibly he had been asleep himself. He carried a musket slung across his back.

Duncan was counting. He counted the horses first – eleven in all, nine long-legged southern cavalry chargers and two Highland garrons. He counted eight men lying around the fire, plus the sentry. A small patrol – no more than a picquet; a junior officer, no doubt, and eight men, on some special duty. But enough to have spelt the end to O'Rourke's dream of opulence.

Those garrons, ten chances to one, were the Irishman's. Duncan's glance, in the flickering firelight, searched their vicinity. There was a certain amount of gear heaped about – stacked muskets, accoutrements, saddlery and provisions. But, yes – he saw them. A little way apart. Four small barrels. Gunpowder kegs.

So O'Rourke also had recognised the value of the kegs as disguise! Duncan had scarcely expected four kegs. Two would have been enough for seven hundred gold pieces, surely? Perhaps it was for easy handling, by one man . . . ?'

The sentry, who presumably felt the cold or perhaps did not like the dark, was heading back whence he had come – no doubt for more fuel. Sure enough, in a few moments there was the sound of more chopping, and presently he emerged once more into the circle of firelight dragging a second branch, ruddy-brown and obviously dead. Duncan noted that he carried no axe this time.

Swiftly the MacGregor's mind worked. The man had left the axe behind. There must be a dead fallen pine there – and he must intend to go back to it for more wood. He was alone on guard – since the number of sleepers and himself coincided with the number of saddle-horses. And his musket was strapped to his back.

Action followed swiftly upon these observations. Moving round as silently as he might from bush to bush and tree to tree – with fortunately the hiss and crackle of the now well-going fire, as well as the splash of the wavelets, to cover sound – Duncan worked his way to the area where the chopping had taken place. He found the source of the fuel without difficulty – a great giant of a Scots pine, uprooted in some early winter's gale. Where the amateur woodman had been hacking away was very evident, even in the dark, and closer inspection revealed a small hatchet there, its blade dug into the red trunk.

Duncan did not hesitate. He withdrew the axe from the wood, but placed it on the ground just underneath. Then clambering over the thick trunk itself, he sank down amongst the prickly brushwood and the shadows immediately beyond. And waited.

For a while he was left wondering whether his reasoning had been correct. The sentry, after breaking up more of the wood already transported, unslung his musket and took a stroll down to the edge of the loch. He remained there, staring out over the dark water, for a while. Then he came back to the sleepers, and commenced to pace up and down slowly. Cramped amongst the brushwood, and frowning now, Duncan was considering whether he ought to try some other plan, when tossing some more wood on the fire, the other evidently decided that the store of fuel was still inadequate. Slinging his musket on his back again, he came stalking over towards the fallen tree. Duncan, tensing, gave thanks for the swift-burning qualities of Scots pine.

Events, after this period of inaction, took place swiftly. The sentry reached the tree, stooped to peer for the axe, perceived that it must have fallen to the ground, and bent right down to feel for it below the trunk. And at the other side thereof, Duncan, holding his breath, rose, and all in the same lithe movement leant over and brought his right hand down hard to the back of the other's head. Clenched in that fist was his dirk – but it was the blunt haft that he smashed down expertly. The felt of the dragoon's cocked hat was scant protection against such a well-placed and calculated blow, and the man folded up with a single grunt, collapsing amongst the tree's debris.

Duncan glanced back to the fire, hurriedly. No one stirred there. He had toyed with the notion of donning the sentry's scarlet coat and black hat, but discarded the idea, deciding that speed was more important. Keeping out of the circle of firelight, he ran round light-footed to where the horses were tethered. First things first, he went to the four kegs. They were linked two and two with a sort of rough rope harness. An eye on the sleepers, he lifted one. It was less heavy than he expected – only half-full apparently. Taking two together, he was able to carry them, by their harness, and stagger over with them to the garrons. It took most of his strength to hoist them up over the back of one of the beasts, one on either side. With his dirk he cut through the rope tethers of both garrons. Then he went back for the remaining two kegs. Throughout, his eyes were never off the huddled sleepers for more than a few seconds at a time. One man kept jerking and stirring alarmingly; perhaps he was only a restless sleeper.

With the second pair of kegs placed on the pony behind the first, he paused, panting. To be off at once, or to cut the tethers of the cavalry horses and seek to scatter them, to delay pursuit? That would take some little time – and he was worried about the stunned sentry regaining consciousness quickly and making an outcry. On the other hand he could not hope to move off the scene with the two garrons without arousing the camp.

The decision was taken for him. Suddenly one of the men, not the restless one, groaned loudly and sat up straight, to stare owlishly around him. Whether what his eyes must see, if dimly, over at the horses, registered immediately on his sleep-dazed mind, Duncan did not wait to discover. Grasping the cut tether of the laden horse, as leading rein, he vaulted on to the back of the other garron, and dragging its head round, kicked the poor tired brute violently into motion. In a hollow pounding of unshod hooves, he headed the two beasts away from the loch and straight up into the hillside woodland.

Behind him a great shouting broke out. It crossed Duncan's mind that this was not unlike his introduction to Scotus, the difference being a mere two hundred *louis*. Under the influence of gold he was becoming as inveterate a horse-thief as any of his MacGregor forebears.

More anxious thoughts than these however quickly filled his mind. With something like consternation he realised that the beast that he was riding was lame. There was no doubt about it; the creature's halting gait, slow pace and extreme reluctance was only too apparent. He would have to abandon it and share the other garron with the gold – no hopeful proceeding with an already tired animal.

Ragged musket-shooting began to follow him – though he was only aware of the noise of the reports. Duncan crouched low on his unhappy mount. Fortunately the trees fairly quickly engulfed him. He wished now that he had had time to loose and scatter those saddle-horses.

On the steep hillside his beast promptly slowed to the merest limping walk. This was quite hopeless. Duncan threw himself off, and clambered on to the back of the other garron, straddling uncomfortably between the two sets of kegs. He abandoned the lame brute.

This animal was clearly almost as unwilling as the other for vigorous motion, especially with the double burden. It took the hill only half-heartedly, despite all its rider's kicks and thumps. Even when he pricked the poor creature's rump with the tip of his dirk, only a very slight access of pace resulted. Duncan was not long in recognising that this would not do.

Only the probability that these troops would not be bareback riders, and would waste time in saddling up their chargers, was presumably giving him this present breathing-space.

Beyond question, it seemed, this weary animal could not carry both himself and the gold to safety. Almost, he would be better on foot. But he certainly could not carry the money, himself. He had to get rid of the gold, therefore – hide it, where the dragoons would not find it. And quickly. Then look after himself. He had little fear for his chances on the hill at night, with any clutch of Southrons, mounted or otherwise. It was the heavy gold that was the problem.

How and where to hide it, then? Water again? A burn? The hillside was scored with burns. But small ones. Could he find one suitable? In time?

Since pools large enough to hide the kegs were more likely to be come across on the lower levels rather than up on the steep hill, he turned his mount's head half-right, westwards.

The first burn that he crossed was a miserable trickle, useless. He halted the garron for a moment, to listen. Distinctly he could hear crashings and stampings and cries below and behind him. The chase was on. His task was going to demand every second that he was likely to be granted.

The next burn, a few hundred yards westward, was rather better-sized, though still too small. But he had no time to pick and choose. Far from liking the process, he turned downhill alongside it. He felt as though every step was bringing him closer to his pursuers.

Duncan dismounted, to lead the garron, the better to see the stream's potentialities – and also with some idea that he might be able to reduce the noise that he made. There were precious few pools at all on this fast-flowing little watercourse, and such as there were would scarcely hide one keg, much less four. Nothing for it but to go right to the foot again. At least his enemies would not be likely to expect that.

The decision made, he delayed no longer at the upper burn-side. He went straight down almost at a run, the pony jouncing and swaying behind with its uncomfortable burden.

From the sounds, it seemed as though the chase was scattered fairly wide. This could be an advantage – and the reverse. Fewer to deal with at once, but more chances of being cornered. Some appeared to be unpleasantly close, too. Let him have but a minute or two at the foot of the hill . . .

But at the foot of the hill this wretched burn formed no pool. It spread itself, yes – but only as a sort of apron of surface water over the greensward. The fugitive cursed his luck.

There was only the loch itself, now. Plenty of water there. Under the bank, somewhere? Had he time? There were alder trees there, flanking the water. Their roots partly undermined. There. Only fifty yards or so . . .

He dragged the garron thitherwards across the grassy level at a trot. He could hear men beating about in the thickets directly above him.

Before ever he reached the water's edge he had the first two kegs dragged off the pony's back. Straight into the shallows he splashed with them, up to his middle, to plunge over and push the things under the projecting alder-roots. Fortunately the water seemed to buoy up the kegs a little, aiding him. Panting, he scrambled out again for the second pair, his wet kilt clinging about his legs.

He practically fell into the loch with his burden this time, strained almost to his physical limits. Somehow he got the awkward and unwieldy objects beneath the roots, the rope getting entangled. He hoped that they were hidden – and would remain hidden in daylight. He dare not delay longer. Sobbing for breath he stood back. One last task. Drawing his dirk, he marked a little cross-shaped score on the bark of the tree.

Staggering up on to the shore again, he slapped the garron on the rump, to drive it away. He would be better without the brute now.

The animal was too tired to move, however. It just stood. Certainly it could not be left there, to draw attention to the hiding-place of the gold.

Grabbing the tether, Duncan began to lead the creature westwards. He was too exhausted himself, for the moment, to run.

He had not gone far when there was a crashing of bushes directly in front of him. One of the horsemen, at least, was down on this path ahead – and close ahead.

There was considerable noise just above him. They seemed to be concentrating. He must have been heard. He dared not try to bolt up there now, as he had intended. Desperately he turned back, eastwards – not the direction he wanted to take.

Leaving the garron he began to run, his wet kilt hampering him at every stride.

A dozen yards he had gone, no more, when a dragoon burst out of the trees above and came hurtling down upon him, his charger's hooves scoring weals through the bracken.

With some notion of swimming for it, Duncan swerved to race in the only direction left to him – towards the loch. Could he reach the water's edge before the trooper with his drawn sabre?

He did – but he did not know it. A few yards from it, troubled by his water-heavy kilt and far from watching his feet, Duncan tripped over a root and sprawling, fell all his length. Part-winded, dizzy, he scrambled up and went staggering on, all too well aware of the drumming of hooves immediately behind. The water only a yard or two off, he glanced round – and saw right above him the terrifying sight of the rearing charger and the down-bent and grinning dragoon, sabre raised for a downward slash. To avoid that fearsome steel he flung his unsteady body sideways – and went directly under the horse's flailing hooves. His whole head seemed to explode in a burst of brilliant lights.

Duncan MacGregor pitched forward, unconscious, his upper half splashing into the shallows of Loch Arkaig.

CHAPTER 14

THOUGH vaguely aware of many strange sensations, much general and unlocated pain and discomfort, and the passage of an infinity of time, it was daylight before Duncan recovered fairly full consciousness and any awareness of his surroundings. He recognised, then, firstly that what seemed to have been obscurely puzzling him for some time by its hazy and hypnotic motion was in fact the gracefully swaying bough of a birch tree with its pale green heart-shaped leaves, nodding in the breeze above him, and intermittently almost hidden behind rolling clouds of blue wood-smoke; secondly, that his head ached and throbbed with an intensity and comprehensiveness that he had never hitherto known or imagined – indeed his whole body seemed to be sore in all its stiff entirety; and thirdly, a little later, that the said stiffness was not wholly muscular, but was partly the result of his wrists and ankles being bound.

That was enough for his notably hazy wits for the moment.

The next assault on his consciousness took the form of a man bending over him and addressing him. There was not so much doubt about his manifestation, for the speaker took the precaution of kicking Duncan in the ribs with the toe of a cavalry boot to emphasise the reality of the situation.

'Well, you,' his visitor observed. 'So you ha' come round at last, eh? And you ha' taken your time, b'God! Now, you better do some talking, see.'

Duncan was prepared to talk. 'God save King James,' he thought would be a suitable remark. But, though his lips found the words, no such pious sentiments emerged.

The boot drove home its clear message to Duncan's already sensitive ribs that this effort was inadequate. 'Talk, I said – you bloody rebel!'

The prisoner moistened his lips, and cleared his throat. 'You . . . are . . . the . . . rebel,' he said, and was pleased to hear the words coming distinctly and with authority. 'King James . . .'

He got no further in this brief conversation. A vicious back-handed swipe across the mouth jerked his head back, unbearable pain flooded over him, and he slipped forthwith into the much more friendly embrace of oblivion.

For how long he remained unconscious he had no idea. But when he came round once more, two faces were bending over him, one younger and more intelligent-seeming. Unfortunately the other was still that of the earlier interrogator.

It was the younger man, not much more than a boy indeed, by his looks, who spoke. 'Can you hear what I say?'

'Yes.'

'Good. Answer my questions then. You are one of the Young Pretender's staff?'

Blankly Duncan looked at him. He perceived that the young man was an ensign of dragoons, and the older one a sergeant. Desperately he sought to gather his wits. How had they come to connect him personally with the Prince?

As though to supply the information, the other said: 'Come, sir – silence will do you no service. Nor lies. We know that you are Captain Duncan MacGregor, so-called, of Glengyle's Regiment in the rebel army. You were carrying a letter on your person, signed Charles P. That is the Young Pretender, God curse him, is it not? It was dated but seven days ago. Where is he now?'

So that was it! The Prince's authorisation, ordering him to take over the gold that Scotus had brought. He had carried it in his doublet pocket. Just what had it said? Duncan racked his brains, bemused as they were, to recollect the wording.

His efforts were cut short by a rude shaking from the sergeant. 'Speak, damn you! Don't think that we will let you play dumb.'

'I do not know,' Duncan said.

The sergeant raised a hand to strike, but the young officer stopped him.

'That matter may perhaps wait. There is another, more immediate, of which you cannot disclaim knowledge. What did you do with the gunpowder, sir?'

Duncan stared, and his mind reeled. Gunpowder? Did he mean, where was the ammunition that was landed from the French ships? He shook his head – but swiftly desisted at the pain of it.

'Do not be a fool!' the ensign ordered sharply. 'You took it from here, with two horses. One of the horses we found – but not the gunpowder. Where have you hidden it?'

The truth dawned on the prisoner. They did not know about the gold. They had taken the powder-kegs at their face value. They had not been full, of course – not so very heavy. The coins could not have chinked or rattled. Perhaps even they had been covered over with some of the powder.

'I am waiting,' the officer said ominously.

'I . . . I threw it in the loch,' Duncan told him.

'You did? That is what I thought. Where was your man taking it?'

Duncan's head was in no condition to cope properly with all this, and its implications. They accepted that he had thrown the gunpowder into the loch. They must look on the kegs of powder as important in their own right – to the Jacobites, at any rate. As they would have been, of course, even a week ago. They were concerned about the powder's destination. They assumed that O'Rourke was carrying it for him.

163

'To . . . to my father's regiment. Glengyle's,' he lied. 'He is short of ammunition.'

'I daresay. Where is Glengyle's Regiment now?'

'Far away. North of Inverness.' Cumberland's forces must be well aware of this fact, for they had spies widespread.

'And you were taking the powder there?'

'Yes.'

'Well, no treacherous rebel guns will fire that powder, after it has been in the lake,' the young officer said, with obvious satisfaction. He rose. 'We will move at once. Sergeant. We need not have wasted so long, spent so much time over this matter. It is as I thought. Get this fellow tied behind one of the men. Or better, in front. He may need holding up.'

'Yes, sir.'

Duncan's frail and elusive consciousness did not even survive the rough handling of hoisting him up on to a charger's back before one of the troopers. He swooned right away before ever he reached the saddle.

It was a nightmare journey that followed. How far they went, in what direction they rode, or for how long, Duncan had not the least idea. All that he was aware of was continual awakening to jolting agony, and happily as frequent slipping back into blessed insensibility.

At some stage, a lifetime later, he felt himself to crash down on to something hard, grievously solid – but at least something that did not jolt and jerk. He asked no more of existence, just then – nor knew any more.

'Do not deceive yourself, MacGregor. You will talk, sooner or later. They all talk, eventually. Captain Miller, here, has the art of extracting real eloquence. Unfailingly. I suggest that you spare yourself a demonstration.'

Duncan eyed the speaker as levelly as he might, considering the state of his head. This was no youthful ensign, to be beguiled, but an experienced senior officer, Major Monroe of Culcairn, one of Loudon's staff, the man who had burned Achnacarry Castle and practically every other Cameron house in the area – including no doubt Glenpean House. A spare stern man with a strong Lowland Scots accent, he had a cold and hooded eye.

'I cannot tell you what I do not know, Major,' he said, steadily.

'But what you do know, you will tell us. Of that I have no doubt. We shall make it our business to see you do. Eh, Miller?'

The third man in the comfortable sitting-room of Clunes House grinned unpleasantly and flexed the fingers of a great hand in and out, in and out. He did not speak, but his appearance lacked nothing in its own eloquence. A huge man, almost as broad as he was long, with a bull-like head and neck, his muscles seemed to be bursting out of his scarlet coat, his massive shoulders splitting the seams. He had his own fame also, this Captain Miller of Guise's Regiment, a professional prizefighter turned King George's officer. He boasted, amongst other feats, that he had raped eight women in one day's operations in Glen Moriston.

Duncan moistened his lips. 'I would remind you, gentlemen, that I am an officer in the army of His Royal Highness the Prince of Wales. I demand the treatment to which a prisoner-of-war is entitled.'

'Pish, sir! You are a bloody rebel, entitled only to a hanging. Or a musket-ball. Which you will get, I assure you, if you do not talk. And quickly. Where is the man Charles Stuart?'

'I have told you – I do not know.'

Captain Miller strolled forward casually, looked the younger man up and down unhurriedly, grinning, and then, hit him suddenly, viciously, first just under the ribs, and then, as the other doubled up, with a chopping blow at the side of the neck. Duncan sank to the floor, choking.

He was not allowed to lie there. The big man hoisted him up by his torn and stained tartan doublet, and threw him like a sack across the table behind which Major Monroe sat, holding him there lest he slide down again – for the prisoner's own hands were still pinioned at his back.

Monroe spoke on evenly, unmoved, as though nothing had happened. 'You may not know that young man's exact whereabouts, but you will certainly know his approximate location, MacGregor. You were with him only nine days ago. You are attached to his personal staff. From the letter you carried on you, I take it that you are an extra aide-de-camp, or something of the sort. Were it not for that fact, sir, you would have been shot out of hand.'

Duncan did not doubt that. Apart from the example of
O'Rourke, in the two days that he had been a prisoner he had
seen evidence in plenty of the Government troops' fondness for
enough to carry in his pocket had preserved his life. So far.
such summary methods of dealing with prisoners. And not only
prisoners; it seemed to be considered suitable treatment for
practically anyone encountered in the Highland area. He had
seen an ordinary small farmer who had brought in an old sword
and a fowlingpiece to deliver up – as according to Cumberland's
proclamation all must do – shot in the back as he left to go
home. He had seen a boy in his early teens cut down with a sabre
because he did not speak English. He had seen an old Cameron
woman, half-blind, shot for not being able to tell where Locheil
was hiding – and raped before she was dead. He did not dis-
believe Major Monroe that the letter that he had been unwise

Gasping for breath, sprawled on the table, he found words.
'If you know . . . that I am . . . one of the Prince's staff officers
. . . how can you deny that I am . . . a prisoner-of-war? Entitled
to protection from hired bullies!'

Captain Miller picked him up, turned him round, drove his
bent knee into Duncan's groin, and flung him back over the
table again, a squirming mass of pain, biting savagely at his lips
to keep himself from yelling out.

Monroe hardly paused, maintaining the same tone of voice,
slightly prim. 'We have three possibilities. One, that Charles
Stuart is still in the Arisaig area. Two, that he is skulking
amongst the islands. And three, that he sailed for France in one
of those ships which brought your gunpowder. I do not think
that he did the last. How do you say, MacGregor?'

Duncan had difficulty in making his lips obey him. His first
words were an unintelligible mumble. 'I . . . I cannot tell you,'
he got out at length, panting. 'I was not present . . . when the
ships sailed.'

Miller reached out his vast paw again, but the Major halted
him.

'A moment, Captain,' he said. 'Perhaps MacGregor does not
know about the Government's great generosity? The Duke of
Cumberland, my friend, is offering a vast fortune, no less than
thirty thousand pounds, for information leading to the apprehension of the Young Pretender. You could do much with such

a sum, I have no doubt, sir? And I have no doubt, also, that a pardon for your past treasons would go with it.'

Duncan found words fast enough now, raising his head from that table. 'I cannot stop you misusing me,' he gulped. 'You keep me bound, so that I cannot defend myself against your baboon here! But, by God – you will not insult me, into the bargain!'

Miller laughed raucously, and began to peel off his tight-fitting gold braided red coat.

'Be gentle with him, Captain . . . about the head,' Monroe mentioned. 'Watkins declared that the least tap about the head, and out he goes! Concussion, or something of the sort, I believe. Unfortunate. It would be a pity if he was to miss any of your educative efforts, would it not?'

Captain Miller made his first spoken contribution. 'Watch me! Just watch me, Major,' he said, in a thick London voice.

He grabbed the prisoner and swung him round. Duncan, bent double and swaying, leaned back against the table-top, holding away. But as the other reached to drag him to him, the bound man, summoning every ounce of his remaining strength, forced himself from the table and hurtled unexpectedly forward. Head still down he butted the big man in the middle with all his force and weight.

Miller, sucking air convulsively, and now doubled up in turn, winded, staggered backwards. He fell over a chair and crashed to the floor.

Duncan fell on top of him, unable to control his rush. But difficult as it was with hands bound behind him, he managed to get to his feet. Those feet were not bound. Raising his right brogan, tottering dizzily, he smashed it down with all the fury and loathing that was in him on to the great fleshy face – once, twice, thrice. He would have continued so to do – but sounds behind him, turned him round. Major Monroe was advancing upon him, arm raised. In his hand was a heavy pistol, grasped by the barrel.

Reeling, everything aswim before his eyes, the younger man lowered head and shoulder in a desperate attempt to repeat his former butting tactics. This time, however, there was no surprise. Monroe, shouting for the guard, saw the rush coming, and brought down the pistol-butt, probably with less nice judgement than he had intended. The blow struck the side of the

MacGregor's head, and smashed down on to his shoulder with a sickening crack.

Duncan collapsed on to the floor beside his would-be educator, as unconscious as ever he had been.

He was aware of the groaning for some considerable time before he realised that it was not in fact his own groaning. His body being nothing more than one vast and comprehensive pain, the groans seemed to match it most naturally. It was only when, seeking to raise a hand to his aching groin and finding that he could not do so, he groaned in weak frustration – and doing so, he thereafter perceived some difference in the groans and their quality. Presently, reluctantly, he opened his eyes, and perceived that the major groaning was not his.

He had a companion in the stable of Clunes House – a bundle of blood-stained tartan rags and twitching limbs, that muttered and moaned and cried out. He had been alone before, he thought.

Duncan was not greatly interested in this noisy fellow-sufferer. His own agonies and miseries were much too vivid and pressing for him to have much attention left for others. But the man's reiterated denials and refusals that interspersed his groans, the babbled mixture of no, no, no and curses and pleas, struck an answering chord in the MacGregor, and he roused himself sufficiently to give a little more heed to his companion in misfortune.

It was only then that he perceived that this was, in fact, Cameron of Camusbuie, one of Locheil's captains, an older man for whom he had no great fondness, and whom last he had seen riding off to Loch Morar from Borrodale with the rest. How came he here? And in this state?

Duncan tried to speak – but words came only haltingly to his lips. Anyway Camusbuie did not seem to hear.

Much became apparent without the other's conscious answering, however. The man had obviously been as roughly handled as he had himself – more so, possibly, for his features were almost unrecognisable, so bruised and swollen and cut were they. Such extensive damage could only have been caused by deliberate beatings about the head and face. That he had been put to the question was equally clear – his continual denials and objurgations presumably witnessing to the quality of his answers. But how had he been captured? Did this mean that there had been an action? That Locheil's company had been surprised?

Duncan was still wondering about this, between bouts of much more personal concern and the growing conviction that he had a broken collar-bone, when the stable door was flung open and three soldiers came in half-carrying another tartan-clad victim. He was thrown down on the cobbled floor beside them. As they turned to leave, one of the troopers turned back, and picking up a pail of water from a corner, tossed its contents in a single swing over all three prisoners. He went out, laughing, and the doors were locked and barred again. Whether this was done as something of a kindness, or the reverse, would have been hard to say. Perhaps the latest sufferer had been asking for water.

Duncan recognised the man at once, despite the blood all over his face – and despite the fact that he was sobbing convulsively. It was strange to see so fiery a warrior as Ewan MacDonald of Scirinish sobbing. He did it in a curious fashion also, quite openly, vehemently, angrily. He was one of Clanranald's lairds – the one who had demanded most insistently that the French gold should be shared out amongst those who had fought and suffered for the Prince. Now he lay and beat on the cobble-stones with his already broken clenched fists, and such a stream, a flood, of furious and profound profanity issued from his swollen lips, in the Gaelic, in and amongst his savage sobs, as Duncan had never heard in all his days.

When the paroxysm had worn itself out, Duncan spoke. 'What happened, Scirinish? How came you here? You and Camusbuie? Was there fighting? Locheil – is he safe?'

The MacDonald swung on him. 'They are swine, foul and filthy swine!' he cried. 'God burn and blister them! God broil and brand them eternally! May the stink of their roasting choke the very devils in hell!'

'No doubt,' Duncan acceded. 'But yourselves? How came you here?'

The other neither knew to whom he spoke, nor cared. He was in no mood for answering questions, at any rate. 'I told them nothing – nothing! Not even that he had sailed. Nothing, I tell you – save what to do with their accursed money! They thought to buy a MacDonald! Or frighten one!' He was sobbing again. 'By the Holy Ghost, I curse them – living and dying, waking and sleeping, eating and drinking, their sons and their daughters . . . !'

The vehemence of these execrations, or perhaps the splash of the water, seemed to have aroused Camusbuie. He spoke lucidly now, if thickly.

'You did not say that Himself had sailed, Scirinish? In the French ships? You did not tell them that?'

The other went on with his cursing, unheeding.

'*I* did not,' Duncan assured. 'I thought of it, yes – but told them nothing. And you?'

'Nothing,' the Cameron said. 'When I would not tell them if he was still in the country, they wanted to know about the French ships. If I had said that he had gone, they would have spread the word that the Prince had left us. To all. That he had gone away to France. It would have been the end of the Rising, the end of all hope . . .'

'Aye.'

'They tried to make me say it – God, they tried! And the money – that accursed thirty thousand pounds! Did they think . . . ? But, Scirinish? Perhaps he said that Charles went in the ships?'

'He says that he told them nothing. Nothing, at all.'

'Thank God! But they will try again! Heaven have mercy upon us – they will try again!'

Duncan could not deny it. The thought was like lead at his heart. It all but choked the words in his throat. This was just the beginning . . .

Thankful to speak of other things, he told briefly of his own capture, and learned details of the others' misfortunes. There had been no general action. Locheil and the rest, as far as Camusbuie knew, were safe. From Kinlochmorar he and a party of Camerons had been sent out on a patrol, by Locheil. There were rumours that the Lord Lovat was hiding in the vicinity, and they were to find him. Scirinish came with them, as it was Clanranald country. They never found Lovat, but were trapped on an island in the loch where it was said that he might be hiding – the Redcoats must have seen them rowing out to it. That was all that there was to tell. The rest, of the Elector's forces' treatment of its prisoners, was no news to him. No doubt these two had not been shot for the same reason that he himself had been preserved. Only for questioning, for torture. The

Prince's apprehension was all important, it seemed. Otherwise they would be but three corpses, by now.

That night, in between fitful bouts of uneasy sleep, which pain never allowed to be prolonged, Duncan had time and to spare for much thought, much dread, and some wonder. Most of the thought, like the dread, comforted him nothing; but the wonder remained. Wonder chiefly on two scores – that men could so debase themselves, far below the level of the animals, could so debase all mankind, as to treat their fellows in the way that they were being treated here; and at the strange tricks and contrary aspects of character as revealed in these two companions in sorrow. Both had clamoured to get their hands on the treasure landed from the French ships, Camusbuie claiming a home burned and family savaged and scattered, Scirinish wounds in battle and losses amongst his men. The gold, which had been sent for the Prince's use in his efforts to gain his father's crown, they would squabble and fight for without conscience, apparently; but this other treasure, Cumberland's vast thirty thousand pounds, the price for betraying the same Prince, they would shun more fiercely than the plague, they would suffer the extremities of agony and indignity rather than compound with. They were Highland gentlemen, who could never betray for gold. And yet, was not the avidity for this other a betrayal? Would not all the rest think the same way? Barrisdale and James Mor, even?

What did he know of his fellow-men, Duncan asked himself? What did he know of himself, indeed? How much more torture could he stand, before proud will gave in to craven agonised body . . . ?

To the prisoners' surprise, they were left alone all the next day – save for the brief visit of a regimental surgeon, a Welshman, whose duties they took to be inspection as to how much more questioning each could stand rather than healing. He did confirm to Duncan, however, that he had a broken left collar-bone, and went so far as to bind that arm tightly to its owner's side, with a sling to support the forearm – an arrangement which necessitated, at last, the untying of the wrists bound at his back and a retying in front. Otherwise they received no attention, not even food – and though they shouted for water, the pail was not refilled.

It was evening before their existence was again acknowledged. Two officers came into the stable, with guards. One was the simian Captain Miller – whose unprepossessing features, Duncan was glad to see, still showed signs of his own yesterday's footwork – but the other was not Major Monroe. He wore the insignia of a lieutenant-colonel and looked an angry man, slight and paunchy.

'Which of these barbarians is the Cameron?' he barked.

With the toe of his boot, and ungently, Miller indicated Camusbuie.

The other stooped down, and slapped the bound Cameron hard across the face. Again and again he did this, until obviously his hand hurt. Then he started to kick instead. He staggered somewhat as he did it, seeming to have but imperfect balance. Undoubtedly he was a little drunk. Panting with the exertions, he gasped out in jerky disjointed phrases,

'Animal! Scum! Vermin! So you would murder one of His Majesty's officers! Cutthroat savages! You shall learn . . . what assassination costs.' In his fury, he had difficulty in enunciating the word assassination, kicking still. 'God help me – I'll teach the whole accursed tribe of you the price of Major Monroe!'

At length, exhausted, the colonel sought to finish his exercise by spitting in the squirming Cameron's face – but, like the rest of this presumably little practised assault, it was not entirely effective and most of what spittle his eloquence had left him went down his own resplendent coat. Miller, who could have done it all so much more efficiently, stood by, almost embarrassed.

'And the other? The aide, MacGregor?'

Eyes narrowing in sheer hate under those low craggy brows, Captain Miller kicked Duncan viciously, a much more telling kick than all the colonel's put together.

'That whelp!' The colonel's lip curled. 'Have him sent under strong escort to Fort William immediately. His lordship wishes to question him in person. As for the other two – take them out and shoot them.'

Miller hesitated. 'Now, sir? Tonight?'

'Good Lord, man – why not? Can your men not aim their pieces unless the sun is shining?'

'I did not mean that, Colonel. I mean sending this man MacGregor to Fort William tonight?'

'You heard what I said, didn't you, Captain? Immediately, I said. Those were Lord Loudon's instructions.'

'Yes, sir. Very good, sir.'

As the colonel stamped outside, Miller bellowed orders to the guards. 'Bring these two out. No — not him. These. And be sharp about it.'

'Dear God in Heaven — you cannot do this!' Duncan shouted. 'This . . . this is murder! Colonel — these men have done nothing. They are prisoners-of-war. They have suffered enough already. Colonel — listen to me . . .'

A kick on the jaw did not exactly silence him, but it certainly reduced his shouting to unintelligibility.

The stable door was slammed shut, and he was alone.

It was only a few grim minutes later that a ragged volley crashed out, close at hand. Duncan MacGregor knelt up on the cobblestones and said a trembling, distracted and not very coherent prayer for the departed.

A little later, when he was led stumbling out of that stable by a lieutenant of dragoons, and set up on a cavalry charger, the two bodies still lay where they had fallen against an outhouse wall. Duncan could not even raise a hand in salute, with his wrists tied together. But at least he could turn and look with loathing and contempt at the officer of his escort — since there was no sign of Miller or the colonel. The lieutenant had the grace to flush a little.

So, in the grey evening, Duncan left the House of Clunes, that sat so snugly at the end of the Dark Mile. He rode in the midst of half a troop of dragoons. And though he might bite his lip at every other jolt of the trotting horse, his conscious mind hardly registered a pang of physical pain.

CHAPTER 15

'I AM told, sir, that you have a shoulder broke. It will make painful riding, I do not doubt. If you will give me your parole, let me have your word of honour that you will make no foolish attempt at escape, I think that I may be able to ease your discomfort somewhat.'

The officer spoke stiffly. After half an hour's riding at the head of his column down the wooded shore of Loch Lochy, he had dropped back to Duncan's side. He was a man of approximately the MacGregor's own age, square-built, stocky, very fair-haired. His stiffness seemed to apply to all of him, not just to his present tone of voice. He frowned as he spoke.

'Honour?' Duncan repeated. 'Word of honour? A strange term, I think, on the lips of one of the Elector of Hanover's officers?'

That so stiffened the other that he became quite rigid, a ramrod in his saddle. His lips slashed a straight line across his square features, and clamped that way.

Yet, after perhaps five minutes of silence, the lieutenant spoke again. 'Your parole, sir?' he snapped. But it was a question.

'Is my own, sir. All that is left to me, it seems. I shall keep it.'

Again silence. The officer moved his horse forward a little way from the other.

But presently he was back at Duncan's side once more, his voice stiff as ever, the words seemingly forced out with difficulty from between those tight lips.

'You must not judge all King George's officers by those you have seen here,' he said. 'Here is only the dregs of an army.'

'I do not doubt it, sir. And taking its tone from your German George's brother!'

The other did not answer that. 'The true soldiers are all away fighting the French. In the Low Countries,' he said. 'Would to God I was with them!'

Surprised, Duncan turned to look at him. 'You do not enjoy torturing and shooting prisoners-of-war, and killing defenceless women and children, sir?'

'I do not.'

'How unhappily placed you must be, Lieutenant! How do you manage to pass your time?'

The other snorted. 'You are bitter. I do not wonder at it,' he jerked. 'What was done today was inexcusable. But it was done by a frightened man.'

'Frightened? The ape Miller, frightened whatever?'

'Not Miller so much. Colonel Walton. He it was who gave the orders. He killed because he was afraid. That it would be his

174

turn next. Shot from behind a bush. Any bush. And this country is full of bushes!'

'Why so?'

'Do not say that you have not heard? That no one has told you? Monroe . . . ? Man, Major Monroe was shot this morning. From behind a bush. By the lakeside. By Cameron of Clunes.'

'Dead?'

'Aye. Notably so.'

'*Dia* – so that was it. And Clunes? What happened to him?'

The lieutenant paused. 'I would rather that you did not ask that,' he said, at length.

'I see. Clunes must have felt . . . strongly! Did I not hear something about his wife . . . ?'

'Aye. There is the nub of it! It was Lockhart who did that. Major Lockhart who took over Clunes House and ravished Clunes' wife. Lockhart went to Fort William to see General Loudon two days ago. But he had a white Arab stallion, a handsome beast, which he left behind. Monroe chose to ride it this morning – when he was shot.'

'So-o-o! That was the way of it. Poor Clunes. I never knew him, but he was esteemed a quiet and honest man.'

'You do not say poor Monroe!'

'I do not. Myself, yesterday, if I could have killed Monroe, I would have done it! Any way that I could!'

The silence descended again upon the two men.

It was Duncan who broke it on this occasion, finding that talk, any talk, served to keep his mind off the gnawing, grinding pain of his shoulder, in some measure.

'What makes you, Lieutenant, so different a man from your colleagues?' he asked.

'I am a soldier,' the other answered, stiffly as ever.

'So are these others, are they not? Colonels, majors and captains.'

His companion shook his head. 'I warrant that five years ago not one of them knew one end of a musket from the other! Tavern-captains, chamber-majors and lordlings' fancies – that is the style of them.'

'And you are a trained soldier?'

'Aye. From a boy, almost. I was wounded at Fontenoy, and sent home. When I was fit for duty again, damn them if they did not send me up here, with a troop of replacements scoured from the London sewers! My regiment is still in the Netherlands. Soldiers, not bloodthirsty brigands! I would that I was with them.'

'And I that there were more Englishmen like yourself, Lieutenant.'

'Do not blame the English, Captain,' the other retorted. 'There are villains of all races. But the worst here are your own people. Scots. Monroe was a Scot. So is Lockhart. So is that devil Grant. And the ship's captain Ferguson. Lord Loudon himself is a Campbell, is he not? How they can treat their own folk thus, I cannot tell.'

'Nor I – God forgive them!'

They had left the foot of Loch Lochy and were following the road down the west side of the river, a thin rain falling. The lieutenant, who gave his name as Carter, offered his prisoner a cavalry cloak. Duncan refused it, for any weight bearing on his shoulder was too much. Food and drink the other gave him also, the first that the prisoner had received, actually, for two whole days – and though, because of the constant pain, Duncan had not realised that he was hungry, he ate and drank thankfully. There was nothing to be gained through physical weakness – and much to be lost, perhaps.

The possibility of escape was never far from the captive's mind, however improbable such a thing might appear, one man against thirty. Certain circumstances, however, might just conceivably count in his favour. Because of the rain, it would be a darker night than usual; he knew the terrain fairly well; his injured state might make his guards less wary; and the surgeon's tying up of his wrists had never been renewed and was not very tight, or effective as a shackle, so that he believed that he could free his hands whenever desired. Another quite important consideration, which probably did not occur to his escort, was that when savage questioning and almost certain torture face a man at the end of a journey, he is not likely to be seriously worried about any dangers in an escape attempt.

The journey of twenty difficult miles to Fort William would take practically all night. Around midnight, and approximately half-way, Carter halted his company for a brief spell, after having crossed the ford where the River Loy came out of its glen to join the Lochy. No escape possibility presented itself here.

Carter guarded his prisoner well, however, humanely. The professional, he took no chances.

Duncan sought, in his tired and aching head, to visualise every yard of the route ahead. Or not all the route, for in only five miles or so they would issue out into the flat low ground of the Corpach Moss where escape would be out of the question and would remain so practically all the way to the fort. Anything to be attempted must be done in the next few miles. He was restricted to the hill-foots of the Locheil mountains, steeply sloping woodlands cut up by innumerable burns rushing down to the Lochy. The road forded all of these, as he recollected it, save one – where the Laragain came cascading out of its high steep glen in a furious torrent. There, to avoid the deep chasm cut by this river, was a bridge.

Duncan's thoughts concentrated on that bridge. It was high and narrow, a pack-horse bridge, a single arch with a steep hump in the middle of it and a stone parapet.

It might be possible, just possible. And with the last two days' rain . . .

Again Lieutenant Carter rode beside his prisoner – and though Duncan appreciated his strange jerky camaraderie, he could have wished him elsewhere. Also, he recognised that what he was contemplating might seem an ill way of showing that appreciation, for if by any chance he made a successful escape, it must result in serious trouble for this the only enemy officer who had treated him decently. He was unhappy about this – but presumably that was war. This professional soldier would no doubt recognise the fact – and almost certainly would attempt the same in a like situation.

Duncan fretted about his shoulder, also. How much would it hamper him? How much might the pain of it, as well as the lack of the use of his left arm, affect the violent physical efforts that he must attempt?

As the land, and their road, began to slant down into the deeper, wider gap in the long hill rampart which they were following, which was in fact part of the western wall of the Great Glen of Scotland, Duncan was working away with the fingers of his right hand to loosen his wrists. Carter had been silent for a while – for however civil, he clearly was no conversationalist; his charge was concerned that he might notice the manipulations at his wrists, and wished that he had accepted the offer of the cavalry cloak, as cover.

They came to the bridge itself, over the Laragain, sooner than
Duncan had anticipated. Suddenly the noise of the rushing river
was loud, as they rounded a bend of the road. The jostling and
breaking of formation of the ranked dragoons in front, as they
first bunched and then strung out in single file to cross the
narrow pointed bridge, was all the warning that he received.
Although that stringing-out was what he had hoped for,
depended upon.

It just would be possible for two horsemen to cross side-by-
side, he believed; would Carter stick close to him?

No. At the bridge-end, the lieutenant gestured for his captive
to go first. He would have preferred to be behind – but better
this than that they should ride together.

Duncan braced every nerve and sinew as his mount climbed
the steep cobbled ascent to the hump of the bridge. He had
deliberately allowed the trooper in front to get a good couple of
lengths ahead. In the clatter of hooves on stone he could not be
sure just how close Carter might be behind – and he dare not
look round.

As he topped the hump, he drew a great breath. He had
forgotten his collar-bone, his pain and weariness. Every sense
was concentrated on immediate action.

The hump passed, he acted at once. He was glad that this was
a tall saddle-horse. Keeping his left foot in the stirrup he kicked
the right free, and standing up on the left swung his right leg
over the saddle. For a brief moment he stood poised there, as he
twisted his right hand out of its slackened bonds. Then he
leapt – two leaps. The first took him the mere three or four feet
on to the top of the parapet, and the second straight downwards
as, without pause, he jumped into the void below.

The fall seemed endless to the man. If he had miscalculated,
if his memory had played him false, if somehow he had jumped
a little way to one side or the other – then he would probably be
dead in a matter of seconds. Or almost worse than dead. The
gorge was narrow and deep beneath the bridge – possibly
seventy or eighty feet. There was a large pool there, in a sort of
terrace between a series of rapids and falls. How deep he did not
know, though it had looked black when last he saw it. But the
entire width of it was probably less than ten yards. He had
sought to drop straight downwards, but if his jump had taken

him too far to one side . . . ? Or even too far outwards, for the pool would shallow fairly quickly he expected . . . ?

It was extraordinary how much of fear, doubt and agonising conjecture could be crammed into what could only have been a second or two. The rock walls on either side were steep and jagged, with thrusting buttresses. The river should be high after the rain, but . . .

He hit the water with an impact which drove the air out of his lungs. No doubt it savagely wrenched his damaged shoulder, but he felt no pain. He did not feel the cold either, or know any sensation other than the sheer terror of the rocky bottom rising up to smash at his feet and legs.

Then he knew himself to be gasping and fighting for air. He was drawing air into his mouth, but not down into his lungs, which seemed to be closed up, clamped off. It dawned on him, then, that he must have come to the surface again, that he had not been smashed by the rocks, that he was only winded in some measure by hitting the water.

Gulping, choking, Duncan sought to strike out. Having only one arm to swim with, he seemed to go round in circles; or perhaps it was a whirlpool motion in the river. He felt himself being dragged down – his clothing losing its air and becoming waterlogged. It was dark down here in the gut of the chasm, and he could not tell which way to swim. But struggling desperately against the direction that he seemed to be pulled, and gasping for air, he felt a stouning pain in his knee. Another in the other knee told him that he was in shallows. Clawing his way forward with an access of crazy energy, he collapsed, gaping like a stranded fish, on a shelf of rock covered by only a few inches of swirling water, and there lay.

Great as was the temptation to do nothing but seek to regain his breath, to rest his trembling and misused body, the man forced himself to consider, to plan, to establish his position. He seemed to be on the north side of the pool. He thought that dimly he could distinguish the black mass of the bridge away above him. He could hear nothing of what was going on up there because of the noise of falling, rushing water. The walls of the chasm were very steep, near the bridge, and it seemed unlikely that any dragoons would be able to get down to his present position save by going up or down stream some distance, climbing down where it might be less steep, and then working back by the riverside. Certainly none could do this mounted. Probably he had some minutes of grace, therefore.

How to use them?

He must do what they would not expect of him – that was certain. What would they least expect? That he should come back to the bridge and the horses. Could this steep cliff-like bank be climbed? In his present state? Could it be climbed at all?

Duncan MacGregor was an expert rock-climber; no Mac-Gregor boy, brought up on the cliff-girt north-east shores of Loch Lomond was likely to be otherwise. But he had the use of only one hand; and he was dizzy.

He staggered to his feet, and peered upwards. It was impossible to see much of detail in the darkness, but the thought that at least this northern bank was less precipitous than the other. Here, then – or above the bridge? Since he had made his jump at the lower side, the dragoons would be likely to look for him on that side first.

He picked his way upstream therefore, clambering over the rocks, splashing through the shallows.

He did not risk going much beyond the level of the bridge itself, for Carter was no fool and would be sure to send searchers upstream as well as down. Since he could not pick out one place as better than another, by sight, he turned to face the bank almost immediately. At least he could see that a scattering of small trees sprouted from it, which argued crannies, soil, ledges.

The motion of climbing was painful; the injured shoulder was like a leaden weight that had to be hoisted separately and individually at each step. Although the arm was still strapped to his side, it seemed as though it was not part of the rest of him, at all. Each move that he made, each upward lift, each sapling or tussock or outcropping spur of rock that he pulled himself up by, had to be considered in relation to the effect on this grinding shoulder. Sweating, panting, biting back the groans which started to his lips, Duncan fought his private war with that shoulder.

Step by step he fought it and cursed it and beat it.

It was only when, sick and for the moment exhausted, he sank down, leaning against a small but stalwart rowan-tree, he came to realise that he was in fact most of the way up the bank, that the worst of the climb was over. So intent had he been of combating that shoulder that the problem of the actual ascent had more or less taken care of itself. As often was the case, it could not have been so steep as it appeared.

Up here the noise of the river was less loud. He could hear shouting, but it was some distance off, and downstream.

Encouraged, he moved on again, in his dazed, zigzag, crabwise one step-at-a-time climbing. There was more of raw earth than of rock, and although it was slippery with the rain, taken slowly and using every root and tree and handhold, it was possible.

At the top he lay outstretched, gasping, for minutes on end. The road was just in front of him, and the bridge-end dimly visible to his right. Neither men nor horses were to be seen on this side.

Forcing himself up, Duncan made for the bridge itself, seeking to screw every sense to the alert. He reached the stonework. Still no movement, no sign of life around him. Keeping close to the right-hand parapet, he climbed the cobblestones of the steep hump. Just before the crest he crouched down, to peer over. He was only a couple of yards from where he had made his leap.

He could see the dark mass of the horses, waiting beyond the southern end of the bridge. He could not distinguish guards — although there were bound to be such. How many? And where?

Carter would want every man that could be mustered to search for his prisoner, undoubtedly; only the very minimum would be left to watch the horses — not more than three or four out of the thirty, probably.

Still bent almost double, to keep below the level of the parapet, Duncan moved on. Thirty horses can take up a lot of space, and these necessarily overflowed the narrow road on either side. The man reasoned that wherever the guards were, they were unlikely to be up on the rising ground behind the road, where the trees came down. Thither he made his furtive way.

In the event, the entire manoeuvre was ridiculously simple. Duncan saw no sentries from first to last. Slipping from tree to tree, he found himself amongst the outermost of the great concourse of horses. He did not wait to pick and choose. The beasts' reins seemed to be tied together in bunches of four. Taking that group nearest to him, he untied the reins, finding a little difficulty in doing so with one trembling hand. Retaining one set, he managed to haul himself up on to the back of the beast they belonged to. With no more ado, and no more valid selection, he dug in his heels and rode away.

He rode carefully, of course, slowly, so as to make as little noise as possible. Not that he greatly feared in that respect, for the stirrings and hoof-scrapings of thirty horses should mask the sound of his one. He rode uphill since he dared not recross the bridge mounted – but not directly so, slanting over to the left, south-westerly, once again reasoning that this would be the last direction that he might be expected to take.

Up through the trees he went, at a walk, a sense of unreality strong upon him. He had to keep feeling the rippling silky muscles of the beast below him to assure himself that this was not all some sort of hallucination caused by pain and weariness.

Dare he believe that he had won free?

Whether any actual pursuit ever developed, Duncan did not know. No hint of it reached him as he rode up the long side of Meall Banavic.

When the trees began to thin away, on the higher ground, he pulled over to the right again, northwards, to retain their cover for as long as he might, and also to regain his desired direction. He wanted to work back to the trough of Glen Laragain, and to follow it up to its head. That way lay safety, and the empty Cameron territory.

He did not push his mount. The animal was a Lowland cavalry charger and no sure-footed Highland garron. With little instinct or training for the hill, on rough and broken ground it could readily damage a leg.

It was a relief when they reached the upper glen. Duncan risked riding down into it. He was two miles above the bridge here, at least, and he could not anticipate that any searchers' would come up this far. There was a track of sorts running up the riverside, and he turned along it. His horse did not require so much attention on this.

Duncan forced his lethargic and reluctant mind to weigh up the situation now. Although all of him cried out for the comparative easement of just riding quietly up a track, he dared not linger in this valley for long. It might be quite some time before Carter gave up the search in the chasm, but once he did, once he reassembled his men, and discovered the loss of one horse, he was almost bound to send at least a small party up here, hot-foot. Anyway, this glen trended away south-westwards towards its head. Somehow he must get over the ridge into Glen Loy, north-westwards. And then, God helping him, over the higher ridge beyond into Glen Mallie. Then still a third ridge lay between him and Arkaigside.

Duncan's whole being protested and rebelled against such a programme, such grievous forcing of himself against the grain of that upheaved land, in his present condition. These ridges were miles wide, up to two thousand feet in height, and awkward, punishing terrain even in daylight. At his most optimistic calculation it would be fifteen savage miles to Loch Arkaig, this way. For consolation, all that he could tell himself was that it had to be done, and that nothing of it was likely to be so desperate and formidable as what he had already accomplished.

Another mile up, therefore, steeling himself, he turned his beast's head off the track at the first sizeable burn coming in from the north, to climb in its company towards the first unseen ridge.

That night's travelling remained ever afterwards little more than an evil dream, a nightmare, vague, undetailed, timeless, in Duncan's mind, without coherence or sequence. He could recollect incidents; his mount stumbling and throwing him off part-way down the heathery side of Glen Loy – for how long he lay thereafter before dragging himself to his feet and on to the brute's back again, he could not tell; the creature getting bogged down in a peat-moss somewhere, and the curses of weak fury and frustration that he had shouted aloud at all Creation as he lurched about, seeking to lead the animal and himself out of it; his getting lost in a vast and benighted wood, he who had prided himself that he could never be lost in all the Highlands, day or night – it must have been the great pine woods of Glen Mallie – and the actual shameful tears that he had wept for himself there, tears for poor damned and lost Duncan MacGregor of Glengyle. These and others of the like stood out; the rest was just pain and endurance and eternity.

Grey dawn found him climbing, so very slowly, the last and lowest of the ridges, still dotted with black pines, between Mallie and Loch Arkaig, leading a jaded, mud-spattered, head-hanging charger. When later, at the summit, he stood swaying and watched the sun rise behind the frowning mountains of

Lochaber, to reflect its first red gleam on the leaden waters of the long loch below, it was to sink down with a groan of thankfulness. Crumpled up as he was, he slept where he sank – and the horse moved no foot as the reins dropped into the heather.

It was mid-afternoon when he wakened, with the sun in his eyes and cramped agony in all his person. Wits sufficient were spared to him to recognise that the open summit of a ridge was not the wisest choice of hiding-place for a fugitive in occupied territory, and he dragged himself and the waiting horse over the crest and down to a nearby thicket. There he sought sleep again, and found it without difficulty.

The shadows of evening were long before he roused himself, and slipped downhill towards the loch. He felt but little rested, he sweated profusely with every exertion – indeed almost certainly he was feverish – and his shoulder was if anything worse. Man and horse drank deep at the first burn that they came to.

Duncan took no great note of where he reached the loch-shore, but he was thankful to mount again and turn westwards along it in the dusk.

It was the blackened remains of a fire on a grassy flat, a large fire, that attracted his wandering and hazy attention presently, and he perceived that he was back at the camping-place where he had first been taken prisoner. And where he had recovered O'Rourke's gold. The gold! He had not so much as thought of it for days. How many days? Three or four? Or more? He could not tell, for the life of him. But the gold . . .

He had no difficulty in locating the spot, at the water's edge, where he had hidden the kegs, the alder-tree with the cross scored on it. Despite the toil and misery of manhandling heavy objects with one arm useless, something compelled him to wade into the water and fight and struggle with those four kegs, dragging them out from under the roots, heaving them on to the bank, and then, worst of all, hoisting them up by pairs on to the horse's back – so high a back. It took him a long time to do it – a man who despised the power of gold over other men.

Hardly able to keep himself upright in the saddle thereafter, he set his mount pacing slowly westwards along the shore track. The beast was left to make its own pace, and largely its own way.

It was late that night when Luath the wolfhound wakened all the mountains to welcome Duncan MacGregor to the dark shieling of the Allt Ruadh. Loud and long she bayed, before she changed her tune to ecstatic yelpings as she leapt and bounded around the foundered horse and the hunched and drooping rider.

Caroline Cameron was first to the cabin's doorway, a plaid wrapped around her, staring out into the gloom at the tall strange horse. Then something revealed to her the identity of the slumped figure thereon.

'Oh, Duncan! Duncan, my dear!' she cried, and came running, arms open, plaid quite forgotten. 'Thank God – oh, thank the good God!'

The newcomer tried to say Amen to that – but was not very sure that he managed it. He was not really very sure of anything, thereafter, save a great chatter of voices, including that of Scotus, strong arms reaching up to enfold him, lift him down, and then a glorious feeling of complete surrender, utter lack of any responsibility for whatever followed. That was bliss, beautitude. In an act of blessed relinquishment that was almost deliberate, he sank away, smiling.

CHAPTER 16

FROM a sort of hell to a very heaven – was ever a man translated so swiftly and completely? Duncan asked himself that question time and again, and always received approximately the same answer. It was pleasurable in itself, however, just to go on asking.

There will be flaws even in the celestial Heaven itself, no doubt – as here. Scotus was overmuch in evidence; Anne and Belle, though excellent children, and kind, were distinctly demanding; and his shoulder ached and ached. These, nevertheless, served only to highlight and emphasise his felicity. To lie on a couch of sweet-smelling heather, in the sun, with no activities, no decisions, required of him, nursed, succoured and cosseted, his every need ministered to by Caroline Cameron, the object of admiration, concern and devotion – what more could man desire? To bask, that was all that he had to do. Duncan bent his whole attention on the business.

No very great concentration and drive was demanded for this – for the man was aware of, indeed cherished, a certain lack of vigour, mental as well as physical. Caroline declared that he had a fever, and perhaps she was right. Certainly the cold-water pads which she kept placing on his brow were very pleasant – even though the tight bandaging and strapping with which she had bound up his shoulder were less so. And her insistence on him lying quite still and in one position was a little trying when his comfort was her avowed objective. But then women, however delightful, were inconsistent ever; was she not asking him questions innumerable, but checking her sisters from doing the same – and indeed telling him to be quiet and not talk when he tried to answer them?

'What harm is there in talking?' he wondered. 'A man cannot be speechless like a dumb animal.'

'You must rest,' she said.

'I am resting, whatever. And the sort of questions that I am asked here are no trouble to answer. Unlike some that I was asked elsewhere.'

'They questioned you? Sorely? They . . . they hurt you, Duncan? In the night, you were moaning and refusing . . . '

'Aye. They did. But not as sorely as they did to others. Camusbuie and Scirinish they killed. But, before they killed, they tortured. Savaged. To have them tell where the Prince might be. To betray him. And they did not speak. The money – they offered them that damnable thirty thousand pounds. Cumberland's reward. They spurned it. These men – I misjudged them.'

'They are dead?'

'Aye. They were men that I thought ill of. Men I believed to be next to traitors, God forgive me. Because of the gold *louis*. They shouted aloud for the French gold – these two amongst others. They would have squandered all the Prince's money. Yet this other money, this reward, they would have none of. They would suffer the pains of hell rather than betray their Prince for gold. Yet the Prince's own gold they coveted. They

186

would have betrayed him in that. Why? Why the difference? How can men act so?'

'I do not know, at all. But do not worry about it.' She laid a hand on his head. 'Do not fret yourself, Duncan. This is what I feared. You should not be talking . . .'

'I have learned that I do not understand men as well as I thought. Men are not always what they seem.'

'That I have learned my own self!' Caroline declared, smiling a little. 'Nor women either.' She bit her lip. 'Oh, Duncan – I . . . we were afraid for you. Terribly afraid. When you did not come back in two days, three days, we feared for your safety. Then your garron came back, on its own. And we feared you . . . dead! I did, at any rate. John had more faith, more confidence. He said that you would came back. He said . . . he said . . . ' Caroline's voice quivered. ' . . . that MacGregors could only be killed by hanging! For cattle-stealing . . . !'

John Scotus was John now! 'He may be right. I seem to have been stealing a deal of horseflesh, of late. But I am sorry that you were anxious for me, *a graidh*.' That was a lie if ever he told one.

'What did you expect?'

He did not answer that. 'Scotus would be a tower of strength to you, I have no doubt!' he said.

'He is very good,' she admitted. 'And cheerful. The girls love him.'

'And you?'

'I like him very well,' she said lightly, and wringing out a fresh cold-water pad, placed it on his brow. 'Now, hush,' she commanded.

Scotus himself, with the younger girls, arrived with the milk from the high corrie. He appeared to Duncan to be growing almost fat, a picture of rude health, well-being and smug self-satisfaction. He had something of the aspect of a family-man, which the other found quite insufferable. Obviously the life of the shieling agreed with him – *this* shieling, at all events.

'Milk for the MacGregor!' he cried. 'Saps for the sufferer! The pity that we have not a tender chicken. But we are going to catch a trout from the burnie for your dinner. Faith, we will make a man of you, yet!'

'Be quiet, John,' he was told. 'Duncan is resting. Put the milk in the cabin, out of the sun.'

'Yes, my dear.'

'John milked the cow today, himself. The black one.' Belle reported giggling. 'He squirted milk all over Anne and me!'

'Then he ought to be ashamed of himself. You all should.'

'Is Duncan better now? Can we ask him questions yet?' Anne demanded.

'I am better,' the invalid told her.

'Ask him how he got the gold from O'Rourke? And what he did with the body!' Scotus suggested.

'I buried it under a pile of stones, at the loch-side,' Duncan said. 'At a bay with a whitened tree-trunk.'

There was a sudden and shocked silence at that flat and factual statement. Even Scotus looked shaken.

'You killed him?' Anne whispered. 'That poor tired Irishman . . . ?'

'Anne!' Caroline blazed abruptly. 'Be quiet! Duncan would never do such a thing. How dare you!'

Startled, her sisters turned their stares on her.

'Not I – the Redcoats. A patrol, a picquet, met him, and shot him. I found the body.'

'For the gold?' Scotus exclaimed. 'They got the gold? And yet – you brought it back with you? In those kegs. They are down in the lochan now, with the rest. It *was* gold in them . . . ?'

'Gold and gunpowder mixed, I think. O'Rourke was clever – but not clever enough. He fooled the Redcoats – but only after they had killed him!'

'But how . . . ?'

Even Caroline forgot to halt the invalid's explanations thereafter – until he himself lay back, silent, tired. Then she was all contrition, miscalling herself, hustling the others away, ordaining absolute quiet, repose.

When, presently, she brought him a horn beaker filled with milk mildly laced with whisky, he did not protest as she raised his head gently and held it to his lips; nor did he spurn the stuff nor gulp it down with any unseemly haste thereafter when he found his head pillowed and supported on a warm, swelling, but firm and distinctly-divided bosom that stirred with a gentle rhythm – even with Scotus grinning at him from the cabin doorway. It was most satisfactory, too, when the MacDonnell and the girls went off down to the burn in the foot of the glen to guddle for trout, and Caroline refused to accompany them;

188

he found that he had been almost dreading her going. Not only for the lack of her presence; the vision of her long graceful legs splashing in the peat-brown pool, and Scotus watching . . . !'

Men can be bewitched and subverted by more than gold.

It was a pity that he fell asleep in the sun almost immediately thereafter, utterly wasting the occasion – and moreover dreaming of much less pleasant things.

Delectable days of sun and light and good company, of cheer and youthful spirits, of tenderness and regard – and of inner strains and stresses too, of course, of longings and questionings and doubts, of the touch of hands, the flash of an eye, sudden laughter, of the interplay of femininity and masculinity frank or covert. Two young men living close to three of the other sex – and even Belle not so much of a child as to be unaffected by the situation.

Nights too, in the dark windowless cabin, when sleep was by no means the foremost preoccupation in any mind, and an atmosphere almost electric in its tension could be generated without a word spoken, when a faint stir of movement, a deep breath drawn, even, from another unseen couch, could set all therein taut, rigid, waiting, or stirring and sighing in their turn. Secret waves that pulsed and eddied unuttered, yet vehement enough to cause a flush or a bitten lip or a slow quiet secret smile. Awareness, too, all the time, of the watching, brooding mountains all around.

Duncan mended apace, with a sound foundation of basic fitness to aid him. So long as he kept his left shoulder tightly strapped and unmoving, the pain was not too trying. Caroline, however, was urgent that he should be seen somehow by a medico as soon as possible; the collar-bone clearly required to be set properly. And the only medico available to a Jacobite in fifty miles and more undoubtedly was Doctor Archie Cameron.

The last word as to the whereabouts of Locheil's party had been brought by a pair of MacIan's men making south for Ardnamurchan, a day or two before. They declared that they had left the company at Tarbet, between Loch Morar and Loch Nevis, where they had made contact with Lord Lovat who was hiding in the area.

Could Duncan ride as far as Loch Nevis in his present condition? Caroline pronounced most definitely in the negative, whatever anyone else might say and despite her anxiety about the shoulder. But good kind John could go, perhaps, and fetch Doctor Archie here to Allt Ruadh?

Scotus saw difficulties. The Doctor might not be at Tarbet any more. He was a very important man, as well as brother to Locheil, with more to do than come scurrying half-way across the country for a broken bone. And the girls should not be left alone at the shieling with what amounted to a cripple to guard them.

It was Duncan's turn to smile. He pointed out, while remaining entirely uncommitted on the need for the doctor, that Scotus could always leave his bodyguard of three MacDonnell gillies behind him.

Satisfaction was only partial when this thorny problem solved itself by the mountain coming most of the way to Mahomet of its own accord. On the evening in question, and with the matter still undecided, Donald Cameron of Glenpean arrived in person at the shieling. Locheil's whole party was back in the Arkaig area, the Morar district having become too hot to hold them, word of Lovat's persence there seemingly having reached the authorities. The company, and Doctor Archie with it, was encamped for the time being in a small and hidden corrie up on the mountain behind Murlaggan, not ten miles away.

Great was the joy at the Allt Ruadh over Glenpean's arrival — and not only there but all over the uplands where his people were scattered. Quickly the news travelled, and soon clansfolk were coming straggling in. It could only be a brief visit, however. Matters were moving at last, it seemed, and there was the hope of action again. Lovat was bestirring himself. The Frasers could still field a thousand men. There was to be a full-scale council-of-war the next day. Lovat would be there. And Lochgarry. And Keppoch, nephew to the old chief who had died at Culloden. Even the survivors of Cromartie's brigade had been sent for from the northern Mackenzie country; Lovat's lieutenant-general's commission, long a source of heart-burning, could now prove its worth as an authority to issue orders to suchlike brigadiers and colonels. Duncan's own father, Glengyle, had been summoned along with MacLeod of Raasay.

Duncan was glad that he would be seeing his father – but unhappy that Lovat was moving into the centre of the stage. Lovat in any circumstances was a dangerous man, he said – not to be trusted; as leader, general, he could be the ultimate disaster.

The others, who had not met the Fraser chief, were less prejudiced.

Glenpean, sworn to secrecy, was told about the recovered gold – both consignments. He accepted and agreed with the young men's decision not to hand over the large hoard; he urged, indeed, that the same should apply to O'Rourke's lot. It was pointed out that this was only being surrendered in the interests of diverting suspicion.

Glenpean stayed the night at the cabin above the lochan, and next morning at sunrise set off back to Arkaig-side. Duncan and Scotus rode with him – and it required a determined parental veto to prevent Caroline from accompanying them, to watch over the invalid, put his case properly to the doctor, and generally assure herself that mere men did not ruin all her fine nursing. As well as O'Rourke's four kegs, dredged up from the lochan, they took with them garron-loads of smoked sides of venison and beef, sacks of oatmeal and other provisions, for the feeding of Locheil's party was a problem indeed.

Duncan rode, shaky but determined.

CHAPTER 17

ALTHOUGH the corrie on Sgor Murlaggan was less than ten miles away, they went by devious ways to give a wide berth to the new Government post in Glen Dessary, and slowly, for Duncan's sake. It was mid-forenoon before they reached their destination.

The place was well guarded, and they were challenged twice before attaining the corrie. It was an admirably chosen defensive position, as well as being suitably secret, with two emergency exits and plenty of wild country immediately behind it.

If the Allt Ruadh party expected their arrival to create even a mild sensation or stir, they were disappointed. The place was already astir with excitement, it seemed. The newcomers were scarcely noticed. MacShimi himself had but newly arrived, it appeared. Men had attention for none other.

This was scarcely to be wondered at. Lord Lovat was ever conspicuous, spectacular, in all that he did – and Lovat in the heather was something to be marvelled at indeed. He had adopted the fullest fig of chiefly Highland dress for the occasion, his great gross figure positively swathed in tartan, studded with silverware and jewellery, and hung with dirks, *sgian dubh*, pistols. He had come, over twenty miles and more of the roughest terrain, in an extraordinary and enormous litter, not slung between garrons but borne by no fewer than a score of running gillies, a thing shaped like a double-sized sedan-chair, with canopy, cushions, a table, containers for flagons and glasses, and even, as an ultimate refinements, a chamber-pot. MacShimi set a new standard in heather-skulking. He skulked too, with a hundred-man escort.

The Fraser dominated the camp by his very presence, irrespective of his lieutenant-general's commission. Sitting up in his litter like some vast grinning Buddha, gouty thick legs outstretched before him, all men must come to him. Beside his gross bulk, toadlike ugliness, hail-fellow bonhomie and sheer overpowering personality, even the noble Locheil seemed dull and ordinary, the tall swaggering Barrisdale a mere lanky posturer, and Young Clanranald a callow youth. As for Murray of Broughton, he might have been some humble if soured scribe in the great man's employ.

Having failed to see Locheil alone, or indeed away from Lovat's side, Duncan sought his brother, Doctor Archie Cameron, and spent a somewhat painful half-hour with him. After a deal of poking, probing and manipulation, the doctor expressed himself as ever wondering at the healing properties of nature as against the idiocies of men, admiring Caroline's ministrations insofar as they went, but highly critical of Duncan's own share in the business. He should have sent for him, not come riding here. He must keep the shoulder more tightly strapped, and so in position. He must not think that he could play ducks and drakes with a broken collar-bone without being permanently affected. Did he want to be a twisted object of pity with a withered arm for the rest of his days? He must return to Glen Pean forthwith and take care of himself. Move as little as possible for a month and more. Broken bones did not knit together in a few days. Some men were born fools, but others only reached their full folly in maturity. Etcetera.

Duncan MacGregor retired abashed.

The arrival of his father and young MacLeod of Raasay completed the company. They were weary, having travelled almost without stop for two days and nights, from far Kintail. They brought messages of support from the northern leaders – and to Locheil not to Lovat.

Duncan rejoiced to see his father. They were good friends. They had much to say to each other.

It was in the midst of confidences and questionings that the council-of-war was summoned – and it was Lovat who summoned it. Field officers only were to take part – that is, majors and above – and all others must keep their distance. Duncan, therefore, and Glenpean and Scotus and other captains, even Sawny MacLeod the Prince's aide, were excluded, much to their indignation.

The council was held round the Fraser chief's litter, and seemed to consist of a question-and-answer enquiry conducted by Lovat rather than any sort of debate. There were raised voices occasionally, protests, objections, but by and large Mac-Shimi maintained everything comfortably in his own hands. With bewildering changes from sweetest reasonableness and genial goodfellowship to savage irony, devastating wit and roaring intimidation, the aged and belated lieutenant-general who had stayed at home throughout the entire Rising took charge of all. Clearly he had made his decision before ever he had come to the meeting. Colonels of regiments, like Locheil, MacDonnell of Lochgarry, Stewart of Ardshiel, Barrisdale, Clanranald, Keppoch and Glengyle, stood or sat silent for the most part. Yet there were smiles, chuckles, too, and nods of agreement, for Lovat was shrewd and lacking nothing in intelligence. He played on practically every emotion represented before him. Undoubtedly he had studied human nature closely throughout a long and eventful life.

At least it was one of the briefest councils-of-war of the entire campaign – there was that to be said for it.

When it broke up for refreshment, Gregor MacGregor came stamping over to his son. 'As Royal's my Race,' he burst out, 'never have I known the likes of that! The man is beyond all belief – beyond all bearing, too! Does he take us for bairns, sucklings? *Dia* – that I should have ridden a hundred miles for this!'

'From here,' Scotus said, 'he seemed to be giving orders rather than taking counsel?'

'Aye, that was the way of it. MacShimi, the God-sent warrior! The Lord's own anointed!'

'What has been decided?' Glenpean asked. 'I care not who gives the orders so long as we fight, so long as we resume the campaign. Hit back at these women-fighters and house-burners and torturers. Is there action planned, Glengyle – united action, at last?'

'M'mmm. Something of the sort is implied, I think,' the giant MacGregor said grimly. 'If only as excuse for the other.'

'Other? What other do you mean?'

'The money. This gold that has come from France. The sharing out of the gold. That is Lovat's main concern, I think. And not only Lovat's!'

'But . . .'

'I might have known it!' Duncan exclaimed, bitterly 'I might have realised that it was the gold that accounted for Lovat's sudden concern for the Prince's cause! That only money would have brought him to the stage of drawing the sword at this late hour. Aye. How is it to be done? How is the rape to be legalised?'

'Each colonel is to declare how much money he requires to field his regiment's fullest available strength. Some will need more than others, he claims – the large more than the small . . .'

'The numberless Frasers more than any, no doubt!'

'That may well be. First requisitions are to be made up forthwith, and money will be paid out this very afternoon. I told him that my Gregorach did not require gold *louis* before they took the field for their Prince – but he told me not to be a fool, that any soldier is worthy of his hire . . .'

'Hirelings, now, does he make us, 'fore God!'

'What does Murray say to this?' Scotus asked. 'He was for keeping the money in his own hands.'

'He does not like it, that is certain. But he cannot stand up to Lovat. He will balk him if he can, no doubt.'

'But Murray is no more to be trusted with the Prince's

money than is Lovat! He would but have the distribution of it in his own fingers.'

'Is it so . . . ?'

'Enough of the damned money!' Glenpean interrupted. 'Forget it for a moment, if we can! I swear, we are all bewitched by it. What is it all for? This distribution? What are the regiments to be fielded for? What action do we take?'

'The plan is to assemble in Glen Mallie, as many men as can be raised,' Glengyle told him. 'When, was not decided, but as soon as practicable. Locheil's, Lochgarry's, Clanranald's and Barrisdale's Regiments to assemble there. Then to move across Lochy, to join up with Cluny's and Keppoch's, on the Lochaber-Badenoch border. At the same time, Cromartie's Brigade and my own Regiment, with others from the northern clans, to move down through Kintail and Glen Moriston, to link with Lovat's Frasers, then to come up with the others across the Corryarrack. The object is to cut off Inverness and the north-east from Fort William and the south – to cut the Highlands in two.'

'It is ambitious enough, whatever,' Glenpean admitted. 'Was this Lovat's devising?'

'In the main, yes.'

'He would thus have his own territory freed early on!' Scotus pointed out.

'No doubt,' the Cameron acceded. 'But let us not split hairs, so long as we have action at last. Lovat could raise three regiments, at least.'

That seemed to be the mood and reaction of most men in the corrie of Sgor Murlaggan.

The frugal meal over, the business of distributing largesse went forward forthwith. Lovat sat at his table in the litter, with barrels and kegs of gold all around, and Murray of Broughton at his side, pen in hand, paper before him, for all the world like some jovial Samaritan and his disapproving articled clerk. Before this pair chiefs and colonels and great lairds must queue up for their doles, as it were cap-in-hand. Not all relished the procedure, obviously – but to stand out, to refuse altogether to take part, would be a costly gesture indeed when others were obtaining large sums. After all, every commander had been dipping his hand deep into his own pocket for months. This was no more than their due, was it not?

Although the Mackinnon chief was first in the line, by the merest accident, and after much clearing of throat and humming and hawing decided that he needed fifty gold pieces — and was allotted forty — it was Barrisdale who came next and who set the tone and standard of the proceedings by demanding a cool and neat one thousand. Even Lovat looked staggered and at a loss for words at this, and Murray gobbled like a choking turkey. Unabashed the MacDonnell repeated his claim.

'My God!' Murray got out. 'This is fantastic, absurd! You are asking for a fortune, man!'

'I am asking for what is required to put my men once more into the field. Modest enough, in all conscience, I swear.'

'Perhaps the good Barrisdale will let us have details?' Lovat suggested, recovering his breath. 'Some indication as to how he arrives at this sum?'

'Certainly. Two hundred and fifty guineas for immediate payment of the men, re-equipping, horses and provisioning. Fifty to defray debts that the regiment has unavoidably run up in Strathcarron in these last weeks. And seven hundred arrears of pay for four months.'

'Ah! Umm. But I would point out, sir, that arrears of pay are not being dealt with at this time,' Lovat said smoothly. 'Only requisitions absolutely necessary for putting the men into the field. The rest must wait.'

'In the Fiend's name — why? The money is there, enough for all. The arrears paid, the men will but fight the better.'

'That may be so, friend — though do MacDonnells fight but for money? Nevertheless, we have to abide by what the council decided — that this payment is concerned only . . . '

'What *you* decided, Lovat! You, who have no arrears to pay whatever! You who stayed at home . . . '

'Mother of God — d'you speak to MacShimi so!' the Fraser roared, smashing fist on table and setting the stacks of gold coins a dance.

'Aye — and to any who would cheat me of what should be mine!'

'Gentlemen!' Locheil exclaimed. 'This is unworthy . . . '

'And nothing is yours, Barrisdale,' Murray declared, thin-voiced. 'All is His Highness's. To be used to best purpose in his cause ...'

'And let him remember that himself, the same Murray!' Duncan commented.

'Aye – but there is point in what Barrisdale says,' Scotus, his cousin and fellow-clansman asserted. 'Arrears of pay do not interest Lovat, for obvious reasons. That old fox looks after himself.'

'Of course he does. So do they all, it seems.'

Glengyle cleared his throat. 'In a situation such as this, a man must pay some heed to the requirements of his own men, his regiment,' he said.

Duncan looked at his father sharply. 'Aye,' he said.

Lovat was whispering to Murray. He managed a smile again, as he looked up. 'Barrisdale,' he said, 'I will forget what you said in the heat of the moment. We cannot go beyond the decisions of the council, however. Arrears of pay will have to be dealt with separately. On another occasion. The two hundred and fifty and the fifty guineas we shall accept, meantime. Mr. Secretary will count out three hundred for you.'

Murray scornfully jerked his head at an underling, who could perform such menial tasks, and held out a paper for Barrisdale to sign.

With a flourish, but without change of expression, that man appended his signature. 'You will hear more from me, my friends,' he said, and gestured for one of his people to collect the gold.

'Who is next?' Lovat wondered. 'Ah – Ardshiel.'

The lieutenant-colonel of the Appin Stewart Regiment hesitated. With the example of Barrisdale before him, he might well have been rapidly readjusting his requisition. 'My regiment is not so large as Barrisdale's ... now!' he said. 'Because we lost a deal more men at Culloden Moor! By that very token, I need more money. More to bring in and equip new men. To arm and victual them ...'

'No doubt, Ardshiel,' Lovat interrupted. 'I commend your fervour. But that is for later. Just now we are concerned with only an immediate muster. It is the costs of that only that we seek to defray, meantime.'

'Two hundred guineas, then,' the Stewart said abruptly.

'I suggest that you might find one hundred sufficient for the moment, Ardshiel? Indeed, I do. Mr. Secretary – one hundred? Very good. One hundred for the Laird of Ardshiel. Lochgarry – are you next?'

Sitting watching, Duncan MacGregor could not contain himself. 'This is beyond all belief!' he exclaimed. 'Hucksters and pedlars at a fair, I swear, could show more dignity! The best blood of Scotland lining up like beggars before that, that basilisk! Bargaining for as much as they can get of their Prince's money. Bah – it turns my stomach!' He gripped Glengyle's arm. 'You? You are not going to touch any of it?' he demanded.

His father tugged at his still-blond beard. 'Well, now,' he said.

Duncan swallowed. 'You would not consider it? His Highness's money? You?'

'Och now, lad – not so fast.' Gregor MacGregor's frank and open countenance was troubled in most unaccustomed fashion. 'I do not see it quite so. It is not the Prince's private fortune, at all. It was sent, was it not, by the French king, for the furtherance of the true cause . . . '

'But not to go into the sporrans and pouches of the Prince's officers! It was for an army in action.'

'Aye. But to get that army into action again will take money . . . '

'If the gold had not come? If not one penny of it had arrived from France, but just guns and ammunition – would the army not have re-assembled? Given the call. Would any regiment have refused to march? Would the Gregorach? Would a single clansman lay down his sword and say that he would not fight?'

The older man shifted his great frame on the barrelful of gold on which he sat. 'Maybe not, Duncan. But the money *is* here. These others are taking it. If the MacDonnells and the Stewarts and the rest get extra money, extra food, gear – will not our MacGregors desire the same? And rightly. The men have earned it better than some of these . . . '

'The men!' his son said scornfully. 'How much of it all will the men get? How much, think you, of Barrisdale's three hundred *louis d'ors* will his MacDonnells glimpse? Since when have clansmen followed their chiefs for money? *Dia* – most chiefs have never seen fifty gold pieces in all their lives!'

Glengyle shrugged. 'I am not Barrisdale,' he said. 'My

people need clothing, garrons. Most of them are barefoot. Would you have me fail them, in this?'

'Fail *them*? See you.' Duncan leaned forward and dropped his voice a little, subconsciously. 'If you must take the money, give it to me, afterwards. To take away and put with the rest. To keep it safe for the Prince. That little more, at any rate.'

His father looked at him blankly, saying nothing.

Slowly, awkwardly, the younger man got to his feet. His shoulder, after all Doctor Archie's attentions, hurt him damnably. 'Then . . . I am going. I shall not stay to watch you shame your own self and the name of MacGregor!' he said, voice trembling. 'I have seen enough, this day . . . !'

'Son!' Glengyle rose up in his turn. 'Here is no way to speak. You are sick – beside yourself . . .'

'May be. But not because of a broken shoulder! I am going back – back to the shieling. And taking back what I brought.'

It was Scotus's turn to start up. 'You mean . . . ? The money? O'Rourke's gold?'

'Yes. It goes back. They have enough here to squander, in all conscience! Thirty-five thousand gold *louis* should be enough, surely – even for this highly priced company!'

'But . . . Locheil? You were going to give it to Locheil.'

'Only to divert suspicion from the rest. But Locheil has been too much taken up with Lovat even to notice that I am here. None know that we have this gold, none are thinking of it. None know that it is here, save you three.' Duncan looked away towards the distant skyline. 'Unless my father feels so strongly . . . that it should go into the general pool . . . that there may be the more to distribute? And tells Lovat!'

Glengyle drew a sharp breath – and then closed his lips tightly.

Duncan turned his back abruptly. 'Do you come with me, Scotus – or no?' he asked.

'Och, wait you, MacGregor. There is no hurry, man,' the MacDonnell declared. 'Here are friends a-many. Many to speak with. We have much to learn . . .'

'I have learned enough, I think. You wait. I go.' And without another word to any of them, he stalked stiffly off towards the horses.

Glenpean half-started after him, but Gregor MacGregor held him back. 'Let him be – let the boy be,' he said, deep-voiced. 'I know him. Let him alone. But . . . God go with him . . . and God pity us both!'

It was quite some way on the road back to the Allt Ruadh shieling before Duncan MacGregor gave voice to his own prayer. Suddenly, to the empty heather hillside in front of him he shouted it aloud.

'God's curse on this damnable gold! Curse, curse, curse it!' And he beat his good fist on his knee.

CHAPTER 18

'YOU were right – right, I tell you. It is evil! Once you said that it was, and I laughed at you. I said that there was nothing wrong with the gold – only the foolishness of men. But you spoke truth. It is evil, devilish! Would to God that it had never come amongst us! It has corrupted us all. All. Aye, myself with the rest. I think gold, dream gold! I said unforgivable things to my own father . . . '

'Hush you, hush you, Duncan *a graidh*,' Caroline besought him. 'You are ill, in pain – not yourself. Forget it all, just now . . . '

'How can I forget it? It is there – the evil, the folly, the corruption. Can I forget what I said to my father? Or what he did? What they all are doing? Not only adventurers like Barrisdale and James Mor, but good men. Ardshiel, Mackinnon, Clanranald – even Locheil. These were heroes but a few short weeks ago. Now what are they? Lickpennies! Merchants, trading men for money! Defeat and gold unlimited have been too much for them.'

'It may be so – I do not know.' The young woman shook her head unhappily.

It was very late, fully two hours after midnight. Duncan had arrived back at the shieling alone, in a state of near-collapse. The double journey, in his present state, had been too much for him. Now he lay in a corner of the dark cabin, propped against Caroline's shoulder, while she pressed food and drink on him,

200

and her sisters peered, wide-eyed in the gloom, from their bunks.

'I brought back the money,' he went on. 'O'Rourke's money. I could not give it to Locheil. Just more to be grasped at by the others . . .'

'Yes, yes. You know best, Duncan. But eat this, now. All that can wait. It is my fault. I should never have let you go. You were not fit to go . . .'

'Scotus stayed. Spanish John – that is what they call him, there – would not come. He said that there was no hurry.'

'Perhaps he was right. Since you had gone, you should not have come away. So soon. It was foolish of you, Duncan. But sip this. It is milk and whisky. It will help you.'

'I had to come. I could not stay there. The place was choking me! All those men . . . men I have fought with . . . my leaders and comrades . . . accusing each other, outdoing each other, hating each other! And myself also. For dirty, filthy money. When I thought of the Prince. And all who had died for him – at Prestonpans and Carlisle and Falkirk and Culloden! Aye, and Camusbuie and Scrinish, there, at Clunes . . .'

'Och, Duncan lad – do not distress yourself so.'

'I had to come away, Caroline. To come here. Here is the only place where there is sanity. Here with you. I had to come.'

She made no comment to that.

'You see, don't you? You understand?'

'Och, och – quiet now! Hush, you. There, now. You are feverish again, I do believe. Do not talk, *mo charaid*.' Like a child, the girl gentled him, humoured him. 'Just lie there. Lay your head here, against me. Close your eyes, Duncan. Rest, now.' She began to stroke his hair, lightly, slowly, rhythmically, and presently she was crooning a soft lullaby, without words, without beginning or end, repetitive, calm, inevitable as the tide on a long strand.

Slowly the tension went out of Duncan MacGregor, his breathing deepened, and quite suddenly he slept. Anne and Belle slept too, and Luath the hound, lying across the doorway, chittered and shuddered audibly in her half-sleep, to a night-bird's cry. Caroline's eyes remained open for long.

It was thus that Scotus found them, as the dawn reddened the sky to the east, having ridden, with his gillies, through the night. The young woman wakened swiftly, completely, silently, and raised a finger to her lips before pointing it downwards. She breathed a hush to the low-rumbling dog.

Spanish John, gazing in, grimaced and shook his fair head. 'You never did as much for me, lady,' he complained in a conspiratorial whisper. 'What must *I* do to spend the night on your delectable bosom?'

She smiled at him, and said nothing. But she pointed again, to where the food and drink lay near her.

As the man tip-toed elaborately past, his hand went down to touch her shoulder lightly, to slip up the long column of her neck, behind her ear, and over her hair.

She smiled again, warmly, luminously, but did not otherwise move her lips. Nor her person, cramped as it was.

Scotus went to the heap of skins that constituted his bed near by, and sat, munching bannocks and watching her. Once she turned her head slowly towards him, and their eyes met. The next time that she looked, he too had fallen asleep, head sunk down between his knees.

The girl watched the sunrise, alone.

It was almost mid-forenoon before the little company were up and about that morning – and Duncan, even so, was only out and not about, on Caroline's sternest orders; the fine spell of weather continued, and he was permitted to sit out in the sunshine. Scotus had had a word or two with Doctor Archie, it seemed, and brought back instructions, which, when transmitted to the young woman, made of the MacGregor an invalid indeed, under strictest supervision. Whether Scotus for his own purposes, exaggerated or not, Caroline took doctor's orders entirely seriously.

Scotus brought back with him more tidings than these. There had been a council within a council, it seemed, secretly held the previous afternoon, at Murlaggan. Convened by Murray of Broughton himself, with Lord Lovat not invited. Present had been Locheil, Doctor Archie, Clanranald, Glengyle, Sawny MacLeod, Sir Stewart Thriepland and Major Kennedy. Murray had been highly concerned about the way the money was going. Lovat, undoubtedly, using his lieutenant-generalship, would take complete charge of all the remaining gold – if he was allowed to. Somehow they must prevent that – or they might see none of it again. That had been agreed, and it was decided that a goodly portion of what remained should be securely hidden somewhere that same night. Fully half of it, for preference.

'And what did remain, after yesterday's work?' Duncan demanded from his seat in the heather amongst the urgent bees.

Something over four thousand *louis d'ors* had been disbursed, he was told – which should have left approximately thirty thousand. Anyway, a small group, consisting of Doctor Archie, MacLeod, Thriepland and Kennedy – who was close to Murray – secretly left the camp after dark, with fifteen thousand gold pieces. Scotus grinned.

'I thought that it was perhaps my duty, as well as conveniently on my way back here, to follow them! Not too obviously of course!'

He could not complain of lack of attention on the part of his listeners.

'They rode right round the head of the loch and down the south side. About three miles down, just beyond the mouth of Glen Camgarry. There, almost opposite Callich on the north shore, they left three parcels, each of five thousand gold pieces, one thousand to a bag. One parcel they hid under a rock in the mouth of a burn, and the other two in holes dug in the ground near by. I saw it all. I marked the place well, in my mind.'

Duncan nodded in approval. 'Fifteen thousand. This is better news than I had hoped for. Murray, I swear, will not intend to leave it there for the Prince – even though the others do. Still, it is safe for the moment.'

Scotus grimaced. 'Except that, I am afraid, others beside myself thought of following the four good gentlemen! Twice I glimpsed others dodging and hiding. It is not impossible that others glimpsed me, likewise.'

'*Dia* – that is bad! So others know where this gold is hidden, also?'

'It seems likely.'

'You do not know who they were? These others?'

'No. In the dusk . . .'

'They could have been Lovat's men! Barrisdale's! Anybody . . .'

'They could, yes.'

'What do you intend to do?' Caroline asked. 'What *can* you do?'

'Two things we can do,' Duncan said. 'We can set a watch on the place, day and night. Or we can take it ourselves – dig up the gold and bring it here, to safety. To put it with what we have already.'

Curiously, this second suggestion seemed to shock his hearers, however logical a development it might be of existing policy.

'I' faith man, we can't do that!' Scotus protested. 'There is a limit, whatever. That would make us almost as bad as these others . . .'

'No, no, Duncan – not that!' Caroline cried. 'How can you think of it! It would be shameful!'

'What difference – five thousand or fifteen? What matters it who removes the gold, and to where – so long as we hold it safe for its true owner, the Prince? It is only what we have been doing already, on a larger scale.'

'No – this is different,' Scotus insisted. 'Taking it from Doctor Archie and these others. *They* have not stolen it.'

'Nor do we. But . . . there is this, that if we take it, when the loss is discovered, a great search will be put in hand, a great outcry will arise. And you may have been recognised, Scotus, by those others who followed. That might undo all – bring everyone down on us. No – it had better be the watch, day and night.'

'But . . . how can we do that? Only the two of us?'

'We can do it. With your gillies, and some of the Camerons here. We can do it. We must.'

'It will be a weary, taxing business.'

'No doubt.'

'I will help,' Caroline said.

'And I,' Anne put in – and her sister, of course.

'But for how long, MacGregor? We cannot spend the rest of our days on the shores of Loch Arkaig, watching!'

'Until the Prince comes back – or we receive his instructions. Did you hear any word of him, at Murlaggan?'

'Only that he is being chased all over the Long Island. By sailors from the naval ships. That is why the French frigates would win into Loch Nan Uamh so easily. He would like to make for Skye, it is said.'

'Skye? If that is so, then he is for working back. Back towards the mainland. That he should never have left. We may not have so long to wait.'

'We have no proof of that. It is only hearsay . . . ' Scotus shrugged. 'But, this watch. Allowing that we do set it up – what then? A watch, of one man or two, could not prevent an armed party from making off with the gold.'

'That is why there should be two men, if possible. One to follow the raiders, and one to bring us word.'

'But it is seven or eight miles from here, at least. By the time that word reaches us, where will the raiders be, man?'

'We must do what we can . . . '

'Signals,' Caroline suggested. 'With smoke. Smoke by day and fire by night. We could see that, from here.'

'To be sure. That will help.' Duncan nodded. 'It would save much time. A signal from the top of yonder small hill.' He pointed, screwing up his eyes into the south-easterly sunlight. 'That is at the mouth of Glen Camgarry.'

'Even so – what then?' Scotus went on. 'If we catch the robbers? If it is a large party, we cannot hope to master them.'

'No one intending to steal gold will take a large party to do it,' Duncan asserted. 'Secrecy would be their aim.'

'But equally it must be ours. If we fight them for the money, our own identity will be known. Unless . . . it is intended that we silence them for ever!'

'No! God forbid!' Caroline exclaimed.

Duncan rubbed his chin, at a loss.

'Masks!' Anne cried. 'Masks. Like the outlaws wore, of old! The MacGregors would wear masks, I am sure, when they were being outlaws? I shall make you masks. Then none shall know you!'

'The MacGregors had no need of masks!' Spanish John hooted. 'Their deeds were enough to identify them! But it is a notion, I grant you.'

'Tartans that could not be recognised,' Caroline added. 'Stained in peat-broth.'

'That would serve,' Duncan agreed. 'We can only do what we may . . . '

'And you,' the young woman pointed out determinedly, 'are going to do none of it! Except to give advice, perhaps. For a very long time to come. That I promise you.'

'That remains to be seen,' her patient returned, but with no great sense of conviction.

CHAPTER 19

CAROLINE enlisted eight of her father's people, and with Scotus and his gillies to make up the dozen, the watch was commenced. That she trusted her clansfolk entirely, as Scotus trusted his men, was not extraordinary. It was not from such quarters that the Prince's gold was endangered. To the ordinary Highland folk, the people of the glens, gold was too remote and exotic a commodity to offer any real temptation. None would have known what to do with a single gold piece, much less a barrelful. Coin of any sort they would seldom see. It was their betters whom the gold could corrupt. O'Rourke, an Irish mercenary, had been in quite a different category.

The watch was established, in pairs, in a specially-prepared hide close to where the gold was cached. This was simplified by the terrain, which was very rough and broken, selected for just that reason. A code of signals was arranged, and fires laid.

Their trap made a catch only the second night that it was set. Barely had Scotus arrived back at the shieling after a spell of duty at the lochside, with the darkness, when a pinpoint of red light, gleaming far down the glen, raised the alarm. Cursing, he donned black-stained kilt and plaid again, whilst Caroline put the warning system into operation to assemble the others – Duncan cursing even more vehemently that he was not permitted to ride with the party. In only a short time seven men set out, both looking and feeling highly theatrical in their masks – to the great excitement of Anne and Belle, who equally with Duncan had to be restrained from accompanying them.

It was almost dawn before the group got back, triumphant. Three riders, at nightfall, had raided one of the buried hoards at the loch-shore. When they had moved off, one of the watchers had followed them, and the other, after noting the direction taken, had hurried to climb the little hill and light the beacon. He had been waiting for Scotus's party when it reached the scene.

The raiders had gone south-westwards up Glen Camgarry, and as arranged, the other watcher had left signs behind him as to the route taken – an arrow scored here, a new-broken branch there, three stones to form a tiny cairn elsewhere. Since, all unsuspecting, their quarry had held to the track up the glen of Camgarry, it had all been ridiculously easy. The pursuers had come up with their scout in a couple of hours riding, waiting to tell them that the trio were camped for the night just directly ahead. The rest had been simplicity itself. The nine of them had crept up on the sleeping marauders, who had not even troubled to set a sentry. There had not been so much as a struggle. The culprits had proved to be MacDonald of Suiladale, one of Clanranald's lesser lairds, and two of his gillies. Scotus, seeking to disguise his voice, had berated and upbraided them, in the name of the Prince, Locheil, even Murray. He had confiscated the money – which turned out to be a mere fifty *louis* – and sent the alarmed MacDonald off with the warning that if he ever came back for more, or so much as breathed the whereabouts of the hiding-place to others, his life would be short indeed.

They had been nearer to Glen Pean than Loch Arkaig by this time, so they had come straight back here. They could replace the fifty gold pieces the following day.

Why do any such thing, Duncan demanded? Add it to their own store in the lochan, rather, where it would be safe from such gentry. With the other site known, and being raided, it would be folly, and a waste of time, to replace it.

Five thousand seven hundred and fifty gold *louis*.

The next addition to their accumulation came from an unexpected quarter. Glenpean, with a part of his company, came briefly to the shieling one night, urgently requiring forty of his cattle-beasts, for the use of the regiments presently assembling at Glen Mallie for the projected action. Late as it was, all hands were set to the task of rounding up the animals scattered wide over the high night-bound pastures. It was after her father and the beasts were gone that Caroline Cameron came to Duncan who had been left alone at the cabin, breathless and upset. She all but threw a small leather bag at him.

'There!' she cried. 'Take it! More of your gold – your horrible accursed gold! Take it. Add it to our hoard.'

The now so well-known chink of coins came from the bag, as the man held it in his hand.

'Where did you get this?' he asked, astonished.

'From my father. My own father – Heaven forgive him! Whom I would have sworn would never have touched it!'

'But ... but ... ?'

'He gave it to me, to keep for him. He took it, as payment for the cattle.'

'But that is different, Caroline – that is but honest dealing . . .'

'It is not. Do not you make excuses for him! Before this, he *gave* his beasts. He does not ask money for his men, does he, from the Prince? Must he now have it for his cattle? And even so, a golden guinea for each beast! That is what he has taken. Thirteen pounds Scots each! Oh, it is shameful!'

'M'mmm. I think that you are too hard on your father, *a graidh*. It is a good price, admittedly – but the times are hard . . .'

'Is that any reason for robbing his Prince? The sorrow of it, he says that Doctor Archie has done the same. Sold another forty at the same price. I . . . I told him, the more shame on Locheil's brother, then! I had thought better of them both.'

'Och, but this is not the same at all, lassie. I cannot take this money. To put with the rest. This belongs to your father . . .'

'You will take it! You must. Or don't you ever speak to me again about the Prince's money! It goes with the rest. I told my father so. But . . . do not tell my sisters, Duncan. Please.'

Two days later there was another attempt on the lochside cache. Scotus and a companion had just arrived there, to take over a spell of the tiresome duty, and the pair whom they had relieved were about to depart, when, in the opposite direction they spotted a single man coming up the shore, on foot. That he came furtively, secretly, though in broad daylight, was evident in every line and movement of him – a Highlander with a single feather in his bonnet. He kept to the cover of the trees whenever possible, and every now and again he gazed behind him.

The four watchers waited, slipping on their masks.

At the hiding-place area, the newcomer, whom Scotus recognised at Lieutenant Rory Cameron, brother to Camusbuie who had suffered and died at Clunes, began to line up landmarks and pace out distances, before eventually pinpointing and commencing to uncover the same buried and hidden third of the cache which had already been raided by MacDonald of Suiladale.

Scotus and his men descended upon him then.

The Cameron, startled, had his pistol half-drawn before he perceived that Scotus had his own already levelled at him. Snarling like any cornered wildcat, he crouched at bay.

At a loss to know what else to do with him, the MacDonnell treated the man to the same homily and threats that he had given Suiladale. The Cameron protested to highest heaven that he had only been going to take two or three guineas, money that was owing to him for garrons that he had handed over to the regiment. Nothing more. Scotus, treating that with the contempt it deserved, repeated the warning about any second attempt or any revelation of the secret to others – and let him go. What else could he do?

Later, Duncan marvelled that he had seen the same Rory Cameron, on the battlefield of Falkirk, go out alone under fire to carry back on his broad shoulders, three times, badly wounded men.

It was decided, at a conference at the shieling, that short of removing all the gold at the lochside to their own store, as Duncan had first suggested, they should take up the buried parcels – not only the one which had been raided but the other also – and put them beside the third consignment in the stream close by, which did not seem to have been discovered. That this would much bewilder those who had deposited it all, when they came to uplift it, could not be helped.

The following night the transference of the buried gold to the adjoining burn was effected – save for one bag of a thousand *louis* which Scotus, with a certain amount of embarrassment and much explanation, brough back with him to the Allt Ruadh. It all just would not go into the said pool without showing, he reported. They had tried every way. And one bag showing might give away all. Rather than hide it somewhere else near by, where it might eventually be overlooked, he thought it wise to bring it back here to add to their own lot.

Duncan MacGregor smiled to himself.

This distinctly unhealthy preoccupation with the gold was upset in salutory fashion the following evening. One of Clanranald's captains, who had been left for liaison with Locheil, brought them grievous news, at Glenpean's request, as he hastened back to Moidart to warn his chief. The assembly in Glen Mallie was no more, broken up, dispersed and abandoned. They had been betrayed. It could only have been treachery. Of the four regiments to muster there, only about six hundred men had so far arrived, most of them Camerons, naturally – when down upon them descended the Earl of

Loudon himself with a large force – three regiments of dragoons, one of hussars and two of his own Campbell militia. He had come directly to Glen Mallie. Locheil had had barely an hour's warning. Disorganised and unready as they were, the Jacobites dared not wait to face a disciplined force four times as large. The order to scatter had been given. Locheil, unfit for fast riding, with Murray and Thriepland, had only escaped by taking a boat across Loch Arkaig. Where they were now, heaven alone knew.

Appalled, the little group at the shieling listened. Here was an end to hopes indeed.

'And . . . our father?' Caroline managed to get out. 'Glenpean? What of him?'

'Most of the Camerons fled southwards. Making for Glenfinnan and the head of Loch Shiel – those who could travel fast. I was sent to warn my chief, Clanranald, who is gathering men in Moidart. I need a fresh horse . . .'

'Yes, yes,' Scotus interrupted. 'But you spoke of betrayal, treachery? Who so base . . . ?'

'Well may you ask! We do not know – we have no proof. But we suspect – aye, indeed we do. Suspect friends of your own, gentlemen!'

'Eh . . . ?'

'What do you mean, man?'

'Barrisdale and James Mor MacGregor left the camp the night before.'

'But this is ridiculous! Barrisdale would not do such a thing.'

'Somebody did. Mallie is a secret and secure glen. And long. Ten miles of it. Thickly wooded. Yet Loudon's brigade came directly for the spot where we were gathered.'

'An enemy scout may have spotted them,' Scotus said. 'Or someone else betrayed them. His own men were there – Barrisdale's Regiment was one of those assembling in Glen Mallie.'

'Aye. One hundred and fifty of them. Even so, he left. And in anger . . .'

'It is nonsense. Ignorant and malicious talk.'

'James Mor is no friend of mine, cousin though he be,' Duncan added. 'But I do not believe that he would be a party to betrayal. Outright treachery. Never that.'

The other shrugged. 'Yet they have been behaving strangely for some time. They were suspicious of all, seeming to bear a grudge against all. Especially against Lovat and Murray. It was the money, I think . . .'

'Aye – the damnable money! Always it is the gold,' Duncan grated.

'And what *about* the gold?' Scotus asked. 'The rest of it. Where is it now? Who has it?'

'Only God knows! Murray took some with him – but fleeing in a small boat, he could not take more than a few bags. Lovat had taken some, of course, when he left for his own country some days before. Not as much as he would have wished, I swear! Barrisdale himself got another two hundred, the day that he left – two days ago. For arrears. He wanted a deal more than that. That was why he left in anger . . .'

'Aye – but the rest? There must still be many thousands . . . ?'

'Doctor Archie and Sawny MacLeod have it hidden at the foot of Arkaig. Somewhere by the loch-shore – just where, none but themselves know. I saw them carrying the bags on their shoulders like gillies. As well that it was the Doctor. None other would have been trusted with it – save Locheil himself.'

Duncan and Scotus exchanged glances.

'How much is hidden there?' the latter enquired.

'I do not know. Ten bags? A dozen? I do not know. I had more to do than count.'

'So-o-o! The good Doctor and Captain MacLeod can lay their hands on the major part of the French money! If I add it aright, nearly thirty thousand . . .'

Frowning, Duncan was hurriedly going to interrupt him when Caroline forestalled him.

'Oh, enough of the wretched money!' she cried. 'Can no one think of anything else? Gold pieces, guineas, *louis d'ors* – that is all that you ever think of! What of the greater things? What of the men? Men's lives? What of the Prince's cause? Is all lost?'

There was a moment or two of silence and discomfort. Then the MacDonald shook his head. 'There was no time to make plans,' he said. 'Locheil said something about trying to win over into the Fraser country, where the northern regiments were to come to join Lovat. Then, again, over to Badenoch, to link up with Cluny and his Macphersons.' He shrugged. 'That is all but hopes. And if Loudon has been told so much, no doubt he will have been told this also.'

None protested that anything of the sort was unthinkable.

The MacDonald, refreshed, exchanged his garron for one of Caroline's, and rode on through the night to warn Clanranald. Going, he left it as his considered opinion that, in view of Lord Loudon's new close proximity, his young hosts would be wise to evacuate the shieling and move elsewhere.

Those he left behind debated that, and the rest that they had been told, far into the night.

Two conclusions they came to, before they slept. One was that they probably were as well where they were as anywhere else that they could go. This high and inaccessible watershed area, on the direct route to nowhere in particular, was never likely to suffer the intensive attentions of conventional troops; it might well be that they would be safer here, less likely to be disturbed, now that the Glen Mallie concentration was dispersed and the pressure relieved in the area. And secondly, that there was nothing that the young men could more usefully do, in the circumstances, than guard and protect the Cameron girls and keep an eye on the two consignments of treasure.

Who would blame them?

CHAPTER 20

So commenced an interlude that seemed almost to belong to another existence altogether, a different life – at least for the two young captains; a period in which time itself seemed to stand still, war and politics and dynastic struggles withdrew to become at first distant, then quite remote, and finally almost unreal, illusory; a period in which even the gold seemed to lose much of its fatal spell over men – viewed from the high watershed above Glen Pean, at any rate. It was a strange and relaxed interlude, with small and personal matters looming so much larger, more important, than matters national. The serene untroubled mountains, omnipresent yet detached as the drifting cloud-shadows that slid lightly, unendingly, across their noble brows, the all-penetrating, all-infusive light of great skies, the long sun-filled days and brief northern nights when darkness barely touched this high world, the scents and sights and sounds of high summer on the very roof of Scotland – all this, given time, could not fail to work its own peaceable balm of spirit and easement of soul, as well as health of body.

Time it was given, as days lengthened into weeks and, imperceptibly, weeks into months. Though time indeed seemed no longer to matter, in a little while, up amongst the shielings. For Duncan MacGregor, at least, almost the only gauge of time was the slow knitting and healing of his broken shoulder. Burgeoning May passed into scented exultant June, and June into maturely smiling July of the bell-heather.

This idyllic existence was no idle one, however, even for the strictly nursed invalid. Although there was little of hurry or urgency about the tasks to be performed, the life held its own rhythmic round of duties. The basic provision of food and drink and fuel was a daily and unending preoccupation. The cattle had to be herded – and none must be allowed to stray over those faces of the hills which might be viewed, even through tele-scopes, from the low ground of the Arkaig valley and Glen Dessary. Hunting was almost as essential and everyday a pro-ceeding. The digging and dying of bog-pine roots, searching for wild bees' nests for honey, gathering edible fungus, guddling for trout, and seeking for the eggs of plover, curlew and grouse, took up a lot of time, however pleasantly. The curing of hides and the smoking of meat, the fashioning of implements and simple furnishings, were wet weather activities. Secret visits down to ravaged homesteads for items that might be salvaged or adapted, were frequent. Also the watch down at the hidden lochside gold was maintained, although less intensively as time went on and no further raids eventuated – until by mid-July it was only a matter of the gillies taking twenty-four-hour shifts, and one at a time, with Scotus, and presently Duncan also, paying occasional visits.

With the dispersal of the Glen Mallie muster the war mean-time seemed very largely to have receded and left this corner of the Highlands. The enemy was not far away; there was the post in Glen Dessary, only six or seven miles off, and another at Callich across Arkaig from where the treasure was hidden. But these were occupied now by garrison-type soldiers, static troops, not first-rank units like dragoons and hussars – infantry indeed, mainly scratch militia levies of older men dredged up for ser-vice, the scraplings of King George's barrel, with no enthusiasm for climbing hills, bog-hopping or seeking out nimbler adversaries than themselves in God-forsaken secret places.

Word of the doings of Lord Loudon's more active minions came to the ears of the people of the shielings occasionally – of murder and rapine and arson in Clanranald's Moidart and Arisaig, and Glengarry's Knoydart, to set Scotus fearing for his own home, far out on its Atlantic peninsula as it was. Then, one day in mid-June, the war seemed suddenly to come close again.

They were all working on the new extension to the Allt Ruadh cabin, the two men less than enthusiastically – for this was a separate apartment which Caroline, probably wisely, was insisting upon for the accommodation of her guests and the three MacDonnell gillies, and for which neither Duncan nor Scotus could see the slightest need – when two of the Camerons brought to them an exhausted and frightened fugitive whom they had found hiding in the heather not far away. He had bolted when discovered and had been caught only with difficulty – although he claimed to be a Fraser and a fellow-combatant.

'You are far from Fraser country,' Duncan charged him. 'And your clan has scarcely been eager for combat! Why did you run from these Camerons?'

'I was afraid,' the other, a small foxy, darting-eyed fellow, told them frankly. 'To one man in the heather, all others are enemies, whatever.'

'There speaks an evil conscience, I'll be bound!' Scotus declared. 'As well it might – for I would not trust one of your name, from MacShimi downwards!'

The little man drew himself up with an access of unexpected dignity. 'MacShimi – the great MacShimi,' he said sadly, simply. 'God rest the soul of him.'

They stared at him. 'What do you mean by that?' Duncan demanded.

'He is not . . . not dead?' Spanish John said.

'If he is not, then he is as good as dead,' the Fraser asserted heavily. 'Himself is taken. Captured by the Redcoats. Even now they are carrying him off to London to his death.'

'*Dia!* Lovat . . . Lovat captured!' Duncan looked at the others. He had no love for the gross Fraser chief, but it seemed somehow scarcely conceivable that he could be apprehended like any felon in the midst of his own Highlands, where he had ruled like little less than a king, one of the most notable men

214

and proudest lords in all Scotland. 'You are sure, man? This is not just some rumour ... ?'

'The truth it is whatever. I am one of the gillies who bore his litter. I saw Himself taken. Och, an ill thing it was, an ill thing. They were after catching him in a hollow tree, no less. Where he had hid from them. On the island in the loch – Loch Morar. Damned may it ever be! They came in boats, many boats. Treachery it must have been – God's everlasting curse on the man who betrayed MacShimi!'

'Caught in a hollow tree?' Scotus all but choked. 'Lovat – that great mountain of flesh! Lord ... !'

Caroline spoke, with a swift compassion for the obviously grieving gillie. 'They will not kill him, perhaps. Indeed, I think that they will not,' he said. 'He is a great lord. He did not take any part in the Rising. Do not grieve too sorely ...'

'They will take off his head,' the other announced with sad conviction. 'I heard them telling Himself the same – the Redcoat officers. He goes to London to die. The man Cumberland has sworn it.'

They sought to comfort the man, and presently sent him on his way back to his own country of Stratherrick, but neither of her guests at least believed that Caroline would prove right in this instance and the Fraser wrong. No actual tears were shed for Lovat, up there by the Allt Ruadh – yet a gloom temporarily descended upon them all. MacShimi had the power, always, of dominating any issue with which he was involved – as no doubt he would dominate even that London stage on which his scaffold would be built. That he had managed to keep a clever head upon his broad shoulders through four Risings and eighty as difficult years as the country had ever known, only made this present debacle the more ominous.

Less sure word of others for whom they cared more reached them from time to time, often very indirectly indeed. They heard first that Locheil, with Murray and Thriepland, had reached Glencoe, well south of Fort William. This seemed to indicate that the proposed linking with the northern regiments and the Frasers had been abandoned. Later this was confirmed; the Mackenzies no doubt wisely in the circumstances, had refused to venture out of their northern fastnesses, and Lovat had never so much as attempted to raise his clan. Doctor Archie was said to be still in Lochaber – but the next word as to his

215

brother, Locheil, put him as far south as the MacGregor country of Balquhidder in Perthshire; what he was doing there was not explained. Murray, it seemed, had now left him, heading for his sister's house in Glen Lyon on his way south to Edinburgh in disguise, taking with him, it was said, a vast treasure in gold – although Duncan calculated that in fact it could not be more than about three thousand *louis*. Other chiefs and leaders seemed to have dispersed to the remotest corners of their domains.

These sad tidings had their effect on the young people on the watershed, inevitably – but less grievously so than might have been expected. There was unreality about it all, a lack of personal impact. Almost it was like a story that had been told – and one which required an actual effort of will to relate closely to themselves and their situation.

That was Caroline's fault – if a fault it was. Consciously or otherwise the young woman effected a kind of transfer of allegiance and interest on the part of her two self-appointed protectors, in some degree and at least temporarily, from the shattered Jacobite cause to her own more vital one. Any personable young female, in the circumstances, most likely would have been able to do something of the sort. But Caroline was not just a personable young female. In addition to her notable good looks, she was possessed of a sunny nature most aptly to match the sun-filled summer days. She was indeed a true daughter of the lightsome pastoral life of these high places, a laughing, lively vital presence that was the perfect antidote of the atmosphere of despair, treachery, corruption and folly that King James's cause now seemed to engender. When Caroline was happy, she was very happy indeed – infectiously so; conditions had to be very grievous wholly to quench that happiness. And despite the fact that she and her sisters were homeless refugees in the wilderness, her father was a fugitive somewhere unknown, her brother wounded and far away, and the long-term prospects for them all uncertain to a degree – despite all this, immediate conditions up there on the watershed between Arkaig and Morar that summer of 1746 were far from grievous. Was it her fault that she held both young men ever more securely in her gay and zestful thrall, to the undoubted detriment of their Prince's hold over their hearts and minds?

This supplanting thralldom did not however make the two

216

victims move any closer in brotherly comradeship, as to some extent had that which it superseded. Despite all Caroline's efforts, Duncan and Scotus drew no nearer to love and affection than are any pair of stiff-legged dogs circling the same single and desirable bone. The gold, and the need to co-operate in their private campaign, had indeed brought them together in some measure, with each at least perceiving and acknowledging the other's qualities – or some of them. The halcyon days of that summer did not enhance this appreciation; their mutual delight in the young woman did not cement the bond. They grew but the more critical of each other, in fact, the more suspect of each other's motives. As a sad example, Duncan judged the other's preoccupation with doctor's orders, his insistence that a damaged shoulder should be safeguarded against practically all movement for weeks on end, as no more than a device to keep Caroline's company to himself in most of the many energetic activities of shieling life; whereas Spanish John managed to perceive in Duncan's consequent helplessness only an underhand and unfair appeal to the girl's sympathies and an invitation to intimate ministrations.

Restricted in movement as Duncan was, the same did not apply to Scotus. He did not remain solidly at the shieling as the weeks passed, making occasional and clearly reluctant journeys north into his own country of Knoydart, on family and clan affairs. He did not speak much of these, but it appeared that he had a semi-invalid father alive, as well as a mother and younger brothers and sisters, whose affairs merited certain attentions from himself. Whatever he contrived to do for these relatives, and for the Scotus property generally, he never allowed it to keep him away from Glen Pean for very long. Duncan could have wished him to be more painstaking on his family's behalf. Always during these brief intervals the MacGregor opened up and flourished exceedingly with his eldest hostess – although any progress that he seemed to make in that direction tended with sad regularity to be lost whenever Spanish John returned, and Caroline welcomed him back with quite unnecessary and unsuitable warmth, like some prodigal.

Throughout that summer intelligence of a sort reached them with quite astonishing frequency and detail as to the Prince's wanderings – considering that the authorities were feverishly ransacking the land for him, searching as with a fine tooth comb, shouting aloud their vast reward for information as to his whereabouts. By the end of June they knew that he had managed to cross from the Outer Isles to Skye, and by mid-July that he had in fact come back to the mainland – even to such minutiae as that he had passed three nights at Mallaigbeg in North Morar, not twenty miles away as the crow flies. There had been some discussion then as to whether possibly Scotus should hurry thither – although it would be a long and dangerous journey for any but the said crows – to inform Charles of the gold situation. Whilst still debating this they heard that somehow the Prince had eluded the innumerable Government patrols, and was now down in Moidart. They heard nothing thereafter until, curiously enough, one day towards the end of the month, a Glen Dessary man of Doctor Archie's sent home to collect some cattle for beef, told them that His Highness had been for a week north again in Glen Moriston – surprising news, for that glen was some fifty or sixty miles north of Moidart. What Charles was doing there was not known. But to get there from Loch Shiel in Moidart, where they had last heard of him, he must have passed very close to their own Glen Pean – possibly as near as the head of Arkaig.

His captains did not know whether to be disappointed or relieved.

'What does it mean?' Caroline asked, by the cabin door. 'What is he doing? Why does he rush about the country so? To go down from Mallaig to Moidart, through Morar and Arisaig where the Redcoats are so busy, and then back north again to Moriston? Over so many miles of this hard and dangerous land. Punishing himself . . .'

'It may be just that keep moving he must,' Scotus said. 'That he dares not to stay in any one place or district for more than a day or so, lest the Redcoats catch up with him.'

'Yet it seems that he has been in Glen Moriston for a week. What does he there? Is he raising men? More soldiers?'

'Not in Moriston, no.' Spanish John shook his head. 'I fear not. The Grants there, though on the right side unlike most of their clan, are too few to form even a company. Anyway, the glen has been ravaged, devastated.'

'Nothing that we have heard says that the Prince is seeking to raise men,' Duncan observed sombrely. 'He keeps but two or three close companions, that is all. The Irishmen. Like a hunted stag, he is – and no cornered boar. No further fight he seeks, I fear, but ... '

'And will you blame him for that?' Caroline demanded strongly, the loyal one, now. 'Can you wonder at it?'

'Perhaps, not. But ... he must know now the love that the Highlands bear him. Thousands must have known of his presence, in all these wanderings – yet not one has betrayed that presence for this great reward, it is clear. He must be aware by now of the gold, and of the arms and ammunition landed. Yet it is notable, is it not, that this area which he has come back to, and which he seems to circle around and traverse – it has Loch nan Uamh for its centre! Loch nan Uamh where first he landed, where the gold was brought, where the French ships were ordered to keep calling. Despite the fact that the Government ships are ever watching it closely. I fear ... I fear that, gold or none, guns and powder though we now have, even with the call to muster the regiments gone out anew – even so the Prince has but the one intention; to return to France as soon as ship can take him. To leave all. I had hoped ... ' He left the rest unsaid.

There was silence.

Scotus broke it at length, almost with a sigh. 'France is a fair country,' he said. 'Less harsh than this. Where a man is not always battling. *La belle France* – a fair and generous land.' He turned to look at Caroline. 'You would like it, my dear,' he said. 'You would be happy there – safe.'

The girl said nothing, and the silence returned, Duncan all but scowling.

Presently the young woman rose to her feet, and touched them both lightly. 'France is far away,' she said. 'But so, probably, are those wicked cows of ours! It is time that they were milked. And were we not to get a pannierful of flat stones from the lochan for the new fireplace? And whose turn is it to teach my hoydenish sisters their lessons?'

Thankfully, they returned to the life of the shielings, uncomplicated, essential. The hint, the shadow of change, however, was there for all to perceive.

CHAPTER 21

THE shadow of change at first grew only slowly, like a small cloud on the horizon. It was fully two weeks later before the electrifying rumour came up Arkaig that the Prince was back here again in the Cameron country – close at hand, indeed, near Achnasaul at the foot of the loch. Doctor Archie was there, it was said, with two of Locheil's sons and the Reverend John Cameron, Presbyterian minister of Fort William. Charles Edward had joined them. Duncan and Scotus could delay no longer.

The same night they made the journey down to the foot of the loch. Although still calling for circumspection, the venture was not so hazardous as formerly – otherwise of course neither the Doctor nor the Prince could have dared to linger in the vicinity. The scarlet-hued tide had largely ebbed – for the time being. The Government posts at Glen Dessary, Callich and Clunes House were lightly held and only sporadically aggressive. Nevertheless, the two men went cautiously, keeping to the uninhabited and rough side of the loch as far as the mouth of Glen Mallie, where a boat was hidden, and rowing therein across the dark water to Achnasaul.

It proved a fruitless journey. Charles and Doctor Archie were gone, both. Left the district that very day, they were told, for Cluny Macpherson's country in Badenoch.

Surprised, the young men returned whence they had come. What did this mean? Badenoch was a far cry from Loch nan Uamh. Cluny Macpherson, though his castle was burnt, was still able to maintain some sort of chiefly state in the inaccessible mountains around Ben Alder, his clan preserved from the worst ravages, his regiment more or less intact. Why had the Prince gone to Cluny? Could it be that Doctor Archie was persuading him to a more militant course, after all?

No word percolated through from distant Badenoch to answer such questions.

At the beginning of September, with the heather clothing all the mountains in its richest purple and the bracken of the lower slopes already turning golden, people from the west told them that ships were beginning to haunt the mouth of Loch nan

Uamh once more, having been glimpsed not a few times against the screen of islets that lay off it; whether French or English was not known — but the fact that they clearly took pains to hide themselves was probably significant.

It was a few evenings later, with the nights already commencing to creep in, that for the first time for months a gleam of red light from the east announced that the beacon on the hill by the lochside was lit again. Duncan and Scotus were almost indignant, wondering indeed whether the thing could have been discovered and lit mischievously by somebody or other. The Cameron on duty was not one of the brightest. It was in that frame of mind, and with only the three MacDonnell gillies, that less swiftly than formerly, they trotted off down the glen to investigate. Caroline had to call them back, to give them their masks.

Their watcher on duty met them by the lochside path a few hundred yards west of the hiding-place. It had been no false alarm, he assured them. Just as dusk was falling a fair-sized party of men, Highlanders, had arrived at the site of the hidden gold, and had gone straight to the position of the hoard that had been raided formerly. When, digging, they could find nothing there, they had begun to dig up the entire surrounding area. He had left them at this, and gone to light the beacon. When he had got back, they had been gone. They did not seem to know anything of the treasure in the burn itself; he had checked, on returning, that the gold was still there, undisturbed.

'Who were they?' Scotus demanded. 'Did you recognise any of them?'

The other shook his head. 'No. There was a tall swack fellow that gave the orders and swore with a pretty tongue. But, och, I could not be seeing right. There was ten of them, at least.'

'Ten? If they did not know about the gold in the burn, then they were not sent by Doctor Archie or Murray or MacLeod,' Duncan said. 'It was thievery again. But they have taken their time. Months, it is . . .'

'Perhaps Suiladale told them. Or Rory Cameron,' Scotus suggested. 'But they have gone, it seems. Empty-handed. You will not know which way they went, man?'

'I was up the hill there. Lighting the fire . . .'

'Aye. We should never have reduced it to a one-man watch.'

'So long as they are gone,' Scotus said. 'We have not the strength to deal with ten or more, anyway.'

They rode back to the shieling, since there seemed to be nothing else to do.

Belle Cameron came running to meet them, all but in hysterics, before ever they reached the cabin.

'They have taken them away!' she cried, sobbing brokenly. 'They have taken them – Caroline and Anne!'

'What?'

'Who have taken them? What do you mean, child?'

'The men. Horrible men. They came and took away Caroline. And Anne. They were horrible. Cruel. They hurt my arm . . .'

'*Dia* – you mean the Redcoats?' Scotus actually shook her, in his agitation.

'No, not Redcoats. Just ordinary men.'

'Our own people? Highlanders?'

'Yes.'

'Who were they? Do you know?'

'I do not know. They twisted our arms . . .'

'Belle – it will be all right,' Duncan told her earnestly. 'We will find them for you – get them back. Never fear. Just think. Carefully. When was this?'

'I do not know. A long time. You have been long, long. If you had been here, they would not have done it.'

'Perhaps not. I am sorry, Belle. How many were there?'

'I do not know. Many . . .'

'Ten, perhaps?'

'Yes. At first they were nice. They asked for food. They said could they rest here. We gave them food. They asked where you were . . .'

'They did? Us – by name? They knew about us?'

'Yes. They said they were friends of yours. Then they asked us where the gold was hidden. They said that you had stolen it!'

'Ah! So that is it.'

'When we would not tell them, they got very angry. They said that you were thieves, stealing the Prince's money. And that we were very wicked to be helping you. They said that they would have to take Caroline and Anne away.'

'God's curse on them, the vile hypocrites!' Scotus declared.

'But you escaped?' Duncan put to her. 'Why did they not take you away, too, Belle?'

'I was to wait here and tell you. That is what he said. I was to wait here – not to move. Not to go and tell anyone. Until you came back. Or . . . or he would hurt my sisters. I thought that you were never coming . . . ' She was sobbing again.

'And what were you to say to us? When you saw us?' Duncan asked, putting his arm around her. 'Think now, Belle. Something he would have you tell us, to be sure?'

The girl gulped. 'To go to him at our house – our old house. Alone. He said that you must go alone. And unarmed, he said, too. Or . . . or Caroline . . . '

'Glenpean House? To take them there!' Scotus interjected. 'The dastard!'

'Remember, it is alone that you must go,' the girl insisted, clutching at Duncan's wrist. 'He twisted my arm. So that I would not forget it, he said. He was horrible. In that mask . . . '

'Mask? You mean that this man was wearing a mask? Like ours . . . ?'

'Yes. Like the ones we made. Only the one of them. This tall man.'

'Masks!' Scotus said. 'This links them surely with Suiladale or Cameron. They will have been told of our masks. It could be one of them, again.'

'But someone who knew of us here. At this shieling. That brings it still closer.'

'Aye. But what matters it who it is? They have us, and know it. We can only do as they say. Go down to Glenpean House.'

'You have to go alone,' Belle reiterated urgently.

'Yes, yes – we will go alone.' Duncan frowned. 'The devil chose well. He knows what he is doing. The ruined house, out there in the open at the head of the loch. There is no cover near it, to hide any approach. We cannot trick him there, with more men in hiding. All round is clear, open.'

'We can only go there. Hear what he has to say . . . '

'You know what that will be! There is no doubt what the man will say to us.'

The other nodded unhappily. 'We have no choice,' he said.

They left Belle with the gillies, torn between desire to accompany them and see her sisters, and fear of the threat that had been impressed upon her as to the consequences of the men not being alone. After only a brief debate, they left their arms behind also.

Practically wordless the two men rode together down Glen Pean once more, thinking their own thoughts. Was this to be the end of their vigil, their long struggle on behalf of the Prince? Were they trapped – trapped in their most fatal weakness? Had this devil taken their measure?

Where the mouth of the glen opened to the wide levels at the head of Arkaig, they paused. Dimly they could perceive where the roofless house stood. No light gleamed there – only the faint glimmer of once-white walls.

Grimly, still silent, they went on across the flats.

Presently Scotus spoke, low-voiced. 'There are men creeping along behind us, I think,' he said.

'I know it. Three of them, there are. He takes his precautions, this one.'

'I do not like it.'

'Did you think to like it? We can do nothing but go on.'

As they neared the house, other men materialised on either side of them, silent, menacing.

They were almost at the former front door, now gaping black, when a voice from the shadows on the right, that had been the byre and barn, halted them.

'I am glad that you have come, gentlemen. And so promptly. So, I feel sure, are the ladies. We knew that you would, of course.' Ridiculously affable and normal that voice sounded, in the circumstances. There was something familiar about it, too, undoubtedly – even although its owner might well be seeking to disguise it somewhat.

'Who are you, damn you?' Scotus burst out. 'Who in Heaven's name could behave this way?'

'John!' Caroline's voice rang out, from within the ruined barn.

'We are here, Caroline! We will get you out of this scoundrel's hand, never fear!'

'Excellent sentiments, my friend – save for the epithet. That is quite undeserved, I swear!' The speaker stepped out from the deeper shadows, a tall man, muffled in plaids, but obviously lean and lanky. A mask made only a black smudge of his face.

'The epithet is entirely just, James Mor!' Duncan said quietly. 'God forgive Clan Alpine for producing you!'

There was a gasp from Scotus, and silence from the masked man. Caroline's cry rose again, with Anne's joining it.

'Duncan! Duncan!'

'Fear nothing, *mo caraidh*. All will be well. I apologise to you for this man that I must call cousin.'

James Mor was clearly put out. 'You have sharp ears, Cousin – to match your tongue!' he said. 'But you would be well advised, see you, to keep that tongue in check. You and your friends are not in a happy position, I would remind you.'

'In the company of you and your bullies, I agree!'

'Good. Go on agreeing, Cousin, and you will be wise. First of all, you had better dismount.' James Mor snapped a word or two aside, and gillies leapt out to grasp the heads of both garrons. Naked steel gleamed in the gloom.

Since they had by no means come here to bolt, the younger men got down.

'If Miss Cameron and her sister are in any way hurt, Mac-Gregor,' Scotus said through gritted teeth, – 'as God is my witness, you will die for it. I will make it my life and purpose . . .'

'Tush, man – spare us the dramatics! They are not in the least hurt, either of them. We have been having a most interesting conversation. Moreover, it is in your power to see that no hurt nor yet distress comes to them hereafter . . .'

'You to speak of distress – who have dragged them here, of all places, to their ravished home!' Duncan charged him. 'You could have spared them that. Your own home was ravished once, you'll mind.' Thirty-three years before, with James a child, Inversnaid House had been burned over his head, his mother raped while it burned, and his absent father Rob Roy made outlaw. 'Your father would not have done this, James Mor.'

'My father had his own methods,' the other returned briefly. 'In an important matter like this, in the Prince's service, I cannot afford to be over-squeamish, over-delicate.'

'The Prince's service! *You* talk of that?'

'To be sure. What else? I am an aide-de-camp to His Highness. Have you forgotten?'

Duncan swallowed. 'This is . . . this is beyond belief! I

would not have thought that you would have as much as dared to mention the Prince's name!'

'Why not? For yourselves, I can understand some such hesitation. But *I* have not stolen the Prince's gold! On the contrary – to recover it is my mission. On His Highness's behalf.'

'*Dia* – what foolishness is this?' Scotus cried. '*We* have not stolen the gold, man . . .'

'My information, sir, is that you have! Excellent and circumstantial information. Only, unfortunately, lacking in details as to where you have deposited the money. Hence these, er, dispositions.'

'But it is not true, MacGregor! You have it all awry. We have been guarding it, nothing more. For the Prince.'

'A likely story! Is it worth while, think you, to insult my intelligence, MacDonnell? Come, my friends – let us be frank. You have taken the money. Many thousands of gold *louis*. Since you still linger on in these parts – in delightful company, I grant you – it seems clear that you have hidden it again somewhere in the area. Where you can keep an eye on it, no doubt? I intend to find out where.'

'You have it all wrong,' Scotus insisted. 'You are mistaken, sir, entirely.'

'I told him that,' Caroline's voice came again, from the barn. 'I told him that you had not stolen it. He will not believe me . . .'

'I do not think that he is mistaken, at all,' Duncan said quietly. 'I believe that James Mor knows the true situation very well! It but suits him to pretend otherwise.'

'The true situation, as you term it, Cousin, unfortunately is all too clear. You cannot deny, I think, if you have any truth in you, that you have removed the gold – for whatever purposes you may see fit to claim. Do you?'

No one answered him.

'Exactly.' James Mor nodded. 'You do not deny it. Now, where have you hid it? For it must be returned to His Highness.'

'That was our intention,' Duncan said shortly.

His cousin smiled. 'Forgive me if I seem to doubt your word, Duncan *a graidh*. But I prefer to do the handing back myself.'

'Liar!'

'Come, now – that is no way to speak. Especially to your

senior officer! You will tell me, in the end. You would not wish to cause the Misses Cameron further . . . inconvenience?'

'So there we have it? Caroline and Anne Cameron, it is, for the gold!'

'I' faith – you are crude, Duncan man! Say that I must use all means that I may, in the Prince's cause. That is, if you refuse to obey the commands of your senior officer! I am, after all, major in the regiment of which you are only captain! And I am speaking in the name of the Captain-General.'

'I doubt it. I do not suppose that you have seen His Highness since you refused to follow him after Culloden.'

'How suspicious and ill-natured you are, Duncan. I spent two days with him, but a week ago, in Cluny's refuge on Ben Alder. When he sent me on this mission. So important to his cause.'

'His cause!' Duncan snorted. 'Your own, do you not mean?'

'My cause and the Prince's are, h'm, inextricably bound up!' the other returned, smiling beneath his mask. 'I trust that you can say the same?'

'Oh, enough of this foolery!'

'Aye – enough, as you say! Foolery is right.' Suddenly James Mor changed his whole attitude. Grimly authoritative, his voice hardened. 'Think you that I brought you here to listen to your childish insults? You, who are thieves, rogues, traitors? I tell you, I should arrest you here and now, and take you before the Prince. He is not so far away. To meet the fate that you richly deserve. Only . . . the money is all important. Charles must have it. At once. And for these girls' sake, who in their foolishness have aided you, I will be merciful. Also, for the good name of our clan. Take me to the place where you have the gold hidden, now – and when it is safely in my hands you, and they, may go free. And I will endeavour to keep your complicity from the Prince's knowledge.'

'Ah! So His Highness does not already know of our wicked theft, after all? He did not send you to us, on this mission of yours?' Duncan said quickly.

'The mission, of course, was in general terms. Do you take me to the gold?'

'If we refuse . . . ?' Scotus began.

'You will not refuse. Not if you value the well-being of these young women!'

There was silence then, for moments on end. All recognised that wordy sparring was over.

Into the hush, plain for all to hear, came the hurried thud-thud of running footfalls.

Every head turned, as a gillie came long-strided. Straight up to Major MacGregor he ran.

'Men coming, Seumas Mor,' he gasped out. 'Many men. Mounted.'

'Damnation! So – so you think to cozen me, you young fools! You would play tricks on James Mor MacGregor? I told you – alone! Christ God – it will be the worse for you! For all of you!'

'No – it is not these, I think, Seumas Mor,' the runner panted. 'They come from beyond. From the other side. From up the loch.'

'*Dia* – Redcoats?'

'No, not Redcoats. They ride garrons and wear bonnets.'

'Are they after coming this way?'

'Yes. And not far, they are, at all.'

'Quick, then! Inside, all of you.' A pistol had appeared in James Mor's hand, and with it he gestured at the two younger men. 'In, I say. And not a sound out of you. Or you will make no more!'

A gillie guarding the doorway stood aside to let them be hustled into the barn. Scotus was first inside, and Caroline threw herself into his arms. Anne did as much for Duncan, babbling incoherences.

'Quiet, I tell you!' James Mor snapped. Four or five gillies had followed him into the roofless building. 'Dirks,' he jerked at these. 'Hold them fast. See that they make no sound.' He himself grabbed Caroline, and another gripped her sister.

So they waited, a dirk-point tickling the throats of each of the captains.

If the reported party had come from the north side of the loch, they would be apt to pass fairly close to the burned house – but there was no reason to expect them to actually come and look inside. Burned houses were all too common in the Highlands in 1746.

Presently they could hear the beat of hooves, many hooves. Then the clink of accoutrements, and finally the faint murmur of voices.

In the ruined barn the tension was acute. It was the same barn, some corner of Duncan MacGregor's mind recollected, that Charles Edward had inspected with a view to couching in five months before.

The riders were close. How close? It was hard to judge. Would they come – would they stop at the house?

They did stop. At least, the beat of the hooves stopped. But apparently a little way off, still. The voices continued. They must be looking towards the buildings, probably speaking of them. Then the hoof-beats recommenced. Only moments were required to establish that they receded, that the party was moving away.

Caroline screamed. 'Help!' she yelled abruptly. She managed another 'Help!' before James Mor's hand clamped over her mouth. The others heard the thud of his fist striking her, as he spat out an oath.

Anne cried out, before she choked to a whimpered gasping. Duncan, jerking forward, groaned against the agony of the arm twisted behind his back, and felt sharp steel bite at his throat. Scotus too began to struggle – until he sank part-unconscious from a vicious blow with the haft of a dirk.

Now the voices outside were upraised. Clearly Caroline's cries had been heard. Men were dismounting, questions and warnings being shouted.

James Mor MacGregor accepted the situation forthwith. He barked swift orders to his gillies. Duncan suddenly had a bare knee brought up into the pit of his stomach, and he was thrown down doubled-up, winded, upon a pile of rotting bog-hay. Scotus was already lying on the cobbled floor, moaning faintly. Leaving the girls, their captors hurried out through the doorless gap.

Sobbing, Caroline called and called into the night.

Men appeared, after a little, in the doorway, cautiously peering, pistols and drawn swords in their hands, kilted men. To them the girls gasped and gabbled frantically.

'Save us – if it isn't Caroline! And Anne, too!' a well-remembered voice exclaimed. '*Diabhol* – what do you here, my dears? Though och – maybe I should not be asking that, and it your own house. But . . . see you, it is all right. All right. Fine, now – fine. It is just my own self. Archie. Doctor Archie. Och, quietly, quietly now. What is the matter, at all?'

From his hay Duncan sought and struggled for breath to form words – and could only wheeze foolishly.

Other men crowded at the doorway, questioning. Then all fell silent as another voice spoke, an authoritative though melodiously accented voice even in its present urgency.

'Who have you got there, Doctor? Some men seem to be riding off in a damned hurry. From some bushes, down by the lake. *Mon Dieu* – what sort of *tapage* is this? The women – are they still here, Doctor?'

'Yes. It is Glenpean's daughters, Your Highness,' Doctor Archie Cameron said. 'Two of them. Miss Caroline and Anne. There seems to be someone else here, also. Sir. But it is curst dark . . .'

CHAPTER 22

DUNCAN MACGREGOR, still somewhat bent, and breathing with difficulty, stared round the company. It was dark, admittedly, and he was probably not at his most acute; nevertheless, he ought surely to know his own Prince?

Caroline Cameron seemed to be suffering under a similar handicap. 'You say . . . that His Highness is here, Doctor Archie?' she said unevenly.

'Why yes, Miss Cameron – your devoted servant, as ever. I rejoice that, for once it seems, we are of some little service. It has been my lot this long while to take all and give nothing, I fear.'

One man had stepped out from the group outside the barn – and it was at the words only and certainly not the appearance that Caroline, distrait as she was, sank in an unsteady curtsey. Duncan only stared. Perhaps he was sufficiently bowed already.

Charles Stuart indeed was barely recognisable as the gracefully handsome and so notably princely figure of five months before. Bearded, fair hair shaggy and long, topped by a plain bonnet, muffled in old plaid, legs bare to feet that were shod only in rough rawhide brogans, he seemed less tall, as well as lacking all elegance – probably because he had actually broadened and developed muscle out of the grim life of a hunted

230

cateran. Only the voice was the same – and perhaps the smile, though the night's gloom left that in doubt.

'His Highness always overlooks the fact that he gives us what no other can do – faith and renewed courage,' the Doctor said. 'And humility too – or he ought to – in face of sufferings and indignities borne without complaint.'

The girl was speechless.

Duncan found words. 'Highness,' he croaked. 'It is good to see you. My duty. My homage. And my thanks. You came. . . most aptly!'

'My good Captain! Are you recovered? Better? Your shoulder, was it not? The Doctor tells me that you were evilly treated. Shamefully. On my behalf.'

'That was nothing, sir. A cracked bone, no more. Others gave a deal more than that!'

'It is to your honour to put it so, friend.'

'My honour, sir!' Duncan drew a quivering breath. 'My honour was in grave danger this night, I fear. 'Fore God, it was saved only by a hair's breadth, I think. And by your coming.'

'Aye – what is this, man?' Doctor Archie intervened. 'What was to do here? I have not fathomed it yet. Who rode away, yonder? And why?'

A chorus of supporting questions came from the others there.

'That was James Mor. My cousin. Major MacGregor,' Duncan jerked. His brows came down like a black bar across his features. 'What he was about, I had rather some other told you.'

'James?' the Prince exclaimed. 'James left us only a day or two since. Why should he ride off thus . . . ?'

'I will tell you.' Scotus had appeared drunkenly within the barn doorway, leaning against the burnt doorpost for support, his head held between his hands. 'He ran, curse him, because he is a coward who fights women – as well as a thieving scoundrel and a traitor!'

'*Nom de Dieu* – who is this man, who dares to miscall a friend and officer of mine?' Charles demanded.

'He is John MacDonnell of Scotus, sir. A captain in the Irelanda Regiment of Spain,' Duncan told him.

'My cousin, that I told you of, Highness.' That was Lochgarry, standing beside the Prince. 'Spanish John.'

'Ah. I am sorry.' Charles quickly relented. 'His uncle died gallantly for my cause. Scotus, yes. I have heard of you, sir. But . . . you must not miscall my good friend Major James so.'

'Yet what I said is truth, Highness,' Scotus insisted. 'And he is no true friend of yours, I fear!'

'Allow me to know my own friends, sir! Major MacGregor is on a special mission for myself. He cannot have realised who it was who came, or he would never have gone away thus. It is most unfortunate.'

Duncan bit his lip. 'A special mission, you say, sir? About the money? The gold?'

'It was, yes. Much of it has been stolen, unhappily. James believed that he might be able to recover some of it at least, for me.'

Duncan, looking from Caroline to Scotus, was silent.

'Highness – not all men esteem James Mor quite as highly as you do, I fear,' Doctor Archie put in. 'I have told you. Perhaps we are prejudiced. But . . . the matter need not concern us at the moment, need it? We should move from here. This is not the safest place to linger. We are too near the posts at Callich and in my own glen . . . '

'Very well, Doctor. That is probably wise.' The Prince sighed. 'It is sad to see this hospitable house so. We shall move on. Up to yonder cabin of Miss Cameron's belike. Where we stayed once before. A good secure place . . . '

Duncan almost objected. But what point was there in asserting that, since James Mor knew of the Allt Ruadh shieling, it was now unsafe? Clearly the Prince would not accept that as any valid objection. He held his peace.

Their late captors having apparently gone off with their two garrons, Duncan and Scotus, like the two girls, were mounted behind members of the Prince's party – which included, as well as Lochgarry, Colonel John Roy Stewart, Captain O'Neil and one of Locheil's sons. Locheil himself, it seemed, with a number of other Camerons, including the girls' father, was not far away to the south somewhere, travelling independently. Making for Borrodale. There was no sign of O'Sullivan.

In this strange fashion they returned to the Allt Ruadh and the waiting, anxious Belle.

Once again, despite jangled feelings and emotional exhaustion, it fell to Caroline to prepare food and drink for the party, aided at least in theory, by her sisters and Duncan. Scotus, still suffering from the blow he had received, was taking his turn at being nursed.

Duncan had great difficulty in gaining the Prince's private ear. Felix O'Neil in especial never seemed to leave his side. He had indeed become Charles's closest companion, throughout all his wanderings. O'Sullivan, it appeared, had become detached from the Prince by accident just before the latter sailed from the Long Island for Skye, and was now thought to be out of the country. Ned Burke was still in faithful attendance. Duncan had never got on well with O'Neil and could not now believe that he was the best influence to be bearing on Charles – especially where Scottish affairs were concerned.

He did at last gain the Prince's more or less undivided attention – but even so, Doctor Archie was with him. Indeed, it was the Doctor's declaration that he wanted to examine his erstwhile patient's shoulder, and Caroline's seizing of the chance to have Scotus's sore head examined also, that created the opportunity. The five of them, with the two younger girls, had the cabin to themselves for the moment.

Duncan interrupted the Doctor's remarks about his excellent recovery. 'Your Royal Highness,' he said urgently. 'About the gold. It is a bad, a shameful business. But I did what I could. As did Scotus, here. We can now render some account of our stewardship.'

'Ah, yes – the gold. *Dieu de Dieu* – that gold!' Charles was scratching himself in less than royal fashion. 'I must confess, my friends, that I am completely at a loss over all this money. The more I hear of it, the more complicated it becomes! To which gold is it that you refer, Captain? There is so much, so many consignments. The good Doctor has, for instance, two consignments hidden away for me. Large sums. How much in these, Doctor?'

'Twenty-seven thousand *louis d'ors*, sir.'

'Less one thousand and fifty,' Duncan amended.

'Eh? What did you say, MacGregor? *Less . . . ?* What do

233

you mean, man?' The Doctor looked startled.

'H'mmm. The fact is, Doctor, that one thousand and fifty of the gold pieces that you buried opposite Callich there, are now down in the lochan below us here!'

'My God!' The other stared. 'You mean . . . you *took* it? Removed it?'

'Yes. For good reason. The first fifty we retrieved half-way up Glen Mallie – from one of Clanranald's people. The thousand we took later, when we found another raider at your hoard – one of your own Camerons . . .'

'I don't believe it!'

'It is true . . .'

Scotus took up the story. 'We put it all in the burn – the rest of your hoard. From where it had been buried in the ground. All except a one-thousand bag which we could not hide. It would have shown. In the water . . .'

'But sink me – what does it all mean?' the Doctor cried. 'How did you know that the gold was there? Who told you? And these others? It is damnable . . . !'

Scotus eyed his finger-nails. 'I, er, followed you, sir. The night that you hid it all. From Murlaggan. As did others . . .'

'Damn you – you did? Follow us? Spied on us? A pest – you admit it, you scoundrel? Of all the . . .'

'Doctor Archie!' Caroline exclaimed. 'John is not well. His head is hurt. You must not berate him. All he did was for the best. In His Highness's service.'

'My service is indeed more complicated than I knew!' Charles said, cracking a louse between his thumb-nails. 'Proceed, sir – I am fascinated.'

'We had already had experience of what might well happen,' Duncan inserted. 'Scotus only took due precautions . . .'

'Precautions, i' faith! Is that what you call it?'

'It was as I feared, Doctor. Others followed you also. Saw where you buried the gold. I glimpsed them myself. So we set a day-and-night watch on the place. To guard it.' Scotus shrugged. 'Only the second night we made our first catch.'

'I was for digging up all your store, Doctor,' Duncan told him. 'All the fifteen thousand there. To bring it here to our own hoard. For safety. But these others would not have that . . .'

'Your own hoard?' Charles interposed. 'What was that?'

'It was money we had brought from Borrodale, Highness. Five thousand *louis*.'

'*Ma foi!* Five thousand!'

'From Borrodale? *Dia* – then it was you who stole it! At the landing?' Doctor Archie challenged, staring.

'No, no. We recovered it, only.'

'You mean, from the Irishman? O'Rourke, was it?'

'No. That was different. That was only seven hundred. We recovered that also.'

The Prince groaned, and halted in his diligent search for vermin. '*Nom de Nom* – have mercy! I am lost! Confounded quite! Gently, my friends, if you would leave me my poor reason. Fifteen thousand! Five thousand! Seven hundred, was it? Fifty . . . !'

'There is forty also, that my father took for the cattle-beasts,' Caroline put in. 'Do not forget that.'

Charles waved a hand limply. 'Captain,' he said to Duncan. 'If my memory serves me aright, was it not to secure a sum that my brother York sent me that I charged you? Alas, with all your figures and thousands I have now forgot how much it was. All this money which, had it but come a month or two before, could have transformed our cause . . . '

'Aye. That is the sorrow of it. Such *was* the mission you gave me, sir. But that money we have not got, I fear . . . '

'It was five hundred, sir. At least, His Highness of York sent two thousand. But it was stolen from me. At Loch Broom. All of it,' Scotus confessed. 'I regained five hundred only. And that the Secretary Murray took – though we sought to keep it from him.'

'As he did much else,' Doctor Archie agreed. 'He has four thousand away with him now, at least. That is why I put the other twelve thousand in the loch, near Achnacarry . . . '

'A truce! A truce!' Charles insisted. 'This gets worse and worse, I vow! I am dizzy with it all. I have no head for such matters. I was telling James MacGregor that, but two nights ago. He was talking in the same way. You are all as bad as bankers, I swear.'

'What money was it that my cousin was searching for, Highness?' Duncan asked. 'This mission you spoke of?'

'It was . . . *parbleu*, I cannot tell now which of them it was! You have me addled. Doctor – do you recollect?'

'Indeed, yes. It was the original five thousand, amissing at Borrodale. At the landing. He said that he believed that he could find it. Perhaps he knew that you two had it?'

Duncan and Scotus exchanged glances. 'I think, not,' the former said.

'It was *your* hoard, Doctor, that he sought. That he was digging for, when first we came on him,' Scotus informed.

'Mine? By the loch? Damme — is this true? You are sure, man?'

'Aye. He dug up all around the spot. But he got nothing. For he did not know about what was hidden in the burn near by. None of them can have seen that. And *we* had dug up the buried lots and put all with the rest in the burn. Save this one thousand . . . '

'You did that?'

'For safety's sake.'

The Doctor shook his head. 'You think, then, that James Mor meant to steal it? Or some of it?'

'But of course . . . '

'Silence! I will not hear of it!' the Prince cried. 'I told you — I will not hear my friends traduced so. James, no doubt, learned of this, this hoard, hidden by somebody, and sought only to secure it for me. He would not know that it was the Doctor who had put it there. He would think it stolen, like the rest. For the last time, gentlemen, I ask you, I *command* you, to have done with such talk. Such spleen and backbiting amongst my officers and friends is shameful and ill becomes you. There has been overmuch of it, the good God knows.'

There was silence in the cabin for a few moments. Belle had fallen asleep where she crouched.

Charles relented. He always relented where personal matters were concerned, stubborn as he could be otherwise. 'But . . . it seems that you have been very good, true guardians of my interests, *mes braves*. I am confused still, and do not understand how you gained it all. But how much, in all, have you hidden away for me?'

'Six thousand seven hundred and ninety *louis d'ors*, sir,' Duncan told him. 'But one thousand and fifty of it really is part of the Doctor's hoard. We can have it up for you in an hour. Less.'

'Six thousand — here! You have done nobly indeed, my

friends. I am grateful to you. With such a sum, much may be done. And with the Doctor's added . . . How much have you now, all told, Doctor?'

'The Devil knows – or perhaps these young men! For I do not,' the older man said. 'With Sawny MacLeod I hid twenty-seven thousand. But what may be left . . . ?'

'We know nothing of the twelve thousand down near Achnacarry,' Duncan declared. 'But there is still thirteen thousand nine hundred and fifty *louis* down in the burn opposite Callich.'

'So-o-o! Altogether I can put my hands on nearly thirty-three thousand,' the Prince said. 'A goodly sum! A handsome sum!'

'Out of forty-two thousand,' Duncan reminded.

'More,' the Doctor averred. 'For old Sheridan had some other money which was landed on Barra, earlier. A deal of it. Murray took it likewise, I am told.'

'No doubt Murray will return all this to me in due course, in France,' Charles said, and yawned.

Duncan's breath caught in his throat. 'You . . . are going . . . to France, sir?' he got out. 'After all?'

'Why yes, Captain. That is why we are here. We are on our way to Borrodale again. Two French ships are waiting off Loch nan Uamh to take me. At last.'

'But . . . but, Highness – what of the Cause? What of the Rising? If you go . . . ?'

'The Rising, alas, is over. This Rising. The Cause remains – but it must await another day, friend.'

'Another day, yes. But not years, Sir! As it will be if you go away, now. If you return to France. Years!'

'A little time it may take, yes. But I will come back . . . '

'But now is the time, Highness – now!' Duncan was leaning forward urgently. 'With all this money. And the arms and ammunition in the caves at Borrodale. Think what it means – the difference it makes. All the land knows of this treasure, now – knows that you are rich. Use it. Use it as a magnet – not for thieves but for soldiers. Buy what you could not win. The men are still in the glens. The clans are still there. The North is untouched. The people still love you – as witness that none have betrayed you all these months. Raise your standard again. Call on the chiefs once more – and those who will not send men for love of you, will send them for your gold! *Dia* – a guinea a man, and you will have an army greater than anything that Cumberland can field against you! Think of those who have held back. Think of Sleat. Think of the Laird of MacLeod. Offer those two hucksters a thousand guineas for a thousand men, and you will have them in a week!' In his eagerness, Duncan had risen to his feet. 'That is what the gold could do. That is what we have guarded and saved it for – not to pay out in doles and compensations. Or to take back to France!'

The Prince looked up at him sadly, and shook his head. 'It is too late, Duncan – too late,' he said. 'I esteem your devotion, your fervour. But that time is past. The money came too late.'

'Not so, sir. Never say it, with you to lead and hearten us. And already many of Cumberland's best troops have been withdrawn. Sent to the Netherlands. It is the scum that is left. I have it from one of the Elector's own officers . . . '

'Think you that I have not weighed all this? These matters are less simple than you think, Duncan.'

'But . . .'

'Your Royal Highness,' Caroline put in, only superficially hesitant. 'Forgive me for speaking. But . . . if not for the Rising itself, for the fighting – think of the people. All the ordinary folk of the glens. Stay, for their sakes. Our sakes. If you remain, there will still be fight in Scotland, still spirit. The Government will not dare oppress the folk too strongly – not with men and arms and money behind you. But if you go – all is lost. Everyone will know it. And the people will pay. The glens will be worse harried than ever, the savagery unending. With no spark of revolt left, the Redcoats will not be held back . . . '

'You are wrong, wrong!' Charles asserted. '*Au contraire*, when I am gone, and there is peace at last, the Government's ferocities will relax. The fire will be out – they need not beat it so. I am sorry, Miss Cameron – but it is better so. Believe me, I have considered well.'

'The fire will be out! And there you have it!' Duncan declared bitterly. 'The fire is not yet out – not while there are thousands of hands to draw sword for you in the heather! But you will put it out, your own self, if you go . . . '

'Enough, man – enough!' Prince Charles started up. 'You forget yourself! I will not be harassed so, browbeaten! Let me hear no more of it. I am weary of it all. Doctor Cameron was

238

at the same talk, but yesterday. You cannot see beyond these Highland hills; I must take the longer view. Enough, then — my mind is made up. Now — it is time that we were on our way. We have lingered too long already . . . '

'You are not staying, sir? Sleeping here?' Caroline cried.

'No. For many a month now the night has been my time for travelling, the day for sleeping. There is much of this night left to us yet — and we must reach Loch nan Uamh by to-morrow's eve. We press on, Mademoiselle.'

'And the gold, sir? What of the gold?' That was Scotus.

'Ah, yes — the gold. I shall take some of it. Enough for present needs. To see us to France. So that we do not land looking like savages. The French, my friends, would not like that! *Mon Dieu* — how I long for clean linen once more. Respectable clothes. And an end to these devilish lice! Save me — I had not so much as seen a louse before I came to your Highlands! And look at me now — eighty I caught on me but yesterday! Eighty! 'Pon my soul, I am become as good a counter of lice as some of you of gold pieces!' Charles paused. 'Now, how much do I need to take with me?'

None of his hearers sought to make that calculation for him.

Charles seemed to become aware of their quiet, their reserve, for he looked round them all, and smiled, kindly again, no longer haughty. It was to Duncan MacGregor that he spoke.

'I think that two thousand should serve. Or perhaps three — for there will be not a few of us going, and not a groat between us all. It will not do to descend on *la belle France* like whipped curs. That will not help my father's cause. Make it three thousand. But . . . take it from the good Doctor's store, Duncan. Not from yours. *Parbleu* — think you that I cannot see what is in your eyes, man, even in this dark? It was not for such that you fought and guarded it, eh? Not for dressing up a parade of exiles, that you hid and stored and saved the gold! I know it, friend — I know it. So save your own hoard, Duncan, and guard it still. Hold it intact. Safe for me, until I come back. That is my charge for you. Keep it secure, as an earnest of my return. For the purpose for which it was sent, and for which you have guarded it so well — for the winning back of my father's throne. I will come back for it, one day — and expect it at your hand. Six thousand . . . ?'

'. . . seven hundred and ninety *louis d'ors*.' Duncan finished for him.

'*Bon!* As for the rest, guard it also. For the Doctor. He and Cluny Macpherson will use it as they see fit, for the furtherance of my cause meantime, the keeping alight of the flame of resistance, the aiding of those whose need is great and who have lost all for me. You will guard it until such time as they tell you. You understand, Captain? Less the three thousand that I take with me. But not your own store. That you hold direct of me. Till I come for it again. As all here are witnesses.' The Prince held out his hand.

Duncan, blinking, wordless, bent to kiss it, but Charles shook his head.

'Not so,' he said. 'It is a compact, a bargain. To shake *your* hand. The hand of a brave and honest man! It is my privilege, sir. You would not deny me?'

There, in the darkened cabin, they shook hands.

'Now, my friends – we ride. Go you to the Doctor's gold, Duncan, wherever it is, and bring three thousand *louis* after me. For my journey. We have not time to wait. We make for Borrodale, by the most secret way, and will not delay. You will require to ride fast, to catch up with us. You have it?'

'Yes, sir.' Duncan still was not trusting himself with words.

'*Eh bien.* Then, Miss Cameron, it is goodbye. And my deep gratitude for many things. For all that you have suffered, too, and lost, on my behalf . . .'

'Not yet, Highness,' the girl said, stiffly for her, jerkily. 'I also will see you again. At Borrodale.'

'You will? You should save yourself the weary journey, my dear.'

'I will be there,' she said.

'Very well. As you will. Would that I deserved all the devotion of my friends! Come then, Doctor – let us be going. *Allons.*'

'Aye, Highness.'

THE eight garrons were driven nearly to exhaustion before Caroline, keen-eyed however tired, perceived the faint drift of blue woodsmoke rising above the lemon-yellow of a clump of scrub birch ahead, and pointed.

It was mid-afternoon. It had taken the six of them – the girl, Duncan, Scotus and his three MacDonnell gillies, with two led horses – until now to come up with the Prince's party. Charles had wasted no time.

They were down near the head of Glen Beasdale, only a few miles from Borrodale and the sea at Loch nan Uamh. They had thought to have caught up with the others before this.

Without comment, they rode on towards the trees.

At the edge of the birches a hidden Cameron sentry recognised them and let them past. They found the Prince and most of his companions asleep, in a grassy hollow amongst the trees and bracken.

Doctor Archie welcomed them, signing them to be quiet, not to wake the sleepers. They needed and deserved their rest, he said – as no doubt did the newcomers themselves. It was planned to move again, over the last stage of their journey, in a couple of hours or so, in order to arrive at Borrodale as darkness came down. Was all well, he added? The money safe?

'Three thousand on the ponies, there,' Duncan nodded, yawning. 'Ten thousand nine hundred and fifty still in the burn beside Arkaig.'

Scotus said nothing. He had been notably and unusually quiet all that day. As indeed had Caroline. There had been a strange tension about them all.

The Doctor did not require to urge them to sleep; all were nodding almost as soon as they sat down. They had been riding for fifteen hours, with no sleep the night before.

They were not permitted to slumber for long, however. A sudden commotion aroused not only themselves but the entire company. Only one man created it – but his coming was sufficiently emphatic and dramatic to transform the slumbrous scene. It was James Mor MacGregor, alone, on foot, gasping for breath, but vehement.

'Where is His Highness?' he cried out, a sentry still running doubtfully at his back. 'God's death – there is danger! Danger, I tell you! You must get the Prince away. Quickly. Away from here . . .'

All around, men stared at him owlishly.

'Quickly – damn you for fools!' he shouted. 'Would you have him captured? Redcoats are a bare mile away! A squadron of them. And if I could see your smoke, they can!'

The camp came to life like an ant-hill disturbed.

'James!' the Prince exclaimed, jumping up. 'What is this? Where have you come from? Redcoats, you say? Where? What is this?'

'Half a squadron of dragoons, Highness – coming this way. Down the glen, there. Another half-squadron at Borrodale.'

'*Diable!* Dragoons? We dare not encounter dragoons . . .'

'No. You must be off. At once. And unseen. For they are better mounted.'

'This could be trickery, Highness!' Duncan said, level-voiced, forcing himself to the words.

'Curse you, puppy!' James Mor flung at him. 'You were born a fool. Think you that I would . . . ?'

'Do not heed him, James,' the Prince intervened. 'He is not a fool, only distrustful. Care nothing. Here is no time for wrangling. How shall we get away from here, unseen? If they are but a mile off?'

'There is a burn-channel. Just beyond this hollow. I came across it,' James panted. 'Deep enough to hide us. Dismounted. Leading the garrons. We could climb up the bed of it. To higher ground. Where they would not see us. They are down in the floor of the glen. They will not see us, once we are higher, owing to the swell of the hillside.'

Duncan took him up swiftly. 'If they can see the trees, we should be able to see *them*! If they are there!'

'Go you and look, then, Cousin. From up above, there. Look you down the glen.'

Duncan did not even wait for him to finish. He ran up the brackeny side of the hollow, crouching down amongst the tree-trunks as he reached the immediate skyline.

Sure enough, the scarlet coats of many cavalrymen were to be seen plainly enough down there, against the golds and browns of the glen-floor. They seemed to be scattered about, searching over quite a wide area.

Biting his lip, Duncan came down to the others again where all were making ready to move off immediately. He nodded his head. 'They are there, yes,' he jerked. 'Scattered about, as though hunting.'

'My lads seek to make a diversion,' his cousin explained, to the Prince. 'To keep them occupied. While I came on here.'

'Come, then,' Doctor Archie said grimly. 'Down first, and into this watercourse. Then up.'

Caroline, leading her garron, moved off at Duncan's side. 'Are . . . are we wrong about James Mor, Duncan?' she faltered.

'God knows!' he said. 'I do not.'

James Mor avoided any speech with his former captives, and clung to the Prince's side, where Felix O'Neil eyed him without affection.

The formation of the hillside gave them cover once they were over the first small shoulder, as James MacGregor had foretold, and thereafter the curve of the slope kept the valley bottom hidden. They could mount and ride unseen from below.

'You said that there were more dragoons at Borrodale?' the Doctor put to James Mor. 'So we cannot go down there. To the rendezvous? How do you know? Have you been there, your own self?'

'Aye. The French ships are anchored out in the loch. Two of them. The other party – Locheil and Cluny and the rest – had arrived. At the rendezvous. Too many people. The Redcoats were watching the ships. The others were seen . . . '

'They did not catch them?' Doctor Archie interrupted. 'Locheil? He is not taken?'

'My father . . . ?' Caroline gulped.

'No. They scattered, in time. Into the woods. I do not think that they have any of them. Locheil himself had enough men to fight a delaying action. And the woods there are thick. But the Redcoats are alert now. Searching. I knew that His Highness would be coming – guessed that he would come by Glen Beasdale.'

'You came to warn us, James? Risking your own life?'

The tall man grinned wickedly. 'Do not say such a thing, Highness! 'Tis as good as sacrilege! You will mortally affront my cousin Duncan. Probably the Doctor here, too. James Mor could never do anything one half so noble! Say that I happened to be passing – running away from the dragoons. And saw your smoke. I could scarce do less than look in? I left my lads to distract the troopers yonder, and came up here myself on foot. Unseen.'

'Brave!' the Prince exclaimed. 'Gallant! My good James – ever I knew that you were true to me. My grateful thanks, *mon ami*. I shall not forget. But . . . what are we to do? Where are we to go, now, to win to the ships?'

'Locheil was telling the others to make for a new rendezvous. At some hidden place opposite An Garbh Eilean. Where there is an anchorage . . . '

'Doire Fhada,' Glenaladale, one of Clanranald's officers, put in. 'The Long Oak Grove. I know it well. A good secure place, where the ships can come close.'

'That is the name. The Doire Fhada,' James Mor agreed. 'To rendezvous there as darkness comes down.'

'Could you guide us there, Glenaladale?' Doctor Archie asked. 'From here? So that we are not seen . . . '

'To be sure. We must go round the back of this great hill, Sithean Mor. Then cross the headwaters of the Borrodale Burn, and so over into the next valley, of the Brunery Burn. That will bring us down through thick woods to Doire Fhada. But it will take us four hours' riding. Rough trackless going.'

'*Eh bien* – so much the better. It will keep cavalry horses away,' the Prince said. 'Lead on, in that case, Glenaladale.'

'I leave you here, then, Highness,' James Mor announced. 'I must go back to see how my lads fare. Keeping the Redcoats occupied.'

'Must you, James? *Hélas* – of course you must! Tell them of my true gratitude. But . . . will you not change your mind and come to France with me, hereafter?'

The other shook his head. 'I think not, Highness. Not this time. There is work to do in Scotland yet awhile. One day, perhaps, I shall join you in France. But not yet.'

'I am sorry, James. This is goodbye, then, my faithful friend?'

'Call it *au revoir*, as you would say in France, sir.' James actually knelt down in the heather to kiss the Prince's hand –

and even with Charles mounted on his garron, so tall was the MacGregor that he did not require to strain upwards. And somehow, because of a basic element of mockery in the man, even this exaggerated gesture did not appear over-humble or in any way servile. 'God bless Your Highness always, and bring you safe to your father's throne. *Slan leat, Tearlach!*'

The Prince had difficulty with his words, as he bid his devoted friend farewell.

'A touching scene, 'fore God!' Scotus muttered, to Duncan. 'The man is the world's greatest hypocrite!'

'I can imagine what work keeps him in Scotland, whatever!' Duncan nodded grimly. 'He will find the gold if he can – all of it!'

'And yet,' Caroline demurred. 'He could have earned thirty thousand pounds this afternoon, with all the ease in the world! All that he had to do was to go to the Redcoats instead of endangering himself to come here. Nothing would have been more simple.'

Duncan rubbed his unshaven chin. 'Aye,' he said.

'There are two kinds of gold, it seems,' she went on. 'A man can betray his Prince's trust . . . but not his Prince himself!'

'Glenaladale says that James Mor and Barrisdale betrayed the Glen Mallie assembly to Loudon,' Scotus said. 'Presumably not for nothing!'

' I cannot believe that,' the girl declared.

'I do not know what to believe,' Duncan admitted wearily. 'But there goes a very strange man – that much is certain.'

With a gallant flourish of his bonnet to the Prince, a wave to others, and a mockery of a bow to Doctor Archie – who had never trusted him – and no single glance towards his three former prisoners, Major James Mor MacGregor swaggered off, back again into the burn-channel and downhill, a lone but never lonely figure.

'We shall go by a rather different route, I think, to Doire Fhada – for safety's sake!' Glenaladale said, looking after that retreating paladin. But he said it quietly, so that the Prince should not hear him.

CHAPTER 24

DOWN amongst the dense shadowy woodlands that clothed the northern shores of Loch nan Uamh, with the rocky beach opening before them in the last wan reflections of a watery sunset, figures emerged from behind bushes and trees and boulders, many dark figures, to greet their Prince. Locheil came limping; Clanranald ran to kiss his hand; Cluny Macpherson, stocky, burly, middle-aged, strode out sturdily; Bishop Mac-Donald of Morar raised a hand in blessing.

'Father!' Caroline cried, and jumping down from her garron, ran into Glenpean's arms.

With the Prince's party, there were fully a hundred men assembled there, around the deep secluded inlet of the sea-loch opposite the craggy islet of Garbh Eilean. No one, it was thought, had actually fallen into the clutches of the dragoons. These thick woodlands and broken rocky shores were highly unsuitable for cavalry and apt for fugitives. Neverthe-less, there was nothing of elation about that hushed and furtive company. The meaning of their presence there, those who would sail and those who would remain behind, lay upon all their hearts like a leaden weight. This was the end of a chapter, if not of the book itself.

Locheil brought forward a dark-clad man, not in Highland dress. 'This is Captain Dufresne-Marion of the St. Malo privateer *Prince de Conty*, Highness,' he said. 'His ship, with another, the *Heureux*, will move closer in whenever the light goes. Clanranald has a boat out, to guide them here. Then the ships' boats will come for us.'

'Ah, my good Captain – well met! I will confess that I am more than glad to see you! Even if your ship, *Heureux*, is scarcely aptly named for the occasion!' Charles forced a wry smile. 'You must have been very bold, very courageous, putting your neck thus into the very noose, for me. I am only too well aware of the risks that you are taking. I thank you, from the bottom of my heart, sir.'

The Frenchman was peering in the gloom, even as he bowed low, no doubt seeking to reconcile this brawny uncouth figure with the elegant prince whom he had been sent to rescue. 'I but obeyed my orders, Your Royal Highness,' he said. 'But . . . I shall not be sorry to see St. Malo port again, I swear by Mary Mother!'

'I do not doubt it, Captain. Nor you only!'

'How many, sir, sail with you? How many do I carry with you? On the two ships?'

'That I do not know, Monsieur. Locheil? Doctor? Can you tell us? If they would pay heed to me, *mon Capitaine*, all here would come!'

'In my party, I think that thirty will sail, Highness,' Locheil told him. 'Some are still undecided.' He shook his grizzled head. 'Despite your Highness's company, would to God I was not one of them! But . . . I am but a handicap to my friends, here, crippled as I am.'

'You will come back, Donald – never fear,' his brother the Doctor told him. And to the Prince. 'Something over a dozen of our party, sir, intend to sail.'

'Fifty in all, then, Captain . . .'

The other Donald Cameron, Glenpean, had drawn his daughter aside – and the two younger men had followed.

'Lassie,' he said, 'you have come a long way to see a sad spectacle. To see your Prince and your chief leave your country – defeated, hunted men. For Locheil goes too. You should not have come, girl.'

'I had to come,' she said. She paused. 'And you, Father? Do you go to France, likewise? With Locheil?' Her voice quivered.

He shook his head. 'No, lass. Think you that I would? My duty to Locheil and the regiment ends on this shore. I am coming home. Returning to that other duty which, God forgive me, I have sorely neglected these many months – looking after my own daughters, my own people.'

She nodded, unspeaking.

It was Scotus who spoke, abruptly, almost harshly for him. 'None the less, sir, Caroline would be better going to France on the ship,' he said. 'Safer. Not to remain just a hunted fugitive in the heather, any more. She should come to France, to a new life.' It was not really at Glenpean that he looked as he spoke.

They all stared at him.

'Me . . . ? Go to France . . . ?' the girl said.

'Yes. Yes, Caroline. It would be best. You must see it? The winter is coming. The life of the shielings will be very different

247

in winter, in snow-bound hills. No life for you, my dear. And once all resistance is finished, hereafter, the Government will know no mercy. Come to France with me, Caroline.'

'You . . . ? You go?'

'Scotus,' Glenpean intervened, a little unsteadily. 'There is truth in what you say, God knows. But . . . it is not possible. Alone – a young woman? You do not realise what you are asking . . .'

'I realise very well, sir. I am asking that Caroline comes to France with me as my wife. We could be married. Here and now. Bishop MacDonald there would marry us.'

Duncan drew a long breath, but said nothing.

There was silence for moments on end.

At last Caroline spoke. 'You . . . you are kind, John. But . . .'

'I am not kind,' he denied. 'This is not kindness – never think it. You it is that I want. I think that you know it. I have never hidden my feelings for you, my dear. Marry me, Caroline. And come away from this unhappy land.'

Tight-lipped she shook her head.

'If it is your sisters – they could follow us. When we have made a home for them.'

'No, John,' she said. 'I thank you – but no.'

'No . . . ?' The man drew himself up – and suddenly, strangely, he was his normal self again. Gone the jerky hesitancy, the unaccustomed stiffness, almost sternness. He was Scotus once more, Spanish John, easy, assured, debonaire, almost as though a weight had been lifted from his mind. 'Alas, alas – I feared as much!' he said, with a sort of rueful humour. 'Aye – it was too much to hope for. I must continue to travel my road alone, then. Ah, me!'

Glenpean cleared his throat. 'Still you go then, lad? To France? Alone?'

'Why no, sir – not to France. That I would have done only to take Caroline there. To safety. No, I do not go to France – not yet.'

'To Spain, then? Back to your regiment?' That was Duncan.

'Nor to Spain either, my good MacGregor. My lone road is . . . my own. However lonely.'

The girl bit her lip. 'You do not stay with us? To guard the gold? Like Duncan . . . ?'

He shook his head. 'You did not hear the Prince put that

248

charge on *me*, did you? To guard his treasure. Indeed, I do not think that he esteems me greatly. Perhaps it is that I am less enamoured of his royal self than are some of you! I am not Prince Charles's man, you see – but Prince Henry's. The Duke of York's. It is on *his* service that my road takes me, now.'

'Ah!' Duncan said. 'You go north, then? To . . . Loch Broom?'

'Precisely, my friend. I have a little matter to settle still, with the Clan MacKenzie! A matter of a mere fifteen hundred *louis d'ors*. A humble sum – but some responsibility of mine. To recover . . . for His Highness of York, of course!' A flashing smile went with that.

'M'mmm.'

'Must you go, John?' Caroline said.

'I must, yes. And why not, i' faith? What is there for me here, now? The Gregorach has all in hand here, I think!'

'I am sorry, John.'

'So am I, my heart – so am I. But that alters nothing, does it? Faith, it is a sorry pair we are!'

Duncan seemed as though he was going to speak, but changed his mind.

A soft call from the shore announced that one of the ships was nosing in behind the little island. Immediately there was a concerted move down to the beach. Once the ships' boats came ashore, there would be no time to be lost. Captain Dufresne-Marion made it clear that he did not wish to linger close in to this coast.

The Prince, down at the tide's-edge, raised first a hand and then his voice. 'Gentlemen, friends all!' he called. 'In especial those I leave behind me. How shall I say what is in my heart, *mes camarades*? It has been a long fight, a grievous campaign – and the more bitter in that once it seemed that we should win it. And this is the most bitter day of all, God knows. Yet, if the same God wills, it is not the end, my friends. What so many have fought and died for, what so much loyal blood has been shed for, cannot just fade away as though it had never been. Heaven helping me, I will return. For that day we must gather our strength, cherish our faith, maintain our courage. My father's cause is as true, as just, now as when first we drew sword for it, you and I. It has been repulsed only, not defeated.'

'God save King James!' Clanranald cried, and whipping out

his broadsword raised it high. 'King James and the right!'

All around the cry was taken up, amidst the skreik of steel – so that Duncan for one glanced around him apprehensively lest the noise should reveal their whereabouts to prowling searchers.

Charles's voice shook. 'Thank you, *mes braves, mes héros!* I thank you with all my heart. Not only for this pledge, this last assurance of your loyalty and affection, but for all the love and care and selfless devotion that you have shown me – especially in these last months when my very name was a menace to you, my presence a death-warrant. And yet, wherever I went, on whomsoever I threw myself, never was I failed, never once rejected . . . much less betrayed . . . ' He gulped, and faltered. 'I . . . I cannot go on,' he said. '*Pardonnez moi, mes amis . . .* '

Only the draw and sigh of the tide broke the hush. Then a creaking sound, that was too regular and rhythmic for the cries of seabirds, caught all ears – the sweep of oars in rowlocks.

'The boats!' somebody called. 'Here they come . . . '

Farewells were hastily said, brother taking leave of brother, father of son, chief of clansmen. Scotus turned to Duncan, and held out his hand.

'I go now, also – the other way. It is apt. So that I may believe that the fair Caroline sheds one tear for me amidst the flood for Charles Stuart! Think you that she will? Heigh-ho – women are contrary creatures, and never know what is good for them! And you – see that you remember it, MacGregor! It is your good fortune – but ill deserved, I swear! Lord – do not be so solemn, man! If you would but laugh a little, now and then, there might be no holding you! Eh, Caroline?' He shrugged, continental-style. 'Though, sink you – who am I to advise you? Save in this, perhaps – do not wait too long for your Prince to return! That would be foolish, I believe. Especially with six thousand gold pieces comfortably to hand, with no one a better claim to than yourself! In the end a man must look facts in the face.'

Duncan shook his head. 'I shall be waiting still, when the Prince comes,' he said flatly. 'And the gold with me.'

'I' faith, I do believe that you will! And it, too. Poor Caroline!' Scotus turned to the young woman. 'You heard?' he said. 'Be warned, woman. Ah well . . . ' He mustered a smile. 'This is *adieu*, then, my dear.'

Blinking her eyes, suddenly she reached out and gripped his arm. 'Oh, John!' she mumbled.

'Aye, poor John!' He touched her hand lightly. 'Poor Spanish John!'

'You will be back?' she said. 'You also? One day?'

'Oh, to be sure – to be sure, I will be back. In, say, five years! For my second string – for Anne! Ha – Anne will have me! I swear it! And if not Anne, there is always Belle, is there not? Sweet Belle. But a year or two later. What is another year or two? On my soul, I am not done yet! Captain John Mac-Donnell, younger of Scotus, no less! Tell them to wait for me, both of them.' He drew the young woman to him, only for a moment, and held her tightly. Then he pushed her away, and turned.

'Your servant, sir,' he said shortly to Glenpean, and swung about on his heel to go striding off, in the opposite direction to the general drift down to the shingle of the beach, into the shadow of the trees, landwards. Out of the same shadowy trees his three gillies materialised and fell in behind him.

Unmoving, silent, they watched him go – the girl, the young man and Glenpean.

The Prince came up to Caroline, the only woman present – although she could not really see him with her eyes swimming. Instead of offering her his hand, he took hers and raised it to his lips. He did not speak.

Some sort of curtsy she contrived, as silent as he, before he in turn made off, for the boats grounding on the shingle.

Duncan leaned over to take the girl's hand, the same that Charles had kissed. She let him hold it. At her other side, her father tugged at his beard.

'Och, Locheil! Locheil!' he muttered.

A smirr of thin rain blew in their faces, cold and salt from the sea.

'The Elector may now sleep secure for a night,' Duncan said huskily. 'Secure on another's throne.'

'John will . . . will not come back either, I think,' Caroline said.

'I wonder that you do not go your own self, Duncan man,' Glenpean declared, almost bitterly. 'There is little to hold a young man here, now.'

'There is much to hold me.'

'The gold,' Caroline said.

'More than the gold.'

251

'Your father and the Gregorach,' the older man suggested. 'Och, aye.'

'More than these.' Duncan's hand tightened on the girl's. 'I have the same trouble as Scotus. But I have less courage. I cannot just walk away from what I want, what I need. I can but wait. And hope.'

He felt the grip within his own hand tighten in turn, and drew a long quivering breath. Gently he loosened that grip and raised his hand behind her until his arm was around her shoulders. It rested there, strongly, authoritatively, possessively. Words had never been the best of Duncan MacGregor.

'Duncan,' she breathed, the merest whisper. 'Oh, Duncan, my heart!'

One glance they allowed themselves, one long, lingering, shining meeting of eyes that glowed. Then they turned again to watch the shadowy boats and ships and islands merge together into the Hebridean night, and so stood.

Though fifty others stood likewise, staring, they might have been utterly alone. For them the night was no longer dark. It was not the end, after all – only the beginning.

NIGEL TRANTER

MACGREGOR'S GATHERING

The heroic story of one clan's struggle to survive, supporting a king without a crown.

At the beginning of the eighteenth century, one of the most exciting and romantic periods of British history, the famous Rob Roy MacGregor and his gallant nephew Gregor, a fierce young Highlander, loyal to the cause, led the MacGregor clan in battle against the might of the then Scottish rulers, the Duke of Cumberland, and the English army.

Outlawed and landless, they still clung to Glengyle, one small remaining corner of their ancient territories, and held fast in their loyalty to the Stuart King over the water. But in the midst of the political struggle young Gregor still managed to find time to pay court to Mary Hamilton, a lovely girl from the Lowlands who at first rejected his rough Highland ways . . .

POST A LITTLE HAPPINESS

Post·A·Book

A Royal Mail service in association with the Book Marketing Council & The Booksellers Association.
Post-A-Book is a Post Office trademark.

NIGEL TRANTER

THE CLANSMAN

The heroic story of one clan's struggle to survive, supporting a king without a crown.

Rob Roy MacGregor – outlawed supporter of the Stuart cause.

This second exciting novel about the brave MacGregors takes the reader through the dramatic days of 1715. Declared an outlaw by the Secretary of State, the Duke of Montrose, and the Duke of Cumberland, Rob Roy left home and clansmen to avoid bringing disaster upon them.

In his absence, Montrose's factor came to his home, attacking his proud wife, Mary MacGregor, frightening his children and setting fire to Inversnaid House. For which Rob Roy vowed a terrible revenge.

HODDER AND STOUGHTON PAPERBACKS

NIGEL TRANTER

CRUSADER

Alexander the Third of Scotland was just seven when he inherited the throne. South of the border, England's King Henry the Third saw this as his chance to assert his paramountcy over the kingdom. At the age of ten, the boy was married to Henry's daughter.

But, through the hazards of power politics and dynastic marriage — as well as the more natural hazards of lively adolescence — one man stood by the young monarch.

Whether it was shooting the wild geese, helping him escape from the prisonlike confines of Edinburgh Castle or teaching him to stand up both to his ever-threatening English father-in-law and the unending feuds of his own countrymen, David de Lindsay, of Luffness in East Lothian, was his one true and constant friend.

The rolling Lothian and Border country and its compelling history are both brought marvellously to life in Nigel Tranter's magnificent account of a young boy and his destiny.

Tranter's style is compelling and his research scrupulous. He reaches down the ages to breathe life into his characters.'

Frank Peters, *Daily Telegraph*

HODDER AND STOUGHTON PAPERBACKS